HARGRAVE

FANNY TROLLOPE

HARGRAVE

ALAN SUTTON PUBLISHING LIMITED

First published in 1843

First published in this edition in the United Kingdom in 1995
Alan Sutton Publishing Limited
Phoenix Mill · Far Thrupp · Stroud · Gloucestershire

British Library Cataloguing-in-Publication Data

A catalogue record for this book is available from the British Library.

ISBN 0-7509-1201-4

Cover picture: detail from Abandoned *by James Jacques Joseph Tissot (1836–1902) (Roy Miles Gallery; photograph The Bridgeman Art Library).*

Typeset in 10/11 Bembo.
Typesetting and origination by
Alan Sutton Publishing Limited.
Printed in Great Britain by
The Guernsey Press Company Limited,
Guernsey, Channel Islands.

INTRODUCTION

Hargrave was written during 1842 when Fanny Trollope was in her new home, Carlton Hill, just outside Penrith in the Lake District. She built the house to be near her daughter Cecilia and her grandchildren, but the move was a disaster: Fanny found the position too isolated, the neighbours dull, and the first winter unbearably cold. Carlton Hill was abandoned in the spring of 1843.

Hargrave, which was printed in 1843, but set in 1835, was the twenty-first of Fanny Trollope's forty-one books and vividly recreates the lifestyle she had enjoyed ten years earlier in Paris and in the country near Baden-Baden in Germany. Both places were well known to Fanny from visits made to collect material for two of her travel books, *Belgium and Western Germany* (1833) and *Paris and the Parisians* (1835). In the winter of 1839/40 she spent several months in Paris, where her son Anthony joined her for a respite from his hated post office job. From here, in the midst of a whirl of engagements, she wrote to a friend: 'What a winter of dissipation this has been, dear Julia! Once entered into it I found it perfectly impossible to stop. . . . I might truly say that I have never had a single hour disengaged after my first week here.' She was the guest of Lord Granville at the brilliant Embassy Ball held in honour of Queen Victoria's wedding, she attended fashionable soirées and visited Madame Récamier, Lady Bulwer and Princess Belgiojoso. It is this world which Fanny describes in such detail in *Hargrave*, giving us an intriguing insight into the fashionable Paris society of the late 1830s.

Mr Hargrave is a widower with two beautiful daughters, and 'his ambition was as unbounded as his vanity . . . but Mr Hargrave was deeply and desperately in debt'. He decides that if he is to marry his daughters well 'a fête must be given that shall make all Paris stare — . . . and if means are wanting, means must be found'. It is the way in which Hargrave finds these means that is the driving force of this book.

This is no mere social satire, but an enthralling story of suspected murder, mistaken identity, theft and daring escapes, set in the sophisticated magnificence of Mr Hargrave's Paris. Written twenty-five years before Wilkie Collins's *The Moonstone* and twenty years before Mary Elizabeth Braddon's *Eleanor's Victory*, Fanny Trollope's *Hargrave* is one of the earliest known murder mysteries.

The reviewer in *The New Monthly Magazine* was intrigued by the story. 'Certain it is that Mrs Trollope has, on the present occasion, chosen a subject, and adopted a style of treating it, that, while they show her talents in an entirely new light, make a more distinct and direct appeal to mere popular favour than is to be found in any one of her previous works. . . . *Hargrave* is entirely different in its general character and construction from any of Mrs Trollope's previous works . . . where else in fictitious narrative, to find so intensely interesting a tissue of events, so skilfully concentrated together, so exactly fitted for the purposes for which they are brought before us, and so ingeniously developed . . . is more than we know.'

Fanny Trollope (1779–1863), the mother of the now more famous Anthony, was a remarkable woman. Having commenced writing at the late age of fifty-three out of economic necessity, she produced an instant bestseller, and in the space of twenty-five years wrote forty-one books in 115 volumes.

She was born Frances Milton on 10 March 1779 in Stapleton, a village just north of Bristol. Her father, the Reverend William Milton, held the living of Heckfield in Hampshire and was also a Clerk of Holy Orders at St Michael's Church in Bristol. His six children were all born in Stapleton, though only three survived, Mary, Frances (Fanny), and the youngest, Henry.

Their mother died after Henry's birth, and the children were brought up by their father, who was more inclined towards mathematics and mechanical inventions than religion, and from whom they received a somewhat unorthodox education. Fluent in Latin, French and Italian, and at ease with her father's scientific friends, Fanny was less familiar with the more feminine requirements of a young lady of the eighteenth century. Bristol at that time was a major trading port and, in addition to the merchants and slave traders, had a diverse intellectual and artistic population. There was a hot well at Clifton, where it was fashionable to take the waters, a theatre where Mrs Siddons played, a reading library and an Assembly Room where weekly balls were held. It was a world which Fanny was to use frequently in her novels.

When their father resumed his duties as parish priest at Heckfield in 1801, his family went with him. Life in the quiet country vicarage must have seemed very slow after the bustle of Bristol, and when brother Henry took up his new appointment at the War Office in London, 24-year-old Fanny and her older sister Mary were happy to go and keep house for him at Keppel Street.

There they enjoyed dinner parties, whist, charades, and visits to art galleries and the theatre; but in spite of the social whirl, Fanny at the age of twenty-nine remained unmarried. In 1808 she met a friend of Henry's, a barrister, Thomas Anthony Trollope, who lent her some books of verse, which marked the beginning of a courtship which was to lead to marriage a year later. In 1809 35-year-old Mr Trollope married 30-year-old Miss Milton in Heckfield parish church.

Their early married life in Keppel Street was very happy, and they had seven children in eight years. Thomas Adolphus (Tom) was born in 1810, followed by Henry (1811), Arthur (1812), Emily, who was born and died on the same day in 1813, Anthony (1815), Cecilia (1816) and another Emily in 1818. Life became less easy for the family when, after a few years, Thomas Anthony began to suffer from the rages and disabling sick headaches that were to plague him for the rest of his life. He was a strict father, demanding from his boys that they waste no time in 'idling', and initiating the rudiments of Latin into them as soon as they could read. In 1813 the family leased a house, Julian Hill, at Harrow where they could spend the summers, and in 1815 they made Harrow their main home. The boys were destined to be educated first at Harrow, where they were able to go as 'town boys', then later at Winchester and New College, Oxford, where their father and grandfather had been before them.

For several years all went well with the family. Fanny had many friends and enjoyed the social life at Harrow and London. In 1823 she and Thomas Anthony visited Paris, met again Fanny's childhood friends the Garnetts and mutual friend Frances Wright, and went to stay with General Lafayette at his country mansion, La Grange.

The Trollopes were by now experiencing money problems as poor crops and high rents were forcing many farmers into bankruptcy and, in his legal profession, Thomas Anthony's increasing intolerance and irascibility drove many of his clients away.

Henry was also achieving little at Winchester, and so in 1826 it was decided to find employment for the 16-year-old boy in a counting house in Paris. In early 1827 Anthony was awarded a place at Winchester and Thomas Anthony, who was determined to send all his sons to a public school, decided that the family must move to a smaller, dilapidated farmhouse at Harrow Weald, three miles from Harrow, where the rent would be lower. Fanny was appalled at the prospect of having to move from her friends and her beloved Julian Hill. She visited Paris in the summer of 1827 to attend Julia Garnett's wedding and to see Henry. Here she again met the charismatic young reformer Frances Wright, who had founded an idealistic settlement at Nashoba in Tennessee, where slaves worked to earn their freedom. Frances was now in Paris to look for new settlers for the community, and to recover from the American fever. She suggested to Fanny that she and Henry become part of the Nashoba experiment: American living was cheaper, and Henry could find employment. Fanny was keen to go, and eventually obtained permission from Thomas Anthony, leaving Thomas Adolphus and Anthony as boarders at Winchester, and taking with her Henry, Cecilia and Emily, as well as their drawing master, a young Frenchman by the name of Auguste Hervieu.

In December 1827 they arrived in America at the mouth of the Mississippi, and reached the Utopian settlement of Nashoba in January. Fanny was devastated, upon her arrival, to find it nothing but a collection of miserable huts, built on partly cleared land in a fever-ridden swamp. What was she to do now? She was without funds, marooned in a strange land with three children, an artist, two servants and a quantity of luggage. With all possible speed she took her party to Cincinnati, where, supported by Auguste Hervieu, she planned to wait for the arrival of her husband to transport them home.

Bedevilled by his own financial worries, it was nearly a year before Thomas Anthony could join them, and by then Fanny had decided to remain in Cincinnati and build a bazaar. It was to be a community centre where the sexes could mingle socially, with a saloon, art gallery, coffee house and ballroom. Managing this establishment was to be Henry's future. However, the bazaar was a disaster: unscrupulous contractors walked off with the money, and instead of sending money from England to pay the workmen, Thomas Anthony sent out trumpery store goods for sale. The bazaar, later nicknamed Trollope's Folly, was seized by the creditors before it was completed and all the Trollopes' possessions were sold to pay their debts.

There would follow another two years of hardship before Fanny and Hervieu between them could save and borrow enough money to get them back to England. Fanny resolved to write a book about her adventures, in the hope that it might bring her some much-needed income. They returned to England in 1831 to the run-down farmhouse where Thomas Anthony was now living.

Fanny's book was in the hands of the publishers by the autumn of 1831. *Domestic Manners of the Americans* was published in March 1832 and became an instant bestseller. In the first year it went into four editions in England, and a further four editions in America. A truthful, witty, sardonic tale of Fanny's experiences of the inequality of American life, it made the Americans howl with rage. In England the Tories hailed it as a dire warning of the pitfalls of freedom, and the Whigs spluttered that it was a pack of lies. Overnight Fanny became a celebrity.

Meanwhile, Thomas Anthony's affairs had gone from bad to worse; his debts were insurmountable, and all his efforts to rectify the situation ended in failure. From now on Fanny became the main income earner. *Domestic Manners of the Americans* was followed by an unending stream of books. She sometimes wrote as many as three three-volume novels in one year, driven by the need to earn money to support herself and her family. By rising at four o'clock in the morning and completing the required number of pages before the family were awake, Fanny was able to continue her writing while nursing a dying husband and children. Henry died in 1834, Thomas Anthony in 1835, Emily in 1836, and Cecilia in 1849.

As well as travel books Fanny wrote romances, gothic novels and satires. Some of her most powerful books were written to expose social injustice: the evils of slavery, *Jonathan Jefferson Whitlaw*; the injustice of the poor laws, *Jessie Phillips*; the exploitation of children in the factories, *Michael Armstrong*; and the dangers of excessive evangelicalism, *The Vicar of Wrexhill*. She became one of the nineteenth century's most popular writers and was acquainted with, among others, Wordsworth, Dickens, Elizabeth Barrett Browning and George Eliot.

Fanny spent the last few years of her life among the expatriate literary community in Florence, where, at the age of seventy-seven, she wrote her last book, *Fashionable Life: or Paris and London*. She died in Florence in 1863, and is buried there in the English Cemetery.

Fanny's books fell from favour as Victorian morality tightened its grip, and her writing was labelled coarse and vulgar by some contemporary critics. She is now mainly remembered for the satirical *Domestic Manners of the Americans*; however; when read today, Fanny Trollope's books of one hundred and fifty years ago are clever, witty and surprisingly modern.

Teresa Ransom

CHAPTER 1

The gayest house in Paris during the winter of 1834–5 was that of Mr Hargrave. It was a noble and elegant mansion in the Rue de Lille, the whole ground-floor and *premier* of which were occupied by his family, and contained apartments which might have accommodated two or three French families of fashion; but Mr Hargrave was an Englishman of expensive habits, with a very decided taste for comforts and luxuries of all kinds.

The number of his family would not, indeed, have seemed to require such ample range, for it consisted of two young girls only; but it was his pleasure that they should be lodged with greater magnificence than any other young ladies of private station in Paris.

With the undivided possession of the *rez-de-chaussée*, they had undivided possession, also, of the noble garden, which, with its groves of forest-trees and wide expanse of lawn, spread behind it. Mr Hargrave was a man of great taste, and of an inventive fancy, which wantoned in the embellishment of every thing around him; so that his dwelling was not only ample, well appointed, and magnificent, but graceful, fanciful, and picturesque in the extreme.

The two pretty creatures for whom all this elegance was provided shewed well in the midst of it; and the critical eye of Mr Hargrave, as he watched their graceful movements, reflected by polished mirrors, and illumined by a hundred wax-lights, often turned from their brilliant *entourage* to them, and from them to their brilliant *entourage*, in doubt as to which embellished the other most.

He was, in truth, exceedingly fond of both; although the entire sum of tenderness bestowed upon them was by no means equally divided; one only being his own child, and the other the daughter of his deceased wife by a former marriage. Hargrave's handsome fortune had been made in trade; his father having been a highly respected City banker. But though no degradation of any sort could attach to this, inasmuch as his own education was the same as that of the highest aristocracy, and the society of the worthy banker chosen always with a view to the advancement of his only hope and only heir, Charles Hargrave preferred Paris to London for the display of his wealth, because he fancied, not only that it went farther and distinguished him more, but also that its origin was less likely

1

to be inquired into. In this, however, it is probable that he was mistaken; for, let folks think what they like, the ancient aristocracy of France is not worn out yet; and though it may be somewhat the fashion in the market-place to seem to forget the difference between those whose shields won their bearings beneath the *oriflamme* and those whose shields are innocent of any bearings at all, it may fairly be doubted if a *nouveau riche* ranks higher in France than in England.

Be this as it may, Charles Hargrave, having displayed himself for two seasons in Paris after the death of his father, contrived, either by means of his handsome person, or his agreeable address, or his large fortune, or by the power and force of all these combined, to fascinate and lead captive the pretty widow of M le Vicomte de Cordillac, with an income of twenty thousand francs, and no incumbrance save a little daughter of two years old, who was to inherit the property after her.

This union gave birth to a second little girl, born exactly three years after the first; but, notwithstanding this difference of age, the children grew up with the strongest affection for each other: the mother seemed equally fond of both, and the pleasant-tempered Hargrave, although he certainly felt that Adèle de Cordillac was not his daughter, and that Sabina Hargrave was, ruled them both with so silken a rein and such even-handed justice, that the family harmony was never disturbed by this variety of race.

Nor had his wife ever reason to regret that she had selected the rich and elegant stranger in preference to all the native adorers who addressed her. The marriage was, in fact, a very happy one. Mr Hargrave continued to admire his wife to the end of her days; and, what was more important still, perhaps, to their conjugal felicity, every body else continued to admire her, too. Had it been otherwise, it is probable that not all the sweetness of temper, propriety of conduct, sparkling talent, nor even her unchanging affection for himself, would have sufficed to preserve unimpaired the sentiment which had first brought him to her feet, and which continued to render the union a happy one to its close.

Those who have not been led by some accident or other to study the effects of vanity in characters where it greatly predominates, have little comprehension of its strength. There is probably no passion, from the very lowest to the most sublime, from the tenderest to the most brutal, which more deeply dyes with its influence the mind where it takes root. Greatly do those mistake who call it a 'little' passion, — it is a great, an absorbing, a tremendous one. Its outward bearing, indeed, when the feeling is unskilfully permitted to catch the eye, may often seem trivial, and provoke more smiles than sighs; but its inward strength of influence is not to be judged thereby. As little do the graceful sinuosities of the constrictors' wavy movements give notice of the deadly gripe into which they can contract themselves, as do the bland devices which purvey to a vain man's appetite announce the insatiable voracity that is to be fed, or the unscrupulous means which may be resorted to in order to content it.

The death of his wife was a severe blow to Mr Hargrave's happiness. She had been for years the bright and beautiful centre of that system, unequalled for its brilliance throughout Paris, of which he was himself the creator, and by which *his* wealth, *his* magnificence, *his* taste, *his* hospitality, *his* graceful talents, and *his* great importance in the world of fashion, were made known to all the civilised world. It was a severe stroke; and nothing less powerful than the passion which received and smarted under it could have enabled him to rally as he did, and start forth in his career anew.

But this enviable effect of a buoyant and elastic spirit could not by possibility shew itself openly during the first months of heavy mourning, in which, of course, the whole family were enveloped. Inwardly, however, it very soon had its effect; and even while the crape-shrouded Adèle poured out his coffee on one side, and the pale Sabina, clad in sable weeds, tendered him the *Débats* on the other, before either of them had left the house, except to go to mass (for all the family were Roman Catholic), he began to contemplate, more critically than he had ever before done, the peculiar style of beauty of each, and to soothe his widower fancy by picturing to himself the effect they would produce when the time should come for recalling around him all the eyes in Paris worthy to pass judgment, and all the voices capable of bestowing fame.

Little did they guess, poor girls! as they hovered mournfully near him, stilling their own deep grief, lest the sight of it should add to his, that the earnest gaze which was turned first to the one and then to the other fair face, was meditating what colours in the flowery chaplets which his fancy wove, would best set off the clear rich brown of Adèle's cheek, and which decorate with most effect the fair-haired delicacy of Sabina. They fancied, pretty creatures, that his kind heart was wrung by thinking of their motherless condition; and their pity for each other, and their pity for themselves, and their pity for him, were so increased thereby, that, spite of all they could do to prevent it, the tears burst forth anew, till the bright black eyes of the one, and the soft blue eyes of the other, were so miserably swollen and disfigured as to force the distressed widower to turn his thoughts inwards, where he found the only consolation he was capable of receiving, from remembering that tears were invariably set aside at the same time that black dresses were taken off, and that six months would amply suffice for the use of both.

Fortunately for Mr Hargrave, his charming wife was taken from him on the 15th of June; the Paris season therefore was over; and change of scene – that much-vaunted remedy for sorrow – might be administered to his daughters and himself, without losing much of that elixir of life which his soul best loved, and which was only to be found within the charmed circle of the French capital.

'We must leave this sad home of ours, dear girls!' said he, in a voice of profound emotion. 'It is too — too sad for us all! There is no object we can look upon but brings a fresh pang with it! . . . We will but wait for the arrival of your aunt, my dear children, before we set off for some new scene, which, from being unknown to us in the days of our happiness, will, I trust, be less painful to us than this.'

'Dear papa! . . . Dear, dear papa!' said both the weeping girls at once: and they hung about him in a manner so gentle, so caressing, and, as he remarked, so graceful also, that he permitted himself to be comforted by the anticipation of the effect his drawing-rooms would produce next season, when opened under the presiding grace of two such beautiful creatures.

Another point on which Mr Hargrave was singularly fortunate was the facility with which circumstances enabled him to supply his young ladies with that most indispensable article — a chaperone; and not only did he achieve this with ease, but in a manner which, in his estimation, was absolutely perfect.

Madame de Hautrivage, the sister of his lamented wife, was, it is true, as unlike her in most respects as it was well possible for a sister to be; but, fortunately, this dissimilitude did not extend to birth, or station in society, or style of dress, and was therefore comparatively but of small importance. Both sisters were *née de Tremouille*, and both had married nobly, so that no reasonable objection could be made to the arrangement which constituted Madame de Hautrivage a member of his family.

The only point of contrast, however, between the two sisters which caused Madame de Hautrivage any regret was, that on the death of her noble husband, instead of finding herself, as her elder sister had done before her, the mistress of twenty thousand francs a-year, she could not discover, after the most minute and careful investigation, that she could lay claim to a revenue of as many sous. The noble nephew of her noble husband had claimed, and taken possession of, all which his thriftless uncle had left; and how it was that Madame de Hautrivage contrived to retain her place in the first society without any visible diminution of the elegance of her toilet or her equipage, nobody appeared very clearly to understand.

Such, however, was the case; and she was therefore evidently the most eligible person Mr Hargrave could possibly have chosen for the all-important office of chaperone to her two motherless nieces.

The choice of the retreat in which the next six months were to be passed was regulated chiefly by distance; Mr Hargrave, in his then desolate condition, caring little for any thing save the power of finding himself sufficiently removed from all his friends and acquaintance, to permit his recovering his spirits and usual power of enjoyment without impropriety.

Adèle and Sabina rejoiced unfeignedly as they watched this admirable effect 'of change of scene;' and not the less so, certainly, for its having brought them, for the first time in their lives, within reach of some of the wildest and most lovely country in the world. For the retreat chosen by Mr Hargrave for the recovery of his spirits under the calamity which had befallen him, was Baden-Baden, at once the most attractive imaginable to the lovers of pleasure and the lovers of solitude, – to the votary of the gaming-table, and the worshipper of Nature, – to the *blasé* spirits who seek relief from the heavy vacuum of their own inanity, and to the happy, healthful being who can draw ecstasy from the bright torrent of the Mourg, and feel themselves in Elysium when wandering among the dreamy solitudes of the five forests in its vicinity. Mr Hargrave had heard much of Baden-Baden in both ways, and judiciously determined upon making choice of it, because it would enable each individual of his own dear world (the world of Paris fashion) to judge of his occupations there according to their various tempers. The men of pleasure might say, 'Hargrave is right; at Baden-Baden one may learn to forget all things, even death itself;' and the sentimentalist would be sure to declare that no country in Europe could furnish haunts equally favourable to the indulgence of the sadness so dear to the bereaved heart as those purlieus of the Black Forest which may be found in its neighbourhood.

Thus all the mourners were as well pleased as mourners could be; for Madame de Hautrivage assured them all, separately and conjointly, that she had now but one single object in life, which was to see all and every one of them doing, saying, seeing, hearing, and feeling, exactly what they liked best.

CHAPTER II

Those who know Baden-Baden will readily allow, that nowhere could the really mourning sisters have found so much to make them rejoice that they had left the scene of their still fresh sorrow behind them. 'Papa is right, Sabina!' said Adèle, wonder-stricken and enchanted, as she stood upon the mouldering walls of the Alt Schloss, and looked out upon the distant Rhine. 'How well must he know the nature of the human heart! I would not have believed, Sabina, that any thing could have so taken me out of myself, as it were, as do the glorious scenes of this enchanting region. Never, never can we either of us forget our mother! I would rather lay down beside her, in cold forgetfulness of all things earthly, than not remember her. But here something seems to mix itself with the thought of her, that takes away the bitterness, and only leaves a feeling of soft and mellowed melancholy that I would not be without.'

Sabina answered only by pressing the arm she held; with a spirit less capable of kindling at the touch of every happy emotion, the younger girl had, perhaps, greater depth of feeling, or, at any rate, greater pertinacity of sorrow; for it required longer to bring her to the consciousness of all the blessings which Nature had still in store for her. But by degrees she too acknowledged that it was a great comfort to be so far from 'dismal Paris;' and that no one, she was sure, but her own dear, dear papa, would ever have thought upon a scheme so admirably calculated to heal their aching hearts.

There was one point, however, upon which this dear papa could never persuade either sister to agree with him; and this was upon the great advantages to be derived, for their health and spirits, from attendance morning and evening at the public rooms. On this point the two girls felt perfectly alike, and though most lively and affectionately grateful for the tender anxiety which prompted the proposal, they steadily adhered to their first assurance, – that they could not appear in public while they wore mourning, and that they would not shorten the usual period for wearing it by a single day.

To do Mr Hargrave justice, he never, either in his own family or any where else, attempted to obtain concessions by his authority which were refused to his gentle, and, in most cases, irresistible entreaties. So Adèle and Sabina were permitted to have their own way in this; and moreover, with the same indulgence which he had ever shewn to the wishes of both, he permitted them also, with the attendance of a certain venerable Roger Humphries, the only English servant in his establishment, to pass most of their mornings in driving about the singularly wild and beautiful country which surrounded them.

This unlimited furlough for wandering, though it extended pretty nearly *ad libitum* as to the hours of daylight, must not be censured as an indiscretion on the part of Mr Hargrave; for old Roger was no ordinary domestic, and, by way of a protector upon all such excursions as the sisters indulged in, was well worth a dozen chaperons. As it is likely enough that this rather singular serving-man may repeatedly appear in the course of the narrative, it may be as well to explain the origin of his position in Mr Hargrave's family.

Roger Humphries, who when thus appointed to the post of *chevalier ambulant* through the Black Forest had well-nigh completed three-score years, occupied in the days of his youth a far different situation under the patronage of Mr Hargrave's father. How those persons are designated who, being neither principal nor clerk, are constantly visible in a banking establishment, I know not; but Roger Humphries was one of these. If a door was to be opened or shut, Roger Humphries was at hand to do it; and if a letter or packet of importance was to be sent, it was to Roger Humphries that the charge was given. He was a huge man, with a small head, and having large features in a face almost too narrow to hold them. His forehead was high, but had nothing of that ample extent which is supposed to indicate organic accommodation for deep thinking; those, however, who were skilled in reading from external evidence what impulses are active within us and what are not, declared that there was in the character of Roger Humphries an adhesiveness of attachment, which would lead him to do much rather than abandon what he loved.

Some good or attaching qualities he must have had to induce the elegant Hargrave, whose household was *monté* with an attention to general effect which would have done credit to the grouping master (if there be such a personage) of the Grand Opera, – some attaching qualities Roger Humphries must have had to make Mr Hargrave not only retain him in his service, but also to permit his personal attendance upon himself and his beautiful daughters; and that, too, positively without any reference whatever to the effect which the contrast of the old man's appearance, when seen in juxtaposition with either himself or them, might produce.

In truth, Hargrave knew that old Roger almost worshipped him, – he knew that not all the kingdoms of the world, nor the glory of them, would have tempted the old man to leave him, as long as he might be permitted to remain near enough to admire, to love, and to serve him.

It was with this venerable attendant, then, seated beside the coachman in the dicky of their elegant open carriage, that Adèle de Cordillac and Sabina Hargrave penetrated into every approachable recess within ten or twelve English miles of Baden-Baden. Nor were such recesses only deemed approachable to themselves as the carriage could draw near; for the greatest delight of all, to the two girls escaped for the first time from the tameness of French scenery, was to stroll on foot, followed by the faithful Roger (who took the liberty of carrying a stout staff the while), wherever a bolder promontory or a blacker mass of shade than usual seduced their imaginations into believing that something 'new and strange' might be found there.

In this way they probably became more intimately acquainted with all the intricate varieties of this singular locality, than even the Guide-writers themselves; for whereas these persevering and most useful purveyors for all wonder-seeking travellers go only where they think they can in common honesty invite others to follow them, our scramble-loving

nymphs delighted especially in getting exactly where they thought that
nobody else could get; and often they had to employ all their eloquence
in order to persuade Roger, that clamberings and climbings totally
impossible for him were both safe and delightful for them. At first the old
man demurred a little; but repeated experience at length giving him
confidence, both in their steadiness of eye and activity of limb, he ceased
his remonstrances, and usually sat down with implicit obedience on the
spot which the young ladies selected for his repose, awaiting their return
with the imperturbable patience of a faithful dog.

Had any one inquired, either of Adèle or Sabina, if they had
encountered any adventures during these exploring excursions, they
would assuredly have answered, 'Yes, a great many.' For if one of them
found out a cavern of a dozen feet square in a rock, it was an adventure;
or if the other came upon a holy virgin or a martyred saint enshrined
between four narrow stone walls, with an opening of a foot square to
peep out upon their worshippers, it was an adventure; besides a hundred
other childish fancies, too silly to mention, all of which served to give
interest to their rambles, and to figure in their journals. But excepting
such as these, they could not have been said to meet with any; unless,
indeed, a sort of mystical puzzle, produced by the atmosphere at one
particular spot which they visited, may be so termed.

The mountain-road between Baden-Baden and Gernsbach runs over a
ridge connecting, as it were, many separate heights together, each one of
which has between it and its neighbour, on both sides, a deep, wild
hollow; some wider, some narrower, some perforated with rocks of a
thousand fantastic forms, and others covered with fern, or lined with the
dark pine of the region, turning the light of noonday into the blackness
of night.

It happened one morning that the sisters, having in view some object
rather more distant than usual, had coaxed old Roger to eat his breakfast
before the lark had finished hers; and the coachman, faithful both for
himself and his horses, being punctually at the door by six o'clock A.M.,
they set off, on rather a foggy and uncertain morning, with the intention
of driving along this lovely Burgstrosse, descending to Gernsbach, and
then following the course of the Mourg to Eberstein, the celebrated
hunting-seat of the Duke of Baden.

To complete this project without a breakfast *en route* was impossible;
but they had ascertained that at the foot of the pine-clad mountain on
which Eberstein is situated, there was a commodious and right pleasant
gasthaus at which this needful rest and refreshment for themselves and
their horses could be obtained.

A short consultation was held with the servants at the door of the
hôtel, before they set out, as to the chances for a fine day, or the reverse;

and the majority of opinions being in favour of the expedition, the well-pleased girls stepped into the carriage and drove off.

Though the question had been promptly decided to their wishes by those they had consulted, they felt quite aware that the powers of the air were still in doubt about it; for, as they slowly mounted the steep ascent that leads by this mountain route from Baden, they perceived that they were getting at every step into a denser fog, and began to fear that not only had they a good chance of getting wet to the skin, but also that, if they escaped this disaster, they were pretty sure of escaping all knowledge of the objects they had hoped to look upon; for did the same kind of atmosphere through which they were then passing continue to envelope them, it was perfectly certain that they would be unable to see the splendid landscapes of which, on that morning, they were especially in search.

By degrees, however, the aspect of things improved upon them; and by the time they had reached that bit of terrace-like road which, having gradually descended for some distance from the highest level of the ridge, runs along the hill's side for the distance of half a mile, they perceived that beautiful effect of mountain vapour, which takes place when the sun steps forth to skirmish with it. Here and there the landscape peeped through with all the glow of summer brightness; while at other points the white mist still hung like a heavy veil upon it, altogether concealing some objects, and showing others under such delusive forms, as to leave the whole picture shadowy and uncertain. The two girls strained their eyes to ascertain what was water and what was land, and where the heavens ceased and the earth began: but the more they looked at it, the less they comprehended what they saw; and both declaring, almost in the same breath, that the scene was somehow or other a thousand times more beautiful than if it had been fully revealed in the broad light of unmitigated sunshine, they agreed, according to their usual custom when any thing struck them as peculiarly beautiful, to stop the carriage, and indulge in gazing about them with all the freedom of pedestrians.

Adèle ordered the coachman to drive slowly on, and wait for them on the summit of the next hill; and then, accompanied by Roger and his staff, they made their way to a small rocky promontory, which, jutting out from the hill's side, gave, in clear weather, a magnificent bird's-eye view of the valley at its foot. Now, the weather, to say the truth, was still any thing but clear, nevertheless, the scene they looked upon was most strangely beautiful, and they bounded forward to the extremest verge of the rock, in hope of seeing more of it. Here, on this extremest verge, they found a youth seated, with his legs over the precipice, his arms folded across his breast, and his eyes intently fixed upon a particular point of the scene below.

The young man turned his head as they approached, and, by a sudden and active movement recovering his feet, stood before them, cap in hand and bowing low; but he did not seem inclined to retreat, though there was hardly space enough for the four to stand upon the little platform without danger. The view from this point was, indeed, singularly advantageous for shewing the half-hidden scene below. The pines, whose tops were some of them level with the rock, made a foreground as they gradually sloped down from it, dark as the Venetian tints of Titian, when he throws a mass of foliage across his landscapes to set off their silvery light. In the horizon were distant hills, looming high, and with various objects on and near them, considerably more distinct than usual. But all between looked like an inland ocean studded with islands, and at intervals a group of trees, a village spire, or the lofty gable of a farm-house, starting forth clearly to view, with a sort of incongruous brightness that seemed like the effect of magic.

'Does it not look like a glorious archipelago?' said Adèle in French; 'and might not one almost swear, against all the geography books in the world, that yonder misty expanse was a noble lake?'

'It is no *noble* lake which lies before you, ladies,' said the young stranger in German; 'but, nevertheless, there is a lake there, and one, too, of peculiar interest. Just in the midst of that blue mysterious vapour, which seems to have neither definite form nor definite limit, is the well-known Mummelsee, or Fairy Lake, of which so many wondrous tales are told.'

Adèle understood German tolerably well, but spoke it scarcely at all; but to Sabina, who loved its romantic literature and wild legendary lore better than all the other learning of the earth, it was as familiar as either French or English, and she immediately replied, without giving much time to meditation upon the propriety of thus entering into conversation with a stranger, by saying in the same language, –

'Are these wondrous tales connected with facts, sir, or are they merely fairy legends?'

'It is not easy,' returned the young man, smiling, 'to answer your questions, young lady, as briefly as you have stated them, for I could scarcely reply by a simple yes or no to either. That there *are* strange facts connected with that Fairy Lake, none can deny; neither would it be consistent with truth to aver that the excited imaginations of those who watch its capricious influence do not exaggerate in their accounts of it. There is a mixture of truth in both these propositions.'

'Strange facts!' repeated Sabina, whose imagination was decidedly of the excitable class alluded to by the stranger. 'What strange facts, sir?'

'There is at this moment beneath your eyes, and almost close to the foot of this rock,' returned the young man gravely, 'or, at least, it is generally believed so, an extensive castle, partly in ruins, but in part still capable of giving shelter to man – were there any spirits bold enough to inhabit it – yet you perceive no trace of it. Return to this spot again a few hours hence, and it is possible, nay, I believe probable, that exactly where you now see that silvery mass of floating mist, you will behold a seemingly substantial edifice of stone and mortar.'*

Adèle smiled, while Sabina almost trembled, not from fear indeed, but pleasure. And the elder sister, then slightly bowing to the unknown chronicler of the fairies, made a movement which indicated her wish of returning to the carriage; but Sabina appeared to have taken root upon the rock where she stood, and with her eyes intently fixed on the misty world below her, seemed totally to have forgotten all things save the mystical statement to which she had been listening.

But Adèle was twenty-one years old and five months, whereas Sabina was only eighteen and four months; therefore it followed that the more prosaic sister generally regulated on all important occasions the movements of the more poetic one; and feeling a gentle pressure on her arm which sufficed to recall her to things present, Sabina, too, gave a farewell look into the mysterious valley, and with a blush, a vast deal more roseate than any displayed by Aurora that morning, made a bow to the stranger, a good deal less slight, and a great deal more respectful, than that of her elder sister, and yielded herself to follow the way she led.

'Is not this extraordinary, Adèle?' she exclaimed, as soon as they were seated in the carriage, and while she still looked back to the spot they had quitted; where the young man, now as invisible to her as the wondrous castle of which he told, stood shyly ensconced behind a crag, that he might gaze without offence as the brightest vision his waking eyes had ever looked upon passed away.

'I suspect that the young gentleman was only quizzing us,' replied Adèle.

'How *can* you think so?' returned Sabina, in a tone that almost betokened indignation: 'I never in my life saw any one whom I thought less likely to be impertinent.'

'I did not mean to accuse him of impertinence, Sabina,' replied her sister, laughing; 'but you know travellers are always crammed with wonders whenever they think fit to listen with confiding ears to native historians.'

---

* The locality of this delusive obscurity is selected purposely where no castle stands that the facts of the narrative may not be sifted too closely, and declared to be *personal*; an interpretation which has so often attended the writings of the author as to render caution necessary. Such delusions, however, do exist, not only in Germany, but in England. Dover Castle is sometimes perfectly invisible from the heights to the west of the town; from whence, at other times, it is seen in its fullest glory.

'Native historians! I do not know what you mean, Adèle, by native historians: but I will venture to say, without knowing whether that young man be native or not, that every syllable he uttered was most strictly true.'

'And that this Mummelsee is really and in good sooth the haunt of fairies, who build and pull down castles *à volonté!*'

'He never said any such thing, Adèle,' returned Sabina, gravely.

'Did he not? Well! never mind what he said,' rejoined her sister, laughing; 'but just use all your faculties to look at that glorious gleam of sunshine that has burst out over those distant hills. We shall have a fine day yet, Sabina!'

'Indeed, I think so; and I shall enjoy it, oh! so much – so very much – Adèle, if you would make me one promise.'

'What is that, dear?' returned Mademoiselle de Cordillac, playfully kissing her. 'I am ready to promise any thing! That sunbeam has put me most superlatively in good-humour, for half-an-hour ago I was in despair about the day.'

'Will you promise that, after seeing Eberstein, you will let us come back by this same road, instead of going round by the valley, as we settled to do yesterday?'

'In the hope of seeing those fine large eyes and that curly brown hair again, Sabina?'

'How can you talk such nonsense, Adèle! This *coup de soleil* seems to have affected your head very strangely . . . God grant that it may not have made you a fool for life! . . . What I *do* hope to see is the castle, and not the curls. Will you promise to come home this way?'

'I am by no means sure,' replied Adèle, maliciously, 'that I shall not be giving a proof of the folly you deprecate if I say yes. However, I will not abuse the power given either by my age or my wisdom, and by this way we will return, sister mine. But, for goodness sake, do not give all your attention to castles which are in the clouds, instead of looking at the humbler glories of the earth. Was there ever any thing more beautiful than that landscape before us, waking into new life, as it does, from the magic touch of a sunbeam? . . . Trust me, Sabina, Nature is your only magician. I would not give one of the fleeting shadows produced by those retiring clouds for a whole host of fairies. . . . Is it not beautiful?'

*   *   *

Having obtained the desired promise, the young Sabina seemed wisely determined to bring herself back again to the objects before her, and wherever her thoughts might be wandering, she looked at, and spoke of, all that Adèle pointed out. Their breakfast at the foot of Eberstein, at the little inn beside the Mourg, was joyous; and their walk up the long ascent which led them to the castle, in all ways so agreeable, that they forgot they were not upon level ground. They turned aside, with all befitting reverence, to look at the shrine of the Virgin within the little Reingel chapel, and listened to the legend which recounted how the queer little figure, to which so many holy pilgrims still bow, got into it; and, lastly, they stepped out with ecstasy unbounded and inexpressible upon the marvellous terrace that surrounds this most beautiful of all Baden's glorious ducal residences.

In short, the long morning was spent in great enjoyment by both the sisters; but when the time came for turning their horses' heads homewards, it was evident that the elder had yielded herself more wholly to the visible beauties it had given to their view than the younger, for Adèle had forgotten all about the castle in the clouds, and told Roger, as she stepped into the carriage, that they were to follow the course of the river on their road home, and be very careful not to keep papa's dinner waiting. But not so Sabina. Whether the exquisite beauty of Eberstein had put the magical edifice out of her thoughts during the time she was actually looking at it may be doubtful, but most certain is it that the moment she heard this command of her sister's, she exclaimed with very great earnestness upon the sin of broken faith, and declared that she should be more disappointed than she had words to tell if they did not return by the same road they came.

'Mercy on me!' cried the well-nigh weary Adèle, starting forward from the snug corner into which she had thrown herself. 'I had totally forgotten all about it, Sabina. But I would not have you disappointed for the world. Tell the coachman to return by the road we came, Roger, and to stop exactly at the same spot where we got out this morning. But do you really think, Sabina, that you shall have strength enough to get out again?' she added. 'In general I can stand fatigue better than you do; but now, I confess, I am fairly beat; and I hardly think I would get out of the carriage again to see St Peter's. . . . Do you really think you shall get out?'

'Yes Adèle, I think I shall,' replied Sabina, quietly; and no more was said on the subject till the carriage stopped, and Roger appeared at the door to announce that they had reached the place where they had quitted it in the morning.

'Yes! This is it!' cried Sabina, eagerly preparing to spring out.

'You are not really going to leave the carriage, Sabina, are you?' said the half-sleeping Adèle. 'I am quite sure you will see nothing, for it is getting to be dark already. Look out from hence. You will see quite as much as from the rock, I'll answer for it.'

But the younger sister was rebellious; and, promising to come back directly, ran forward faster than Roger could follow. With undeviating steps she reached precisely the same spot on which she had before stood; and looking down into the valley perceived, with a degree of astonishment which made her heart beat, and her colour change, exactly such a castle as the stranger had described, apparently close to the foot of the rock on which she stood. She uttered an exclamation of wonder and delight, and stood for several minutes hanging over the beetling rock, contemplating with ever-increasing surprise the wide extent, the massive strength, and the near vicinity, of a fabric which a few hours before had been utterly invisible.

The first thrilling emotion which this sight inspired being over, she remembered the scoffing scepticism of Adèle, and turning to the old attendant, who had by this time overtaken her, desired he would go back with all the speed he could make to the carriage, and tell Mademoiselle de Cordillac that she must come to her directly.

Roger was not a man to dispute the commands of Mr Hargrave's daughter; and, however little disposed for more walking, he immediately obeyed. But scarcely had he got beyond her sight, than Sabina was startled by the apparition of the same tall figure, large eyes, curly hair, and all, which had greeted her on the self-same spot in the morning.

It is no paradox to say, that had she been less frightened, she would have been more shocked. To a young girl, brought up at a first-rate French seminary, with the strictest attention to Parisian etiquette, the idea of finding herself, by her own imprudence, alone with an extremely handsome young man, on an isolated pinnacle of rock, in, or near, the Black Forest, seven minutes after the sun had gone down, would have been quite enough at any other moment to have sent her flying off with more than Atalanta's speed of foot to join her sister. But now she was spell-bound: not, however, as it was possible that her saucy sister might have suggested, merely by some sudden sympathy with the young stranger himself, – her feelings were of a less mundane and ordinary kind. His sudden and unaccountable reappearance the moment she was alone, had something in it so strangely analogous to the still more unaccountable reappearance of the castle, and to the mystic air of the changed landscape, according to his own exact prediction of it, that she actually trembled from head to foot with a genuine superstitious feeling.

I would here fain say something, if it were possible, to prove that my pretty Sabina was less silly than poetical; more abounding in imagination than deficient in judgment; and altogether, a great deal more to be admired than despised, for the emotion which made her fancy herself on the precincts of another world; – while, in fact, she was only contemplating the clear obscure of a delicious twilight in this. But I am perfectly aware that nothing I can just at present say on the subject would suffice to satisfy such carping critics as would make no allowance for a young lady, deeply versed in all the wild legends of Teutonic *diablerie*, and visiting the land which she had learned to consider as the favourite battlefield of fiends, and paradise of fairies, for the first time. It may, therefore, be wisest to let the matter rest, trusting to the chance of her finding some sympathising friends, among those who are as young and fanciful as herself.

But the species of poetical trance into which Sabina thus fell did not last long. Propriety resumed her accustomed power, and thrusting blushing Imagination into the background, enabled her, when the young stranger exclaimed, 'Said I not truth, lady?' to reply with a very respectable degree of nonchalance, 'Ho, wohl, Meinherr,' and with a slight bow and rapid step, to leave the young magician as he stood, – the gratified hope of her arrival, and the vexing disappointment of her departure, holding him transfixed between them.

Sabina reached the carriage very nearly as soon as the more deliberate Roger, and in time to prevent the reluctant compliance of the tired Adèle with the request she had sent by him.

'Oh! I am so glad you are come back, Sabina,' she exclaimed. 'Then you do not insist upon my getting out?'

'No, Adèle, no,' replied the flustered girl, hastily resuming the place she had left beside her. 'It was no use waiting till you came; it is getting so late; and, besides, I can tell you all about it.'

'To be sure you can; and I shall like it a prodigious deal better, I assure you. Did the curly locks say sooth? Is there really a castle there?'

'Yes,' replied Sabina, in an accent of considerable solemnity. 'Yes, Adèle, there is a castle there.'

'You don't say so! . . . Well, I am very glad of it; and now I shall go to sleep again. I verily believe we must have walked a dozen miles to-day, for I never was so tired in my life;' and so saying, Mademoiselle de Cordillac nestled again into her corner, closed her eyes, and positively did go fast asleep; thereby rendering it quite impossible for Sabina to 'tell her about it' at that time. And it was long before the inclination to do so returned upon her. There is no class of feelings and ideas so completely dependent upon accident and locality as that which belongs to poetical exaltation of all sorts. It was from no want of confidence in her sister, nor from any painful consciousness of feelings that she ought to hide, which for many months prevented Sabina's again alluding to the mysterious castle or to the youthful stranger whom she had seen in its vicinity; for as the world, and the world's prosaic realities, again closed round her, she felt too strongly the childishness of the emotions they had inspired, to wish to talk about them.

This adventure, such as it was, and though, perhaps, hardly deserving of the name, was the only one which occurred to the fair sisters during their summer ramblings round Baden-Baden. In a different way, meanwhile, Mr Hargrave and Madame de Hautrivage pursued their course, also, with considerable enjoyment, though but little variety. The library, the public rooms, and the ever gay and moving scene in the noble portico before them, sufficed, with their late rising, to fill up the day. And thus gradually wore away the months of summer and of sorrow. Not but that Mr Hargrave still very sincerely lamented the loss of his elegant wife, – and her two young daughters would either of them have given a right hand to have brought her back again, – but in exact proportion as their loss was hopeless and irreparable, did unrepining endurance follow it. Such is the benignant lot of nature!

As to Madame de Hautrivage, her philosophy required not the aid of any latent provision of Providence, in order to enable her to support her spirits. For the greater part of her life she had never omitted to repeat at proper intervals, *'J'adore ma soeur! Tout le monde l'adore!'* And her part of the amiable Madame Hargrave's funeral obsequies having been performed by her pronouncing these same sentences with no other alteration than changing the present tense into the preterite, she gave herself without scruple to the agreeable consciousness of having secured a home where she should be able to dress in a very superior style, and save money into the bargain.

CHAPTER III

We must now return to the opening of our story, from which a necessary digression has led us. The gayest house in Paris, during the winter of 1834–5, was that of Mr Hargrave. There was not a single person of fashion, native or foreigner – inhabitant of the *'belle ville,'* or only a sojourner there – who did not share its hospitality and contribute to its splendour. Mr Hargrave himself was ever the centre and main-spring of every elegant scene of amusement which went on there; and much as it may be the fashion among the clever natives of that brilliant capital, while enjoying the costly entertainments of its British visitors, to pronounce them *'gauche et de mauvais ton,'* Mr Hargrave seemed by common consent to be declared an exception to the general rule. Every succeeding *fête*, let it be of what name or nature it might, was declared to be *'le plus parfaite qu'on avait jamais vu;'* and even when no single Englishman was by to listen, it was quite a common thing for them to pronounce among themselves, that, 'notwithstanding he was an Englishman, Monsieur Hargrave was a person *tout-à-fait comme il faut*, and actually graceful and agreeable, though not a Frenchman.'

Of this suffrage, this enviable preference, this intoxicating approbation, Mr Hargrave was fully aware; and not only did it constitute, in a great degree, the glory and happiness of his existence, but there is no exaggeration in saying that there was nothing which he would not have done rather than lose it.

It is not possible to suppose that scenes so splendid, amusements so skilfully chosen, and so ably varied, could fail of being agreeable to the two lovely girls, who seemed eternally to live in an atmosphere of golden light,

'Giving and stealing *brightness*.'

Mademoiselle de Cordillac, in particular, did most certainly enjoy this portion of her existence very greatly. The natural pleasure which a pretty, elegant, and accomplished girl feels, from being duly appreciated, or, in plain English, greatly admired, and the joys of dancing and music, too, where youth, health, a light heart, and a good ear, assist to give them value, are worth something, when they come without drawback of any kind; and when to all this is added the carefully arranged absence of every annoyance, and the sedulously sought for presence of every thing agreeable to existence, it is no great wonder if a very lively and very innocent French girl did find herself superlatively happy in the midst of it. This measureless content of the bright-eyed Adèle was not, however, fully shared by her half-English sister. Sabina had a much less keen relish for the occupations which are resorted to for mere amusement, and was, moreover, apt to fancy that there was less of mental dignity in mirth than in melancholy. She was, too, less anxious to be popular, and derived infinitely less gratification from admiration than Adèle, who knew no greater joy than to feel that every body around was gay and happy, and that some portion of their gaiety and happiness was derived from her. But this difference between them arose wholly from temperament, and in no degree from principle; both being equally pure in heart, and equally ready to have sacrificed any pleasure to what they believed to be their duty.

Many offers of marriage had been received by Mr Hargrave for both the girls, but the answer was ever the same — 'They are in no haste to marry; nor am I in haste that they should change their present state of unalloyed happiness for one more doubtful.' This answer was, of course, without appeal; for though Mademoiselle de Cordillac's pecuniary independence of her step-father was perfectly well known, no Frenchman of sufficient rank in society to be received as a familiar guest by Hargrave, would have been hardy enough so completely to break through established usage as to request the young lady to judge for herself. And even if they had, there was little choice of their receiving any more favourable answer.

But though Frenchmen are not in the habit of requesting young ladies of fortune and fashion to receive their addresses entirely from inclination, and not from the influence of either custom or authority, there was a young Englishman at that time in Paris, who had been educated under a different code of manners, and who, having fallen gradually, but profoundly, in love with Adèle de Cordillac, thought of nothing but making himself acceptable to her, and to her only, without giving a thought to the possible influence of Mr Hargrave. Alfred Coventry knew perfectly well that, if he could be happy enough to win the affection of Adèle, there was nothing in his fortune, connexions, or character, which would render it probable that her inclinations would be thwarted by her friends: and to this sweet occupation of winning his way to her heart he devoted himself, from the moment that he became thoroughly and conscientiously convinced that he could be well content to make the study of her happiness the occupation of his future life.

It was long, however, before Adèle began to understand how very much he was in earnest. Accustomed from her first appearance in society to universal admiration, and equally accustomed to the belief that this had nothing whatever to do with her future settlement in life, she learned nothing from the marked attention of Mr Coventry but that he was infinitely more agreeable than any other man of her acquaintance.

The incessant dissipation in which the Paris season was passed, and the rapid succession of engagements, which invariably included all the most distinguished members of its society, rendered the intercourse between these two people of almost daily recurrence; and they danced together so constantly, and talked together so much, that Madame de Hautrivage, who had early in the acquaintance made what she called proper inquiries in the proper places, began to flatter herself that her beautiful niece was about to form a connexion in every way worthy of her. For some days after this conviction came upon her, Madame de Hautrivage waited with tolerable patience for the proposals, which she felt perfectly certain her brother-in-law would receive, and forthwith announce to her; but finding that nothing of the sort came, and that Mr Hargrave seemed absolutely insensible to the necessity of bringing the business to a conclusion before the end of the season, it occurred to her that she was herself the most proper person to receive the overtures, which, perhaps, the shy young Englishman had hardly courage to make; and, accordingly, she took care at his next visit to have him shewn into an unoccupied *salon*, where she speedily joined him.

Though as far as possible from intending to make an offer of himself to the woman he adored through the medium of any one, Mr Coventry was not insensible to the advantages which he derived from being very decidedly in the good graces of Madame de Hautrivage. He had seen many a flattering admirer of his lovely Adèle sent *ça et là*, upon various frivolous excuses, on purpose, as he very correctly believed, to indulge him with the uninterrupted pleasure of her conversation. For this kindness he was by no means ungrateful, and devoted more time to the being civil to the good lady in return than any other woman, save his beloved, could boast of having won from him.

There is something very peculiar, and demanding a good deal of observation *de près* in order to comprehend it, in the tone taken occasionally in France by a pretender to a young lady's hand towards the mother or aunt of *la belle*. It sometimes happens, without, however, giving the slightest ground for scandal, that ladies so circumstanced, and being still *à prétension*, like to receive, and actually do receive, a very considerable number of sighs, hand-kissings, and tender glances from the identical men who are soliciting their interest with their direct or collateral descendants. In ninety-nine cases out of a hundred this may fairly be understood to express nothing more than a latent regret on the part of the *prétendant*, that he had not flourished at the time when the lady before him might herself have been free to accept his honourable vows; and though, by gentle degrees, this chastened gallantry merges in all well-regulated families into a tone more consonant to the relationship in which the parties subsequently stand to each other, its existence, while it lasts, is productive of a good deal of sentimental coquetry, which in some way or another is probably amusing to both parties.

Madame de Hautrivage was the last woman in the world to think of marrying a niece without coming in for her full share of this species of offering, and was most pleasantly persuaded that she actually did receive it every time Alfred Coventry offered her one arm, while Adèle hung upon the other, during a crowded exit from the opera, or *entrée* to the supper-room of a *fête*.

On entering the elegant little *salon* to which, by her orders, Mr Coventry had been shewn on the morning that she intended should witness the consummation of her hopes for her eldest niece's establishment, she found him engaged in examining a miniature, of which there were many, cased in velvet and gold, lying upon a table. It chanced that the portrait which at that moment occupied his attention was her own, and it was with a sort of tender smile that she remarked it.

'This is very beautiful,' said Mr Coventry, after paying his compliments to her as she entered. 'I have seldom seen a lovelier face.'

'Ah, flatterer!' she replied, shaking her head; 'I greatly doubt your thinking so.'

But for this bashful disclaiming of his compliment, which most

assuredly was not intended for her, though it was for her picture,
Coventry would never have guessed that the one was a 'counterfeit
presentment' of the other; for, although Madame de Hautrivage was still
what is called 'a fine woman,' there was but little resemblance between
her neatly wigged and carefully rouged face, and the blooming little
Hebe he held in his hand. But thus schooled, he of course took care not
to betray his own dulness in tracing a resemblance, and gallantly replied
that nobody could doubt the beauty of the face but herself.

She drew near him, and laid a finger on his shoulder.

'Come, come, my friend,' she said, with a slight sigh, 'no more of this.
It would be great folly to deny that those poor features, such as they are,
have been gazed upon by the eye of love; but this it not a moment for
you to think of it; your thoughts, *cher ami*, are, and ought to be,
elsewhere. French women are proverbially called coquets – I know it! But
trust me, Alfred, we are capable of checking the tenderness of nature,
which leads to this, whenever more important business is to be attended
to. Such is the case now; I think not that I am capable of doubting it.
Speak then, Mr Coventry, and be assured that it is not an indifferent ear
which will listen to you. When Clementina de Hautrivage professes
friendship, it is no weak sentiment which fills her breast.'

As Madame de Hautrivage concluded these words, she placed her right
elbow on the palm of her left hand, and shielding her eyes behind the
richly jewelled fingers thus supported, seemed to await his answer with
that sort of forced composure which arises from high principle when
struggling with sensibility.

Alfred Coventry understood her perfectly. He knew, as well as she did
herself, that she desired he should propose for her niece, and that she was
ready to bind him in chains of eternal gratitude by promising her
influence in his favour. But rather than have conveyed his fond devotion
to Adèle through such a medium, and have suffered the eyes which now
languished at him between diamond fingers to catch from those of his
beloved the first answer to his acknowledged hopes, instead of receiving
that hoped-for answer into his own bosom, he would have endured any
thing – he would have done any thing, even to making downright love to
the disagreeable personage before him.

In truth, he felt himself placed in so very awkward and critical a
situation by this direct and unexpected appeal, that he saw he must make
rather a desperate plunge to get out of it; and knowing that words of the
most unmeaning gallantry are a sort of false coin which is permitted to
pass current in France, without subjecting the utterer to any heavy pains
and penalties, he replied, 'My charming Madame de Hautrivage! can you
believe it possible that in your presence the thoughts of any man can turn
elsewhere?'

Under many other circumstances the exquisite Clementina de Hautrivage might have listened to this, and much more in the same strain, without perceiving in it any thing out of the common way, or calling for any return beyond the dropping of her eyelids, and, perhaps, a slight sigh. But the case was different now. In the first place, she knew, from considerable experience, that the most *volage* of Englishmen are, generally speaking, infinitely more in earnest, for the time being at least, than the most *fidèle* of Frenchmen. Secondly, the unremitting assiduity of the young man before her could not be mistaken. If he was not in pursuit of Adèle de Cordillac, he must be in pursuit of some other of the family. The thing was clear, and admitted not the slightest doubt. Sabina Hargrave it could not be, for he had never distinguished her by any particular attention whatever. But with herself the case was far otherwise; he *had* distinguished her – '*Oh, Ciel!*' could she doubt it!

Her relationship with Madame Hargrave had given her some acquaintance with the English language, and at this critical moment she remembered an anecdote of George the Fourth, which had led to a phrase, now passed into a proverb, always pleasantly recalled by beauties of a certain age.

'Faat, farre, and forté,' she inwardly repeated, and, with all the quickness of thought, reasoned upon it. '*Faat* – grosse? Je ne suis pas maigre . . . *Farre*, blonde ou belle . . . belle donc . . . et n'est-ce pas que je suis belle? . . . *Forté* . . . ça veut dire quarante . . . et bien . . . j'ai quarante ans, je le sais . . . même quelques jours de plus . . . mais qu'est-ce que cela fait? . . . Faat, farre, and forté! Alfred! . . . c'est moi! . . . c'est moi que tu aimes! . . . Ah, Dieu! Comment est-ce que je l'ai jamais douté?'

During the moment thus employed by the lady, Mr Coventry had recourse to the miniatures, and, as ill luck would have it, again opened that of the Madame Clementina. Had any doubt still remained on her mind, this act would have removed it. What *could* it mean at such a moment, but that in the extremity of his emotion, her lover found relief in gazing at her portrait rather than at herself? – a portrait indeed was, as she well knew, a sort of hieroglyphic in love, the mere perusal of which was an act of faith.

But, although Madame de Hautrivage was thus satisfactorily convinced of his passion, there were other things, besides its existence, which it deeply behoved her to know, ere she decided upon her own line of conduct in return. Had the young man been a Frenchman, she would have been less perplexed – but as it was, she had doubts. Did the devoted, the noble-minded Alfred contemplate marriage? There was nothing cruel in the nature of Madame de Hautrivage, and had she felt certain that he did *not*, her education and her principles would probably have led her to pass a very lenient judgment on his indiscretion; but in her particular position it would be vastly more convenient that he should. She felt called upon, therefore, to act with becoming caution, lest any imprudent symptom of weakness on her part might lead him to change the better line of conduct for the worse. But, while fully impressed with the necessity for this sort of reserve, she at the same time felt it to be absolutely necessary that she should ascertain whether the attachment so openly avowed was of the graver or the lighter quality. From her knowledge of mankind in general, as well as from a latent consciousness that she was not quite so young and so lovely as she had been, she might, perhaps, have been prematurely led to the conclusion that Mr Coventry intended nothing more than one of those *liaisons par amours*, for which her happy country was so justly celebrated. But there was a gentle decorum of manner about him, which made her hope better things; and she very nearly convinced herself during the next five minutes' conversation with him, that his views were most strictly honourable, and that she had nothing whatever to fear from the vehemence of his passion, which could militate against the hope – every moment becoming stronger – that his purpose was to win her affections, with no other object than to make her his wife.

After remaining in very idle chit-chat as long as he thought there was any hope of seeing Adèle enter, Mr Coventry's patience gave way, and suddenly rising, he said, –

'My dearest Madame de Hautrivage, I must wish you good morning; and must trust to your goodness to excuse the unreasonable length of the visit I have made. I am not, I confess, without hope that though I have not dared fully to open my heart to you, yet that you have guessed in some degree what is passing here, and that you do not altogether look upon it with displeasure.'

'Thank God!' mentally exclaimed Madame de Hautrivage; 'he has ventured to speak out at last!'

'Mr Coventry,' she replied, 'I will not affect to misunderstand you; such dissimulation would be unworthy of us both; and I am persuaded that I could only lose in your estimation by resorting to it. I scorn to do so, Alfred Coventry, – I scorn the appearance of throwing difficulties in your way, when my own heart tells me that none exist. I have now said enough, I trust, to still the agitation of your spirits, and to make you feel all the delicious calm produced by hope unchilled by fear. One word more, and you shall leave me, Alfred. Be assured that the delicacy which has prevented your explaining yourself more fully is well appreciated by me; and that, though a Frenchwoman, and accustomed, perhaps, to plainer speaking, I am not insensible to the charm of that reserve which seems ever, in your countrymen, to accompany the most perfect faith and the truest sincerity. May I not thus interpret it, dear Alfred?'

'You may, indeed,' returned Mr Coventry, with great earnestness, and not a little pleased at believing that he had succeeded in propitiating the aunt without forfeiting the dear English privilege of himself confessing his love to the woman who had inspired it. But knowing, as he did, what the manners and customs of '*la grande nation*' demanded on such occasions, he could not but feel a vast deal of gratitude to the kind-hearted woman who had thus permitted him to break through them all, without testifying the slightest displeasure at it. In truth, at that moment his heart was overflowing with a multitude of happy, gentle, and affectionate feelings; and not wishing to prolong the dialogue, lest he might be led on to say to another what he had determined to utter only to the ear of Adèle, he relieved the overflowing fulness of his emotions by respectfully impressing a kiss on either cheek of his intended aunt.

Had he not left the room the moment after he had perpetrated his audacity, all the foregone conclusions of Madame de Hautrivage might have been overthrown; and all the satisfactory composure of spirit, derived from the conviction that the sanctity of his honourable attachment had put a bridle on its ardour, lost. As it was, however, no man ever left a lady more completely satisfied with his words and conduct. For many years she had been labouring, with an expenditure of Machiavelism sufficient to maintain the most crafty dynasty that ever ruled, to obtain a second marriage, which might supply the pecuniary difficulties of her first; and now, at the very moment when she had begun to confess to her heart of hearts that her chance of obtaining this was well-nigh gone for ever, behold her in possession of more than her most sanguine hopes had ever represented as possible!

It is, I fear, by no means improbable that the state of things, as thus described, will be censured by my countrywomen as highly unnatural, not to say impossible. But to all such, I would recommend a deeper attention to the character of our fascinating neighbours than they have probably yet given. It must be remembered, in the first place, that though there are doubtless many among us who live, and, fortunately for the happiness of their earthly existence, die in the belief that they are a thousand times more charming than any one else ever thought them, nevertheless, not one of the whole number ever felt that delightful conviction which is common to all Frenchwomen − that if they are ugly, *c'est égal*; that if they are ignorant, *c'est égal*; also, that if their reputation has melted away, not into thin air, but into an atmosphere charged to explosion with

'Little hints of heavy scandals,'

still *c'est égal!* For be they as ugly as Hecate, as old as her grandmother, and with a worse reputation, our fair neighbours have each and all of them the immutable persuasion of possessing a charm, a *tournure*, a style, a tone, – *something*, in short, that is perfectly and altogether irresistible. It is for this that they have invented for themselves a phrase which, in speaking of this extraordinary power of fascination, conveys in four words a description of it. What is the '*Je ne sais quoi*' so fondly boasted of among them, but this innate assurance of being bewitching without any possibility of stating the reason why? Most assuredly, in ninety-nine cases out of a hundred, this inexpressible, universal, irresistible attraction, of which no Frenchwoman scruples to *confess* herself conscious, if strictly inquired into, can only be fitly described by this simple and sincere reply, '*Je ne sais quoi.*' The phrase may, indeed, be safely declined through every possible voice, mood, and tense, and still be found to furnish an answer most strictly true, –

'*Je ne sais quoi.*'
'*Tu ne sais quoi.*'
'*Il ne sait quoi.*'

And when brought to the climax, '*Nous ne saurons jamais,*' it will not, even then, have exceeded its proper limits. Admirable phrase! Perfect alike in its *naïveté* and its truth! All the nations of the earth ought, in common justice, to exclaim in chorus, 'We thank thee, France, for giving us that word!'

Till all this has been duly inquired into and understood, I must take leave to deprecate the sentence which shall declare the satisfaction of Madame de Hautrivage, after her interview with Mr Coventry, to be unnatural. So far, indeed, is this from being the case, that had she even been forced to explain the charm in which she confided, with more specific exactness than the national formula above quoted supplies, she would have found herself at no loss for it, – for she would have proudly answered, –

'I am a Frenchwoman!' An answer, by the by, which none can duly appreciate who have not listened to it in the vernacular. The tone with which '*Je suis Française*' is pronounced, being decidedly more pregnant of innate contentment and self-gratulation than any other in the world.

CHAPTER IV

No sooner was Madame de Hautrivage convinced that Mr Coventry had left the house, than she hastened to the room generally occupied by the young ladies in the morning; not, indeed, with any fixed intention of communicating to either of them the scene which had just taken place, but rather to enjoy the consciousness of her own delightful secret in the presence of those who might fancy, perhaps, that they had a better right to be the heroine of such a mystery than herself.

She found Sabina, as usual, deeply engaged upon a volume of wild German stories, which alternately with the poetry of the same imaginative land furnished one of the greatest charms of her existence. She was, indeed, too completely occupied even to perceive the entrance of Madame de Hautrivage, and continued to read, without raising her eyes. But Adèle, though she had a book before her, was very far from bestowing upon it the same degree of attention; she even seemed glad of an excuse to close it, and when her aunt entered the room, threw it aside, and languidly addressed herself to her embroidery frame.

'Ah! you are happy young creatures!' exclaimed Madame, standing for a moment to contemplate them. 'How devoid of all care is the destiny of early youth! And how little does strong emotion of any kind interfere with your joyous existence!'

'Joyous!' repeated Sabina, looking up, and shaking her head with a sort of mournful smile. 'I do not think, Madame, that you have chosen the epithet well when speaking of Adèle to-day; for I think I never saw her so little joyous in my life.'

'Ah! Is it so?' said Madame de Hautrivage, turning her eyes upon her niece, and immediately perceiving that she did indeed look paler, and less gay than usual. 'What is it, Adèle? Are you unwell, my child?'

'Shall I tell tales, Adèle?' said Sabina, laughing. 'Shall I tell Madame that you certainly expected Mr Coventry to call this morning, and are disappointed because he has not made his appearance?'

'You are a silly child to utter such nonsense,' replied Adèle, gravely. 'But, fortunately, I know that if you really thought any such thing, you would not say it.'

'Upon my word, Adèle, you are mistaken,' replied her sister. 'I am perfectly in earnest in what I say; and the reason why I have no scruple in uttering it is, that I feel persuaded your aunt knows as well as I do, that Alfred Coventry is going to propose for you, – if he has not done it already.'

A much more mischievous person than Sabina might have studied for a month before they could have spoken anything so calculated to torture Madame de Hautrivage as these few words. From one short, sharp moment of painful thought, the intended bride felt uncertain as to what line of conduct it would be most judicious to pursue. She looked at Adèle with a frowning and indignant brow, and a multitude of hateful surmises chased each other through her brain; but there was something so particularly innocent and unconscious of offence in the expression of the sweet girl's blushing face, as she bent her head over her work, that her aunt felt convinced that if Sabina were right, and that the thoughts of

Adèle really did wander towards Alfred Coventry, it was not in consequence of any thing which had yet passed between them, but solely from an impulse of some unjustifiable girlish fancy, which it would have been her especial duty to check, even had she no other interest in the business than that of a maternally anxious and watchful friend.

'Come with me, Adèle, my love,' said she, in a voice of much kindness. 'I wish to speak a few words to you in private.'

Adèle trembled from head to foot. She doubted not at all, more than the gentle Sabina, whose eyes were fixed upon her with a look of the tenderest interest, that Madame de Hautrivage had been commissioned to break to her the proposals of the young Englishman. Pleasure will often shew itself under an aspect that looks like grief; and Adèle could not have looked paler, as she rose to obey the invitation of her aunt, had she been sure that she was about to listen to the announcement of the heaviest misfortune that could possibly fall upon her.

Having reached the *salon* which Coventry had just left, the lady who considered herself as his *fiancée* sat herself down exactly where he had sat, and made a signal to her niece that she should place herself opposite.

'Adèle!' she said, with much solemnity of manner, 'I might, perhaps, as the eldest child of my deceased sister, have selected you as the person to whom I would first wish to communicate the important news I have to tell, even if the silly nonsense just uttered by your childish sister did not render it absolutely necessary. She spoke, my dear, of your having an idea, – that is, of your having taken it into your head; or rather, I think, of her having taken it into *her* head – that Mr Coventry, our English friend, Mr Alfred Coventry, had thoughts of making proposals for your hand in marriage. I trust, my dear, that Sabina Hargrave had no right whatever to say what she did, and that you will be ready to assure me that no such ridiculous idea has ever entered your imagination.'

Madame de Hautrivage here ceased to speak with her tongue; but her eyes, steadily bent upon the face of her suffering niece, carried on the examination with the most inquisitorial severity, and left poor Adèle no resource but to turn away her face, and fix her own eyes upon the ground. Had the words of Madame de Hautrivage suggested to Mademoiselle de Cordillac the meaning they were intended to convey, – had she understood from them any reproach for having hoped in vain for the offered hand of the young Englishman, her manner would have been totally different; for she would not have called in vain upon the pride and delicacy which were strong within her, for power to rebut so offensive a suspicion. But these tremendous words, 'the important news I have to tell,' still rung in her ears, and she understood from them nothing less than a formal annunciation that *some* proposal had been made for her, which the wisdom of her aunt approved. True, Adèle was independent;

she remembered this, and thanked Heaven for it. But the consciousness that her opposition to every proposal in the world but one would, in truth, arise from her having committed the offence so grievous in the eyes of France, – men, women, and children, – of daring before marriage to prefer one human being to all others, completely overwhelmed her, and gave her the appearance of guilt, which she was ashamed either to acknowledge or deny.

'What am I to think of this confusion, – this terrified embarrassment, Mademoiselle de Cordillac?' said her aunt, trembling with passion. 'Is it possible that you have so completely, so eternally disgraced yourself, as to bestow your affections on a man who not only is totally free from all partiality to you, but actually affianced to another? Must I, indeed, believe this possible in the child of my own sister?'

'Affianced to another!' repeated Adèle, unconscious that she spoke at all.

'Yes, mademoiselle, to another! Do you still doubt? Must I go yet farther to make you withdraw this most indecent acknowledgement of unrequited and unsought-for love? Nay, then, you shall be satisfied, young lady. You shall have no excuse for persevering in this fearful degradation from any ill-timed concealment of mine. Know then, Mademoiselle Adèle, that I have this very day, and in this very room, myself received a proposal of marriage from Alfred Coventry!'

'And for whom, aunt?' said Adèle, recovering her usual manner.

'For myself, Mademoiselle de Cordillac!' was the reply. 'You look surprised, Adèle,' resumed Madame de Hautrivage; 'and, I am sorry to say, mortified. But you are old enough to know, my dear, that it is not only youth, and the earliest dawn of beauty, which produces the sincerest attachments, and still less the most frequent offers of marriage. I have never thought it necessary, my dear, to explain to you, or to any one, the exact state of my affairs; but the fact is, I am extremely rich. It is probable that you may have guessed this from the style of my dress and general appearance, but I am aware that you could not in reality know much about it. Perhaps, even, I have in some degree wished to conceal the fact, from the dread of being eternally persecuted with proposals, and this may satisfactorily account for any thing you may have ever heard to the contrary. But the case is altogether different with Mr Coventry. He has, as he most certainly had a right to do, carefully informed himself of the facts in this case; and I have lived too long in the world to think the worse of him, mademoiselle, for selecting a wife whose fortune may enable him to do many laudable acts which he might not be able to achieve without it. I have, indeed, reason to believe that it is his intention to obtain a seat in the British Parliament, – a sign of very noble ambition, which I shall greatly approve, although I am aware of the heavy costs it brings with it. But, be this as it may, mademoiselle, *mon parti est pris*, – I have accepted the offered hand of Alfred Coventry, and his lips have ventured to ratify the contract, not only in words, but by a kiss of affection equally solemn and tender. After this,' added Madame de Hautrivage, with an air of impressive dignity, 'I need hardly add that I consider myself already as his wife!'

The elderly beauty was perfectly right in conceiving that Adèle was surprised, but wrong when she added that she was mortified. It was not mortification that she felt. She was shocked, and she was astonished, – painfully astonished by the information thus communicated to her; but a stronger feeling still was thankfulness, that, notwithstanding the feelings and the hopes which she knew had found a place in her heart, nothing had ever passed between herself and Mr Coventry which could have enlightened him on the subject. She recalled, by one rapid glance over the past, a hundred instances of looks and expressions on his part that seemed to indicate his devotion to her; but not one – no, not the shadow of one, wherein he could have traced any feeling in return that she would have wished to conceal. It is true that of late she had been in daily expectation of learning from Mr Hargrave, or her aunt, that he had declared in the usual form by which such matters were managed in France, the sentiments which she had fancied he wished her to perceive. But most happily for her present tranquillity, the manners of her country, and in which she had been most carefully educated, so guarded and fenced her in from all approaches not made in the usual way, that in the midst of daily intercourse and devoted attention she had still retained the love and manner of a young girl who had never dreamed of love. It was, indeed, this reserve, so constantly, and at all times and seasons preserved by Adèle, which had hitherto prevented Coventry from laying his heart at her feet. Like other young men of large independent fortune and unobjectionable station and character, he had received his share of coaxing from careful mothers and provident fathers; and though still under thirty, had already learned to tremble at the danger of being married for his acres rather than for himself. When first he looked at Mademoiselle de Cordillac with the admiration which loveliness excites when the peculiar style of it particularly pleases the taste of the gazer, he rejoiced at perceiving that her position was so brilliant, her independence so generally recognised, and the admiration she excited so general, that *should* it so happen that his liking grew into love, he might be pretty sure of not winning her unless she loved him too.

It was this confidence, perhaps, which made his long-sought-for heart surrender itself so promptly to the beautiful French girl, despite a few English prejudices which, under other circumstances, might have led him to pause; but certain it is, that before he had been six weeks in the habit of daily and nightly conversing with Mademoiselle de Cordillac, he became most deeply attached to her. Yet still he spoke not the important words which were to place all his hopes of earthly happiness in her hands; for still he doubted whether there could be any feeling capable of being fostered into love in one so very free from every recognised symptom of it. By degrees, indeed, he saw, or fancied he saw, a sparkling brightness in her eye when he approached that made his heart bound as he watched it; and he had pretty well made up his mind to wait for no surer indication of what was passing within, when his fatal interview with Madame de Hautrivage took place.

After listening with becoming gravity, and as much composure as her speaking features could assume, to Madame's history of the parting salute, Adèle rose, and said in a gentle and very tolerably steady voice, 'I am obliged to you for this confidential communication, aunt, and beg you to believe that I sincerely wish you happy. For the emotion you witnessed when you said that you had important news to tell me, you will easily understand it when I confess that I thought you meant to announce some application, with which you were favoured, for myself. I am too happy, aunt, as I have before often told both papa and yourself, to wish for any change . . . and all I ask for is to be permitted to remain as I am.'

'Well, my dear,' continued Madame de Hautrivage, very complacently, 'if that is all, I see no reason whatever for not indulging you . . . You are a very handsome girl, Adèle, and, better still, you have a very handsome fortune, which will always suffice to secure you an eligible *partie*, whenever you shall happen to change your mind.'

Mademoiselle de Cordillac made no reply to this agreeable prediction save a smile and a bow, and then quitted the room, leaving her aunt exceedingly well pleased at the interview.

'Well, Adèle,' cried Sabina, as her sister re-entered their boudoir; 'what is it all about? Is it an offer of marriage from Mr Coventry that Madame has announced to you?'

'Yes, Sabina, it is,' replied Adèle, with a languid smile; 'she has, indeed, announced to me an offer of marriage from Mr Coventry. But it is not for the person you are foolish enough to suppose, – it is not for me, Sabina.'

'For whom then? Not for me, I am very sure.'

'No, my dear; it is for neither of us. It is to Madame de Hautrivage herself. Mr Coventry is going to be married to my aunt.'

'Adèle! what can induce you to amuse yourself by talking such nonsense?'

'If there be nonsense in the business, Sabina, it is not mine. I have repeated to you very exactly, the information I have just received from Madame de Hautrivage. She tells me that she is affianced to Mr Coventry, and that she already considers herself as his wife.'

'And it is without laughing that you say this, Adèle?' said her young sister, looking at her grave face with the most unfeigned astonishment. 'I wish to Heaven you would explain yourself! I cannot bear to be mystified about any thing serious, and particularly about any thing which concerns you.'

'Believe me, Sabina, there is no joke in the matter; and you should be glad, dearest, that if I do not laugh, I do not weep either. I am shocked to think that, partly by your flattery, and partly by my own, I had very nearly persuaded myself to believe that this gentleman had treated me with particular attention; and, what is worse still, that I was exceedingly well pleased that so it should be. Had I in any other way been thus suddenly obliged to give up all the thoughts and . . . why should I deny it to you, my Sabina? . . . all the *hopes* which have sprung from this wild idea, the pain – the disappointment would have been hard to bear. But now, Sabina, what is there in it more terrible than awaking from a dream? There is no such man as the Alfred Coventry by whom I fancied myself beloved; and though my vision was a very pretty vision, and that all it wanted to be perfect was that it should be true, I am not weak enough to sit down and break my heart that it is not so.'

'God forbid you should, dearest Adèle!' exclaimed Sabina, who, now that the truth was forced upon her, looked, if possible, paler than Adèle herself, – 'God forbid that you should ever waste another thought upon one so utterly contemptible! And yet, merciful Heaven! how is it possible to believe it? Madame de Hautrivage on one side, and Adèle de Cordillac on the other, and a man is found who prefers the former to the latter! Oh! it is monstrous, Adèle. And though I no longer suspect you of meaning to deceive me, I cannot help believing still that our poor aunt deceives herself; for, without any great degree of self-love, you must surely be aware that such a preference is absolutely unnatural.'

'Perhaps it would be so,' replied Adèle, with another of her altered smiles, 'were it not for the motive which Madame de Hautrivage herself, with a total absence of vanity or self-delusion of any kind, explained to me. The confession was certainly too *naïve* to leave any doubt of its veracity. She told me, Sabina, what we neither of us ever knew before – and no wonder, for I am sure we never bestowed a thought upon the subject, – she told me that she was very rich, and that Mr Coventry had many objects of laudable ambition before him, which his union with her would enable him to achieve. So, at least, we must allow that, however much my own vanity has led me to deceive myself, Mr Coventry has evidently not attempted to deceive her.'

'A very noble degree of sincerity, indeed,' replied Sabina, 'and well worthy of the parties between whom it has been displayed! Now then, Adèle, let us never mention this hateful man's name again. He has put himself up to sale, and, as I presume, the highest bidder has got him. Were I you, I would most cautiously avoid all intercourse with him. If he really be paying his addresses to this good lady – if he is really to become your uncle, it may, and must be, I suppose, impossible to keep wholly out of his way; but, were I you, I never would permit him to converse with me again.'

'And so display to him the profound impression which his light gallantry has made upon my too sensitive heart? No, Sabina, if you were me, you would do no such thing. Let me tell you honestly, my sister, how it stands with me: – There are some painful feelings that I could bear, and, as I hope, bear well; but there are others which I could not bear at all – or, at any rate, very ill indeed. I believe I could bear well the mortification and disappointment consequent upon finding that a gentleman whom I had first endowed with all the virtues under heaven, and then laid at my feet as my lover, was about as far removed from deserving the first as the last of these imputations. Yes, Sabina, I could bear this, and feel, perhaps, in the course of time, that it was a very useful lesson against presumption of all kinds. But what I could *not* bear, is the thought that Alfred Coventry should read the disappointment of my silly heart in my countenance or in my manner to him. God forgive me, Sabina, but I think that, rather than bear this, I would die! Then save me from it, dearest – dearest love, as you pity me!'

Inexpressibly affected by the manner in which poor Adèle uttered these words, so totally unlike any thing she had ever heard from her before, Sabina knelt on the footstool before her, and, throwing her arms round her, exclaimed, 'Oh, Adèle! Tell me only what you wish me to do or to say that may comfort you, and it shall be the first object of my life to obey you.'

Adèle returned her caresses, and a few tears escaped from the bright eyes of both; but in the next moment the smile with which the elder sister reproved the weakness of the younger shewed that it was not in the *larmoyant* strain that she intended to seek for consolation.

'I will tell you,' she said, 'what it is I wish you to do; and all I wish you to say, my own gentle, sweet Sabina, is, that you will endeavour to support me in the line of conduct which I intend to pursue. What you must do, love, will not be very difficult; for it is only to treat Mr Coventry, and our aunt too, exactly in the same manner as you have ever done. Can you do this for me, Sabina, even if it should sometimes cost you a slight struggle with your inclinations?'

'A slight struggle!' Sabina repeated with a sigh. '*Mais c'est égal.* I question whether I have the power of being a very skilful actress under any circumstances, but I will do my best to please you, Adèle.'

'Thank you, dearest! I ask no more. All the skill needed is merely to avoid all occasions of testifying coldness or dislike. And now, Sabina, we will talk as little about this unpleasant blunder of mine as may be, and do not fancy that I am going to pine in thought. I do assure you, sister mine, there are many points on which I ought to be most especially grateful, and I trust I am so. First, for instance, I KNOW that I have never betrayed myself; and secondly, I know also that this time drawing aside the glittering veil with which my false prophet was invested will very effectually prevent the peace of my future life from being injured.'

Sabina Hargrave had the very highest possible opinion of her sister's judgment and high principle, as well as an attachment for her, as firm and devoted as it was possible for one human being to feel for another; it was, therefore, with the most docile obedience that she complied with these injunctions: but it was not without difficulty, for her feelings towards Mr Coventry had more of bitter dislike in them than any injury offered to herself could possibly have produced; and as for Madame de Hautrivage, there was a mixture of scorn, pity, and disgust, in the sentiment she excited, which made it a pretty severe penalty to converse with her, and no slight one to treat her with the respect which her near relationship demanded.

CHAPTER V

Alfred Coventry, meanwhile, passed out from his interview with Madame de Hautrivage in the happiest state of mind imaginable. He had been quite aware of the sort of expectation to which it was probable his attentions to Adèle had given rise, and was inexpressibly relieved by the subject having been satisfactorily discussed without his having been driven to send in, *en règle*, a statement of his wishes and pretensions, of his hopes and his rent-roll.

'It will not, then, be from the elegant *nonchalant* father-in-law, or from the made-up *maniérée* aunt, that I shall learn whether Adèle de Cordillac is to be mine or not!' thought he. 'It will be from the matchless eyes of the bright angel herself that I shall learn my destiny, and may God give me strength to bear it like a man; for either way the sentence will be enough to overpower one. Should it be, "*No, sir, no! I can never be yours!*" which way shall I turn? Whither shall I go? How shall I be able to look at her and live, if she tells me this? And − merciful Heaven! − should she say to me − or should she look as if she meant to say to me − "Alfred, I am thine!" what will become of me then?'

But wayward as these fancies seemed to be, hope so joyously predominated, that though he really endeavoured to examine his chance as doubtingly and modestly as possible, his step was light, and his gay eye as bright as the sunshine it encountered, as he walked across the splendid bridge which leads from the Chamber of Deputies to la Place de la Concorde.

Too much occupied by his own busy thoughts to know particularly well which way he was going, Coventry was passing the gates leading to the Tuileries Gardens, when he was accosted by a young Russian nobleman of considerable talent and great acquirement, with whom he had formed an acquaintance of more intimacy, perhaps, than with any other foreigner whom he had encountered during his residence abroad.

'*Mon cher!* You look as if you were setting out on a ramble from earth to heaven!' said Count Romanhoff, suddenly stopping him by laying his hand on each of his shoulders; 'and yet you turn your back on the Elysian Fields, which shews you to be greatly ignorant of the way. But truly, for the present, I would rather you should miss than find it, for the sight of your countenance is refreshing. You are the only man I have seen to-day who does not look as if he must step with caution, lest he should stumble as he walked and get his brains knocked out in some unaccountable manner or other before he knew who was near him.'

'What mean you, Romanhoff?' returned Coventry, laughing. 'Why should I expect to have my brains knocked out?'

'Only because it is so very much *la mode!* But, upon my honour, I begin to doubt if you even know of the adventure which has made all the men of fashion in Paris turn pale?'

'Nay, you may do more than doubt, – you may be very sure of it. I know no more what you are talking about than if I were returning from the journey you were pleased to mention, and this moment descended from the moon.'

'Then you have not heard that last night, for the third time within the last month, a gentleman leaving Riccordo's *salon de jeu*, with a considerable sum of money won there, was robbed, and left bound hand and foot in a corner so remote as to have been discovered only this morning?'

'No, truly, have I not. Three times within a month! And coming from the same place, too! This does not speak much in favour of the Parisian police, methinks.'

'Oh! for that, it is quite an exceptional case; and it would be hardly fair to blame the police for not interfering to prevent what it would have been so perfectly impossible to foresee,' replied the Russian.

'I don't suppose that any robberies are absolutely foreseen, Romanhoff; for in that case, of course, none would be perpetrated: but certainly it does seem rather strange that so very bold and atrocious an act as that you describe should be repeated three times under circumstances so similar.'

'So it does; but it will be repeated no more with impunity, for all Paris is in commotion about it now. Hitherto, it should seem as if the strange audacity of the deed rendered it so improbable it could be repeated, that both the first and the second crime were suffered to pass by, with no more preparation for preventing their recurrence than if an earthquake, unprecedented in the latitude, had swept away the street where it occurred.'

'What is this deed, Romanhoff, that

"Roars so loud and thunders in the index?"

demanded Coventry, who of late had thought so little, and cared so little, for any subject save one, that if the direful adventure alluded to by his friend had been related in his hearing, it had not made sufficient impression to rest upon his memory.

'What is it? Have you been out of Paris, Coventry?' returned the truly astonished Count.

'No; not positively out of Paris,' said Coventry, laughing. '*Mais fais comme si je n'y étais pas, mon cher*, and I shall understand you better a great deal than I do at present.'

'*Eh bien, mon hermite de la Chaussé d'Antin* thus it was: – Three weeks ago last Monday – and this you know, or I presume you know, is Wednesday – three weeks ago last Monday, M Jules Roland, the eldest son of the rich Roland, had won a very considerable sum at Riccordo's. How much it was I cannot exactly tell you, but I know that a portion of it consisted of a thousand napoleons and five hundred sovereigns, won from an Englishman, because the set who had been watching the play jested about the weight of it, and told Roland that he must look about for a trusty ticket-porter to carry it. To which he gaily replied, "*Merci, mes amis*," quoting with his exquisite accent –

"De labor ve delaught in, phisiques pin."

Upon which old De Nolonville ejaculated an oath or two against English, but added in a friendly tone, "At any rate, young man, keep to the open Boulevard."

"'Not a bit of it, M le Comte," replied Roland; "I shall do no such thing, but cut across as usual by – by –", Diable! I forget the name, but it was some obscure, little, dark street which lay in his way home. Eh, bien! we all saw him leave the room about two hours past midnight, and several followed soon after; but, as he himself positively states, nobody left the room with him. He says, too, that he did exactly as he said he should do; that is, he turned off the Boulevard into a dark narrow street, and before he had traversed half its length, he was seized from behind in the arms of a tall powerful man, who contrived so effectually to twist his (Roland's) cloak round his arms and over his mouth, that he was rendered as completely defenceless as if a strait waistcoat had been fastened on him, and as incapable of uttering a cry as if he had been gagged. This done, the villain rifled him of his gold and his notes, and then of his silk pocket-handkerchief; with which last article, however, he did not make off, but employed it in tying the legs of the unfortunate Jules so tightly together, that he was rendered as incapable of flying as of fighting – and thus he was found by the first passer-by on the following morning.'

'Did he see the face of the fellow who treated him thus?' demanded Coventry.

'No, not for an instant. The whole of the operations were most skilfully performed from behind him; which led the police to suspect, when they were applied to the next morning, that the scoundrel was some one who knew he should be recognised if seen. Besides, Jules bears testimony to the very gentlemanlike gentleness with which he was gagged and bound; not an atom more violence having been used, he says, than was absolutely necessary to effect the object in view: from which it is shrewdly inferred that the thief must have been one of the society present when the money was won, and the winner's purpose as to his route declared.'

'How dreadful,' exclaimed Coventry, 'is this idea of consorting with pickpockets and cut-throats! Will not this, Romanhoff, suffice to keep you in future from haunts where you are so little likely to meet companions deserving the honour of your fellowship?'

'I suspect that you rate that honour too highly, my good friend,' replied the young Russian. 'There is fellowship to be met in the *salons* of Riccordo, which my superiors in every way might be well pleased to fall in with.'

'In every way!' returned the Englishman. 'I doubt it, Romanhoff. But, at any rate, the set who really know each other there ought to ascertain with all despatch who it is among them who can by possibility be subjected to so horrible a suspicion.'

'And that is exactly the business upon which every man of fashion in Paris, except yourself, Coventry, is at this moment occupied. Of course the police is giving us all assistance; but they declare now, that, as nearly as possible, the very same thing has been repeated once and again, precisely as they did at first – that the case is so entirely out of the common way, and so removed from all possibility that their well-organised acquaintance with rogues and vagabonds should assist the discovery of the culprit, that but little is hoped from their interference. It unquestionably is a devilish disagreeable predicament in which we all stand, for there is not one among us, you perceive, who may not be the culprit; and it is certainly paying a very marked personal compliment if any one of the society looks at another with full and perfect assurance that he is not the man.'

'And do you mean to return again to this very mixed society, Romanhoff?' said Alfred, with a good deal of friendly anxiety.

'Why, do you not see, my dear fellow, that in the present state of affairs it would be as much as a man's reputation was worth to be absent from Riccordo's *salon*? Any *habitué* who should venture to withdraw himself at this crisis would be very suspiciously *noté*, you may depend upon it.'

'Then I can only rejoice the more that I am not one of them,' returned Mr Coventry, gravely; 'and most sincerely wish, my dear friend, that you were in the same category.'

'Nonsense, Alfred; you positively look at me with as pitiful a visage as if you thought that, whether going to the *salon* or staying away from it, I was equally liable to suspicion. Why, think for a moment of the noble names to be found in the set you are thus condemning wholesale? I am not the only intimate you have among them: there are D'Obigny, Castello, Reindenberg, De Bruton, Hargrave, Fitzjames, D'Arusez, and a dozen others at least, – all your right good and very intimate friends: are they all to be as profoundly pitied as I am?'

'No, Romanhoff, very few of them; for very few of them are so greatly capable of doing better. However, God made us all, as Beatrice, or some of her kindred, says. I will detain you no longer from your quest, and honestly wish you all success in it.'

While this conversation lasted, the two young men had walked across the gardens to the Rue Costiglione, where they paused; Alfred intending to mount his horse for as quiet and meditative a ride as the Bois de Boulogne could afford, and Romanhoff having a gossiping visit to make in the Place Vendôme.

'*Eh bien, donc,*' said the latter, after their different projects had been explained, '*sans adieu*, we shall meet to-morrow night, if not before, *chez votre digne compatriote M Hargrave. Dieu! comme il est magnifique, cet homme! en tout ce qu'il fait, c'est véritablement un prince. Eh que les demoiselles sont adorable!* – It is only the aunt,' he added, with something approaching to a shudder, 'that makes the advantage of the *entrée* there doubtful. But that woman is a horror, – she positively expects one to make love to her.'

'Does she?' said Coventry, laughing. 'I hope, at any rate, that one does not mean all?'

'Oh! but it does though . . . nobody can escape her. *Cependent*, I shall venture to-morrow, notwithstanding. *Au revoir!*'

And so they parted; Coventry thinking of the morrow's ball, of which his friend spoke so lightly, with a degree of emotion which almost turned hope into fear, and pleasure into pain: for he had fully made up his mind to seize an opportunity at this ball, amidst the often-found seclusion of a crowd, to open his whole heart to Adèle, and learn from her the destiny of his future life, while others were diligently occupied in selecting their partners for a dance.

CHAPTER VI

How little we are apt to think as we enter some crowded rendezvous of fashion, and throw a light glance over the light throng entering with us, — how little at such a moment are we apt to think of the various cares, sorrows, fears, and anxieties, that may be entering along with them; they all look so smilingly, or so proudly, or so richly, or so beautifully, that it never enters one's head to remember that every bosom there, be it as fair as it may or as bold as it will, let it palpitate behind a transparent inch of lace, or swell beneath the weight of a dozen decorations, has each its own little museum of cares, which, if laid bare before us, would make the outward coating seem wondrously flimsy.

Not one of all the lovely girls who moved about those splendid rooms of Mr Hargrave's, like so many full-dressed peris in Paradise, looked more gay, more beautiful, more animated, or more happy, than did Adèle de Cordillac; and yet she would gladly, thankfully, have resigned the chance of ever being present at another *fête*, could she thereby, unknown and unseen, have escaped from this. But she had screwed her courage to the desperate pitch of going through all the dreaded hilarity of that terrible evening, without giving Alfred Coventry the satisfaction of perceiving that she had the slightest objection to receiving him in the character of an uncle. She was shocked herself, poor girl! at the agony which this struggle cost her; but she believed that, could she find strength to get over this first trial, all that followed after would be comparatively easy: and it was this idea which urged her to the feverish energy of exertion which gave such a lustre to her eye, and such a glow to her cheek, as Alfred Coventry thought had never before been equalled on earth.

Nor was poor Adèle's the only heart which throbbed painfully amidst the elegant festivity of that splendid evening. Alfred Coventry's, too, beat painfully, — but this was as much, perhaps, from hope as from fear; and Sabina Hargrave's heart beat painfully, — for it swelled with scorn and indignation towards some; dislike, that approached antipathy, towards others; and towards her sister a degree of pity that positively wrung her to

the quick, and made it a task of no easy achievement to keep tears from
starting every time she looked at her.

Nor was the condition of Madame de Hautrivage entirely *couleur de
rose*; though she considered herself as decidedly the heroine of the hour,
and fully believed that, were her interesting situation known, she should
be envied by every woman present. But she could not altogether shut her
eyes upon the radiant beauty of Adèle, or the youthful loveliness of
Sabina; and she certainly did think it unlucky that they should both of
them have been dressed so very peculiarly well on that night.

It is probable, therefore, that if among our very restricted acquaintance
with the party which filled Mr Hargrave's magnificent rooms we are able
to name four who were ill at ease, it may be safely inferred that the
observation was a just one which pointed out the fallacy of festive
decoration as a symbol of enjoyment. When it is added that the identical
individual who had committed the three audacious robberies by Count
Romanhoff was actually one of the party, and by no means the least gay
and graceful person present, it will be allowed that, in the present
instance at least, some strong degree of anxiety must have mixed itself
with the festivity of the meeting, and of more kinds than one.

Nevertheless, to all outward appearance, every thing went well. *Blasé* as
the majority of the company probably were to all sorts of splendour, the
tasteful extravagance of Mr Hargrave contrived to elicit admiration, and
almost astonishment, from even the most veteran gazers upon Parisian
elegance; and, excepting such young ladies as were too deeply engaged in
flirtation to see any thing, there was scarcely a single individual in the
company who was not quite aware that the whole scene was one of the
most splendid they had ever looked upon.

A part of the extensive garden, with its magnificent conservatory, was
on this occasion added, at an immense expense, to the suite of rooms on
the ground-floor. A wide space between two rows of acacia trees was
roofed in, forming a gallery supported by a succession of illuminated
arches, and terminating in the green-house, now converted into a retreat
for lounging and conversation; while its exotic tenants were scattered in
blooming groups along the gallery, enriching the air with their fragrance,
and receiving on their dark leaves and brilliant blossoms the soft light of a
thousand waxen tapers, mysteriously enhancing their beauty, as it does
that of all the other pretty things it falls upon.

The more than common splendour of this sumptuous entertainment
had a more specific object than Mr Hargrave could, in general, have
pleaded in excuse for his boundless extravagance. The youthful brother of
a sovereign prince had, during the whole winter, which was now
drawing to its close, permitted himself to be the load-star of every *salon*
upon which the stamp of fashion was sufficiently impressed to authorise

his being invited to enter it. Gallant, gay, animated, and handsome, he was, of course, not only a first-rate personage, but a first-rate favourite wherever he appeared; and happy was the fair one whose hand he selected for the dance. On none had this selection fallen so often as on Sabina Hargrave, and to none had his manner been so respectfully attentive. The mere honour of this distinction would probably have been more keenly felt by any individual of the fair society than it was by herself; but this proceeded not from any sublime contempt for the *prestige* communicated by rank to all other *agrémens*, but to the fact that when the prince, at his own request, was first presented to her, his appearance, despite the insignia that glittered on his breast, so forcibly recalled that of the very simply clad youth she had seen on the rock, whence she gazed on the Mummelsee, and the spectre-like castle beside it, that it was surprise and pleasure, rather than gratified vanity, which his notice excited in her.

However, as he never, in any of the conversations that followed, alluded to the adventure which had befallen her there, and had shaken his head, as a negative, when she had once asked him if he had ever visited Baden-Baden, she was compelled to believe that this resemblance was merely accidental. Nevertheless his rank never produced any flattering or agreeable effect; on the contrary, it only made her conscious of a very painful distance between them. But with her father the case was widely different. His ambition was as unbounded as his vanity; and both together led him to think that, however incongruous such a connexion might be considered in any other family, the pre-eminent distinction to which he had attained in the world of fashion, together with the unrivalled beauty of his young daughter, would render it a very natural occurrence in his.

This notion once conceived, strengthened with every hour that passed over him, and speedily became the object to which every thought and every act was directed. Mr Hargrave must be very thoroughly known, and every circumstance of his situation very thoroughly understood, before any adequate idea can be formed of the manner in which such a hope was likely to work within him. That he loved Sabina tenderly and devotedly is most certain; but not all the joy which the investing one so fondly cherished with all which, in his estimation, made life worth having, would have sufficed to excite the feelings which now possessed him. True, such a marriage was every thing he could have wished on earth for her; it was every thing he could have wished on earth for himself: but this was not all; and what remained behind was, even in his estimation, and despite the besotted vanity which still raged within him, of more vital importance, ten thousand-fold, than any marriage which she could make, or any connexion, were it thrice royal, that he could obtain.

Mr Hargrave, in fact, at this time stood upon the brink of a precipice, one steady glance down which would probably have sufficed to make him a maniac for life. This steady glance, however, he had never yet given; nor was there the least chance of his doing so, as long as these buoyant hopes and meteor-like expectations, begot between self-love and imagination, continued to float before him. But Mr Hargrave was deeply and desperately in debt. The large fortune he had brought with him from England had gradually been dissolving away from the year of his marriage with Madame de Cordillac; for her comfortable little income of twenty thousand francs was but a drop in the ocean of extravagance, into which the glory of outdoing the noblest and the wealthiest of her high-born connexions immediately plunged him. From that period, the income of his handsome fortune never sufficed to supply his annual expenditure; and the process of supplying the deficiency, by drawing upon his capital, though at first apparently a slow one, might have awakened any man to its inevitable consequence who had not lapped himself in the elysium of a variety of visions, all as extravagantly wild as that on which he now seemed determined to risk his last stake.

Prince Frederic of ——, the hero of the romance thus wildly woven in the brain of Hargrave, decidedly thought Sabina Hargrave the prettiest girl he had met in the *salons* of Paris; and never doubting that his station must render the expression of his admiration an honour, unaccompanied by any danger to the young lady's tranquillity, he expressed it on all occasions without the slightest reserve, and to no one with so much flattering enthusiasm as to Mr Hargrave. It was some complimentary boast of this kind which had put the notion of this splendid *fête* into the head of the speculating father. He knew how delicate, how beautiful, how sweetly tranquil, his Sabina looked, while moving about the splendid halls of his pride, and occasionally brought forward to notice, by the duties which hospitality demanded of her.

'He shall see her in all her glory,' thought the intoxicated Hargrave: 'he shall see her as no Paris beauty of seventeen was ever seen before – he shall see her as a king's son might glory to see his wife! And should it come to pass, as my prophetic spirit tells me that it will – should I see my Sabina borne to the feet of her brother-in-law's throne, what will it matter to me as I follow her thither, and with all the affection of a devoted father consent thenceforward to reside beneath her princely roof, what will it then matter to me how many scurvy creditors ungratefully murmur, because a few, among countless thousands, remain unpaid? A *fête* must be given that shall make all Paris stare – it must be done – all things must be done rather than fail; and if means are wanting, means must be found. What is the difference between a man of genius and a dolt, but this – that the one controls circumstances, and that the other yields to them?'

This sapient meditation, with the flourish at its conclusion, was quite sufficient to put Mr Hargrave in action; and he set about the needful preliminaries with a feeling of conscious superiority, which made him look almost with an emotion of pity upon every one he met. In short, all the complicated machinery necessary for so great an occasion was set in motion. The gardens were filled with workmen, the invitations sent out, the most desperate efforts made by those who were not of the elect to obtain admission, and means found to supply such an amount of ready money as was absolutely necessary for the undertaking.

Assuredly no preparations ever succeeded better. The royal lips of Prince Frederic expressed again and again his delighted admiration of the brilliant scene; and, better still, no sooner was the waltz over, by which he opened the ball with Sabina, than he asked her to gallop; and no sooner had the gallop ended, than he asked her to walk through a quadrille. In short, if every body but Mr Hargrave had not perceived that the royal guest was anxious to prove, by his attention to the daughter of his host, his sense of the compliment paid him by this splendid entertainment, others might have thought as he did, that the royal youth was very decidedly in love.

And in truth, had not the prince been as loyal as royal, he might have been tempted that night to have expressed the admiration he really felt with more tenderness than would have been strictly honourable; for never had the unconscious Sabina looked so beautiful, or acquitted herself so gracefully. Her dearly loved father had told her that this *fête*, given avowedly in compliment to the prince, must greatly depend for its success upon her; and this gave her a motive for exertion which not all the princes of the earth could have excited without it. Perhaps even, so well did she obey her father's bidding, there might have been moments, ere the morning came to chase the enchanting revellers of the night, during which Prince Frederic might have wished that the maiden had been as royal as himself, or he of no higher lineage than her own. But if so it were, Sabina did not find it out, though it may be that her father did; for as the night advanced, his spirits became more and more exhilarated; and his handsome person, as he graciously paraded it among his guests, seemed to dilate, till he towered above them all.

Meanwhile the fevered Adèle, who had nothing to do in this royal game, proceeded with her own design with undeviating courage and perseverance, and alas! with most perfect and most lamentable success.

If every timid swain, when he finds himself blessed by an occasional *à porte* conversation in a ball-room, knew how exceedingly easy it was for the fair lady to avoid it, if such were her will, he might consider himself as more blessed still.

Mademoiselle de Cordillac, of course, met Mr Coventry's eager greeting with a charming smile; and when, surrounded by a dozen gay friends, he addressed himself to her alone, she answered him with the most courteous attention: nay, when he asked her to waltz, she waltzed, and, with a heart sinking with disappointment and sorrow, whirled lightly away before a circle of admiring spectators, with an aspect as bright as her spirit was heavy. But when this was over, and with anxious watchfulness he sought for an opportunity of whispering one sentence in her ear, a sun-beam as it darts from an April cloud is not less amenable to the persuasive 'stay!' than was Adèle.

'She did not hear, or did not understand me,' thought Alfred; and another hour wore away in ceaseless efforts on his part to arrest an attention which could not be caught, and to give an ear that was deafer than that of any adder in the universe. Yet still he would not admit the belief that she avoided him. 'Avoid me!' he murmured, as he watched her light figure glide away at the very moment that he fancied every obstacle removed. 'Adèle avoid me! Why should this be? How can I believe it? Has she not danced with me, – smiled upon me? Why should I thus torment myself?' Yet still the night kept wearing on, and still he was no nearer to his object.

Adèle, meanwhile, paid little or no attention to what might or might not have passed between Mr Coventry and her aunt. Not an atom of the littleness which in a mind of less elevation would have mixed itself with her misery, found place in hers. Her soul was wrung with shame and sorrow, because she was conscious that she had loved ere she had been wooed; and she threw no thought away upon the probable absurdities of the courtship which, upon such excellent authority, she knew was going on. She watched not to see how ridiculous Madame de Hautrivage might be making herself, or how well, or how ill, her contemptible *futur* played the part of her lover. Had her mind been sufficiently commonplace to permit her looking out for all this, it is possible that she might have seen enough to shake her faith, even in the solemn asseveration of her mother's sister; – and Alfred Coventry might not have left the house, among the very last of the lingering guests, bearing in his heart the conviction that Adèle de Cordillac was the most accomplished coquet in France, and himself the most unhappy Englishman who had ever suffered his peace to be wrecked in pursuit of an object so every way unworthy.

Poor Madame de Hautrivage, indeed, did not long enjoy the sweet delusion into which she had fallen. No acknowledged beauty of twenty, however, can ever have dressed for conquest with less apprehension of failure, and more assured certainty of success, than she did upon this eventful evening. During the two hours thus occupied, and the delicious twenty minutes afterwards given to the contemplation of the finished work, and in which the pride of the artist joined itself with the pride of the woman, – during this interval the faded, yet glowing Clementine de Hautrivage, was in a truly enviable state of mind. But here ended her portion of the evening's enjoyment. It was not her wish to make her *entrée* while the rooms were empty; she knew that the assumed grace with which a fine woman, *avec une toilette irréprochable*, wins her way on entering a suite of rooms about half full, especially when she is at home and has to dispense her smiling welcomes as she moves along, produces an effect which triumphant generals might envy, and nymphs of sixteen wish for in vain. Mr Coventry, therefore, was already in the room when she swam into it; and desirous, in the first instance, rather of attracting notice than of bestowing it, she contented her fond heart by placing herself where she was quite sure of being seen by him; and there awaited the eager and delighted salutation of the man she favoured. But, alas! it came not. That he saw her, unfortunately admitted not of the slightest doubt; for during the space of three seconds his eyes were directed towards her, and he performed one of those slight, but civil bows, which, in general, can be neither flattering nor offensive; because, for the most part, they are just what the occasion requires, and no more. But in the case of the unfortunate Madame de Hautrivage, a pistol aimed and discharged at her head would have been infinitely less affronting.

'For one moment, and no more,'

the delightful possibility that some new and unexpected effect in her brilliant costume might have deceived him, and that he recognised not the splendid figure before him as his affianced Clementina, – for one short moment this hope sustained her, but in the next it was gone for ever: for she perceived, beyond the possibility of mistake, that he spake something to Adèle, with whom he was conversing, which caused her to turn her eyes towards her; and the half-melancholy smile with which she nodded to her aunt, and then glided away among the crowd, shewed plainly enough that on perceiving her she had with perfect propriety avoided the *gaucherie* of detaining her lover from her side, although it probably cost her a pang to resign him.

But what did the lover do? Did he profit by his release to fly to her? Alas! no. With the most perfect indifference as to being remarked or not, Coventry looked after Adèle, and then followed her in a way which, to an eye so experienced as that of Madame de Hautrivage, left not a shadow of doubt as to her being at that moment the object which wholly occupied him.

'*Je m'y connais!*' thought the unhappy lady. And the thought expressed no vain boast of her skill. She really did understand all such matters perfectly; and the acuteness of the Frenchwoman overpowered the vanity of the venerable coquette. 'I see it,' she inwardly exclaimed, – 'I see it all. *Bête! – Bête Anglaise! – Dieu merci!* no Frenchman could be thus equivocal!' Yet, notwithstanding this movement of gratitude for native blessings, her feelings were far from agreeable; nor were they rendered at all more so by this same keenness of awakened observation during the remainder of the evening. The unfortunate *bévue* concerning the portrait had so completely mystified her, and her long-established habits of love-making so assisted the mistake, that she really and truly believed the young Englishman had fallen in love with her, and the more easily laid herself under 'the soft impeachment,' from not being able to assign any other cause for his *not* proposing for her niece, when she had so obligingly opened the way for him to do so. But now that English *bêtise* suggested itself as an interpretation of all these lamentable mistakes, she perceived her blunder with very disagreeable distinctness.

As far as the young man himself was concerned, the accident did not give her the slightest uneasiness. She detested Englishmen, and from her very soul scorned their ignorance of all the graces of *légèreté*, and of all that is beautiful, moral, and sublime, in that species of *amour volage* which her countrymen (and women) alone understood; where change has no mixture of inconstancy, and where infidelity is a sin and a sorrow unknown. Yes! Madame de Hautrivage detested Englishmen, and would have felt a marriage with the wealthy Coventry a tremendous sacrifice to the tyranny of circumstances; therefore the loss of him might have been easily endured. But she perceived, in the course of this long night's observations, that she had – quite unintentionally, good lady! – thrown the prospect of poor Adèle's excellent match into utter confusion. She saw that the gentleman was more devoted than ever, but that the lady, too young as yet to comprehend the probability of his making love to two women at once, and, in short, simply believing the extremely false tale she had told, shunned every opportunity of being drawn into conversation by him, and would now unquestionably consider any offer of marriage from him as equally offensive to her aunt and to herself. This was exceedingly disagreeable; but it was by no means the only penalty she had to pay for the folly of believing that a coarse-minded, unpolished Englishman was as capable of choosing an old woman in preference to a young one as a Frenchman. She had also, as she well knew, to undergo the ceremony of appearing in the eyes of her young nieces as *avoir été jouée* by an Englishman! – It was dreadful!

It was only towards the close of the entertainment, and during her fourth attendance at the supper-table with some guest whom she particularly wished to honour, that, just after having once more refreshed herself with a glass of champagne and iced water, it suddenly occurred to her that she might pass off the whole matter as a jest. Coventry, she clearly perceived, had not the slightest suspicion of the blunder she had made; and as it was equally evident that he was as much occupied with Adèle as unoccupied about her, she easily persuaded herself to believe that matters would speedily be set right between them. All, therefore, that she should have to do would be to laugh at her niece for the facility with which she had received the hoax played upon her; and no living being but herself would be aware that the *chère amie* of so many gallant hearts had at last listened to a declaration of love to her niece, and fancied that it was intended for herself.

The eye of an Asmodeus, in looking down upon the crowded haunts of men, can descry what is passing among them with much greater rapidity than he can record it; and, in like manner, the historian, however gifted with the power of discerning, must content himself with relating a vast deal less than he sees. Many curious and interesting sketches of the easy, amusing, and varied tone of the cosmopolite circle usually assembled in a first-rate English *salon* at Paris might here be given, were there time and space for it. But it may not be; the narrative concerns but a few, and a few only can appear in it. Enough has, perhaps, already been said respecting such of those as were present at Mr Hargrave's ball, to give an idea of the manner in which they spent the evening; excepting, indeed, that one very general subject of conversation has not been alluded to, which, as it pervaded every group, and appeared to interest every individual present, could not, of course, be altogether uninteresting to any of them.

The recent outrages practised upon the successful players, as they pursued their way from Riccordo's to their several homes, was still so foremost in all men's thoughts, that few spake together for many minutes without its being brought upon the *tapis*.

Many of the gentlemen present belonged to the society which, at that time, assembled nightly at this fashionable rendezvous for idleness and high play; and those who did not felt scarcely less interested than themselves in the discussion of an affair which seemed to involve the safety of all Paris, and to compromise very disagreeably the high reputation of its police. Nor were the ladies a whit less anxious to hear all that was to be gathered on the subject than the gentlemen; whoever appeared to have any thing to say upon it was eagerly listened to, and happy was the man who had picked up any atom of intelligence upon this thrilling theme.

Of all the talkers on it, Count Romanhoff was, perhaps, the one listened to with the greatest avidity; and there were many good reasons for this. In the first place, he was extremely handsome; in the second, he was extremely voluble, omitting no single circumstance which could excite interest, and speaking with such perfect facility, both in English

and French, as to make him answer all questions in the language in which
they were asked, and thus making himself equally intelligible to all. In
addition to this, he had all the charm in speaking of this extraordinary
occurrence which is given by a lively imagination, when the subject
discussed is peculiarly exciting to it. Never, as he declared, had any thing
so strongly interested him before; and the fact of his having, for nearly
two years, constantly frequented the *salon*, rarely passing a night during
some part of which he did not enter there, being freely avowed, and
pretty generally known, gave such authority to all he said, that

'Where he stood there men did congregate;'

and his version of the story soon became the ground-work upon which
all other talkers constructed their own.

Among his other listeners, he had the honour of attracting the ear of
Prince Frederic, who, seated on a sofa surrounded by a circle of fair
ladies, most of them sitting with the partner with whom they had just
waltzed leaning on their chairs, chanced to catch a word or two of the
oft-repeated tale from a group at a little distance, of which Romanhoff
was the centre. His Royal Highness, who was well acquainted with him,
called to him by name, and the young Russian was in an instant before
him.

'Were you at the *salon*, Count, when this last unlucky gamester walked
forth with his gold, unwarned by the adventure of his predecessors?'
demanded the Prince.

'I was there on that night, Monseigneur, and on both the preceding
ones, when the former outrages took place.'

'May I ask, without indiscretion, if you were playing?'

'Twice out of the three times, Monseigneur, I was not.'

'Were the rooms crowded, Romanhoff?'

'No, your Highness; certainly not at the time that the winners left
them.'

'Have you any recollection,' resumed the Prince, fixing on him a look
that expressed much interest, – 'have you any distinct recollection of the
persons remaining in the room when the tables at which the successful
gamblers played broke up?'

'I distinctly remember several, your Highness, though probably not all,'
replied the Count, with a slight embarrassment of manner.

It is probable that the Prince perceived this, for he changed the subject;
and addressing Sabina, who was seated beside him, said, –

'I trust you are not tired, Mademoiselle Hargrave, and that your
kindness will accord me another waltz before your charming party breaks
up?'

'I shall be very happy, Monseigneur,' she replied, with all the smiling satisfaction she could muster; but at that moment her eye chanced to be fixed on Adèle, whose feverish animation having faded away, had left her pale, languid, and fatigued. She had joined the circle round the Prince expressly to elude poor Coventry's evident desire to speak to her, and had endeavoured, with all sincerity, to listen to what was going on, in the vain hope of being able for a moment to forget him.

Prince Frederic, as he spoke to Miss Hargrave, remarked the direction of her soft and sympathising eye, and, turning his own in the same direction, was struck by Adèle's pale cheek and weary aspect.

'On my honour I fear we are indiscreet,' he said, 'in keeping up these delightful revels so long. Mademoiselle de Cordillac's fair cheek ought to be on her pillow. Is it not so?'

'Oh, no, Monseigneur,' replied Adèle, rousing herself. 'I have been listening with only too much interest to your Highness's questions, and the Count Romanhoff's replies, concerning these horrible adventures; and I only wish your Highness had proceeded, – I long to hear more.'

'*Ah! ça cher Comte, poursuivez donc, je vous conjure,*' said Prince Frederic. 'But take care,' he added, 'that you do not make your narrative too interesting, for it has certainly blanched one lovely cheek already.'

'Alas! your Highness, the more the story is dwelt upon, the more profound must the impression become; and, perhaps, Mademoiselle de Cordillac had better listen to no more of it.'

'Nay, nay, you suspect me of more weakness than I feel, Count Romanhoff. I shall hold myself greatly obliged to you, if, with his Royal Highness's permission, you will go back exactly to the point where you stopped, and tell us if you remember, on all or either of these occasions, having remarked the presence of persons who were apparently strangers to the society, and whom you did not remember to have seen before?' said Adèle.

Every eye was turned upon Count Romanhoff in anxious expectation of his answer.

'I cannot say I did,' replied the Count, after a pause.

'Where is papa going?' said Adèle, affecting, perhaps, more interest than she felt. 'Though he does not play, I know he is often at the *salon*. – Let us examine him.'

Mr Hargrave, though he had not danced with either of the ladies seated near the Prince, had nevertheless, in his character of host, ventured to approach the little circle, too happy at perceiving the juxtaposition of his daughter and his royal guest; but having satisfied himself, as it seemed, that all in that quarter was as he wished it to be, he was moving off, when Prince Frederic, at the suggestion of Adèle, stopped him by saying, –

'Let me entreat you not to leave our *coterie*, Monsieur Hargrave. We want you to assist Count Romanhoff's memory with yours. Were you at Riccordo's on either of the nights in question?'

'Yes, Monseigneur, I was,' said Mr Hargrave, quietly.

'*Mais oui, mon cher Monsieur*,' said the eager Romanhoff, 'you were there on all the three evenings.'

'No, Count, I think you are mistaken there,' said Mr Hargrave. 'On the first, and on the last, I was not only there, but remained, if I recollect rightly, till the rooms were quite empty. I was interested on both evenings, as I well remember, by a game of piquet that I was watching. But on the second evening I think I was at the Opera.'

'Pardon, Monsieur!' said a voice from behind the chair of a fair duchess, who had placed herself in front of the Prince in the hope of being selected by him for the next dance, – 'Pardon, Monsieur!' said the gentleman who had been her partner in the last, 'but I think you were at the Opera and the *salon* both on the night of the second outrage.'

'It may be so,' returned Mr Hargrave, bowing to him with a courteous smile, for he was a man of very distinguished rank; 'and it is, indeed, highly probable that your Excellency is right: for I am so much in the habit of dropping into Riccordo's to see how things are going on, that my coachman often stops there without my bidding him.'

'Ah!' returned the same gentleman, 'the horses and servants of you men of fashion pay a dreadful penalty for the interest excited by the tables at Riccordo's. Do you never feel a touch of pity for them, M Hargrave, and walk home?'

'Indeed I do, your Excellency,' returned Mr Hargrave. 'I very often send my carriage home from thence, and follow it on foot.'

'Excuse me, Monsieur l'Ambassadeur,' interrupted the Prince – for the personage who had joined the conversation was of no lesser rank, – 'but you have stopped M Hargrave, who, I believe, was going to tell us, in reply to the very pertinent question of his charming *belle fille*, whether, on either of the eventful evenings in question, he remarked, in Riccordo's *salon*, any person not absolutely an *habitué* there? – This is, surely, very important. I am aware that the society accustomed to meet there is numerous – too much so for any one of them to feel capable of answering for all the rest, as he would for his familiar friends. Nevertheless, it would certainly be very agreeable for all these gentlemen, could it be proved, that on each of the three nights in question, persons, or some person, totally a stranger to them all, had been remarked there. You, M Hargrave, as well as our friend the Count, seem to have been present on every one of these occasions – did you remark any individual whom you were not accustomed to see there?'

'I think, your Highness – I think I did,' replied Mr Hargrave slowly, and apparently giving great attention to the question, but not feeling perfectly certain how to reply to it. 'But the fact is,' he added, 'that my attention is always so devoted to some particularly interesting game or other (which saves me, your Highness, from the danger of playing myself), that I am the last man in the world to give such an account of the company as may be depended on.'

'The circumstance of your not playing would seem, on the contrary, to point you out as one of the very first to whom we should apply,' said the ambassador. 'Do endeavour to recall every thing that occurred, M Hargrave. If you have an idea, however vague, that you really did remark some figure which you were not accustomed to see there, you must, I presume, have also an idea, if not a distinct one, as to what sort of figure it was. Is it not so?'

'How admirably Monsieur le Diplomate examines!' exclaimed the Prince, starting up, and presenting his hand to Sabina. 'But, unhappily, the process must always be rather tedious, and there is something very like sin in wasting such moments as the present by turning a court of beauty into a court of law!'

These last words were for Sabina alone, and uttered nearly in a whisper, as he led her to the top of the ball-room. But his movement indicated, with sufficient clearness, that he thought the subject of the robbery was pretty well worn out; and this was quite enough to make it *mauvais ton* to talk of it in any voice above a whisper for the rest of the evening.

The evening, however, or, more properly speaking, the night, was drawing to a close. The appearance of his Royal Highness, walking up the room with a fair *danseuse* on his arm, was a signal for the weary orchestra once more to pour forth notes that might revive the worn-out energies of the most lazy of listeners. His Excellency, meanwhile, with an air *tout soit peu piqué*, took his departure, and Mr Hargrave once more indulged in the soothing occupation of watching the lofty head of Prince Frederic bending itself to the level of the fair Sabina. Oh! what a world of happy emblematic augury was there in that spectacle! Neither the consciousness of ruined fortunes, nor any of the anxieties which ensued from it, could prevent Mr Hargrave from tasting again all the exquisite pleasure of gratified vanity and strengthening hope.

As he made his way to a convenient sofa, from whence, without being too conspicuous, he might enjoy the spectacle which gave birth to this delicious reverie, the dispirited and miserable-looking Coventry passed him in his way out. He had not intended to address Adèle again; but she, too, was in his path, and he stopped, almost involuntarily, to speak to her.

'You are going, Mr Coventry,' she said, with an air of gay reproach, and looking at his hat, which he carried in his hand.

'Indeed I think it is time, Mademoiselle,' he replied; 'even your roses have somewhat faded since the ball began, and I never saw your father look so ill.'

'Does he?' said Mademoiselle de Cordillac, looking towards him with some anxiety: 'I have not remarked it.'

'Then, perhaps, it is not so. Perhaps I only see the reflection of the weary, wretched feelings of my own heart! – Farewell, Mademoiselle de Cordillac!'

And without even waiting for a look in reply, Alfred Coventry disappeared.

'Wretched and weary feelings!' murmured Adèle, remaining on the spot where he had left her, and unconsciously keeping her eyes fixed on the door by which he had passed out. 'What can he mean? – Oh! what can he mean by calling his feelings wretched? – Why should Alfred Coventry be wretched? He has chosen his bride – he has wooed – he has won her! There can be no wretchedness in this, let her be who or what she may; for, was it not his choice? Why should Alfred Coventry be wretched?'

But it was in vain she continued to gaze through the vacant door, no one appeared there to answer her. She looked round the room for this chosen bride of the unfortunate young man who so frankly avowed himself to be wretched, despite his success, and almost determined to name him to her, that she might mark her countenance, and so learn if any thing unpleasant had passed between them. But Madame de Hautrivage was nowhere to be seen; and feeling herself, now that all reason for exertion was over, hardly able to stand, she, too, stole off, leaving a whirling circle of lighter hearts than her own to watch the daylight of a bright spring morning, peeping through the windows of the conservatory, as if to scatter the rear of dancers within, as it had already done the rear of darkness without.

CHAPTER VII

'Well, Adèle!' said Madame de Hautrivage, on joining the late breakfast-table on the following morning, and addressing her niece with a sort of mystifying air, intended to appear extremely jocose – 'well, Adèle, have you found me out? And are you ready to confess that you are the very readiest *mouette* that ever was led off upon a false scent?'

'Confess what, aunt?' returned the heavy-eyed Adèle. 'I do not understand you.'

'*Charmant! – Admirable! – C'est parfait! – mais c'est parfait!*' returned Madame de Hautrivage.

Perfectly unable to comprehend what all this might mean, Mademoiselle de Cordillac shook her head, languidly attempted to smile, but said no more.

'*Et toi*, Sabina! have you not, with all your prodigious reading and meditative sedateness, – have you not wisdom enough to discover the delicious trick I have played upon your sister? – *Mais c'est incroyable!*'

'*Vraiment, ma tante*,' replied Sabina, while a feeling nearly resembling contempt curled her pretty lips, 'I am totally unable to comprehend you.'

'Then you are, both of you, the very silliest pair of children I ever met with. You still believe, then, Adèle, that M Alfred de Coventry is about to be taken by me *en seconde noce?*'

'I cannot do otherwise than believe what you told me, madame,' replied Adèle, but with considerable less languor than before. 'But if I misunderstood what you intended to say, I shall be obliged to you if you will explain yourself farther.'

'*Eh bien, donc, ma pauvre petite!* don't look so tremendously grave, because it is too ridiculous to turn *les petites plaisanteries d'un esprit, gai comme le mien*, into sober earnest! But the fact is, that I told you all that long story about M Coventry merely to try a little experiment. I wanted to find out whether you really were as vulgarly in love, in *la mode Anglaise*, as I suspected. Of the young man's attachment to you, though he has not yet taken courage to make his proposals in form (*excusez, ma chère, mais les Anglais sont tout peu bête*), – of his attachment and intentions towards you there could be no doubt; but, feeling that there would be something offensively indelicate in hinting to a young person like you, Adèle, that I thought it possible she could like one man better than another, I resolved, if possible, to obtain the information I wished for by stratagem. But little did I imagine, my dear, that you could be *bête* enough to let *ma petite supercherie* continue in force after you had seen your lover. For shame, Adèle! – how could you be so foolish as to imagine that I was going *myself* to marry young Mons. Alfred de Coventry?'

All the suffering which this deception had brought upon her – all the lost happiness which she might have enjoyed during the hours of the preceding evening, flashed through the mind of Adèle in an instant. But she was constitutionally sweet-tempered and constitutionally gay; and, instead of resenting the misery her aunt had, by her own account, thus wantonly caused her, she was *almost* ready to embrace her for the joy her present statement brought. Never, as she told Sabina when they were again *tête-à-tête*, never had she known before what happiness meant!

'Surely, Sabina,' she said, 'the good God must have sent sorrow into the world in order to make us value, at its worth, the blessings he sends with it. Is it a sin, dearest, – is it indelicate, to feel so very, *very* much delighted as I do at remembering all the love I read in poor Alfred's eyes last night? Oh! he did look so wretched when he left me! And I behaved to him, Sabina, — you can have no idea how I treated him! So much civil contempt and gay indifference! Dear Alfred! And he, all the time, being, I do verily believe, almost as wretched as I was myself. But, thank Heaven, it is passed! Where do you think I shall first see him again, Sabina?'

'Not here, I fear, dear Adèle,' replied her sister, with a look in which anger and vexation still lingered: 'he can hardly be expected to volunteer a visit after being treated as you describe.'

'Then he must be invited, Sabina,' said Adèle, laughing. 'I do not intend to stand upon much ceremony with him now, I promise you. If I could but make you comprehend how I treated him last night, you would be aware of the necessity of being a little more than commonly civil to him now. Had I any doubt about his loving me, it would be a different thing, you know; but even in the midst of all my misery last night, I saw that. In short, I believed him to be as audaciously false as he was meanly mercenary, — at once a traitor to my foolish aunt and to me. And, after unjustly loading him with such foul suspicions, think you not, Sabina, that I owe him some atonement? Think you not that we might, without impropriety, desire papa to invite him here?'

'Indeed I do,' returned Sabina. 'Prince Frederic told me last night that papa had invited him to dinner; and if his gay-hearted Royal Highness has not made a blunder, I will beg my father to let Mr Coventry be one of the party invited to meet him. Shall I, Adèle?'

'Yes, dearest, yes! It will be a most flattering mark of distinction. How sweet of you to think of it! But I had no idea, Sabina, that the Prince was coming to dine here. What an extraordinary man your father is, Sabina! Where will you find another man, without rank, title, or political importance of any kind, holding the situation that he does here? He certainly has most charming talents; and I like Prince Frederic for the marked distinction he shews him. It really will be a great compliment paid to a private English gentleman. I don't think he can have made any blunder about papa having invited him: do you?'

'I do not feel quite sure about it,' replied Sabina; 'and I do not think the Prince felt quite sure about it himself, because his phrase was, "*Si je ne me trompe pas, votre aimable papa m'a prié*:" but he did not say a word about the day when this honour was to fall upon us.'

'Let us go to the library and ask papa all about it,' said Adèle, rising gaily from her chair. 'I suppose he is up by this time; though poor Coventry's last words, by the by, just before he left the rooms, were that papa looked ill. I dare say he must have been excessively tired. Miserable as I was, I could not help observing how admirably he did the honours.'

'Dear, dear papa!' returned Sabina, fervently, 'how I do love him! And do you know, Adèle, I am quite convinced that all this immense trouble that he takes is for us. I cannot bear to see him look as pale as he did last night while that tiresome Count Romanhoff was prosing away at such terrible length about the business at Riccordo's. It struck me instantly, as I observed it, that he had been exerting himself beyond what could be pleasant to him. . . . I hope, if he *does* give this dinner, that it will not fatigue him, as I am certain the ball did last night.'

'Fatigue him, Sabina! Oh! nonsense, my dear! I know no person in the whole circle of Paris *bon ton* who appears to enjoy society so much as your father; and as to *receiving*, it is evidently his delight: so don't you go, you foolish girl, and endeavour to persuade him that he is too delicate in health to preside at a dinner without danger of turning pale before the end of it. I should excessively enjoy this *dîner des élites*, I confess. Come, Sabina, let us go to him.'

Nothing could be more amiable or more endearing than the terms on which the graceful widower lived with the two young girls whom his beautiful wife had left in his charge. An excellent library – one of the rarest accompaniments to domestic comfort and elegance to be found in the French capital – was the room in which Mr Hargrave always took his breakfast and spent the first hours of the morning; but there was nothing sulky in this retreat, for Adèle and Sabina were not only permitted egress and regress without restraint, but were made very clearly to understand that they could in no way please him better than by coming to chat with him there on all the *petits politiques* of the *salons*, and that with as much freedom and unreserve as if they were still gossiping to each other in their own boudoir.

It was, therefore, with all confidence of a cordial welcome that the two sisters took their way, arm in arm, to the library; but when Adèle laid her hand upon the lock she found that the door was fastened from within.

'Good Heaven! he is not up yet!' cried Sabina, with a feeling of alarm. 'Indeed, Adèle, I am afraid he is ill!'

'No such thing,' returned her sister, gaily. 'I am sure I hear him in the room.' And playing a light tattoo with her delicate knuckles on the door, she cried, '*Ouvrez, monsieur, s'il vous plait.*'

The summons was immediately answered, not by the opening of the door, but by the voice of Mr Hargrave, who, apparently too busy to come to them immediately, said, cheerfully, '*Attendez, mes belles, pour un instant;*' and for a few minutes they remained standing at the door. This was so unusual, that when at length Mr Hargrave, still *en robe de chambre*, opened it to them, Adèle, whose spirits, always gay, were now exuberant, seized upon him as he appeared within it, exclaiming, 'What have you been about, *notre papa*? I arrest you *au nom du roi*. Nothing short of having some treasonable correspondence to hide could have made you, the most *preux des chevaliers*, keep two beautiful damsels waiting so long at your door.'

Sabina, who with her loving eyes fixed on her father's face, was waiting for her morning salute, till her sister should have released him, almost screamed at the sudden change in his complexion which she remarked, as with smiles and caresses he returned the address of Adèle, and after the interval of a moment, extended a hand to each and led them towards the fire.

'You are not well, papa!' she exclaimed, 'I am quite sure of it. Adèle says that Mr Coventry remarked last night——'

'Remarked what?' interrupted Mr Hargrave, abruptly. 'Who remarked? What do you mean, Sabina?'

'Only, dearest papa, that Mr Coventry remarked your looking pale and fatigued last night; and I cannot help thinking myself that you are looking unwell to-day. I suppose it is impossible for any body to be so completely the centre of a large circle as you were last night – so entirely the mainspring of all that was agreeable and animated throughout the whole evening – without feeling fatigued by it.'

'You little flatterer!' exclaimed Mr Hargrave, fondly kissing her, and at once chasing all fears for his health by the gaiety and animation of his manner. 'There were others, methinks, who were more like a mainspring of all that was agreeable than your antiquated father, Sabina. What say you, *par exemple*, to Prince Frederic?'

'Oh, certainly, he was very agreeable too!' replied Sabina; 'and it is exactly about him that we are come to talk to you, papa.'

'Exactly about him, papa,' joined in Adèle. 'Is it true that you have invited him to dinner?'

'Invited him to dinner! No, indeed, I have not. Though I am sure if I thought the invitation would be agreeable to him he should have it directly. What was it put this notion into your head, Adèle?'

'Nay, papa, not into my head. It was put into Sabina's head, and that by no other than his Royal Highness himself.'

'Is this so, my dearest Sabina?' demanded Mr Hargrave, his whole countenance suddenly lighted up with an expression of hope and joy that might almost be described as ecstasy. 'Did the Prince express a wish that I should invite him to dinner?'

'Why, no, papa, that is not exactly the way I should describe what passed. Prince Frederic said, he *thought* you had asked him to dinner, and most certainly he seemed very well inclined to come. But he did not say that he hoped you would ask him,' replied Sabina.

'The difference is but trifling, my love – very trifling indeed,' rejoined her father. 'Of course there is no doubt, my dear girls, about his being asked. The only question remaining to be solved is, whether it shall be a

state party, as I may call such a one as I *could* give him, or a domestic one.
I must have your judgment upon this, my dear girls, before I definitively
pronounce my own. What is your opinion, Sabina? Which of these styles
do you think he would prefer?'

'Before I answer, papa, you must tell me what you mean by a state
party,' replied Sabina.

'By a state party, dearest, I mean one consisting entirely of personages
of the very highest rank that I can venture to invite; and I am happy to
say that this excludes very few, even of the very highest. Of course, if the
entertainment be given upon this footing, every thing must be in
accordance with it – every thing must be in the very highest style of
splendour, and no one whatever of plebeian rank admitted,' replied Mr
Hargrave, with great animation. 'But, on the other hand, Sabina,' he
added, after the pause of a moment, and fixing an inquiring gaze on the
face of his daughter, 'on the other hand, Sabina, if you think he would be
equally well, or better pleased by being received almost, as it were, *en
famille*, of course I can have no objection to it.'

'Well, then, papa, that is what I think he would like best,' eagerly
replied Sabina, whose predominating idea through the whole
conversation was the getting Alfred Coventry invited. She had
sympathised too sincerely with all that Adèle had suffered concerning
him not to feel as desirous as herself that all things should be set right
between them; and she was, perhaps, more alarmed than her sister by the
idea that the apparently capricious treatment he had received might cause
a lasting separation. An invitation to meet Prince Frederic at dinner,
especially if the party consisted of a few only, could not fail of being
acknowledged by him as a very flattering distinction; and every word she
uttered on the subject had this origin and this object. Poor Sabina! she
little guessed the importance of every syllable she spoke.

Mr Hargrave listened to her as if his life, and her life too, hung upon
what she said; and the joy – the rapture, which thrilled through his
whole frame as he heard Sabina frankly acknowledge, with her innocent
'well then, papa,' that she thought Prince Frederic would like a domestic
party best, actually brought tears into his eyes. But he felt that this was
not the stage of the business at which it would be wise to let such
emotion appear, and stooping to arrange the fading embers of the fire, he
contrived to subdue this vehemence of feeling before it was observed.

'And you, Adèle,' he resumed, turning gaily to Mademoiselle de
Cordillac, 'what is your opinion on the subject? Do you also think that
his Royal Highness would rather be received here *en bon ami* than *en
grand seigneur?*'

Now the fact decidedly was, that Mademoiselle de Cordillac had
thought less about his Royal Highness Prince Frederic, his merits or

dismerits, his likings or dislikings, than any other individual in Paris, perhaps, who had been equally often in his company. Young ladies, as much in love as was our Adèle, will not attribute this remarkable indifference on her part to any radical contempt or aversion to princes or princedoms, but to a cause which they will perfectly well understand. However, when Mr Hargrave thus demanded her opinion on a point upon which she fancied that somebody else was concerned as well as Prince Frederic, her countenance betokened a little confusion, but no indifference, as she replied, –

'From what Sabina says, papa, I have no doubt that he would prefer a small private party to one that was stately and ceremonious.'

There were two distinct feelings which caused Mademoiselle de Cordillac to blush as she said this. The first arose from the consciousness that Sabina had, in truth, said nothing whatever to her which might justify her forming an opinion on the subject; and the second from feeling that what she was saying arose from a motive so decidedly selfish, and so utterly impossible to be acknowledged, that she was very nearly ashamed of herself for uttering it.

But what would she have felt, could she have guessed the interpretation put both upon her words and the blush by which they were accompanied? Mr Hargrave, in common with every one well acquainted with her, had a very high opinion of Adèle's judgment and powers of observation: the delicacy and genuine modesty of her character were equally well known to him; and it was pretty nearly impossible that she could have expressed herself in any manner better calculated to impress him with the belief that her opinion of Prince Frederic's views was exactly the same as his own. At that moment his happiness could scarcely have been augmented by hearing the young man declare his passion in form. All doubt – all hesitation vanished entirely from his mind, and he only longed to be alone, that he might give himself up to the unrestrained enjoyment of the prospect before him, and to the means by which the costly splendour which surrounded him might be sustained till his Sabina became Princess Frederic of ——.

'Now, dear girls, you must go,' he said. 'You remember that I was very busy when you came, – so much so, as you perceived, that I locked myself in; a precaution exceedingly rare for me to take, because as you both, I believe, pretty well know, the oftener I see your saucy faces peeping in upon me, the better I am pleased. But the fact is, that I have various papers which I am anxious to look over and arrange, and shall therefore certainly suffer no one but your two fair selves to break in upon me.'

'We will vanish instantly, papa,' said Sabina; 'but I have one very great favour to ask before I go, and I do assure you that I have a very particular reason for it, which, perhaps, one of these days I will tell you. Will you be so very kind, when you invite Prince Frederic, as to invite Mr Coventry to meet him?'

A score of merry smiles seemed playing about Mr Hargrave's mouth as he answered her. He had not been insensible to his distinguished young countryman's attention to his step-daughter, and was sufficiently well informed of his fortune and position in society to make him exceedingly well pleased at believing that he would propose for her. This marriage would be such as even Prince Frederic might approve, and it would, unquestionably, be much more desirable that Adèle should be married, than appear at the court of —— as a hanger-on upon her sister. That *he* should accompany her, share her greatness, watch over her happiness, and augment it, as he had ever done, by his devoted affection, was in every way desirable. But this was enough; it was better she should have no more relations thrown upon her.

'Mr Coventry must be asked, must he?' was the question by which Sabina's petition was answered; but it was uttered in a tone that left no fear for its success. 'And does Adèle,' he continued, 'approve this also?'

'Never mind, papa, about that,' replied Sabina, laughing, and leading off her sister. 'I am your own daughter, you know, and I shall think it very cruel if you refuse me, and be jealous as a Turk, I assure you, if you should deem it necessary to apply to her about it.'

'Very well then, Mademoiselle Hargrave, I will take my orders from you, as in duty bound. Mr Coventry shall be asked, and will, I dare say, have the kindness to excuse its being only a sort of – of family party. Next Wednesday, I presume, will be distant enough for so unceremonious an invitation; and when you have fairly disappeared, young ladies, I will write a note to Prince Frederic, another to Coventry; and, if you object not, I will also invite le Duc et la Duchesse de Vermont, which will take off, – that is, I mean, will give a better air to the party.'

The young ladies having distinctly expressed their approbation respecting every part of this arrangement, and each received a kiss from its projector, retired; leaving Mr Hargrave one of the happiest, if not the very happiest, man in Paris.

CHAPTER VIII

Nothing could exceed the general feeling of hilarity which seemed on that day to pervade every part of Mr Hargrave's family. The cause of his own intoxicating exhilaration has been already sufficiently explained, as well as that of the so lately wretched Adèle. Sabina's contentment, sweet soul! arose from believing that she had set matters *en train* for reestablishing a good understanding between her sister and the man she so evidently loved, despite all the laws of French etiquette and established usage. Nor was Madame de Hautrivage much behind the rest of this happy family in contentment; for she was greatly relieved from sundry tormenting fears by hearing that Mr Coventry had been invited to dinner, in a manner so flattering as, beyond all question, to atone for any offence he might have received from the altered manners of Mademoiselle de Cordillac; and, moreover, she was very far from being insensible to the honour and glory of being one of a family where a royal prince was invited to dinner with as much freedom as a private gentleman. Of her brother-in-law's ulterior views she knew nothing; that gentleman having very judiciously decided in his own mind that her participation in the business might very probably do harm, but could by no possibility be productive of good.

Before the family met at dinner, an answer had arrived from the Prince, most graciously accepting the invitation, and couched in terms of such amiable condescension that Mr Hargrave felt, as he read it, as if he were already his son. The answer given at the hôtel where Mr Coventry lodged, was, that he was out of town, but that the note should be given to him as soon as he returned.

This seemed to satisfy them all: even Adèle would not suffer herself to feel disappointed at not receiving a less doubtful answer, reasonably consoling her spirit with the reflection that, even if Alfred Coventry did not return in time to accept it, the conciliatory object of the note would not be lost upon him, and that it was not very likely he should omit coming to thank her father for it.

The late hour at which they had all retired to rest on the preceding evening disinclined them from any engagement; even the Italian Opera was given up, and they all lounged round the tea-table in the library, lazily engaged in discussing the brilliant effect of the last night's entertainment, and the style of that to be given to the Prince on the following Wednesday, particularly as to the hours after dinner; when it was hoped the *prima donna* of the season would vouchsafe, for the consideration of some thousand francs, to favour them with a little of her precious breath.

'Ah! *c'est ça!*' exclaimed Madame de Hautrivage, upon hearing Mr Hargrave propose this exquisite *finale* for the day. '*Il faut avouer que mon beau frère s'y connait;*' and then, after a few moments of more silent reflection than she often gave to any subject, she addressed herself to the two girls, and very gravely inquired what dresses they intended to wear.

They both laughed at this extraordinary anxiety for their beautification, but declared that they had not as yet taken the subject into consideration, and that they did not imagine the choice of their dresses on the occasion would be a matter of any very great importance.

'I beg your pardon, there, my dear children,' said Mr Hargrave. 'Madame de Hautrivage is perfectly right. It really is a matter of importance. It is precisely one of those circumstances in which the greatest tact is required. To be too plainly dressed would be disrespectful, and in every way to be avoided. Yet a costume in any degree approaching full dress would, if possible, be worse still; because it would be most decidedly *mauvais ton*. However, I have no fears but that all this will be perfectly well arranged. You have, both of you, my dear children, very excellent taste in dress; and the reputation of Madame de Hautrivage on this point is established upon the basis of universal applause. It therefore must appear superfluous for me to give an opinion on the subject, nevertheless——' Here Mr Hargrave stopped, and looked round upon the three ladies with a sort of timid smile, as if fearful of giving offence by too rashly interfering on a subject of so much delicacy.

'Oh! do go on, papa,' cried Adèle, eagerly. 'I would rather consult you upon this point than all the *marchandes de modes* in Paris. You have the most perfect taste of any person I have ever known. Do tell us what it was you were going to say when you so very cruelly stopped short.'

'You are most flatteringly kind, my dear Adèle,' returned Mr Hargrave, laughing, as if in jest, yet at the same time very evidently wishing to accept the office offered to him. 'And if Sabina is equally condescending, I would take advantage of it by indulging my fancy for you both. You, Adèle, with your fine dark eyes, rich chestnut tresses, and your "nut-brown" skin, I would dress, very literally, *couleur de rose*. But the robe must be of no ordinary quality, observe. I should wish to see you in the very richest satin you could purchase, made perfectly plain, and with no ornament whatever, except earrings, brooch, and bracelets of pearls; no flowers in the hair, no garniture, no finery of any sort.'

'*Si fait!*' exclaimed Adèle, gaily clapping her hands. 'In this manner will I be dressed, and in no other. I went dress-buying with Madame de St Aubin the other day; and in a *magasin* to which she took me I saw the exact thing papa describes – pale as the eglantine – rich as the state robe of Madame de Pompadour. The fate of my toilet for that day is fixed beyond appeal. And now for Sabina?'

'For Sabina,' said Mr Hargrave, proudly turning his admiring looks upon his daughter, – 'for Sabina I would have something that should almost make her look like a young queen, by its costly, yet simple richness. The delicacy of her complexion, the lightness of her figure, and the peculiar youthfulness of her general appearance, pretty as I confess it to be, might be in danger of sinking into insignificance in the plainness of a dinner-dress, unless it were redeemed by its intrinsic elegance and splendour. Sabina must be in rich white silk, brocaded with small satin flowers – all white, of course. Her little feet must be in black silk, her hair must be braided with pearls (the young lady's casket, any more than your own, Adèle, is not poor in that article), and her brooch, bracelets, and earrings, must be *en suite*. *Vouée au blanc*, excepting the black shoes, she must not permit any mixture of colour to approach her; unless, perhaps – but of this I am not quite certain – she should place in her bosom a sprig of myrtle in full blossom.'

Mr Hargrave uttered these oracular words with his eyes half closed, as if by shutting out external objects he could render more perfect the image that his fancy was sketching within. When he had finished, he looked round upon the three ladies with an air, half-serious, half-jesting, and as if ready to fall into either vein, according as they might seem disposed. Nevertheless, it was not very difficult to perceive that in all he said he was quite in earnest, and really desirous that the suggestions thus lightly thrown out should be acted upon.

'Exquisite!' exclaimed Madame de Hautrivage: '*Et puis moi?*'

'For you, dear lady, I can only say,' replied Mr Hargrave, gallantly bowing to her, 'that I would wish you to adorn yourself on this occasion with the same admirable taste and propriety which you invariably display on all others.'

'The dress you have imagined for Sabina, papa, will be very becoming to her,' said Adèle; adding, after a short pause, 'But will she not look almost like a bride if she is to be so entirely in white? Change but the myrtle for an orange-flower, and she would be perfectly ready for the altar.'

A smile, which he seemed disposed to conceal by turning aside his head, passed over the countenance of Mr Hargrave, but he immediately resumed his gravity, and replied, –

'Changing the myrtle for the orange, Adèle, would indeed make all the difference; but that all is much. Well then! will you be good girls, and do exactly as I bid you?'

'To be sure we will!' was the joint and separate answer of both. 'We must start upon our shopping the moment breakfast is over to-morrow morning,' said Adèle; 'for truly we shall not give our dressmaker too much time. But there is one preliminary that you must perform, papa, if it so please you. We are going to a *marchand* who knows us not, and I shall therefore choose to pay for what I order. We have been so gay and so busy that I have never found time to ask you for our usual settlement of the last quarter's account, and I am absolutely *sans sous*. Will you recruit my empty purse?'

'Will I, dearest?' said Mr Hargrave, rising with great alacrity. 'Yes I will; though you are a naughty child for not reminding me of this before.'

Being quite *en famille*, the party were sitting in the library; and in order immediately to comply with his step-daughter's request, Mr Hargrave opened a Bramah-locked drawer in his elegant library-table, which, with many other costly articles of furniture, had been imported from his native London, and taking out a handful of gold coin, locked the drawer again; and returning to the table at which the ladies were sitting, threw the glittering treasure before the two girls, saying – 'There, *mes belles!* Divide them between you. Only tell me, when you have counted them, how many fall to the share of Adèle, that I may enter it on her account. Every farthing of your income which you do not receive, my love, goes, as you know, into the funds, and increases your snug little fortune. So do not be too extravagant.'

'Nay, papa, I am not in the least inclined to be economical just now – especially when I see such a splendid heap of gold before me!'

'Is it not magnificent, Adèle, to have money paid us in this style?' demanded Sabina, with childish glee. 'Where in the world, papa, did you get all these beautiful sovereigns?' she added, beginning busily to employ herself by dividing the pieces into two equal portions.

But Adèle, who seemed inclined to resign the finance department to her sister, happened to have her eyes fixed on her step-father as this question was asked, and was surprised by seeing him bite his under lip, and contract his brows into a frown, which it was very rare to see upon his usually bland and smiling countenance. But the painful feeling, whether of body or mind, passed away in an instant, and he replied, –

'Where did I get this gold, Sabina? From that fertile source of all good things, the banking establishment of Messrs Lafitte and Co. Is it enough for you both? If not, say the word, and I will produce as much more; and that, I think, will about empty my hoards of your admired metal for the present.'

Adèle was startled by hearing him say this: for when he had left his place to seek the money, her eyes accidentally followed him, and she was so placed as to perceive that the small drawer he opened was full of gold pieces, so full, indeed, as to make her more than share the wonder afterwards expressed by Sabina at the sight of a small portion of them. The assertion, therefore, that another such handful as he had laid on the table would 'empty his hoard', was unintelligible. She sought not, however, any explanation from his countenance; a very painful feeling caused her, on the contrary, to look away from him, and to fix her eyes upon a book that lay before her; and while her father, her aunt, and Sabina, continued in a light and lively strain to discuss the various particulars of the flattering visit they were about to receive, she sat in deep abstraction, pondering the circumstances which had just occurred, and vainly searching for any possible interpretation of it which might satisfy her.

That her step-father had uttered a decided falsehood was certain. But his reason for doing it appeared so perfectly inscrutable, that she harassed herself in vain to find any plausible explanation of it. That he should wish to deceive herself or Sabina upon such a subject, or indeed upon any other, seemed impossible. It might − it must be her aunt, from whom, for some mysterious reason or other, he wished to conceal the fact that he had in the house a large sum in gold. Was it not within the reach of probability that he might think the good lady likely to wish for a portion of it, by way of a loan for her card-purse, when, perhaps, he had obtained it for some similar purpose for himself? But why not wait for her demand, and refuse it when it was made, in any manner which he might think best? Why volunteer an untruth for any purpose? Why so wantonly have recourse to it upon an occasion so very insignificant?

But Adèle was weary of conjectures long before she could end them. It was of no use that she told herself again and again, that, let the cause be what it would, it *could* not be a matter of any consequence; but, of consequence or not, her restive thoughts would turn to the subject, nor did it leave her in peace till she fell asleep. Long before that time, however, she had become perfectly convinced that her excellent stepfather was blameless, that he was right, and must have been right in doing what he had done, and that she alone was to blame for the pertinacious weakness with which she permitted her thoughts to fix themselves on the subject.

In this frame of mind she would have deemed it a sin had she mentioned to Sabina the subject which had thus worried her. 'It is quite enough,' thought she, 'that I should virtually insult the kindest of men by dwelling so absurdly upon a word, which after all, perhaps, I misunderstood. It certainly is not necessary that I should give his acts and words into the hands of his daughter, in order that they may undergo the same undutiful process.' And accordingly they parted for the night with much less of perfect sympathy than usual. For Sabina's head was running upon snow-white robes, anticipated good looks, and a multitude of other agreeable thoughts, which made her totally unobservant of the heavy, absent look of her sister − or, if she saw it at all, it was only with the conviction that the late hours of the night before had made her sleepy.

In some degree, perhaps, this conjecture was correct, for it was late before the bright April sun awoke Adèle; and when it did, though it was not long before the prevailing thought of the preceding night recurred to her, it came less painfully. Sunshine and morning air are the finest specifics in the world against moody musings; and before the gay breakfast was over, and the three ladies decided as to what shop they should first honour with their presence, the golden treasure of the drawer had very nearly melted into thin air, and Adèle, like her companion, began thinking about rich fabrics and becoming forms.

Beautiful young ladies are, generally speaking, considerably less difficult in the choice of their suits than ladies less young and less beautiful. Adèle and Sabina found, in what Madame de Hautrivage thought a wonderfully hurried manner, the pink and the white so accurately described by Mr Hargrave, and their purchases were immediately made. A large and beautiful assortment of 'fancy goods', as they are technically termed, has, unquestionably, and beyond the power of honest denial, a decided tendency to occupy the female mind, and withdraw it, for a time at least, from mightier matters. And so it was with our beautiful Adèle; for, despite her interesting misunderstanding with the young Englishman, − nay, despite, too, the teasing, puzzling thoughts which had been so lately tormenting her, she was as much present to the rainbow show before her as her more light-hearted sister; and it was only when at the same moment they both drew out their purses, in order to pay for their purchases, that the sight of the English gold so far brought them back as to make her slightly sigh as she looked at it.

'*Ah! . . . des sovereigns, mesdames?*' said the shop-keeper. 'We can only allow twenty-five francs, ladies; for the trouble of changing them is fully worth the difference.'

'Very well,' said Adèle, laying down the necessary sum; '*ça ira.*'

'What could induce my brother to take cash in this troublesome coin?' said Madame de Hautrivage.

'National partiality, I suppose,' replied Sabina, laughing.

'National partiality!' inwardly repeated Adèle. 'To be sure it is! He thought Madame would laugh at him if he confessed that he had taken so many sovereigns, which must be decidedly less convenient than the coin of the country. Dearest papa! It was only a sort of joke then after all!'

Perfectly satisfied by this interpretation, Adèle's spirits rose in exact proportion to their former depression; and the remainder of that morning's important business was performed with equally gay animation and enjoyment by them all.

CHAPTER IX

Whether accident or skill most favoured Mr Hargrave when he was particularly desirous of giving an entertainment, perfect in every point, it might be difficult to say; but no person, fortunate enough to have made one at any party thus sedulously cared for by him, could possibly deny that his success upon all such occasions was ever brilliant and ever unfailing.

On the day when he had the honour of receiving Prince Frederic of

—— to dine with him, Aladdin's lamp could hardly have furnished a
more perfect entertainment. That it was in one respect a failure in the
opinion of poor Adèle cannot, however, be denied; for Alfred Coventry
was not of it. But as the repeated inquiries made at his hôtel always
received for answer that he was not returned to Paris, the sorrow
occasioned by his absence had no admixture of despair in it; for even
Adèle herself never doubted that she should see him again in a few days;
and in this hope she shook off, as far as might be, the feeling of
disappointment which his absence occasioned her, and very amiably
exerted herself to the utmost to enliven the conversation of the small
circle permitted to share the honour of the royal guest's companionship.

The Duc de Vermont and his beautiful Duchesse were the only
strangers admitted, making a party of but seven persons round a table
glittering with gold and crystal, blazing with lights, and fragrant with
successive viands of the most exquisite *recherche* and variety. But the table
was a round one; and though large enough, perhaps, to accommodate a
dozen, lent itself gracefully to the less crowded occupation of the select
few who now surrounded it. Adèle thought that if Coventry had been
there, the party would have been perfect, and every one else thought it
perfect as it was. The Prince, though still a very young man, had already
become weary of the stately entertainments to which alone, in the
common course of things, it was his destiny to be invited, and enjoyed
exceedingly the contrast which this delicious little banquet afforded.
Though he certainly admired the delicate Sabina beyond all the other
beauties of the Parisian paradise, he was far from being insensible to the
sparkling loveliness of Mademoiselle de Cordillac, or to the gorgeous,
sultana-like attraction of the graceful Duchess. Neither was he at all
incapable of appreciating the conversational ability and perfect tact of Mr
Hargrave, the truly French vivacity of the Duke, or the rare and exquisite
quality of the wines which inspired it. In short, and to express the whole
result in one single emphatic word, the Prince was pleased.

And, in truth, however strong might be the internal emotions of
thankfulness and joy which swelled the bosom of Mr Hargrave at perceiving
this, there was nothing very surprising in it; for there really were abundant
elements for the pleasant passing away of an hour or two, unless the royal
young man had had within himself some antidote to social enjoyment,
which most assuredly was not the case. And then, every body else was so
evidently delighted when they looked at and listened to him, that nothing
short of a most vilely churlish temper could have prevented his testifying
some amiable feelings in return; and as all that could be wished for in this
way sparkled in his eyes, smiled on his lips and dropped in words of polished
courtesy or playful ease from his tongue, it cannot be wondered at if all the
little circle were delighted as well as the accomplished host.

Many royal personages seem to have discovered that music is one of the few enjoyments bestowed upon human beings by all-bounteous Heaven, which comes to them unvitiated by the pomps and vanities of their illustrious position; and they often appear to value it accordingly. Prince Frederic was one of these; and it was well known to all the world, who knew any thing, that there was no gratification which seemed to give his Royal Highness such unequivocal delight as listening to the inspired harmonies of the best composers, who breathed upon his ear by that choicest of musical instruments, the human voice divine — provided that the organ thus employed in his service was not a French organ; for the *criand* tone of which he had conceived an abhorrence, that alone, of all the feelings of which he appeared susceptible, shewed itself strong enough to conquer the habitual restraint of politeness, for since his arrival in Paris he had never been known to sit out the vocal performance of any native.

Fortunately, neither Adèle nor Sabina were musical exhibitionists, though the latter was no bad performer; and the family vanity, therefore, was in no degree wounded by its having been decided in the Committee for Ways and Means to furnish amusement for this royal visit (which had sat for the despatch of business as soon as the invitation was accepted), that Grisi, Lablache, and Tamburini, were to be put in requisition for the occasion, instead of having recourse to Parisian talent, either public or domestic.

The *café, chesse café*, albums, annuals, and miniatures had each and all done the duties required of them towards speeding the flight of time for the first hour after dinner; the light and laughing tone, engendered by good-humour and champagne, was just fading into something less animated, and Mr Hargrave had cast one single anxious glance towards the alabaster time-piece, when the outer door of the suite was thrown open and the above-mentioned constellation announced.

'Possible!' exclaimed the Prince, with a countenance expressive of the most unequivocal satisfaction, adding in a half-whisper to Sabina, beside whom he was seated, 'There is no one in Paris, mademoiselle, who understands how to arrange an entertainment like *monsieur votre père*.'

Sabina had never before conversed with Prince Frederic otherwise than by that safe and ordinary mode to which young ladies should always confine themselves, unless they wish to express more than they choose to say; but at that moment such a feeling of gratitude and delight seized upon Sabina, that her eyes spoke her thanks much more eloquently than any words could have done, and so sweetly, innocently beautiful, did she look the while, that the poor Prince felt for the first time that there was danger near him. He behaved incomparably well, however: for though he vehemently longed to say to her, 'You are the very loveliest creature that ever Nature made!' he did no such thing; but smuggling away a sigh under the disguise of a short cough, resolutely left his place, and advanced to offer his princely homage to the harmonious triumvirate.

Who is there that has not felt, on one side the Channel or the other, the ineffable enchantment which these three Italian magicians have the power of throwing over the senses? So few, that it can be scarcely necessary to observe that Mr Hargrave could not possibly have hit upon any expedient so likely to detach the thoughts of the Prince from his daughter, as well as from every thing else in the world, as by setting them to sing at him, for three hours altogether, with little interruption beyond what proceeded from the entry of ices, and such little interludes of conversation with the performers themselves as the gracious Prince deemed necessary, in order that they might be made aware of the exquisite pleasure they were bestowing, and thus become sharers in it themselves.

The anxious host watched the operation of his costly entertainment from beginning to end with the most acute and undeviating attention, and there were moments in the course of it during which he *almost* lamented the having had recourse to any other enchantment than that of his lovely Sabina, who certainly did appear to him, and perhaps really was, more touchingly beautiful on that evening than he had ever seen her before. In fact, she had never before enjoyed any hours so completely. Her love of music was as strong as that of the Prince himself, and perhaps even more fastidious. She always declared her own performance too bad to endure, though in fact it was better by many degrees than that of ninety-nine out of a hundred of the amateur pretenders to the divine science. But what with her *exigeante* delicacy of ear, and a temperament leading her greatly to prefer ease to labour, the luxury enjoyed at the Italian Opera was so greatly beyond any she could procure for herself, that she rarely played at all, excepting when quite alone; and then it was rather with the capricious uncertainty of the Æolian harp, which sends forth its sweet sounds in voluptuous wantonness, than with the studious laboriousness of science. Had she been brought up a very poor, instead of a very rich girl, it would have been otherwise; for rather than not have had good music at all, there can be no doubt that she would have contrived to obtain it for herself. But it was quite sufficient for her to have her own corner in her own box at the Italian Opera, and there it was her wont to lose herself in sweet unconscious reverie, her senses 'lapped in Elysium,' and her shapeless, unsettled thoughts careering away vastly beyond the reach of common sense, but generally into regions of poetry, peopled with beatific visions, all exceedingly unlike the full-dressed realities around her. All this had happened to her often, and had decidedly furnished the greatest enjoyment of her young life; but the magic witchery of scenic representation, with all its adventitious aids of orchestra and so forth, had always, in some degree, divided her attention, or at any rate left her with the persuasion that her enjoyment was produced by the united charm of all she saw and all she heard. But now, when Grisi first raised her voice, almost unaccompanied, and ran up to the very top of her compass, and then sunk into the plaintive sweetness of a nightingale that serenades the moon, she could hardly help exclaiming

> 'Can any mortal mixture of earth's mould
> Breathe such divine enchanting ravishment?'

and remembering the sort of dreary delight this same voice had so often given her before, when it had

> 'Lulled the sense,
> And in sweet madness robbed it of itself;'

to add (which she might have done in very sober truth) that

> 'Such a sacred and home-felt delight,
> Such sober certainty of waking bliss,
> *She had never felt* till now.'

It was easy enough to perceive that, of all the little party thus exquisitely regaled, there was but one beside herself who felt it as she did; and it is vain to deny that, as she observed this, she felt that there was pleasure – great pleasure, in listening to music with any body who loved it as well as one did oneself.

The last trio had been asked for by the Prince, and performed as if the three wondrous voices had not sounded a single note before; and then the professors retired, leaving the hero of the *fête* with a feeling of having tasted more perfect enjoyment than any entertainment had afforded him since his arrival in Paris. He, too, rose to take leave, and extending his hand to Mr Hargrave, thanked him for the pleasure he had afforded him with a degree of sincerity which rarely accompanies similar words.

'Your Royal Highness makes me too happy,' returned the delighted host, with truth equally rare; 'but let me beseech your Royal Highness not to leave my humble roof without partaking of the refreshment prepared in the little *salon* there. It is impossible, I believe, to listen to the music with the enthusiasm which you, *mon prince*, appear to feel, without experiencing somewhat of fatigue and exhaustion. Will your Royal Highness permit us to follow you to the next room?'

By no means displeased with the proposition, Prince Frederic nodded a smiling assent, and immediately afforded his arm to Sabina. Was it because he remembered that she was the daughter of his host, and that her eldest sister was not? Or was it because the temptation was too strong to be resisted, and that he really could not help it?

Mr Hargrave was perfectly right. Fatigue and a feeling of exhaustion are inevitable upon attending to any thing earnestly for three hours. It was half-past one o'clock, and the supper was the very perfection of a French supper – which means, that though as light in appearance and as tastefully ornamented as a banquet on the stage, it had, nevertheless, such a portion of real comestibles amongst its prettiness as courageous people venture to address themselves to when they are hungry, let the hour be what it may. It is exactly for such a repast as this that champagne seems invented, and such champagne as Mr Hargrave's the Duc de Vermont declared must have been made on purpose for the beautiful lips now invited to sip it. On himself its effect was exactly what his watchful entertainer would have desired. His gay spirits mounted and effervesced as brightly as the sparkling beverage he quaffed, occupying and delighting every one, save only Prince Frederic of ――― and the fair young creature at his side.

With what feelings Mr Hargrave watched this exception to the laughing hilarity of the little party could be guessed by none unacquainted with the inmost secrets of his soul; and as for the repository of these secrets, he had never chosen any confidant: save himself alone, none could guess the ecstasy of that hour. Sabina, too, now shewed for the first time that as she listened to the Prince the distance of rank was forgotten and nothing remembered but himself. Had the delight which the observing this occasioned to her father been caused by believing that the union, which he now fancied was within his grasp, would lead to her happiness as much as to his own, much might have been forgiven him. But it was not so. He saw in it nothing but an additional charm whereby to work upon the passions of the youthful Prince, and watched it with no better feeling than that with which a spider may be supposed to watch the subtle complexity of the web that is twisting itself about the unwary insect who has approached it. Hargrave felt sympathy with no human being but himself – not even with his lovely and most loving child, and deserved not that any should feel sympathy with him.

At length the evening closed, and the guests departed, no two of the small company feeling in the least degree alike on the subject of the entertainment they had shared. Madame de Hautrivage was simply *abîmée* with fatigue, and yawned till her jaws were very nearly dislocated as soon as the royal and noble guests were beyond the reach of seeing or hearing her. The Duc de Vermont, – who, since the Prince had ceased to listen to the *feu de joie* of witty words with which he had enlivened the meeting, had devoted himself to Adèle, – had nearly yawned too, as he perceived how entirely *la belle demoiselle*, who he feared was *tant soit peu Agnes*, was thinking of something else. The beautiful Duchess roused her husband from his sleepy fit as they drove home by her exclamations of envy and astonishment at the enormous wealth of the English. '*Mais qu'ils sont bête*,' she added, '*après tout*. What Frenchman would have given an entertainment that must have cost at least three thousand francs, and then set down four women and three men to partake of it? *Quelle bévue ridicule!*' Adèle was indeed so mindful of all that was going on, that she would have been greatly puzzled to give any account of the day when it was over. Sabina – the pure-minded, innocent Sabina – had been so very, very happy, that all criticism upon the winged hours, and all judgment upon any thing that had passed in the course of them, were swallowed up in a general conviction that her dear papa was the most delightful man in the world for knowing, as the Prince said, so much better than any body else how to arrange a delightful party!

And the Prince himself – the hero of this deeply-studied *fête* – what did he think of it? His only objection to it was, that he was conscious of having found it too agreeable. 'There is danger in such hours,' thought he, as he turned restlessly on his pillow. 'That delicate angel is too good, too fair, too fascinating, to approach with impunity. We must have no more small dinner-parties at Monsieur Hargrave's!'

CHAPTER X

Adèle de Cordillac had endured with more than ordinary philosophy the deep disappointment occasioned by the absence of Alfred Coventry at the dinner which has been just described; but not all her resolution could prevent her sister's perceiving, when they met the following morning, that she looked both ill and unhappy.

At no time would Sabina have been unobservant of this, for no attachment could be more perfect or more tender than that by which the half-sisters were united: but now the feeling produced by it was peculiarly strong; for, in the first place, Sabina herself had never in her life felt so happy as she did that morning. The two girls seemed to have changed characters, like the Olivia and Sophia of Goldsmith, and the gaiety of Adèle to have passed into the heart of Sabina, while in return she had received the gentle meekness of her less animated sister.

'What ails you, dearest?' said the younger, kneeling upon the cushion at her sister's feet, caressingly taking both her hands, and raising her beautiful blue eyes to her face with an expression half playful, half tender.

'I will not have you look so woe-begone! I thought that such a day as yesterday must do you good, and almost make you forget the absence of Coventry. Was not the day delightful, Adèle?'

'Not to me, dear love,' replied Adèle, gravely, and with a movement of her head that seemed to indicate many disparaging thoughts concerning it.

'What can you mean, Adèle?' said Sabina, starting up, her delicate colour heightened, at the very least, to the third shade of a moss-rose that goes on blushing *crescendo* to the centre.

'Dear child!' returned Adèle, mournfully, 'I am in no fit state to lecture you – for truly I feel that I well deserve lecturing myself; but if you will have the truth, I must tell you that in my well-intentioned efforts to forget the absent, I looked on with more than usual attention on what was present, and——' But here she stopped.

'And what, Adèle?' demanded Sabina, her complexion assimilating nearer and nearer to the centre of the rose.

'I fear you will be very angry with me! Yet you would not, could you understand me fully, for then you would see that I hold you blameless as an angel,' said Adèle, colouring in her turn. 'But I do think, Sabina, that Prince Frederic is very nearly, if not quite, in love with you.'

'That is not like you, sister Adèle,' said Sabina, sitting down with a look of deep vexation. 'I know not what you have seen in Prince Frederic of —— which can justify your making such an observation. We need not tell each other – you and I, I mean, – that love from him to me must be an insult. And what has he ever said or done to deserve such a suspicion?'

'Nothing, Sabina, nothing! – that is, there is nothing to deserve the suspicion that he would offer you an insult; which, as you most truly say, any mention of love from him to you must be. But there is much to make me fear, rather for his sake than for yours, Sabina, that he admires you more and more every time you meet; and that it is terribly likely, without any act of the will, that it may end by his becoming most devotedly and unhappily attached to you.'

'And pray, sister, do you think I am likely to become most devotedly and painfully attached to him?'

'No, dearest Sabina, I do not. With so excellent an understanding as yours, and principles of the quality which I know yours to be, there can be no cause for such fear. But this young Prince——'

'Forgive me, Adèle, for interrupting you,' replied Sabina, with vivacity; 'but you must permit me to say that this young Prince, as you call him, has never, for a single instant, given us any right to suspect that his principles are of worse quality than our own; or that his princedom, or his youth either, need be pleaded in extenuation of any thing he has ever done or said. Let none of your fears, therefore, be directed towards him, Adèle. As for myself, I will not sit in judgment on the wisdom of having felt all the admiration for him of which I was conscious yesterday; but, believe me, there is no danger of my forgetting that

> "It were all one
> That I should love a bright particular star,
> And think to wed it; he is so above me."

I know all this, dear sister, as well as you could possibly wish me to know it, − and let that suffice you.'

'It shall − it shall, dearest: but do not turn away as if you were vexed with me, Sabina. I am very ready to believe that the uneasy fancies which have been floating about my silly head have no wiser origin than my own low spirits. Sabina, I am very miserable.'

'My dearest Adèle! and I have been cross to you!' returned the penitent Sabina. 'Oh, forgive me; and yesterday, then, while I was gayer and happier than I ever remember to have felt before, you were pining for the absence of Alfred Coventry.'

'Less for his absence,' replied Adèle, bursting into tears, 'than for the cause of it. I cannot forgive myself,' she continued, 'for having listened to any thing such a person as my aunt could say, in preference to trusting to what I myself know of his character. He would not have so treated me, Sabina: and when I recall his manner to me on the fatal night of that detestable ball, and the number of times I insultingly evaded his earnest − oh! so evidently earnest wish to speak to me, I lose all confidence in the hope of his return, and feel irresistibly persuaded that he has left Paris to return to it no more. Am I not punished for my contemptible jealousy and pride?'

'What makes you think that he would take so very strong a measure?' demanded Sabina. 'Surely, if he believed that you had blamed or suspected him unjustly, his best method of proving this would not be the flying off from Paris, post haste, in this way?'

'No, no, it is not that; I gave him not the slightest clue by which to discover the senseless jest which had been played upon us. What he must believe, Sabina, is that I am the most heartless coquette that ever France produced. Every hour that I spend in recalling all that has passed between us makes me feel more strongly the odious light in which I must appear to him. No one can judge of this so well as I can do, Sabina; and indeed − indeed, I think that his only course was to turn away from me for ever, − and that he has done so I can doubt no longer.'

'My dear Adèle, I cannot but think such a persuasion is premature: at any rate before we receive it, let us send to his hôtel to know whether his return is still expected there; whether he has left servants, horses, or carriages behind him; and, in short, find out, − as most certainly it must be very easy to do, − whether he has finally taken his departure or not.'

'Sabina, I would give my right hand to do it!' returned Adèle. 'But the means, dearest? I cannot ask papa to despatch a servant with such strangely curious inquiries, and still less can I do it myself!'

'What say you, Adèle, to our sending old Roger, confidentially, upon this expedition? Is there any thing within the reach of possibility, think you, that the dear old man would refuse to do for us?'

'But even to old Roger I shall feel ashamed to betray the deep interest I feel in this message; yet, unless I do so, what chance is there that he will execute it effectually?'

'None whatever,' replied Sabina, laughing. 'If Roger fancies that he is sent trotting to the Rue de Rivoli upon any business that an ordinary domestic could execute, the embassy will be very unprofitably performed, depend upon it. You know perfectly well that the act of traversing one of your magnificent bridges appears to him an enterprise only second to setting off for Pekin. Therefore be assured, that without a motive proportionably strong, he will set about it very reluctantly, and perform it vilely; but only just let him suspect that he could render you an important service, Adèle, and one, too, with which none other of the household could be trusted, and the only difficulty remaining will be to make his venerable body keep pace with his eager soul.'

'You plead eloquently, my sister, and most convincingly,' replied Mademoiselle de Cordillac. 'But must I then,' she continued, 'shew forth all the secrets of my heart to the worthy Roger, and tell him in good set terms that I am very heartily in love, and am in need of his good services to bring my wandering lover back again?'

'Upon my word, my dear, I fear you must, or we shall make nothing of him. You cannot fear his breathing a single syllable of any thing you say to him in confidence? I am convinced that he would consent to be torn to atoms rather than suffer any human being to share the trust so confided in him.'

'I know it, – I know it, Sabina! No, I have no fears of dear old Roger. Only it is rather disagreeable to send any page on such a mission. But it shall be done, my dear, bold counsellor. I have paid enough for my pride's sake, and now I will make the offending rebel smart a little.'

So saying, Adèle de Cordillac deliberately rose and rang the bell. 'Send Roger to me,' she said to the servant who answered it: and the old man stood before her, smiling, and well pleased to be summoned to her presence, considerably before she had determined how to explain her singular mission to him.

'This is a glory and a pleasure to me, ladies,' said the delighted old man. 'God bless your sweet young faces! Is there any thing to be done in which I can be useful?'

'Indeed there is, Roger,' replied Adèle, taking courage, and determined that her embassy should not fail from her averseness to explaining it. 'We know that we can trust you, Roger, with any secret, and what I am going to say to you now must be for ever kept from all others.'

'Miss Adèle,' replied the old man, earnestly, 'the only great pleasure that I think God could now give me in this world would be finding out that I had the power of doing either my beloved master or your dear young sister some real service; except, indeed, the seeing that you are not afraid to trust me.'

'God bless you, old friend,' returned Adèle, affectionately; 'you shall judge then if I am afraid to trust you.'

She then explained to him at some length, and with perfect clearness, the *mauvais tour* which Madame de Hautrivage had played her, and all the painful consequences which ensued from it; adding, 'But for this, my good old friend, I do in troth believe that I should now have been affianced to this gentleman. Go, then, good Roger, and discover for me if Mr Coventry is expected to return, or whether the people of the hôtel believe that he has left Paris altogether.'

It was quite evident that the honest man perfectly understood his commission, and no less so that, if his zeal in the cause could avail, it would not have been given to him in vain.

While this important business was transacted in the boudoir of the young ladies, affairs of at least equal moment were going forward in Mr Hargrave's library. He had retired thither immediately after breakfast, chiefly with the intention, perhaps, of quietly enjoying in review the honours and success of the previous day. Never before had he felt so delightedly assured that all he wished was near. He had often, as he smilingly told himself, observed unequivocal admiration and the most marked attention on the part of Prince Frederic to his daughter, but never till the last night had any expression of positive tenderness beamed from his royal eyes as he gazed upon her. His beautiful daughter, too, – that sweet epitome of his own grace and elegance, – could she have kindled as she did, while listening to the low-toned conversation poured into her willing ear, had no mixture of wooing sweetness lurked in it? Triumphant was the answer that his very soul received as he asked himself this question; and his reverie changed from contemplation of the past to the most intoxicating anticipations for the future. He seemed to feel upon his heaving breast the delicious weight of stars and crosses of orders innumerable. Sweet sounds murmured in his ears as of whispering throngs of nobles, whose words, being interpreted, were 'See! that graceful, noble gentleman is the father of the Princess Frederic!' Long suites of gorgeous rooms opened in a palpable vista before him, and among them his heart told him he should find his home. 'Ay,' he murmured softly, stretching himself on the sofa, whereon he had thrown his 'graceful length of limb,' in order to indulge these meditations, – 'Ay, there will be my resting-place, and without the cursed – cursed necessity of seeking means to pay for it! – Oh, blessed chance! Just at the very hour when all resources fail me – all! – just at that frightful hour to open upon a mine of glorious state and costless luxury, which shall wait upon me to the last hour of my existence, without a single racking thought, by day or night, as to how it is supplied!'

Exactly at the moment when Mr Hargrave had reached this climax of hope, the knock of an intruder was heard at the library door. 'Come in,' he said gently, and without greatly changing his position, for he doubted not that he should see, when the door opened, the lovely form of his daughter, which he had ever admired as being a softened copy of his own majestic beauty, but which he now felt ready to kneel before and worship, as the source of all the golden joys which he saw before him.

The revulsion of feeling produced by the disappointment which followed was really terrible. Instead of Adèle and Sabina, whom he expected to see enter, the slowly opening door admitted the form he most hated to behold, namely, that of his house-steward, who had long been in the habit of receiving all his bills, and of very punctually paying them as long as his elegant master had punctually furnished him with means.

After the first shock, however, occasioned by the contrast between what he saw and what he expected to see, Mr Hargrave recovered himself; for he did not at that moment anticipate any particularly pressing claims upon him. A few weeks before, indeed, this same unwelcome individual had painted with such hateful accuracy the inevitable consequence of continuing any longer the system of paying in promises instead of francs, that Hargrave's buoyant and bold spirit had almost sunk before it; but he had not only rallied, but by some way or other found means to satisfy, or stop, the claims which had very nearly overwhelmed him; and he now felt very tolerably secure that, for the present at least, his extravagant establishment might go on without any danger of immediate consequences, and shew forth, as he hoped, the same brilliant surface of wealth to the public, till the marriage of Sabina should render it no longer necessary.

Scarcely, however, had the prospective father-in-law of a royal prince looked in the face of his steward, than his heart misgave him; for he saw symptoms there of the same gloom and anxiety which had been so recently removed by efforts to which Mr Hargrave was well aware he could not, for many reasons, resort again.

'What is the matter now, Jenkyns?' exclaimed Mr Hargrave, suddenly springing from the sofa: 'you look as if every ounce of plate I have in the world had been stolen. For God's sake explain the meaning of your doleful visage instantly!'

'It is easy enough to do that, sir,' replied the man, who had led a very easy life while the resources of his lavish master lasted, and was as little disposed as his principal to witness the end of so brilliant a career. 'I only wish I was sure that it would be as easy to cure the mischief as to explain it.'

'What the devil do you mean, Jenkyns?' demanded his master, turning very pale; for thoughts of a possible danger shot through his brain, considerably more appalling than any which had gone before.

'The old story, sir,' replied the steward, knitting his brows, and shaking his head very significantly.

'Hoh!' exclaimed Hargrave with such a heavy 'suspiration of forced breath' as seemed to denote a feeling of relief. 'But you can surely skirmish with them a little longer, Jenkyns? I thought you told me that the money I have lately given you – in pretty tolerable abundance, God knows – would suffice to keep the people quiet, and ready to go on for some months to come?'

'And I answered for no more than was true, sir,' returned Jenkyns. 'The tradespeople are all in high good-humour again, and I don't expect we shall hear any more grumbling. Somehow or other they had taken fright, but your coming down, sir, so freely with ready money again has set all that right, and I dare say we shall hear no more of their bills till towards the end of the season.'

'Then why, in Heaven's name, my good fellow, do you look so confoundedly dismal?' said Mr Hargrave, gaily turning on his heel, and looking in the mirror over the chimney for a more agreeable object than the puckered visage of the old steward.

'I am afraid, sir, you have forgot all about Monsieur Jules Marsan. You know, sir, that just before your good lady died, you borrowed a hundred and fifty thousand francs of him – at terrible high interest, to be sure – but it was but a trifle, and it could be of no great consequence in our large way of going on; and, therefore, when he came into my bureau this morning, looking as black as thunder, I went on sipping my tea, as easy as may be, thinking that the little matter of interest in arrear, which couldn't be above six or seven thousand francs, might easily be settled. However, I soon found out that we were not to be let off so easy; for that he was come to insist upon having his principal back again forthwith, which he swears you promised to pay on demand any time after two years from the date of the loan; and that he wrote to remind you of this, and to give you notice that he wanted the money: to which letter he declares you have given no answer whatever. And this it is, I suspect, which has made him so savage; for he swears lustily that he will have the money in his pocket, or you in a gaol, before the week is out.'

'I declare to you, by the honour of a gentleman, Mr Jenkyns, that I have never seen any such letter,' replied Mr Hargrave, with great dignity;

'and I desire that you will let him know this without loss of time; assuring him, likewise, that if he will only indulge me now with the same notice he intended to give when he wrote, his money shall be punctually paid him.'

'And how long, I wonder, would that give for finding the money?' said the steward, giving a furtive glance at his handsome master, who had again turned to recruit his spirits by looking at himself in his favourite mirror.

'A month, Jenkyns,' replied Mr Hargrave; 'and that will suit me perfectly well.'

'And, I dare say, that will suit him too,' replied the well-paid servant, taking his departure without giving any hint of having discovered how very lightly the honour of his elegant master had been pledged.

Unpleasant as this very urgent claim must have been at any other moment, it now only acted as a spur upon the already excited temper of Hargrave; and he immediately set to work to invent some new and reasonable excuse for again inviting the Prince to his house; satisfied that a very little more opportunity for fostering the passion he had conceived, was all that was required to bring on a declaration of it.

While thus engaged, he was again interrupted; but this time it was by nothing more annoying than his verbose sister-in-law. This accomplished Frenchwoman was in many ways extremely useful to him; and he received her now, as he was always accustomed to do, with a most courteous welcome.

'*Ah, ça!*' she exclaimed: 'I find you alone, my brother – that is well, for I have business to discuss with you.'

'*Eh, bien! ma soeur,*' returned the gentleman. 'What is it?'

'*Mais* – you shall hear. I have been making a visit of consolation to Madame de Tours. You know her husband is just ordered to Africa. *Eh, bien!* she could not talk of that, she could talk of nothing but the diamonds of Madame Bertrand, the rich banker's newly-married wife. Madame de Tours assures me positively that she has been taken at the Opera for the Infanta of Spain – by somebody, of course, who did not know the Infanta's person – for they say that Madame Bertrand is an extremely pretty young woman, and that she is to be the beauty, *par excellence*, for the remainder of the season. All Paris is wild to see her and her diamonds. *On dit*, that she is absolutely covered with them from head to foot – literally from head to foot! *Imaginez!* – nothing is so much the fashion as to invite her. *Et voilà mon affair.* I want our cards to be sent instantly, together with an invitation to a *fête*. You have always been the first in every thing, and I would not have you the last in this: *comprenez-vous, mon frère?*'

Mr Hargrave assured her that nothing could at any time be so agreeable to him as complying with her wishes; and that, à propos of the subject on which she had been so kind as to express them now, her feelings and opinions were precisely his own.

'A la bonne heure!' exclaimed the animated lady, springing from her chair with the playful grace of sixteen; 'vraiment, mon cher – mais, vraiment, vous êtes divin! – Allons donc. When shall it be? Do not fix a distant day, lest all the world shall have been before you.'

'What say you, dear lady, to this day week?' said Mr Hargrave.

'Nothing can be better,' she replied. 'Sans adieu, donc, I go to consult nos demoiselles on their dresses;' and Madame de Hautrivage, kissing the tips of her fingers, tripped away.

Here then was another opportunity for Prince Frederic! Having, as usual, made out a list of the company he wished to invite, for the use of the person whose office it was to send forth invitations, Mr Hargrave himself addressed a note of homage to the Prince, in which he alluded, with graceful playfulness, to the Paris whim of hunting all novelties. Each family, he said, considered it a duty which they owed to society, to catch the short-lived wonder for a night, and, holding it in soft bondage, to exhibit it for the amusement of their friends and acquaintance. In performance of which modish rite he was going, he added, to request the élite of the beau monde to assemble in his drawing-rooms on the 19th, for the purpose of looking at a certain beautiful Madame Bertrand, who appeared at the present moment to be the centre of all attraction. Could his Royal Highness condescend to turn his eyes for an hour or two in the same direction as the multitude turned theirs? If this might be hoped for! &c. &c. &c.

> 'When honours come, they come not single spies,
> But in battalions.'

Not only did Prince Frederic accept this invitation, and that, too, by a few gracious lines written by his own royal hand; but in his turn he invited Mr Hargrave and the ladies of his family to favour him with their presence at a fancy-ball, for which he was about to send out invitations for the 1st of May.

This written document seemed to complete the process of Mr Hargrave's infatuation. There was not a word in it but he turned and twisted till it became to his fancy a solemn assurance of all he wished; and, had every other line failed to furnish the desired interpretation, that in which his royal correspondent so clearly stated that no one else in all Paris was as yet invited to the projected fête, would have perfectly sufficed. This fancy-ball, then, was given for Sabina! Did she decline the invitation, it was clear as light that the whole thing would fall to the ground. This princely entertainment was to afford the royal lover the opportunity of declaring his passion. It was no new device. Such arrangements had been often heard of before. When king's sons married from love, and not from policy, it was not likely they would lose the dear joy of witnessing the emotion their generous devotion must cause in the fair object of it, — it was not likely they would ceremoniously demand consent of friends, and so forth. 'No!' murmured the thrice Happy Hargrave; 'I have not lived so long in the very centre and heart of society without learning to interpret the signs and tokens belonging to it. Sabina is the elected wife of a prince, and I am destined to stand in the position of brother to a king! — And poor Jenkyns thought to scare me by talking of a pressing claim for a few thousand pounds! What a whimsical incongruity it seems!' And Mr Hargrave laughed — laughed heartily at the jest he saw in it; and then sat down again at his elegant *écritoire*, and composed an acceptance of Prince Frederic's invitation, with as much eloquence as it was possible to throw upon the subject.

That the unfortunate Hargrave, despite the *savoir vivre* on which he so greatly piqued himself, was most egregiously mistaken in all these calculations, is most certain; nevertheless, his daughter Sabina was in truth the origin and cause of Prince Frederic's fancy-ball: nor had she appeared at all less lovely in his eyes on the evening they had last passed together than her ambitious father supposed. But the result of his admiration, as well as the motive for giving this *fête*, were as far as was well possible from what his inflated imagination conceived.

Prince Frederic, through many a bright gala, had danced and talked with the beautiful Sabina without a serious thought beyond what was necessary to decide his opinion that she was the loveliest blossom of the bright *parterre* which (by the help of exotics) a Parisian *salon* of the first class is sure to display. Many were the balls, concerts, and operas, which had passed over them before he became in the least degree conscious of any change of sentiment towards her; but, of late, he had begun to be a little aware that he liked better to talk than even to waltz with her. He felt that it was a pity to lose the expression of her marvellously sweet eyes when she looked timidly in his face as he spoke to her. He acknowledged to himself, — without, however, much thinking that it signified, — that Sabina Hargrave was not only the fairest girl in Paris, but, to the best of his knowledge and belief, the purest, gentlest, most intellectual lady in the world: and, soon after this, the thought struck him that it was a pity she was not of a royal house. But still he was in no way alarmed; feeling convinced, as many a good man has done before him, that he was master of his will, if not of his wishes, and that, while he remained so, there could be no danger of any kind in the intercourse.

It was on the evening of Mr Hargrave's dinner-party, that this noble-minded scion of a royal stock first became aware of his own danger; and perhaps, also, that it was not impossible there might be danger for Sabina too.

It is '*de notoriété bourgeoise*' that, in the intercourse between gentlemen who are royal and ladies who are not so, the *perfectly* well-conducted of the fair sex, particularly if they are young and beautiful, take more especial care to be discreet in words and looks than on any other occasion; the consequence of which is, that these illustrious sons of kings rarely catch a beam of unquenched feeling from the eye of the most charming, because the purest of human beings: and it was probably for this reason, that when Sabina, for an instant forgetting his rank, looked up in the face of Prince Frederic with unrestrained gratitude and delight, upon his paying a compliment to her father, it seemed to him that he had never before seen any thing so exquisitely beautiful as her countenance; and he might have exclaimed, like the eighth Henry, though in a far different spirit, –

'Oh, Beauty!
Till now I never knew thee.'

'Oh! how those eyes could speak!' thought the stricken young man, 'if one but dared to question them!' But, to his honour be it said, not once again in the whole course of that delightful evening, – not even during the gay hour of unreflecting enjoyment which followed the exhilarating supper, did Prince Frederic seek to fix the glance of that innocent eye upon his own, or attempt in any way to make her understand how deeply he was touched by her loveliness. Had he felt less, perhaps, he might have been less cautious to conceal that little than he now was to hide, to struggle with, and overcome, what he felt was strong enough to frighten him.

Before he left his apartments on the following morning his resolution was taken, and his plans perfectly settled and arranged. He wrote to a noble friend in London, announcing his intention of immediately prosecuting his scheme of travel by proceeding to that capital, and requesting him to bespeak suitable apartments, to be ready for him in a fortnight. He then summoned the principal *employé* of his suite, gave him notice of his intended change of residence, and informed him, likewise, that it was his purpose, before he left Paris, to give an entertainment on a scale suitable to his rank, the preparations for which he desired might be set about without delay.

CHAPTER XI

To Adèle, the absence of old Roger seemed interminable; and even Sabina, though she was thinking a little of other things, confessed that she could not guess what he could possibly be about so long. At last, however, like other tedious things, his absence ended; and just as Adèle was proposing that they should tell their father how very long he had been out, and request that some active measures might be resorted to for discovering what was become of him, the old man made his appearance, a little out of breath, he said, by the activity he had used, but, in all other respects, in a state of the highest preservation and safety.

'And your news, Roger?' said Sabina, perceiving that Adèle appeared more desirous of hearing than of asking for it.

'Not over good, my dear children, – not over good,' he replied, shaking his head.

Adèle turned very pale, but spoke not a word.

'Speak out and tell all,' said Sabina; 'but do not keep us in suspense.'

The privileged old man looked earnestly in the half-averted face of poor Adèle, and replied, –

'Not for the world, my dears; but it is rather a long story, if I am to tell you all of it.'

'Sit down, old friend,' said Sabina, placing a chair for him; 'and fear not that we shall think the history too long; for, trust me, we would not have you omit a word of it.'

Adèle gave her young sister a very grateful look, and prepared to listen.

'In the first place,' resumed Roger, 'and to give the result of my commission before I go on to any thing else, I must tell you, ladies, that the young gentleman is not in Paris, nor has been, since he left it the day after our last great ball.'

'There is no bad news in that, Adèle,' observed Sabina, cheerfully. Adèle nodded in acquiescence of the remark, and changed her position, so as to see the countenance of her faithful messenger.

'No, that is all very well, my dears, but the worst is to come.' And then, bestowing a good deal more tediousness than was absolutely necessary, Roger Humphries proceeded to relate, that upon asking for Mr Coventry's people at the hôtel, a very decent servant-like body, and altogether an Englishman, came to him, and told him not only what he had just repeated, but also that his master was expected to return in a few days, but probably for a few hours only, as he had sent orders for every thing he had left at the hôtel to be packed up in readiness to start as soon as he came back. 'Now this I should have been sorry for,' said the worthy Roger, 'even if he had said no more; because it was plain enough to me, that you had rather he was not going away quite so soon, my dears. But it was what he said after that made me think the news so very bad; for he spoke of him, to be sure, as if he was altogether out of the common way of ordinary young gentlemen nowadays . . . Such a son! – such a brother! – and such a fortune! And so you see, my dear children, it could hardly help coming into my head that he would be just exactly the very husband for one of you two. Think what it would be, – I ask your pardon, Miss Adèle, – but just think what it would be if either of you was to marry a Frenchman! It would be the death of me, – I am quite sure it would be the death of me. Not that I ought to mention such a reason as that, – for what's my dying or living compared to your having husbands like? Lord have mercy upon me! I needn't name names; – and you, both of you, used as you are to such a gentleman as my master, – you would take to hating him, ladies, in a month, – you would indeed. And, take my word for it, that's a very bad thing, and leads to mischief, as sure as can be. But it is little use to talk about this Mr Coventry any more, I suppose; unless, indeed, you thought there would be any good in my stepping over again, just when he comes back, maybe, and giving him a hint that you would just like to say good-by to him before he goes. It takes a long while sometimes before young folks get to the end of saying good-by.'

At length, to the great relief of Sabina, Roger concluded his harangue, and wiped his forehead.

'Thank you, Roger Humphries, – thank you kindly,' she said. 'Go now, old friend, and get some refreshment; you look heated and weary, Roger. Should we think you could help us further, we shall be sure to call for you.'

The old man uttered his usual fervent 'Bless you! – bless you both!' and departed; leaving both the poor girls discouraged and discomfited, and pretty equally convinced that but little chance remained of ever seeing Alfred Coventry more.

It was now, and now only, that the unfortunate Adèle de Cordillac became aware of the misery which the absurdity of her un-venerable aunt had brought upon her; for it was now only that she was fully aware how wholly she had bestowed upon Coventry the affection of her heart. She spoke not, but she wept bitterly; and not the less so from the conviction that she had used him ill. The genuine worth and unmistakable nobleness of heart, which she had had sufficient opportunity of observing, ought, as she felt but too plainly, to have saved him from such hasty condemnation; and every sad moment of meditation on the past only brought with it the strengthened conviction that she had been loved, and was loved no longer.

In this state of mind it was fortunate for her that she had stolen away

to her own room, that she might weep, unperceived even by her gentle
and sympathising sister, before Mr Hargrave entered the boudoir, all
radiant and glorious with the intelligence he brought of two more balls,
of which Prince Frederic was to be the hero. Certain it is that his news
was not listened to now by an indifferent ear; and it was with a
delightful beating of the heart, which almost answered to her own, that
her father witnessed the beautiful flush which mounted to her cheeks as
he spoke. But much too wise to let her perceive he noticed it, he
turned from her with an air of affected business and bustle, saying, −
'Where is Adèle? − where is your sister, my dear child? I particularly
wish that you should both of you prepare your toilets for these
occasions with more than usual care. At the *fête* given by the Prince, my
dear Sabina, this is especially necessary; as, you may depend upon it,
every lady of any distinction in Paris will make a point of appearing in
the most costly and elegant costume she can devise. It is a compliment
which his Royal Highness well deserves from all, in return for the
gracious affability with which he has entered into the amusements of
the society; and to us, in particular, his condescending kindness has
been so remarkable that any omission on our parts would be
unpardonable.'

'It is you, papa, who must invent our fancy-dresses,' said Sabina,
rather desirous of turning the conversation from the Prince to a subject
so absorbing as that of dresses for a fancy-ball. 'I am quite sure,' she
added, 'that neither Adèle nor I shall be able to do any thing without
you.'

'You shall not need, dearest,' replied the happy Hargrave. 'No man
of taste would desire a more agreeable employment than draping two
such pretty lay figures as yourself and Adèle. But, above all things, my
love, we must keep in mind the important distinction between a fancy-
ball and a masquerade. Nothing which I at this moment remember
strikes me as so offensively *mauvais ton* as confounding them. In a
masquerade-dress, − in the by-gone days when ladies were permitted
so to amuse themselves, − the perfection of a costume consisted in the
learned accuracy with which every circumstance of time, station, and
personal peculiarity in the character represented, was seized; whether
becoming or unbecoming, whether elegant or precisely the reverse, a
masquerading dress, to be approved by persons of real taste, must be
strictly and severely historical, and nothing else. But at a fancy-ball,
thank Heaven! the case is wholly different. The first object is to
ascertain what age and what country furnishes the style most accordant
to the form and features, and then all the skill of the artist employed
must be directed to modify, heighten, or soften, the effect of the
costume chosen, with the most studious attention to what becomes the

individual, and utter disregard to every thing else. In short, my dear child, what is learning at a masquerade becomes pedantry at a fancy-ball; and you know me well enough to comprehend how I should shrink from such an imputation. These are the broad principles upon which our conduct in this affair must be based; and, these established, we run little or no risk of failure. Your style of beauty is so singularly picturesque, my sweet Sabina, that it would be more difficult to fail than to succeed in producing the effect desired. What say you to an Eastern dress, my love? White and gold, — simply white and gold, — arranged in the picturesque style usually attributed to Circassian slaves when transplanted to Constantinople, would become you well, I think.'

'Then such shall be my dress, papa,' replied Sabina; 'your first thoughts are always brilliant. And Adèle, — what shall our pretty Adèle wear?'

'Spanish; those magnificent eyes of hers are decidedly Spanish. But her dress, like your own, dearest, must not be too correct. The general outline may be in your case Eastern, and in hers Castilian; but the detail must be French. I will make a slight sketch of both before your hour for shopping to-morrow, and that, with the assistance of Madame Octavia, will remove all anxiety. But there is one thing, my dear love, that I wish to observe to you. It is rather *mauvais ton*, my Sabina, to run about, purse in hand, to other people's tradesmen. Not, of course, that your paying ready money can be any inconvenience to me; on the contrary, indeed, I think it always saves trouble. But that is not an advantage which can come for a moment into competition with the consideration of what is *bon ton* and what is not; therefore, Sabina, I wish you to procure every thing at the *magasins* where you have been chiefly accustomed to deal, and order your bills to be sent in, as other ladies of fashion do. You understand, my love?'

'Oh yes, papa, I believe so. I am not to carry my purse, and pay ready money — like the little girls going to market for a sous-worth of *oseille* — that is what you mean, is it not?'

'Exactly!' replied her father, laughing heartily at her lively illustration. 'And now, dearest, I must leave you; for, as you may imagine, my habit of giving my own instructions to my *maître d'hôtel* renders such an entertainment as I intend to give Madame Bertrand a matter of business as well as pleasure. But go and find Adèle; tell her of these two engagements, and also that, before mid-day to-morrow, I will prepare for her a little sketch of the style of dress which I propose for her to wear at Prince Frederic's *fête*.'

Mr Hargrave then, with a heart buoyant with hope, and a brow devoid of every trace of care, impressed a kiss upon his daughter's cheek, and left her.

CHAPTER XII

Mr Hargrave was just putting, on the following morning, the finishing touch to his elegant little drawing of Adèle's costume (that of Sabina, as well as one of his own gorgeous Russian uniform, having been completed to his heart's content an hour before), when a timid and rather sinister-sounding knock at the door of the library disturbed the pleasant careerings of his fancy, and obliged him to say, 'Come in.'

It was slowly, and as if with reluctance, that the door opened, and presented to his view, not only the careful face of Mr Jenkyns, which was what he expected to see, but also the dark lines of a sharply-featured and stern countenance behind him, which, after a few seconds of harassing uncertainty, Mr Hargrave recognised as belonging to his creditor, Jules Marsan.

The slight frown which had begun to settle on his handsome brow at the sight of his kill-joy Jenkyns, was in an instant changed into a smile of the very kindest suavity, as he rose and stepped forward to meet this man.

M Jules Marsan moved a little on one side, as if to avoid the hand that was extended to salute him; and fixing his dark, deep-set eye full on the countenance of his debtor, said, –

'This person tells me that you deny having received the letter of notice which I addressed to you, demanding payment (according to agreement) of the 150,000 francs which you owe me.'

'He tells you nothing but the truth, my dear sir,' replied Mr Hargrave, in a tone of polite indifference. 'I question not the least in the world your having sent such a letter, and of course I expect you, my dear sir, to believe as readily that I never received it. The fact is, M Marsan, that my life is spent so constantly among persons whose rank entitles them to command my presence whenever they wish for it, that I have positively little or no time left me for attention to my own concerns. I cannot, however, doubt that the message which I did myself the honour of addressing to you by my steward has been satisfactory, and that the settling this little pecuniary transaction at one month from the present time will in all ways suit your convenience.'

'No, sir, it will not,' replied the thin-visaged Frenchman. 'If you have not received my letter, which was intended to accommodate you by giving a month's notice (not stipulated for in the agreement which I hold under your own signature), so much the worse for you. That letter was sent a month ago, and I must have the money before this day week, whether you have received that letter or not.'

'But, my dear fellow,' returned Hargrave, gaily, 'you cannot reasonably expect any gentleman to have 150,000 francs always ready at a moment's warning.'

'It is not at a moment's warning,' returned Jules Marsan. 'I still give you seven days, which I think, – excuse me, sir, – is considerably more than you have any right to expect: but, beyond that, I will not give you an hour. My resolution is taken; and if you are a wise man, M Hargrave, yours will be taken too before we part. It is no child's play we are upon. My credit, and the credit of my son, depend upon my having the money you stand pledged to pay me by the time I have named. If you fail me, I will at least give public evidence that I had a right to expect from you the sum I have undertaken to pay. You told me again and again, sir, that you could at any time repay this money at five minutes' notice. I have, therefore, now learned that your word is not to be trusted. Do not fall into the error of believing that I pledge mine as lightly, when I tell you that, were you in the presence of the king himself, I would arrest you at the very hour that the week I have granted shall expire.'

Mr Hargrave got up and walked to the window. His complexion was perfectly ghastly; and conscious of sensations he wished not to betray, he remained there for a few moments to recover himself. Then, turning again towards Marsan, with a countenance still pale, but, considering all things, most astonishingly under his command, he said, in the light accent of easy nonchalance, –

'Come then, M Marsan, if it must be so, I will set about this troublesome business directly, and in good earnest. But, to be candid with you, the fact is, that I have recently lost some very considerable sums of ready money at play, and I am by no means quite certain of being able to get hold of the sum you require without longer notice.'

'Excuse my interrupting you, sir,' said Marsan, 'but it is better to tell you now than later that no half measures will be acceded to on my part. I have need – very pressing need of the money you owe me, and have it I will, though you should sell your plate and your jewels at a tenth of their value to supply the sum.'

'Leave us alone for a few minutes, Jenkyns,' said Mr Hargrave. 'I do not wish that my old and faithful servant should witness such a scene as this.'

Hargrave, with all his faults, was affectionately beloved by his dependants, for he was good-humoured, easy, and liberal; and the old steward, as he moved off in obedience to this unexpected command, cast a glance of pity on his master, which proved that, despite the hard-drawn, money-making lines of his wrinkled face, the old man was not altogether unfeeling. But he started when he looked at him, as if he had seen a ghost; for the countenance of Mr Hargrave was so deadly pale, and so completely changed from its ordinary expression, that the man thought he must be seized with some sudden and desperate malady, and stopping short in his course towards the door, he drew near his master, and said, –

'If you feel that this troublesome business makes you ill, sir, don't go on with it for any body. Let me lead Monsieur Marsan back to my bureau, and wait till you feel better.'

'Nonsense, Jenkyns,' returned Mr Hargrave, endeavouring to smile with his usual air of gay indifference. 'Monsieur Marsan's mode of settling accounts is certainly somewhat new to me, and it is likely enough that I may feel a little discomposed by it; but I assure you that I am perfectly well: so leave us, my good fellow, and I will ring the bell twice when I want you.'

Jenkyns left the room, and closed the door behind him. Mr Hargrave remained silent for a minute, and then rising, walked to the door, opened it, and looked out. The glance satisfied him that there were no listeners near, and gently closing it again, he resumed his seat, and said, –

'I have dismissed my steward, Monsieur Marsan, because your urgency drives me to make you a proposition which nothing but the apparent necessity of the case could induce me to think of, and which I shall beg you not to mention, as it betrays a pressure for money which it would be injurious to me to make known, and which, being only the result of an accidental misfortune, will pass over, and leave no inconvenience whatever behind, if it be not made the subject of idle gossip. Now hear me, Monsieur Marsan, and hear me quietly, – you will not expedite the business by interrupting me. To pay you the sum you apply for in ready money, before the interval of one month, is wholly and absolutely out of my power. But this fact produces, as it should seem, no effect whatever on the peremptory tone of your demand. – Be satisfied, monsieur,' continued Hargrave, moving his hand to check the interruption which seemed to threaten him, 'I have no intention whatever of pleading any further for your forbearance. You speak of the sale of my plate and jewels as the means you shall resort to for obtaining what you demand. You are quite right, sir. It is only so, that, at the present moment, it can be satisfied. The time may come, perhaps, and that very shortly, when you may feel inclined to wish that your measures had been a little less violent. But this matters not. Now hear me, sir. Far from opposing your suggestion of bringing such property to sale as can most easily be converted into money, I will assist you in this object to the very best of my power. The magnificent jewels of my late wife are in my possession, and are for the most part unset, having been recently pulled to pieces for the purpose of arranging them anew for her daughters, one of whom is about to contract an alliance which, I am happy to say, will supply her with jewels, if what I can give her should prove deficient. Such a portion of these trinkets as shall fully answer your demand shall be placed in your hands by twelve o'clock at noon on this day week. Will this content you?'

'Why should they not be placed in my hands directly?' said the

Frenchman. 'It will take time to convert them into money, and I have told you that money is necessary to me.'

'If my proposal does not content you, sir,' said Mr Hargrave, with dignity, 'I must leave you to take your own methods for recovering the debt. I can do no more.'

'Can I not have the jewels now?' demanded the anxious Jules Marsan.

'No, sir, you cannot,' replied Mr Hargrave, in a tone of firm, but civil decision. 'It will be necessary for me to shew these articles to a jeweller, before I part with them; both for the purpose of taking an opinion as to their value, and also having others made in imitation of them. I must repeat, sir, that if my placing them in your hands by noon on this day week does not content you, I must leave the business in your own hands.'

'Are the stones diamonds?' demanded Marsan.

Mr Hargrave did not immediately reply. He drew forth his pocket handkerchief, and taking up a rich Bohemian *flacon*, deliberately poured from it a quantity of *eau de Cologne* to refresh himself, as it seemed, under the fatigue of these lengthened details; and then said, with a good deal of *hauteur*, 'When you receive them from me, sir, you will be at liberty to examine them; and should you afterwards bring me any document, signed by a competent and respectable authority, stating that their value falls short of the sum required, I will supply the deficiency. This, I presume, is all that it can be necessary for me to say respecting your part of the business. On mine, I have one favour to request, which I feel not the slightest doubt will be strictly complied with on your part, as I truly believe you, sir, to be a man of honour. I need not point out to you the very obvious fact, that the means to which my imprudence and ill luck have driven me to resort, for the purpose of immediately satisfying your just claim, are in the highest degree painful to me. May I request you, Monsieur Marsan, to pledge me your word that you will not communicate to any one the fact of your having received the jewels from me? I am firmly resolved never to gamble more; and my property is of an extent which will speedily enable me to make such arrangements as will remove my present deficiency of ready money. May I trust to your honour and kindness for this important concealment?'

'You may, sir,' replied Marsan, with more civility of manner than he had hitherto thought proper to display. 'I should be sorry to do you or any gentleman an injury. If your deposit fairly covers my just demand, interest and principal, you shall hear no more either of the debt or the manner of its payment.'

'I thank you, M Marsan,' replied Hargrave; 'I will take care not to err in my estimate of what I am about to make over to you in any way that shall exonerate you from this promise.' He then rose and rung the bell twice; the steward reappeared, and the softened creditor rose to take his leave. Jenkyns looked earnestly in his master's face, but said not a word. Hargrave smiled kindly upon him, and nodding his head good humouredly, said in his ear as he passed out, 'It is all settled very pleasantly, Jenkyns. He has behaved better than I expected. Say no more about the business to him, but offer him refreshment, and speak civilly.'

The greatly comforted old man silently nodded in return, followed the retreating steps of Monsieur Jules Marsan, and closed the door, leaving his master once more alone to the luxuries of his library and his meditations. But it seemed as if the interruption had jarred his nerves and put them out of tune; for he pushed from him the sketches upon which he had previously been so delightfully employed with a frown, and placing his arms upon the table rested his head upon them for many minutes without moving an inch.

Some princely vision, however, then returned to him; once more he raised himself with all his wonted elasticity of mind and movement, and having completed, entirely to his satisfaction, the drawing of Adèle's dress, he took it, together with that of Sabina, to the boudoir of the two girls, and with his usual gay and gallant manner laid it before them. But although he appeared thus completely to have recovered himself, Sabina, happy and occupied as she was, remarked that he looked ill.

'Dearest papa!' she said, 'you are too good – too kind to us! You positively must not fatigue yourself as you do about all our whims. What lazy girls we are, Adèle, to throw all this upon papa! Are not these sketches beautiful? But I must not have you look so pale, papa – I cannot bear it.'

'My dear Sabina,' he replied, while a shade of temper, most unusual to him, passed across his brow – 'my dear Sabina, I do beseech you to leave off telling me that I am pale. Thank Heaven! I never had a very red complexion, my love; and I do assure you that I so detest the idea of it, that did I perceive any symptoms of the kind, I should instantly put myself under very severe discipline to correct it; and if I must let you into my confidence upon the subject, it is what I actually have often done, and still do, whenever I have the slightest suspicion that it is necessary. So never tease me by talking any more about my being pale. Do not look as if I was scolding you, dearest: but remember this, will you?'

Sabina kissed him, promised to plague him no more about his complexion, whispered to Adèle not to look so dismal, and then sat herself down between them, and chattered away so gaily about balls and costumes that it was impossible to resist the contagion; and both her companions appeared to chat gaily too.

'But all this is concerning the Prince's *fête*,' said Mr Hargrave; 'you have not said a word, Sabina, about mine. So now, if you please, let us talk a little of that. By the by, I want you both to tell me something more about this little Madame Bertrand, that we are all making such a fuss about. What is she like? Is she pretty?'

'Yes; extremely pretty, indeed! At least, I suppose so: for M Bertrand, who is immensely rich, only married her for her beauty.'

'And what are all these jewels, that they talk about? It is hardly likely — is it? — that a little nobody, married entirely for her beauty, should have jewels worth making such a fuss about. Have you heard any body mention them besides your aunt Hautrivage?' asked Mr Hargrave.

'Good gracious, papa! One hears of nothing else,' replied Sabina. 'For my part, I think I must beg you to permit my wearing blinkers — I expect to be half-blinded by their splendour. I am afraid to say how many hundred thousand francs they are worth; but it is something perfectly astonishing.'

'And pray is the lady supposed to be in love with her magnificent husband?' said her father.

'Poor thing! I am afraid not,' was the reply. 'They say he is old and ugly.'

'Oh, ho! that's the case, is it? That somewhat accounts for the diamonds. But, by the way, how can one ever know in such a case as this, but that the glittering baubles may be false? All paste, Sabina, depend upon it.'

'By your leave, no, papa. Every body but you — who really seem to have shut your ears against the most important news of the day — every body but you, papa, knows perfectly well that they were furnished by the first jeweller in Vienna; and a great many of the finest diamonds are said to have belonged once to Napoleon. I perfectly long to see them,' said Sabina.

To this girlish tirade Mr Hargrave returned no answer, and seemed indeed to have suddenly turned his thoughts to something else; for after a moment's silence a heavy sigh escaped him.

'What are you thinking of, papa?' said Adèle, looking earnestly at him. 'If you were a graver personage, I should say that you were going, like Jacques, to moralise the spectacle into a thousand similes. But do not sigh about it. I must not,' she added, 'tell you that you are looking pale, lest you should chide me, as you did Sabina: but, upon my word, I doubt your being quite well to-day; and you really ought to take care of yourself, or the fancy-ball, and the diamonds, and Madame Bertrand, and every thing else, will all fall to the ground together, as far as we are concerned.'

'Thank you, dear Adèle,' said Mr Hargrave, rising; 'but I do assure you, I never was better in my life. I sat up reading Balzac's new novel last night till I made my head ache; but it has very nearly left me, and will do so entirely, I doubt not, after I have had an hour's riding in the Bois de

Boulogne. But I must not make you waste any more time. Have you ordered the carriage for your shopping?'

The sisters assured him they had only waited for his promised drawings, and that they should set off with Madame de Hautrivage immediately.

'*Au revoir*, then!' he replied, gaily kissing his hand to them both; 'we shall meet at dinner.' And so saying he left them, with every appearance of recovered health and spirits.

CHAPTER XIII

During the remaining days which intervened before that fixed for Mr Hargrave's entertainment, no further symptoms, either of languor or ill health, were perceptible in that gentleman. Never before, indeed, completely as ball-giving was his vocation, had he manifested an equal degree of taste, ability, and lively interest in all that was going on. Nothing seemed to escape his attention that could in any degree affect the general gorgeous appearance of his magnificent apartments; and his chief object evidently was to produce such novelty of arrangement in the management of them as might strike even those who were the most familiar with the *locale*, as presenting rooms which they had never seen before. In this his success was so perfect, that when on the evening before the *fête*, all the alterations of this kind being completed, and the rooms lighted up, he had summoned the three ladies of his family to accompany him in his review of the whole, their genuine and unaffected astonishment equalled their admiration.

The receiving apartments up-stairs were not greatly changed, being for the most part appropriated to the use of card-players; but in the *rez-de-chaussée*, the whole of which consisted of what might be called state apartments, his love of novelty and surprise had displayed itself to great advantage. In the supper-rooms, indeed, and in the two noble apartments appropriated to dancing, no alteration had been attempted beyond some trifling improvements in the decorations of the orchestras; but among the lesser rooms, and in part of the garden enclosed at his last ball, the genius of Mr Hargrave appeared to have performed the work of an enchanter.

He conducted the wandering trio through meandering passages, which led – upholsterers only knew how – to tents of Eastern splendour in one direction, and to twilight retreats of flowery sweetness in another; all managed with such mastery of deception, that of three apartments constructed in the gardens and approached from the principal *salle de bal*, through the aperture of a banished window, not one could be reached but by a complication of arcades, dazzling with a thousand many-coloured lamps, yet so mysteriously dubious from the labyrinth-like caprice of their direction, that those who should seek the brilliant Eastern tent would be likely enough to find themselves in the shadowy bower of exotics; and eyes, longing for the soothing repose of this dimly lighted retreat, might be dazzled anew by emerging upon a lofty chamber, where gas was made to do its best and its worst, to blind and to enchant, by illuminating the gaudy decorations of a Chinese saloon, superb enough to have constituted the glory of glories of the Celestial Empire.

'I am lost, absolutely and literally lost!' exclaimed Sabina, after attempting in vain to recover the route which led to the pretty *bocage*, whose gloom contrasted so beautifully with the blaze of light which filled the other rooms. 'I do not mean that I am lost in wonder – though there would be truth enough in that too – but I have positively lost my way, and know no more in what part of the mansion I now am, than if I had never entered its doors till this evening. I expect every moment to come to some vista that shall give me a near view of the Invalides, and feel perfectly persuaded that at your next *fête* you will inclose the Champ de Mars by way of obtaining another little ball-room. Prince Frederic is quite right, papa: there is nobody in all Paris to be compared to you.'

'Did the Prince say that, Sabina?' said Mr Hargrave, his colour rising and his eye kindling with delight.

'Yes, indeed, he did, papa. He said so the day he dined here *à propos* of the perfect reception you gave him. And, I confess, I did not think he was very wrong then; but now I am quite sure he was right.'

'I can only hope, my dear child, that upon this less exclusive occasion I shall not lose ground with him. I will not deny that I value his approbation very highly, and it would vex me a good deal if his Royal Highness condemned the sort of whimsical vagaries I have been playing here. By the way, Sabina, I think the best scheme to avoid my suffering from such a disappointment will be for you to take the office of guide and *cicerone* upon yourself. I have now explained to you the sort of effect I have wished to produce by this varied style of decoration, and if you point it out to him exactly in the same manner that I have done to you, it will prevent the danger of his fancying that the whole thing has been arranged by the upholsterers without my having conceived any general design. Will you promise me, my love, to do this?'

'I will endeavour to do so, papa, if it is your wish,' replied Sabina, with some slight degree of confusion in her manner; 'but I think you would do it much better yourself.'

'But that, my dear, would be so exactly like asking him to praise me for my taste and ingenuity that it must not be thought of. Of course, I do not mean to give you the trouble of leading his Royal Highness every where; but if you can, without making any obvious fuss about it, take care that he sees the Turkish tent and the Chinese saloon, I shall be pleased.'

'For my part,' said Madame de Hautrivage, 'I most decidedly give the preference to that delicious *bocage!* In what part of the suite it is, I profess I have not the slightest idea; but, to my taste, it is worth all the rest.'

'I think it is pretty by way of a contrast,' replied Mr Hargrave, 'but, to let you into a secret, madame, I am afraid it is terribly damp. I would have neither of you go there after dancing upon any account. You must all promise me this, or I shall be quite uneasy about it.'

'*Mais, mon Dieu, oui!*' exclaimed Madame de Hautrivage. 'If it is damp I will not approach it for the universe. *Oh Ciel! imaginez! moi, moi, avec une fluxion de poitrine! Quelle horreur!*'

'And you, my dear children, will you both promise to be as discreet as madame? Will you take care to avoid the *bocage* after dancing?'

Both the girls promised obedience, and the party returned to the library, which was almost the only room that had not undergone a metamorphosis.

Poor Adèle, during all this high-pressure preparation for gaiety, struggled hard to prevent any trace of what she felt from appearing on her countenance; but she suffered greatly. The conviction that she had treated Alfred Coventry ill, that her conduct had been regulated by a jealousy at which common sense revolted, and a want of honourable confidence in an honourable man, which rendered her unworthy of his esteem, gnawed at her very heart, and produced a degree of unhappiness which no misfortune, unaccompanied by self-condemnation, could have brought upon her.

But more than one cause led her to confine all this to her own aching bosom. She saw Sabina infinitely more animated and more disposed to kindle at the touch of pleasure than she had ever been since the death of their mother, and for the world she would not have tarnished the brightness of the hours she was now enjoying. The very lightness and apparent frivolity of this enjoyment increased her wish that it should not be disturbed, for had there been any mixture of love in the feelings which inspired her, the sinking heart of Adèle assured her that even if Sabina were happy she could not be so very gay.

Another cause of the reserve in which she wrapped herself was the deep consciousness that her feelings were not understood, nor in any degree appreciated, by her sister. In every conversation they had held together on the subject of Mr Coventry's absence, Sabina had treated the matter as a mere temporary misunderstanding, which, if Coventry were in earnest (of which she had no doubt), would beyond all question be removed at no very distant period; and she reprobated, with more vehemence than she often bestowed on any subject, the idea that her sister had been to blame. 'If you, Adèle, have been weak,' she said, 'in too implicitly giving credence to the point-blank assertion of Madame de Hautrivage, Mr Coventry has at least been equally so in taking an averted look as a signal for leaving for ever a woman that he loved.'

But there was no comfort for Adèle in this. Her judgment of Alfred Coventry, cleared as she now felt it to be of all illusion, was not to be hood-winked by the wish of exonerating herself from blame. The strong attachment for this young man, which had by degrees taken such firm root in her bosom, arose from many traits of character, not quite so uncommon, perhaps, among his countrymen as among her own. Adèle de Cordillac was, nevertheless, a very true-hearted Frenchwoman on many points, and, like all other human beings of high-toned feeling, loved the country that gave her birth, and would have willingly sacrificed much for its prosperity and its glory. But her mother's second marriage had made the language and literature of England as familiar to her as her own, and it may be that she felt a greater excitement of curiosity in developing the character of a country to which she did not belong, though accident had given her a more than ordinary facility of becoming acquainted with it, than she would have felt under any other circumstances. But, be this as it may, it is certain that Adèle de Cordillac had studied the national characteristics of England, as they are found stamped upon her powerful and varied literature, with a degree of admiration which had well prepared her to value at its worth such a specimen of their living excellence as Alfred Coventry.

Many eligible, and in one or two instances even splendid, proposals of marriage had been made for Adèle; but her complete independence had given her a power of rejection, which she exercised with a degree of thankfulness for the possession of it, of which no heart but her own had been at all aware. But although during the whole of this probation she had walked

'In maiden meditation, fancy free,'

presuming *fancy* to mean the 'soft passion of love,' she had ever the *beau idéal* of a possible Englishman in her head, and, more firmly, perhaps, than she was quite conscious of herself, was determined to give her heart to no other.

It is not difficult to imagine how the events of the last few weeks had brought all this speculative feeling into action, or how profound the self-reproach with which she contemplated the conduct which had destroyed the reasonable hope of what had often appeared to her imagination as something almost too precious to be reasonably hoped for.

But all this sadness was deeply buried in her heart, and she listened to all that was said, and sometimes answered it too, with a degree of outward tranquillity that might have done some honour to a Spartan.

★   ★   ★

Once more the Rue de Lille was nearly blockaded by the carriages which sought to reach, or to retreat from, the lofty *porte-cochère* of Mr Hargrave's princely dwelling; – once more the glittering panoply of the patrol which regulated the reins and the whips of the congregated coachmen, proclaimed to every idle passenger the importance of the business that was going on within it; – and once more the elegant *locataire* gave smiling welcome to all that was most brilliant in the society of Paris.

The atmosphere of splendid and well-lighted rooms, in which he acted as lord of the ceremonies, was to Mr Hargrave what the reviving warmth of spring is to the vegetable world. It seemed to breathe new life into him; every fibre appeared to dilate, every faded hue to be renovated; and the very essence and principle of existence, which had before appeared to lie dormant, burst forth with fresh vigour into animation and activity.

Sabina looked at him with delight. Never had she seen her father so gracefully gay, or looking so pre-eminently handsome. Even Adèle was roused for a few moments to more than a mere outward interest in the scene, as she watched the dignified courtesy and polished ease with which he received the wealthy M Bertrand, whom he had never in his life beheld before, and his new-looking little wife, laden with magnificent jewels, which seemed to be brought thither much as a Tyrolese or Bohemian musician brings his gaudy costume, in proof and pledge that he is to be admitted, however much all other circumstances in his appearance might lead the beholders to suppose the contrary. It was long since any *salon* in Paris had thrown the splendour of its mimic day upon gems reflecting them so brightly, and having, moreover, the additional gloss of being new in the eyes of all men. And strange did it seem, to those who thought about it, that any woman, – young and pretty enough to gain favour amidst the rival beauties of a *guinguette*, where she might have skipped about at ease, – should prefer exhibiting those costly wares for the amusement of a throng of perfect strangers, who looked at her for no reason in the world but that they might laugh at the incongruity between herself and her dress. Her husband, however, was neither so old nor so ugly as the romance-loving Sabina had been pleased to imagine; nor was there any reason whatever to suppose that they might not be as fond a couple as had ever been joined together in wedlock, had it not been that the gentleman looked so exceedingly like a showman coming into company to exhibit a puppet or a dancing-dog, and the lady so

nearly approaching in awkward but obedient manoeuvrings to the chief
pet and treasure of such an exhibitor, as to suggest the idea that she was
his property. Yet, after all, this furnished no good grounds for doubting
their mutual affection: fondness shews itself in a variety of ways; and
there is no substantial reason for denying that exhibiting, and being
exhibited, may be among them.

Prince Frederic was by no means one of the latest guests whose name
was thundered through the hall and ante-rooms; and his arrival, with the
peculiarly condescending and even friendly manner in which he
addressed Mr Hargrave and his family, seemed to bring the vivacity of the
graceful host to its climax. Carefully, however, did he guard against
bestowing too much of himself upon this illustrious personage; having,
together with Madame de Hautrivage, marshalled him to the place of
honour in the principal ball-room, in that accredited style of attendance
which announces the dignity of a guest to the ignorant as effectually as a
herald proclaiming his titles could do, he bowed himself to a distance,
leaving the royal young man to amuse himself in any manner that he
might find best suited to his inclination. This distance, however, was not
so great as to prevent Mr Hargrave from taking note as to what manner
of amusement this might be; nor did he give more than seeming
attention to any thing else, till he saw Prince Frederic lead Sabina into
the circle which was forming itself round the room for a waltz.

No sooner had his satisfied eyes given notice to his happy heart that all
was right in that quarter, than he turned all his attention to Madame
Bertrand. He soon discovered that her husband was a whist-player; and
having introduced him to three others, who would all have rather taken
root in their chairs than have left them while another rubber might be
had, and assured him in the most amiable manner that he should in
person have the great pleasure of doing the honours to his lady, he
devoted himself in the most conscientious manner to redeem his word,
appearing unconscious, excepting at short intervals, that any other lady
was in the rooms; and leading her with devoted resolution to join the
dancers in the smaller ball-room, though he was a most accomplished
performer himself, and felt all reasonable assurance that the glittering
danseuse he had chosen would infallibly perform the evolutions of the
waltz, which unfortunately was the dance she preferred, with all the
fascinating dexterity of an ass in a mill.

Many who saw him thus engaged smiled their admiration at him for
his exemplary hospitality; others looked archly, in the belief that he was
making this enormous sacrifice for the purpose of collecting traits of
bourgeoise character, with which to enliven his discourse hereafter.
Madame de Hautrivage knit her brows, and thought he was overdoing
the thing altogether; and Adèle watched him with most unfeigned

astonishment as he continued again and again to lead her to the dance, –
sometimes in the great room, sometimes in the smaller one, but always
with such a display of devoted *empressement* as her own excellent tact told
her was not only unnecessary, but very nearly ridiculous. Adèle was, in
truth, precisely what the French mean when they talk of being *mystified*.
She was puzzled, thrown out, and perfectly at a loss, as to what motive to
assign for so remarkable a proceeding. In any other man it would
certainly have been much less so. However much Mr Hargrave might
deceive either himself, or the world in general, upon other points, there
was no delusion as to the fact of his Chesterfieldian studies having been
attended with the most perfect success; and of this his fair step-daughter
was so fully aware, that while she watched his super-abundant devotion
to his plebeian guest, she felt certain that it could proceed from no
blundering as to what was required of him, but must arise from some
motive – either grave or gay – which she was unable to penetrate.

Had she been in a merrier mood, it is probable that she would have
endeavoured to improve her understanding on the subject, by making her
way to her good-humoured step-father and asking him, *sans façon*, why
he paid such very particular attention to little Madame Bertrand; but,
having given the subject more attention than she believed it possible she
could have given to any thing, it faded from her memory like every thing
else not connected in some way or other with her ceaseless self-
reproaches on the subject of Coventry.

Delicacy, and proper feeling of all kind, however, prevented her
permitting any eye that watched her to perceive that she was no longer
the happy being that she used to be. She danced – danced incessantly, for
this was less irksome than conversation; and the long hours of the night –
long at least to her, though passing with winged rapidity to some others
of the party, wore away; till at length, to her great comfort, a movement
was visible towards the supper-rooms; and she had made up her mind to
steal away as soon as this part of the night's business should be over.

It was during the compression of the crowd towards the door-ways,
which this movement produced, that she was first aware of the presence
of the young Russian, Count Romanhoff, in the rooms. That he had
been invited with the rest of their acquaintance was a matter of course;
and, despite her pre-occupation, his absence had not escaped her, for he
was known to be the intimate friend of Coventry; and more than once
she had looked about her in the hope of seeing him there, but hitherto in
vain.

She now saw him almost close beside her, and, as her eye caught his, it
was evident that he was endeavouring to make his way to her. An
operation of this sort is greatly expedited by both the parties concerned
in it being of the same mind. Adèle greatly wished to speak to M

Romanhoff, and the consequence was, that her arm, either wilfully or of
necessity, was withdrawn from that of the gentleman with whom she had
been dancing, and who was doing his very best to lead her unscathed
through the crowd; while she sufficiently seceded from the throng to
enable the Count very soon to succeed in his efforts to reach her.

'I am happy to see you, Count Romanhoff,' said Adèle, civilly: 'I have
been looking about for you among the waltzers, and fancied you were
not here.'

'I have not been here, mademoiselle, more than five minutes. I have
been passing the evening in a scene far less brilliant: I have been assisting
my poor friend Coventry to prepare for his departure from Europe. He
will leave Paris — for ever probably — in an hour or two. I heard him
order his post-horses for five o'clock.'

What would not Adèle have given to have been at that moment alone!
What words were those for the heart-stricken girl to hear while a
hundred eyes were looking at her! But the urgency of the case supported
her more effectually than any uncertain hope of escape would have done;
and, feeling it impossible to run away, she determined, like many others
rendered desperately brave by necessity, to make the best of it, and gain a
little more of the same sort of torturing information before she made any
attempt to escape. For a moment or two she was silent, for she feared to
trust her voice; but at length she ventured to say, 'How very disagreeable
the crowd is!'

'May I offer you my arm, mademoiselle? Perhaps you will find it more
agreeable to retreat till the pressure is a little over?' said Count
Romanhoff, whose ear had caught the tremulous uncertainty of the
voice in which the once lively Adèle had addressed him, and who had his
own reasons for wishing to converse further with her.

Adèle immediately took his arm. 'I shall thank you very much,' she
said, 'if you can manage a retreat for me;' and then recollecting that by
far the best means of securing the vicinity of the only person present
likely to speak to her of Coventry, would be by placing him next herself
at the supper-table, and thereby securing his attendance, she added, 'If
you can manage to get to that side-door, which none but inmates know
to be the shortest way to the supper-rooms, we shall escape the crush
entirely.'

The Count, with very excellent sympathy of purpose, seconded her
wishes by a little sidelong manoeuvring, which brought them speedily to
the door indicated by Mademoiselle de Cordillac; having passed through
which, they found themselves able to proceed without difficulty, the
passage having been discovered only by a few of those struggling young
men who have a faculty, like mice, of finding their way in all directions
where there is a chance of getting any thing to nibble, and who may be

seen at most crowded parties contesting with the domestics the shortest passages, and most direct access to that goal of all their wishes, the region of *pâté-gras* and champagne. By such as these Adèle and her conductor passed along, without pausing to reconnoitre who they might be; but on reaching one of the turnings by which Mr Hargrave had so skilfully contrived both to connect and dissever the various apartments of the *rez-de-chaussée*, they perceived that gentleman at a point which draperies and temporary *cloisonnage* had converted into a sort of *carrefour*, in earnest conversation with a man who was neither in the dress of a guest nor a domestic, but who had all the air and appearance of that most disagreeable variety of civilised human nature usually classed as shabby-genteel. The position in which Mr Hargrave and this man stood prevented either of them perceiving the approach of Count Romanhoff and Adèle, till they were near enough distinctly to hear Mr Hargrave say, 'I adore her, Ruperto! Manage this matter for me skilfully, and the price named by you yesterday shall be doubled.'

Mr Hargrave spoke in French, but the man whispered a reply in Italian, of which Adèle only heard enough to convince her that her step-father's proposal was agreed to, whatever it was; for her companion, very disagreeably aware that he had led the young lady into hearing what was certainly not intended for her, hastily turned in another direction, which at length brought them, though not without a few more turnings and twistings, to the room they sought: but neither of them spoke a word, for both felt embarrassed by the adventure.

The Count probably thought that there was nothing very extraordinary in the business, and would hardly have heeded the words at all, had they not been spoken in the hearing of Mademoiselle de Cordillac; but on Adèle their effect was very different. She was shocked and astonished much beyond the power of speaking, even if her companion had been one to whom she could have expressed what she felt; and when at last she found herself seated at one of the supper-tables with Count Romanhoff by her side, not even her earnest desire to hear him speak of his friend could enable her to address a single word to him.

The Count, however, was himself determined to speak what he came prepared to say, and was in the very act of pronouncing the name which, far more than he had any idea of, was sure to rivet her attention, when he was himself induced to postpone the subject for a few moments by the entrance of Mr Hargrave leading the Duchesse de Vermont. The smiling composure of his manner as he led the noble lady to a place at the most distinguished table, almost made him doubt whether he had not mistaken the person whose privacy he had just before so unintentionally invaded; but turning towards Adèle, who was so greatly less likely to be mistaken than himself, he saw plainly in the astonished countenance with which she regarded him, that if he had blundered she had blundered too.

This was no moment to do his errand, for he fancied it was evident that she was too completely occupied to notice what he wished to say with the attention he desired to obtain. He therefore contented himself with endeavouring to withdraw her eyes from Mr Hargrave by speaking of her sister, who was seated near the Duchesse de Vermont; while Prince Frederic hung over Sabina's chair in an attitude of very evident devotion.

The eyes of Adèle fixed themselves upon this group, and she sighed, but answered nothing to Count Romanhoff's observation on her sister's '*grand succès dans le monde;*' and before he could say any thing sufficiently interesting to obtain a reply, the attention of both was again irresistibly drawn to Mr Hargrave, who having left the room as soon as the Duchesse was seated, now returned to it with Madame Bertrand on his arm, and leading her to a smaller table at the other end of the room, seated himself beside her, and assumed an air of so much gay gallantry in conversing with her, that Adèle was more than ever bewildered.

Count Romanhoff amused himself for a moment or two by suffering his eyes to take the same direction, after which he turned somewhat abruptly towards Adèle, and said, 'Mademoiselle de Cordillac must excuse me if I venture to intrude upon her attention for one moment, on a subject to which it will probably never again be called. You must permit me, mademoiselle, to speak to you a few words concerning my unfortunate friend, Alfred Coventry.'

He had no longer any reason to complain of Adèle being preoccupied. Mr Hargrave and his mysterious companion in the lobby, Madame Bertrand, Sabina, Prince Frederic, were all equally and entirely forgotten; and her eyes fixed themselves on his face with so earnest and undisguised a look of interest, that, notwithstanding some pretty strong preconceived notions to the contrary, Count Romanhoff perceived that the name he had uttered was not one to which the lady he addressed could listen with indifference. Adèle spoke not, however, but she bowed her head in token that she was willing to hear him.

'I can hardly hope, mademoiselle,' he said, 'to escape the imputation of being a very impertinent person when you shall have heard what I am going to say; but I would rather risk this, than leave it unsaid: for it is just possible I may serve my friend by it, and the chance is well worth a little danger. I only entreat you to believe that the fault, however great, is all my own, and that Alfred Coventry is entirely ignorant of my intention.'

This preface was not very likely to restore the composure of the young lady, but she shewed no outward symptom of the tumult within; and Count Romanhoff proceeded, –

'I do not believe it possible, mademoiselle, that my friend Alfred Coventry can have loved you passionately for three months without your being aware of it. Indeed, in opening his heart to me while I was watching over him, during hours in which reason and madness seemed battling in his brain, as to which should be his master, he clearly stated his conviction that you were *fully* aware of this; and then, with unsparing self-accusation for the weakness, he avowed also that he believed his love returned – You start, Mademoiselle de Cordillac! Is it his presumption or my frankness which offends you?'

'Neither! neither!' replied Adèle, almost gasping.

'I should be sorry to distress you, Mademoiselle de Cordillac,' said the Count, with increased gentleness of tone, 'but my self-imposed duty obliges me to be perfectly sincere. I think it is possible, and so I have told him, that his not having complied with the established usages of the country, by requesting from your friends permission to present himself as a pretender to your hand, may have led you to doubt his purpose of devoting to you his life. If this be so, all may yet be well; for you must be sufficiently acquainted with English peculiarities in this particular, to be aware that Coventry would have been obliged to sacrifice what an English lover considers as his dearest privilege, had he addressed himself to your step-father, or your aunt, instead of to yourself. May I ask you, Mademoiselle de Cordillac, whether any species of offence has appeared to you to have been committed by this omission?'

'None, sir,' replied Adèle with decision.

'I am sorry for it,' said Count Romanhoff; and for a moment he was silent, but then continued, 'There is another point, mademoiselle, on which I would say a few words, and then I will take my leave. All the world acknowledges the grace and beauty of Mademoiselle de Cordillac, – all the world is aware of her honourable descent and high connexions, – and all the world, too, are perfectly well informed as to the fact of her possessing what is held here to be a large independent fortune; all which circumstances might render the addresses of a stranger suspicious from the probability of their being interested, especially when, as in this case, they have not been made in the usual manner. If any such idea, mademoiselle, was the cause of the sudden change of your manner towards my friend, – a change which he assures me left him without the possibility of doubting that it was your purpose to check any further advances towards an explanation on his part, – if any such opinion found admission to your mind respecting Alfred Coventry, permit me to tell you that you have greatly wronged a noble gentleman, who loved you with true and pure sincerity, and whose fortune and position in society are such as would render his alliance an honour to any lady of private station in Europe.'

The manner of Count Romanhoff had varied through the whole of this *sotto voce* conversation, – carried on under cover of all the busy duties of an attentive cavalier at the supper-table, – from gentle to severe, according to the feelings and suppositions which became predominant in his mind during the course of it; but the last words were uttered in a tone of *hauteur* and indignation, which seemed to imply that it must be a very meek and humble-minded response indeed which would satisfy him. Now, Mademoiselle de Cordillac was at that moment in no humour to be humble and meek to any body. All she wished and wanted on earth was before her – all she had ever asked from Heaven during the misery of the last dreadful fortnight was accorded. She was at liberty to open her whole heart to the only man she had ever dreamed it was possible to love; and that by an act of generosity, and not of degradation. For an instant her bright eye met that of Romanhoff; but there was a flashing joy in it that looked to him like triumph, which puzzled and alarmed him. 'Have I undertaken this unauthorised mission,' thought he, 'solely to gratify the vanity of this unfeeling girl?' And again he turned to speak to her; but ere he could do so she had risen from the table, saying gaily, 'I see, Count Romanhoff, that, notwithstanding the extent of papa's preparations, there are many guests still waiting for places at the supper-table: I therefore hasten to give up mine.'

Before the young Russian could recover his surprise at the lightness of tone with which this was spoken, Adèle had quitted his side; and the moment after, he saw her pass with a rapid step towards a door by which she disappeared.

'She avoids me,' thought he, with a deep feeling of indignation. 'Alfred must never hear of this my most unauthorised and most unwise interference. Yet I will describe the light-hearted young lady to him as she deserves. If he has the spirit of a man, I shall be able to cure him of his love!' And with this friendly intention Count Romanhoff hastened to leave the rooms; and finding his carriage punctually waiting for him, he sprang into it and drove back to his unhappy friend, determined rather to rouse him from sleep than permit him to leave Paris without the advantage of knowing that Adèle de Cordillac was the most heartless coquet in it.

Adèle herself, meanwhile, was very actively engaged in a manner which she intended should produce a different result. On all occasions of great parade like the present, all the male retainers of Mr Hargrave were clad in gorgeous liveries; and, whether otherwise useful or not, were made to understand that they were expected to assist the general splendour by shewing themselves. Old Roger Humphries was on ordinary occasions exempted from the fatigue of waiting at table, his especial office being that of personal attendant on the young ladies; but just as Adèle, with beating heart, was listening to the last part of Count

Romanhoff's communication, she remarked the tall stiff old man parading among the supper-tables with an aspect of very pre-eminent dignity.

With the quickness of lightning she decided upon what she would do; and the moment after the Count had seen her leave the room, she seized on the arm of Roger, who had passed out before her, and only pausing distinctly to pronounce the words, 'Follow me, Roger!' glided off to her boudoir, which the old man reached immediately after her.

'Roger Humphries,' she said, struggling hard to speak with sufficient composure to be intelligible, – 'Roger Humphries, do you remember offering to take a message for me to Mr Coventry before he left Paris, if I should wish to send one?'

'That I do, indeed, Miss Adèle,' replied the old man; 'and proud shall I be if you will send me upon such an errand, after all his faithful servant said of him.'

'But, Roger, if this is ever done, it must be done instantly! Mr Coventry will set off in an hour or two for Africa, and I never shall see him more, unless a note from me be first delivered to him.'

'For Africa!' cried Roger, plaintively; 'mercy forbid, Miss Adèle! That's just where the gentlemen are sure to be killed, they tell me. For goodness' sake, miss, don't let him go there!'

'Are you stout-hearted enough, Roger, to set off instantly to prevent it?' demanded Adèle, with trembling impatience. 'If not, I must hasten back to the ball-room, and send my message by one I should be sorry to employ. Speak, Roger, will you go for me?'

All serving-men are stout-hearted at half-past three o'clock in the morning when a ball and supper are a-foot; and even sober old Roger felt somewhat of the contagious inspiration.

'I will go, Miss Adèle, quicker than a younger man,' he replied; 'and surer too, take my word for it. Give me the note, Miss Adèle.'

'I must write it first, my dear old friend,' said his grateful mistress: 'sit down, Roger, – sit down, while I do so.' Roger obeyed, and as quickly as it was possible to write, fold, and seal, Adèle gave him the following note: –

'If Mr Coventry will let me see him for ten minutes before he leaves Paris (for Africa!), I shall be able to convince him that I am all that he believed me to be before our last miserable meeting, at which time I was led to suppose that he was exactly all which he has since thought me.

'ADELE DE CORDILLAC.

'Rue de Lille, half-past three, A.M.
    23 April, 1835.'

'Now, then, dear old friend, lose no time,' said Adèle, earnestly; 'and remember, every step you take, that Mr Coventry leaves Paris at five o'clock.'

'Trust me, – trust me!' replied the old man, taking the letter from her, and carefully securing it in his deep waistcoat pocket, fastening every massive button of his coat over it, from the collar downwards. 'My old legs shall ache for it rather than I will fail to get there in time; and I can't make an hour's walk of it, let me go as I will.'

With these consoling words the venerable serving-man disappeared; while Adèle, still trembling with emotion, but far happier than she had ever hoped to be again, stole unchallenged to her bed-room, conscious that, should the dancing be renewed and prevent her sleeping, she had quite enough to occupy her mind agreeably for the remainder of the night.

And here it may be observed that it was impossible Mademoiselle de Cordillac could have chosen a more faithful messenger. His whole heart was in the business, which he understood very nearly as well as his fair mistress herself; and a longing and very thirsty desire for another cup of wine was resisted, that no time might be lost. Old Roger, nevertheless, felt that it was absolutely impossible to walk across either of the bridges in white silk stockings and pumps, so that, of necessity, he was obliged to sacrifice a few minutes, while he changed them for a *chaussure* more suitable to the expedition he was about to undertake. But to the honour of Roger Humphries' fidelity and active walking, it must be noted that this unavoidable delay would not have made him too late, had it not been that Count Romanhoff so well succeeded in transfusing a portion of the indignation which burned in his own bosom into that of his friend, by describing Adèle as by far the most accomplished coquet and the most heartless woman he had ever known, that the unhappy Coventry, roused from his uneasy slumbers above an hour before it was necessary to start, grew so restless and impatient, that the Count rattled all the horse-boys and postilions up, and succeeded in getting Coventry's carriage packed and ready by exactly ten minutes before five. Not another instant was lost in setting off. Romanhoff, kind-hearted as he was vehement, rolled himself and his full dress into a large cloak, and jumped into the carriage after his friend, ordering his astonished servants to follow him to Calais with all things needful for a week's absence; Coventry having gratefully agreed to defer his departure for another quarter of the globe, on condition of the Count's accompanying him for a few days to London. So that when honest Roger arrived, 'fiery red with speed,' at the hôtel, he had the terrible mortification of hearing that the gentleman he inquired for had driven off with four horses, *ventre à terre*, exactly six minutes before.

* * *

Meanwhile the festivities at Mr Hargrave's were not yet brought to a close. The majority of the company, indeed, departed immediately after supper; but Mr Hargrave had induced the flattered and delighted Madame Bertrand to promise him one more waltz, late as it was; and as her whist-loving husband had not yet left the card-table, no obstacle occurred to prevent her fulfilling the engagement. The grand orchestra was, accordingly, again called upon, and once more a set of unwearied waltzers spun off round the ample floor, as featly as if it had been the first measure they had trod that night.

Though many of the company had departed, this room was still crowded; and all the other apartments being forsaken, except by such lingering card-players and loitering supper-repeaters as sought amusement elsewhere, it appeared to have become the sole centre of attraction.

It was still, therefore, not without difficulty that the most skilful cavaliers guided the conflicting steps of each fair *danseuse* through the host of lookers-on without endangering either flounce or limb. All those experienced in such matters declare that, despite fatigue and the inconvenience of circumjacent pressure, generally increased by the unceremonious movements of persons earnestly bent on departure, or on amusing themselves to the very last, by critical examinations of every portion of the pretty pageant, – despite all this, it is currently asserted that the dance, or dances, after supper, are worth all the rest. Why it should be so, it is, of course, impossible to guess; but certain it is, that the statement could rarely have proved itself more correct than on this occasion, for a general air of animation and enjoyment seemed diffused over nearly every individual present.

In none, however, was this more conspicuously the case than in the youthful bride, Madame Bertrand. Whether it was from admiration of her youth and unsunned prettiness, or from compassion of the shy awkwardness with which she carried her little self and her great diamonds, or from any other cause less obvious and more difficult to trace, Mr Hargrave had devoted himself throughout nearly the whole evening almost exclusively to her. At first, poor little thing! she felt nearly as much oppressed by this as by her diamonds; but Mr Hargrave had not devoted himself to the subtle science, called knowledge of the world, without taking notes as well upon simple ladies as on gentle lords; and so admirably did he practise what he had learned, that even before they had sat down, side by side, at the supper-table, all painful shyness on the part of the lady had vanished, and she permitted him to prepare for her more than one goblet of champagne and iced water, without appearing out of measure shocked at giving so fine a gentleman so much trouble.

How much Mr Hargrave, while recruiting the spirits of his fair partner at the supper-table, had been tempted to enliven his own, it is impossible to say; but undoubtedly he had, during this after-supper dance, every appearance of being particularly gay, and just when the *crescendo* spirit of the waltzers seemed at its acme, he whirled his partner lightly round, and actually danced with her through the draperied opening which led to the various fanciful erections in the garden.

If any noticed this gay manoeuvre, it was only to smile at the appropriate style in which their versatile host thought fit to entertain the pretty *quondam boutiquière*, and the dance went on with unabated zeal.

And now servants entered, bearing salvers reeking with enticing fumes from cups of warm nectar, which might have won applause from gods, even when idle, and which could hardly fail of being welcomed by mortals after such fatigue. And while the lips of the ladies sipped these delicious little draughts expressly prepared for them, the gentlemen deemed themselves privileged to

'Leave their fair sides all unguarded,'

in order to seek from iced wine the refreshment which the fragrant, smoking, little vases of Sèvres china were evidently not intended to afford them.

All this, of course, occupied some time; yet still the yawning orchestra was not dismissed; and presently a cry of 'Cotillon!' was raised, timidly at first, but gaining strength by degrees, till the whole room seemed to echo 'Cotillon! cotillon!' The obedient musicians uttered one low growling groan, and then began to play so invigorating an air that, like the inspired minstrel immortalised at Anster Fair, they seemed not to leave the power of rest in any; and this most whimsical finale of elegant festivities began in a style that did not foretell a speedy ending.

Except the exemplary mothers, who were chained by duty to their seats, and who moved not, and might not move, till the next measure ended, there were but few spectators of this concluding dance, nearly all who were not engaged in it having departed. Sabina alone, of all the beauties who had shone as stars throughout the night, was quietly, and somewhat wearily, awaiting her setting, when time and the hour should permit it. Prince Frederic, with whom in the course of the evening she had as often danced and as often talked as was at all advantageous for the tranquillity of either of them, had departed, as was his custom, immediately after supper, and she had not danced since. Gladly, upon his leaving the room, would she have left it too; but she had seen Adèle quit the supper-room, and having watched in vain for her return, submitted to the necessity of remaining to do the honours till the very latest revellers had quitted the house. Too tired, however, to hope that she could attempt conversing, with any prospect of wide-awake success, with the ladies who still kept possession of the benches, she placed herself in the quietest corner she could find, awaiting the moment when the music should cease, in order to step forward and shew that she was at her post to the last.

Just at the moment when the seemingly endless cotillon was at its highest point of vivacity, Sabina observed her father enter the room by a door leading from the supper-rooms; he was alone, and she was on the point of rising to meet him, when she perceived him very abruptly, as it seemed to her, seize the hand of a partnerless lady, and dart forward with her into the middle of the dance, with an air of frolic and defiance of etiquette both equally foreign to his usual style and manner. Sabina disliked the cotillon, and never danced in it; but she felt now that she disliked it more than ever, as the rude vortex of its mirth seemed to constrain her father to put off his graceful stateliness in order to join in its turbulent evolutions. As the figure of the dance brought him nearer to her, however, an idea occurred greatly more painful than any suggested by the circumstance of his condescending to join in a dance which she did not admire, – she thought he was intoxicated! and the strangely unsettled expression of his eye, as well as a most unwonted want of sedateness in all his movements, fully justified the idea, unsupported as it was by any thing she had ever seen or heard, and totally at variance, as she felt it to be, with all her preconceived opinions respecting him.

Her previous anxiety for the dance to cease was now multiplied a thousand-fold. The idea that her father, of whose finished elegance of demeanour she was infinitely more proud than she could ever have been at any imputed grace of her own, should so distinguish himself, was mortification almost intolerable; and great, indeed, was the relief when, at length, her weary ear ceased to throb under the infliction of the instruments, whose noise seemed greater as their charm grew less, and group after group passed out – carriage after carriage rolled off, – and the entry of servants, armed with extinguishers, gave her notice that she might make her exit without reproach.

As the company departed, she had the inexpressible satisfaction of perceiving that her father had almost completely resumed his ordinary manner. He was, indeed, rather more observant in his adieux to each separate guest than she had ever seen him before, or than usage, as she thought, required; 'But, perhaps,' thought she, 'he is conscious of the effect (so unusual to him!) which wine and over-exercise produced, and may be anxious to prove to all who might have remarked it, that it was of no long duration.' Greatly comforted by this idea, she turned towards the vestibule, to which he had attended the last of the ladies in order to embrace and wish him good night, according to custom; but, instead of finding him alone there, as she expected, she perceived him to be surrounded by four gentlemen, all speaking together, while her father appeared to be listening to them in the greatest astonishment.

'*C'est impossible! – mais, absolument impossible!*' were the first words she distinctly heard, and they were spoken by a gentleman with whose person she was perfectly unacquainted, but who appeared to be one of the guests, and to be suffering from some violent and painful agitation.

'Compose yourself, my dear sir,' said Mr Hargrave, in a voice of the most pitying kindness; 'it is perfectly impossible but that some mistake must be the cause of this most painful alarm. Let me entreat you to walk in, that the fullest inquiries may be made of the servants as to the time your lady's carriage was announced.'

'My wife drive off without me!' replied the personage, who was evidently the hero of the affair, let it be of what nature it might, – 'my wife drive off without me!' he reiterated, in a voice between rage and grief. 'I tell you, that it cannot – cannot be!'

'Explain to me, Monsieur de Beauvet, I entreat you, what all this means?' said Mr Hargrave, turning to one of the other gentlemen. 'This is Monsieur Bertrand, if I mistake not. What is it that has happened to him?'

'The only account I can give of the matter,' replied the person thus addressed, 'is, that this gentleman – M Bertrand, as it appears – M de Soissons, Milor Hartwell, and myself, have been playing during the whole evening at whist. Every refreshment we could wish for has been handed to us; and, therefore, as we all seemed equally to enjoy the *partie*, we have remained at the table till about five minutes ago, when two footmen entered, apparently to extinguish the lights, and informed us, with many apologies for the interruption, that the rest of the company were gone. It so happened that we were in the act of settling for the *partie* just concluded, and, therefore, hastened to descend without further delay. These two gentlemen and myself' – pointing to M de Soissons and Lord Hartwell – 'find our carriages waiting, but M Bertrand has been assured that his lady is gone; and, therefore, has not, I believe, even inquired for his.'

'Depend upon it, then, that all is as it should be,' returned Mr Hargrave, gaily. 'I have no doubt whatever that we shall find Madame Bertrand waiting in her carriage in the court. I am only vexed that she should have preferred this to remaining with my daughters.'

Ere Mr Hargrave had well finished these words, M Bertrand rushed out of the house, and Sabina then came forward to ask for further particulars respecting the alarm from which he appeared to be so severely suffering.

More than one voice was courteously raised to answer her, when the unfortunate bridegroom returned, wringing his hands, and almost sobbing with emotion.

'The carriage is there! – the carriage is there! – *Mais elle n'y est pas!*' he exclaimed, in an agony that was truly pitiable.

'Sabina! when did you last see Madame Bertrand?' demanded Mr Hargrave, with every appearance of anxiety.

'At supper, I think, papa. Yes, certainly, I have not seen her since supper.'

'Gracious Heaven!' cried the unhappy husband, 'that must have been hours ago! Oh! doubtless she was carried off from the supper-table, and must now, with all that mine of wealth about her, be far beyond the reach of pursuit. Yet think not,' he added, with a burst of very genuine tears, – 'think not, gentlemen, that I am wretch enough to think of the loss of diamonds at such a moment as this. Alas! the naming them only shews what I think to be the cause of my loss. She would not have left me, do not think it, gentlemen; she has been snatched away during the hurry and crowding which probably took place on leaving the supper-room, and, ere this time, may have been both robbed and murdered!' And again the poor man wept bitterly.

'At any rate, my dear sir,' said Mr Hargrave, with the most soothing kindness, 'I can prove to you that you are mistaken as to the time; for I myself danced with your charming lady immediately after supper; and, though I will not positively assert it, I cannot help thinking that I saw her dance again afterwards.'

'With whom, monsieur? with whom?' sobbed the unhappy Bertrand.

'Nay, my dear sir, I will not pretend to tell you that,' replied Mr Hargrave. 'I danced the cotillon myself with Mademoiselle de Charmonte, and was too much occupied by her vivacity to notice very exactly who and who were dancing together. But where is your sister Adèle, my dear Sabina? Perhaps she may have been more observant.'

'I believe Adèle was not very well, papa,' replied Sabina, 'for I think she retired immediately after supper.'

'And your aunt, my dear? Madame de Hautrivage will be sure to help us, for she observes every thing.'

'She only danced once or twice, papa, and then went up-stairs to play *écarté*, as she told me, with M de Foar.'

'It matters not greatly at what hour my unhappy wife disappeared,' said M Bertrand, who had listened impatiently to these inquiries. 'The fact which makes me the most wretched of men is clear enough. I have lost her! And I believe her to have been murdered. But heaven and earth shall witness that I loved her; for if money, or labour, or perseverance, to the last gasp of life, can avail to avenge her, she shall be avenged!'

These last words were spoken through closed teeth, and with raised hands rigidly clenched, in a manner which seemed to threaten an immediate commencement of hostilities against the whole human race.

The gentlemen looked at each other as if to consult what could be done with the unhappy man, who at that moment looked so like a maniac, that it certainly seemed doubtful whether some degree of coercion might not be necessary to prevent his doing mischief to himself or others; but before the expression of such thoughts had got farther than their eyes, Sabina, with the courage that genuine pity always inspires, had laid her gentle hand on the sufferer's uplifted arm, and, less by the force of that than by the power of her soothing voice, caused it to drop again, while a fresh burst of tears gave a safer vent to his feelings, and enabled those around him to suggest the only mode of proceeding which was likely to remedy the misfortune he deplored. He could not, however, be persuaded to return to the forsaken rooms; and the consultation which followed took place in the hall, at which the pitying Sabina assisted, and suggested an inquiry, the result of which threw so much light upon the mysterious business, as went far towards proving, even to those who were less confiding than the enamoured husband, that the poor lady had been snatched away with a degree of vehement haste, which spoke strongly in favour of her having done nothing to assist the elopement.

'Has any one inquired for Madame Bertrand's cloak?' demanded Sabina; upon which search was immediately made in the room appropriated to receiving ladies' wraps, and there the ermine-lined white satin capuchin of the lost lady was discovered.

'There can then be no doubt that the unfortunate lady has been removed by violence,' observed Lord Hartwell. 'No suspicion could have been raised,' he continued, 'at any period during the evening had she sent a gentleman to ask for this mantle; and this she undoubtedly would have done had power of choice been left her. M Bertrand must immediately give notice to the police; and it is more than probable – I conceive it to be almost certain – that he will discover where his lady is, and by whom she has been thus spirited away.'

Every voice present joined in seconding this proposal; and Mr Hargrave, in the most hospitable and amiable manner, expressed his hope that M Bertrand would permit a room to be prepared for him in the house, promising that, if he would endeavour to compose himself to rest, he would himself go in search of the police, and make them fully understand the nature of the business on which they were to be employed, and the enormous importance attached to it. But poor M Bertrand was far too miserable to consider rest as a blessing. He civilly, but peremptorily, declined Mr Hargrave's assistance; and, pressing with an air of passionate fondness the forsaken garment of his lost wife to his bosom, waved an unceremonious farewell to the party, stammered out some order to his servants, and threw himself into his carriage.

'Where did the poor man order them to drive?' said Mr Hargrave to the three gentlemen, who remained panic-struck, as it seemed, in the hall. 'I hope, poor soul! that he will not set out upon a wild-goose chase without consulting a *chef de police* as to what he had better do.'

'There is no danger of that,' replied M de Soissons. 'It is clear to me that he has conceived a correct view of the case. It is perfectly evident, *selon moi*, that the poor little woman has been kidnapped for the sake of her diamonds. God forbid they should murder her! Do you think so horrible a catastrophe probable, *mon cher* Hargrave?'

'*Mais non, mon cher*,' replied Mr Hargrave, composedly caressing his *favoris*, 'I really do not. On the contrary, if you ask my opinion of the affair, *en ami*, I will give it to you frankly: – I firmly believe that the pretty little *grisette* has eloped.'

'*Diable!*' exclaimed M de Beauvet; 'what makes you think so, Mr Hargrave?'

'Go to bed, dearest!' said Mr Hargrave, addressing the pale Sabina, who, though trembling violently, continued to stand near her father, as if hoping to hear something which might lessen the terror that shook her frame.

'Murdered!' she exclaimed, as if replying to her father's command: 'how can I go to bed, father, till I know that she is safe?'

'Be assured of it, my dear Sabina,' returned Mr Hargrave, slightly smiling, and in an accent which seemed to speak more plainly than his words. 'It is not possible for me to enter into all my reasons for feeling quite persuaded that this foolish young woman was exceedingly likely to do exactly what she has done. Kidnapping pretty ladies, whether they will or no, is quite an old-fashioned device, I assure you; so go to bed, my love, – there's a good girl! – and do not harm your kind little heart more than is necessary.'

Sabina remonstrated no further, but silently embracing her father, and bowing a farewell to the three lingering guests who still remained in the hall with him, retired to her chamber.

Mr Hargrave continued standing in the midst of the dismayed whist-players, evidently waiting only for their departure to follow her example; but still they lingered, and as soon as the young lady was out of sight their three voices were raised simultaneously to request he would explain the hints he had dropped, and tell them his reasons for feeling so certain, as he appeared to be, of Madame Bertrand's having eloped with her own free choice.

Mr Hargrave laughed. 'It is hardly fair – is it?' he said, 'to examine me so very closely. However, if we did not all look, and as I presume, feel, so very sleepy, I might chance to make you laugh, by repeating some of the sayings and doings of the pretty lady in question, which I have seen and heard to-night. But I cannot say I think there is any thing in the affair worth keeping you out of your beds to discuss. I will, therefore, only say that I believe you may go to sleep in peace, without feeling any alarm concerning the personal safety of pretty Madame Bertrand.'

The three gentlemen smiled, nodded, and looked intelligent; but being all of opinion that they could no longer resist the plainly confessed wishes of their weary host for their departure, hurried away, without entering into any further discussion, and Mr Hargrave mounted to his own room, by no means sorry to be left alone.

CHAPTER XIV

The sisters, though each had much to tell the other, met not that night after the ball was over, nor even till the first sunny portion of the day, which, under such circumstances, is called night, had long passed over them. Sabina, indeed, with her head full of the mysterious disappearance of Madame Bertrand, paused before the door of Adèle as she went by, and greatly longed to turn the lock and enter, for the purpose of relieving herself of the load of fears and conjectures which oppressed her. But she had not the heart to wake her, and passed on. The precaution was kind, but very useless. Adèle, instead of sleeping, had spent the night, from various causes, in a state of agitation which would have rendered the appearance of her sister a real blessing. She had made up her mind to be very wise, and to go to bed as soon as she had despatched Roger Humphries on his mission; and had even proceeded so far towards putting this discreet resolution in practice as to disembarrass her beautiful brow of its wreath, collect the long silken braids of her dark tresses into one rich knot, exchange the delicate tissues of the ball-room for the soft folds of a *robe de chambre*, and all this without any aid from her 'waiting gentlewoman,' for she was in no mood to meet questions, though uttered only by the eye. But ere she had proceeded farther towards seeking the rest of which she stood so much in need, a feeling that she was not yet sufficiently tranquil to find it induced her to open the window of her room, which in general commanded a view of the garden, but at present offered little to the sight, excepting the canvass roofs of the various erections which covered nearly the whole area of what was usually a very handsome lawn.

For some moments she enjoyed the cool fresh breath of the April daybreak on her feverish cheek, and amused herself the while by watching the artificial light emitted here and there through the temporary roofs and walls, battling with the faint but increasing light of the sun, and losing ground before him every minute. While thus engaged, she perceived a figure, or it might be figures, very obscurely moving at the very farthest corner to which the temporary buildings reached, which was exactly where the dark shade of the large forest-trees and underwood surrounding the garden touched the verge of the lawn. This spot, as seen from the window where Mademoiselle de Cordillac stood, would have been but dimly visible even at noon-day; for not only was it thickly planted with evergreen shrubs, but the canvass or boarding of the festive edifice appeared at that point to project into what seemed an irregular sort of porch, or garden exit from the rooms. Seen, therefore, by the grey uncertain light of the morning, rather marred than mended by the gleams proceeding from the illuminations within, it was quite impossible for her to distinguish whether the moving mass she saw were man, woman, or both. But she looked not the less earnestly for that. Woman-like, the less she could make out what she saw, the more eagerly she gazed at it; and while standing thus with her head advanced through the open window, she caught a sound, evidently proceeding from the spot at which she gazed, yet so indistinct, considering the vicinity, that she felt certain the person who uttered it must be muffled by some very close envelopement.

With a quick and almost instinctive movement she turned round and extinguished the light which stood on a table near her, and then resuming her position, gazed with very nervous excitement upon the misty scene below. She again heard the same indistinct sound, which was more than once repeated before it ceased entirely; but the moving object she had seen was no longer visible, and she was about to withdraw and shut the window, when a sudden gleam of brilliant light shot from the porch she had before remarked, and while it lasted she clearly discerned the figure of a tall man pass out. But the flash was so instantaneous, and the dimness which succeeded appeared so much greater than before, that the moment the door or curtain through which it had been emitted closed, she was unable to distinguish any object whatever.

By degrees, however, as the effect of this contrast between strong light and comparative darkness subsided, Adèle again distinguished the trees and shrubs, and even the garden path which wound away amongst them; but nothing living or moving remained in sight, and she stood puzzled, frightened, and uncertain whether she ought to give notice of the baffled cry which she believed she had heard, or whether the whole thing might not have arisen from some affair of gallantry into which she would not be wise to penetrate.

The moment this idea struck her, it was followed by the recollection of the words she had heard spoken by her step-father as Count Romanhoff led her to the supper-room. – 'Ruperto, manage this matter for me skilfully, and the price shall be doubled.' Neither was the explanatory phrase, 'I adore her!' forgotten; and the deeply-distressed Adèle felt convinced that what she had just witnessed was the result of this conversation.

It was more from being lost in very disagreeable reverie than from the expectation or the wish of seeing any thing more that she still retained her position near the window; and just as a feeling of chilliness roused her to the consciousness that it would be better to close the *croisée*, and retire to bed, she again perceived a tall moving figure near the garden entrance to the temporary buildings, which immediately disappeared within it; while, as it entered, another short flash of the artificial day within made the gloom which succeeded wear the appearance of almost total darkness.

Adèle shut the window, drew a curtain over it, and threw herself, shivering and painfully agitated, on the bed. But sleep was now perfectly out of the question. The mission of Roger, and the adventure of which she had just been a spectator, would either of them have been sufficient to make her wakeful; but, together, they caused a degree of nervous agitation and excitement as new to her as it was miserable.

Till the latter occurred, the former, though agitating, had in it a mixture of hope that made her heart bound, even while she trembled at her own temerity; but the latter had thrown a weight upon her spirits, which made her see every thing *en noir*. Fear, and a feeling approaching to self-condemnation, took the place of hope, and she would have given worlds that she had submitted to the desertion of her lover, without having made what now seemed to her so very improper an effort to bring him back. The solitude she had so longed for seemed terrible to her: she fancied that she should have felt less miserable in the ball-room; accused herself of unkindness to Sabina and rudeness to the guests, for having withdrawn; and then tormented herself by sketching in vivid colours the embarrassment and distress she should have to endure when she next found herself in the presence of her step-father. The terms of affectionate and pleasant intimacy on which they had always lived, – the absence of every sort of suspicion of a similar nature during his past life, and his gay habit of challenging every expression on her countenance or that of Sabina, which might chance to be less cheerful than ordinary, – all pressed upon her, and made her dread the meeting. And still the music and the dance went on below, sending up at intervals a sort of joyous swell of sound that seemed to mock her sadness.

At length, however, this ceased, and, by degrees, stillness and silence succeeded to incessant movement and incessant noise. It was a relief: but still Adèle was certain that she should not sleep; and greatly did she long, while listening for the light step of Sabina, who must pass her room in going to her own, to open her door, and invite her to enter. Had all the weight which rested upon her mind been of an ordinary character, – if, even, it had related only to her own too-decisive measures respecting Mr Coventry, it is probable she would have yielded to the temptation that the sound of Sabina's step, at length distinctly heard, brought with it, and would have sprung to the door to let her in. But she would not have mentioned the adventure of the garden to her for the universe, as, with the explanation which must have followed, it would have presented her father before her eyes in a manner so degrading and so painful, as she well knew would make her completely wretched.

Resolutely, therefore, did she determine to bear all this alone; and, breathing a prayer that the dear Sabina's eyes might soon close in the refreshing sleep of peace and ignorance, she turned herself upon her restless pillow, and was speedily rewarded for the sisterly self-denial, by herself dropping into profound repose in less than ten minutes afterwards, and even while she was (in spite of her earnest endeavours to do no such thing) tormenting herself to discover who the object of Mr Hargrave's unholy adoration could possibly be.

CHAPTER XV

The sleep of poor Adèle, sound as it was, did not last long; for, being gifted with a pair of those inconvenient ears which seem to wake while all else sleeps, she was startled, after the interval of an hour or so, by a sound which seemed to be immediately below her windows. She got up, and partially withdrew the curtain. It was now broad daylight, though the lofty walls, and thick but still leafless trees of the garden, threw a deep shadow over the part of the enclosure which surrounded the canvass-covered exterior of the last night's fairy palaces. But this shadow, deep as it was, could not now conceal the objects which it fell upon, as it had done an hour or two before; and if any doubt remained on the mind of Mademoiselle de Cordillac as to who might have been the tall personage whom she had dimly discerned go out and go in during that obscurity, it was now removed, for she perceived Mr Hargrave come forth from under what now appeared to be a heavy mass of canvass, seemingly drawn up in the manner of a curtain, and (carrying some implement in his hand which she could not very plainly distinguish) take his way rapidly, but very stilly, round the corner of the new erections, which then concealed him from her sight.

Almost instinctively she replaced the curtain of her window, for she felt certain he would return, because she knew that there was no outlet from the garden in that direction. But, though nervously anxious to be herself invisible, she could not resist the movement which led her to watch for the return she expected; and, carefully shielded by the drapery of her window-curtain, she managed easily so to adjust her eye as to see while remaining perfectly unseen. She had not waited long in this position before she perceived Mr Hargrave return again to this opening from the garden rooms, and enter by it. He carried in his hand what appeared to be a large silk pocket handkerchief, such as he was in the habit of using; but now it was tied into a sort of pendant bundle, and evidently, from the shape in which it hung from his hand, contained something weighty, though not large. The implement which he had carried when he passed out had been left in the garden, for the handkerchief above described was all that occupied his left hand, while the right remained at liberty, and was employed to assist his entrance by pushing aside the heavy canvass by which he passed.

Greatly did Adèle rejoice at the precautions she had taken for concealment, for just before her mysterious step-father disappeared within the drapery, he paused for an instant, and looking up towards the house appeared to reconnoitre its windows with a scrutinising and anxious glance.

Nothing could be much more tormentingly vague, or painfully puzzling, than the state of mind in which this act of *espionnage* left poor Adèle. Whatever might be the meaning of what she had seen, she regretted most deeply having witnessed it. A malicious sort of fatality seemed to have attended her throughout the night, which had just let her sufficiently into Mr Hargrave's secrets to make her feel herself in some sort a spy upon him, yet leaving her, despite all the strange things she had heard and seen, most completely in the dark as to what had actually happened. If, as she could not reasonably doubt, the stifled cry she had heard proceeded from the person Mr Hargrave professed to adore, how came it that, so speedily after her forcible abduction, he could be occupied so strangely, as to time and place, upon some mysterious business with which it seemed impossible that this lady could have any concern? She could not have been mistaken as to the identity of the person who had spoken the words she had heard on her way to the supper-room; neither could there be any doubt as to who it was that had been collecting in the shrubbery a handkerchief-full of something or other at seven o'clock in the morning, after an entertainment which could not have permitted him to retire to rest before five. All this was certain – and her step-father was the hero of both these incongruous adventures. It was, indeed, possible that she had been mistaken as to the tall figure she had so dimly seen in the garden in the interval between the first and last; yet, while allowing this possibility, it had no effect upon her mind, and she felt little less certain of having seen Mr Hargrave then than upon either the former or the latter occasion.

With her heart beating, her head aching, and her ear nervously on the alert to catch every sound, she had seated herself, cold and miserable enough, in the easy chair which stood at the foot of her bed, and presently heard the door of the library, which opened at a few yards' distance into the same passage as her own, cautiously closed, and the roused and anxious sense even caught the sound of the bolt by which it was secured within.

Alas! how truly might she have exclaimed with Cato, 'I'm weary of conjecture!' Weary she was, indeed, but with that weariness that leads to restlessness, and not to repose. She looked again at the time-piece on her chimney; it seemed to have stood still since she had looked before. It was still but twenty minutes past seven, and there could be little hope of hearing any servant stirring after such a night for the next two hours. Roger, indeed . . . It was just possible that the active old man, who was ever the first of the household to be stirring, might not have gone to bed after executing her commission. How she longed, as this possibility occurred, to leave her room and penetrate to the offices, where, perhaps, she might find her venerable messenger refreshing himself snugly after his expedition, and thus learn, before any ear was awake, save his own, to listen to her inquiries, what had been the result of his embassy.

So strong was this longing at her heart that she would probably have braved the closed windows and expiring lamps in order to gratify it, had it not been that she must have passed the library. Almost equally unwilling to be seen herself in the performance of the errand she had meditated, or to let her step-father suspect that she might by possibility have seen him, she abandoned the project, and determined to wait with all the patience she could for such a general movement among the household as might prevent the opening of her own door from being remarkable.

But what should she do meanwhile? . . . Read? . . . No apartment belonging to Adèle de Cordillac could be unprovided with books; and there, in truth, they stood in goodly rows before her. But had they been made of wood, they would have been fully as interesting to her at that moment; and she shook her head as she remembered the fallacious line about

'Books, those silent friends that *ever* please.'

She would much more willingly have set herself to *parfiller* her silken coverlet than have attempted to exchange the wandering, wavering, vague, and tormenting thoughts which filled her mind, for the most glorious speculations or beautiful fancies that ever beamed upon mortals from the empyrean heights of poetry. No! reading was out of the question, – she perfectly loathed the thought of it; but after sitting for the space of about ten minutes, waiting for sounds which she did not expect to hear for two hours, she felt that she could not bear it, and suddenly determined to dress herself, as she had undressed herself, without the aid of her maid, to eke out this operation as long as she possibly could, and when it was completed, to try her endurance again for as long a time as it would serve her: after which, if needs must, she thought she might brave the chance of being detected as the first person awake in the house, and venture to pass through her own door, and before that of Mr Hargrave, in quest of Roger.

Considerably relieved by having thus sketched her plan of operations, Adèle began her toilet. Having once more tightened the long tresses of her luxuriant hair, till that richest of decorations, withdrawn in all directions from her beautiful face, looked, in its classic simplicity, like a dark casque upon a bust of alabaster, she indulged in that most rousing and refreshing of all ablutions the immersion of the face in cold water. Again and again was this repeated, and each time she arose, like Antaeus from the earth, or (a closer resemblance) like Venus from the wave, braced and revivified by the contact.

There be many reasoners, besides female ones, who are apt to jump to a conclusion; and had any such watched the rekindling hope and spirit of Adèle's eye, as her nerves thus recovered their tone, he might have been tempted to declare that he found in it a convincing proof of the materiality of the fair creature before him, and that it was not necessary any spiritual essence should mix itself in such a frame in order to render it perfect; for that it was as clear as light, 'the body thought.' It was but a proof the more, however, that it was 'divinely wrought;' and, in all respects, a most fitting tabernacle for the holy light that dwelt within.

Conscious of the healthful influence, and thankful for it, Adèle knelt, and prayed to God to give her strength to endure with firmness and resignation whatever awaited her. And then, no longer so childishly restless or so unwisely impatient, she seated herself to perform that most difficult operation of the female toilet (and the only one, perhaps, in which a young girl really wants assistance), namely, the brushing, with arm vainly extended to its utmost length, the abounding mass of silk that, released from all restraint, now flowed around her. The task was new, and Adèle was certainly awkward at it; for ere her uplifted arm had twice repeated the necessary effort, the treacherous implement flew from her grasps, and struck with rebellious violence against the corner of her table.

The noise occasioned by this unfortunate concussion was, as she instantly felt, ten times more startling than any she would have been likely to produce had she yielded to her wish of leaving the room; and she sat in trembling expectation that some symptom would reach her of its having been heard by other ears than her own. Nor had she long to wait for a confirmation of this very painful fear, for, in the next moment, she heard the bolt of the library door withdrawn, the lock turned, and then a step, which distinctly approached her door.

Adèle trembled from head to foot; but the prayer she had just uttered seemed to return to her own bosom; and remembering that she was, in truth, engaged in no unlawful act, her courage rallied, and she remained quietly waiting for what should happen next.

The sound she expected followed. A gentle knock was heard upon her door, and she immediately rose and opened it. Adèle certainly was not surprised at seeing Mr Hargrave, for, in fact, she would have been greatly surprised had she seen any one else; and yet she started, for she had not expected to see him look so ill. It is probable that, though at least as much a watcher as Adèle herself, he had not as yet had recourse to either of the restoratives she had employed. In other words, that he had neither breathed a prayer nor washed his face; for he looked haggard, pale, and agitated.

The beautiful composure of her countenance, however, seemed in some degree to restore him; for he smiled, and said, in a voice not quite steady, but of perfect gentleness, –

'You are up, then, my dearest Adèle? I was afraid I heard you. What makes you leave your bed, my dear child, after so late a party? I trust you are not ill?'

'Oh dear, no, papa!' she replied, inexpressibly glad that the first words were spoken. 'I am perfectly well. Only, being wide awake, and seeing the sun shine so brightly, I got up without much considering what o'clock it was.'

'Not yet eight, Adèle: no servant, as I take it, can be moving yet,' replied Mr Hargrave. And he then added, after the interval of a moment, during which he looked in her face with an earnestness that was painful, 'What has made you so restless, Adèle? Have any sounds disturbed you during the night?'

But before she could answer this he spoke again; and she was equally relieved and surprised by his saying, –

'I feared, indeed, that this would be the case; for after you retired last night, circumstances occurred which, for some time, led to great confusion, both in the house and out of it.'

'And what was that, papa?' she said, with quickness, anxious both to receive his answer and to avoid making any herself.

'Nay, my dear child,' he replied, yawning violently, 'for all that I must refer you to Sabina, who was herself a witness to the painful scene; for, unfortunately, tired as I am, it is necessary that I should finish a sort of *procès verbal*, which I promised to write before I closed my eyes; and I give you my honour I can hardly keep them open. Go, therefore, to your sister, my love, as soon as you hear she is awake, and she will tell you quite as much about this disagreeable business as I could do.'

Inexpressibly comforted by these words, and readily persuaded that all her foregone conclusions were wrong, Adèle replied, with even more than her usual affectionate sweetness of manner, –

'Go – go, dearest papa; do not let me detain you a moment longer! Make haste to get through what you have to do, and lay down for a few hours, or I am quite sure you will make yourself ill.'

Mr Hargrave smiled affectionately, kissed her cheek, told her he should most strictly follow her advice, and then added, –

'I wish you would also follow mine, dear child. Darken your room, Adèle, and endeavour to take another nap.'

Adèle escaped replying to this by returning his caress, and then waved her hand in token of her anxiety that he should lose no more time in talking to her.

'God bless you, dearest!' he said, in a tone which shewed that he too was glad to be released; and then kissing his finger-tops with a touch of his ordinary gay and gallant bearing, he returned to the library.

Once more alone, Adèle returned thanks to Heaven that, though all she had witnessed was still involved in mystery, she was relieved from her worst fears concerning her father's share in it. It is true she would much rather not have heard the words which she had connected, as it now seemed so unjustly, with what she had seen; but she determined never to allude to the irregularity of conduct which those words betrayed to any human being, – to use her very best endeavours to forget them herself, and, above all, to conceal from Sabina all she unfortunately knew, and all she had unwarrantably suspected concerning her beloved father.

'And now, then,' thought Adèle, 'there can be no danger in my going down-stairs as soon as I am dressed, and endeavouring to find old Roger. It will be something new if fatigue of any kind keeps him in bed till nearly nine o'clock.'

Skilfully or not skilfully, all that remained of her dressing operations was speedily performed; and Adèle, her heart throbbing with both hope and fear concerning the answer she might receive from Coventry, hastened to leave her room. Though undoubtedly she no longer felt the same dread of encountering Mr Hargrave as she had done before their interview, she almost, unconsciously perhaps, wished, if possible, to pass his door unheard. Not that he could guess her secret reasons for thus wandering about the house; he had never heard her mention the name of

Alfred Coventry since the day on which the abortive invitation was sent
him to meet Prince Frederic at dinner, and she had no fears whatever of
his penetrating her secret. But she dreaded the necessity of more evasion,
which was as foreign to her habits as to her principles; and rejoicing that
her door had fallen to without the lock having caught, she opened it
without a sound, and noiselessly stealing over the richly-carpeted passage
and staircase, reached the hall below, without having the least cause to

'Startle at the sound herself had made.'

She then turned into an open passage which led to the offices, and
knowing that she was now in a region from whence noises of many kinds
might at that hour be heard without exciting attention, she walked
fearlessly on to the sitting-room of the upper servants, where she fully
expected to find the comfort-loving old Englishman enjoying his never-
forsaken luxury of a cup of tea. But in this she was disappointed. Not
only was no Roger Humphries there, but it was evident that no such
notable individual had that morning entered the room, for no spark of
fire was on the hearth, and no gleam of light entered it save by the door.

She had, then, to live on yet longer without knowing whether she was
about to be the very happiest creature on the earth, or one of the most
wretched! What should she do now? Return to her own cheerless
chamber, and there await the summons of the tardy old man? Her
courage sunk before the idea of this anxious interval; and, after a
moment's reflection, she resolved to find her way through the lately
bright, but now dark, labyrinth which led to the new buildings in the
garden.

As long as the hope of immediately learning the result of Roger's
embassy lasted, all curiosity respecting the mysteries of the preceding
night seemed in abeyance: she had happily ascertained that her step-
father had no private connexion with them; and the subject, therefore,
compared with the news she expected from her confidential servant,
appeared one of the most perfect indifference. But now that perforce she
must wait a while longer for the former, she felt disposed to set about
investigating the latter. To Sabina she was still determined not to apply till
the morning was more advanced; but she thought she might gain
something like information by visiting the spot behind the garden rooms,
from whence she had seen Mr Hargrave return with his heavily laden
pocket-handkerchief.

For this purpose she made her way by such glimmerings of light as
crevices admitted to the flowery retreat, which her knowledge of the
local geography had last night taught her to discover was the termination
of the intricate suite: and here the bright light of the morning sun again

greeted her; for the entrance she had seen used while watching the spot from her window, was still open – the canvass being suspended by a pole that had been drawn away from a large orange-tree, which it had supported.

Adèle paused to look about her. Her first feeling was that which must be common to every one who ever gazed upon the *débris* of a gala. All that under the cunning influence of tasteful arrangement, and the delusive brilliance of fictitious light, had appeared graceful and gorgeous, now looked like the wreck and remnants of a paltry world made up of paint and pasteboard. The very flowers which, blushing beneath the glances of unnumbered tapers, had a few hours before given to this spot an air of almost supernatural beauty, now looked pale, and sick, and sorrowful!

'What a frightful contrast!' murmured Adèle. 'It is a blessing that Nature manages her eventide and morn better than we do. How terrible it would be after every star-lit moon-embellished night, were we, on awaking in the morning, to find every thing looking as dirty and dismal as our manufactured world does here!'

Having concluded her philosophical survey, she was about to pass into the garden, when she was struck by the evident care which had been bestowed in the construction of the building to render this place of exit both easy to use and difficult to see. She perfectly remembered the aspect which that portion of the seeming wall, which was now suspended by the pole, had presented on the preceding evening. The painting upon it represented a magnificent arch; and two splendid orange-trees, stationed on each side of it, had assisted to lead the eye through its well-managed perspective to an imagined world of courts and corridors beyond.

'When I so greatly admired that arch last night,' thought Adèle, 'I certainly had no idea that it would be so easy a matter to walk under it.'

The garden, though a magnificent appendage to a metropolitan residence, was not large enough to make it difficult for Mademoiselle de Cordillac to find the exact spot to which she had seen Mr Hargrave direct his steps the last time she had watched him quit the building in the morning; for, in fact, the erection reached on that side to within a few feet of the surrounding wall, and the whole of the space was thickly planted. But, from the direction in which she had seen him disappear, it was quite certain that he must have passed through this narrow, and almost tangled, bit of shrubbery, though the doing so was no easy matter.

'What could he have wanted here?' thought Adèle. 'He was scarcely long enough absent to have reached the space left on the other side of the building.' Wrapping her dress round her, however, she entered the little thicket, determined to make her way through it, as he must have done before her. But, ere this resolution had been tested by encountering any of the thorny obstacles it seemed to promise, her steps were arrested by the sight of a trowel, such as masons use. She stooped and took it up. Could this be the implement which she had discerned in her step-father's hand as he went out? – she thought not. She had distinctly seen what appeared to be a longer, a slenderer, and a lighter-coloured handle than that of the implement she had found, and she let it drop on the place from whence she had taken it. Before she passed on, however, she gave another glance to it as it lay upon the ground; and as she turned her eyes from it, with the conviction that it was not what she had seen in the hand of Mr Hargrave, they were attracted by the gleaming of some bright but minute object, lying at the edge of a heap of withered leaves which seemed raked together from an abundance of others with which the ground was covered. She moved the moist and dirty-looking mass with her foot, for its appearance was not inviting to her ungloved fingers; but this daintiness speedily vanished before what her foot disclosed; and stooping, without further ceremony, she plunged her hand into the wet mass, and drew thence a long chain of gold, the clasp of which had evidently been torn off, as well as something which had been attached to the centre, for the link from which it had hung had been wrenched asunder.

Terrified – she hardly knew why – Adèle turned about, and was hastily returning with her valuable though mutilated treasure to the house, when it occurred to her that she had but very imperfectly looked through the mass of leaves which appeared to have been collected to conceal this trinket; and stepping back she took up the trowel which lay in her path, and set about examining the heap with more care. No more gold, however, peeped out from it; but, having reached with her trowel the bottom of the mass, she clearly perceived that the ground under it had been recently moved, and, instead of being as firm as the soil around, lay loosely raised above the surface.

Adèle's courage almost failed her. What might she discover if she removed that loosened earth? The evidence of guilt and robbery seemed before her: her step-father, perhaps, had sought such proof in vain – but it was now before her; and, with greater agitation than seemed reasonable to herself, she knelt upon the ground, and used the instrument she had found to remove the soil. There was no difficulty in the task; it lay, lighter than the moist leaves which had concealed it, over a rudely-crushed mass of trinketry, hidden at the distance only of an inch or two beneath the surface.

But this was not all: beside, or rather in the midst of this strangely bruised, but still glittering mass, lay a hammer, with a long, white, slender handle, exactly resembling that which she had seen in Mr Hargrave's hand when he left the building.

It was not suspicion — Oh no! it could not be suspicion which for an instant suspended the pulsations of her heart. 'What a fool I am to be thus terrified!' she said aloud. 'What is it I am afraid of?' and having thus chid the weakness that for a moment had made her feel so deadly sick, she lifted the golden fragments from the earth, and then perceived that they consisted entirely of settings, from whence gems had been violently torn. But, while gazing on these unequivocal traces of rapine and violence, and completing the theory by which she accounted for the manner of Mr Hargrave's going and coming, her eyes suddenly became fixed and distended; the things she held dropped from her hands, and she would have fallen with them had she not seized the branch of a tree, and, resting her head against it, sustained herself till the sudden faintness had passed.

A moment before Adèle had accused herself of weakness, but now she wondered at her own strength, which enabled her to stand upright and in full possession of her senses, while convinced — perfectly, soberly convinced — that the ornaments she had just held in her hand were in many places spotted with blood! Alas! the dreadful tale this told was but too legible. Not robbery alone, but murder had been committed on the premises, fatally laid open to the wretches who must have been lying in wait to perpetrate these fearful crimes by the frailness of the substitute for doors and windows, which the temporary buildings had supplied!

This, then, was the event to which Mr Hargrave had alluded; for the explanation of which she was referred to Sabina, and to which the *procès verbal* he had mentioned of course referred. It was now evident that, by some chance or other, he had been led to examine the spot where she stood, and had doubtless left it as nearly as possible in the same state in which he had found it, in order that it might be so seen and examined by the officers of justice. The hammer must have been left there in forgetfulness; and the contents of the handkerchief? — it was impossible to explain it all, nor was it needful. She should hear every thing ere long, and hear too the name of the unfortunate victim. These thoughts were succeeded by others more personal. Most deeply did she lament the curiosity which had led her to penetrate so far into this dreadful business; and the idea that, from having moved the articles, she might be called upon to give testimony in the cause, suggested itself with a force that perfectly dismayed her.

Had she trembled less violently, it would have been no difficult task to replace every thing exactly as she had found it; and, even as it was, she did so in all essential points, and felt no scruples of conscience interfere with her resolution of keeping her terrible adventure secret. Having completed this agitating task, poor Adèle returned to her own room, silent and unseen, with no spirits even to renew her search for Roger, and heartily hoping that, for an hour or so, Sabina might contrive to slumber, that she might avoid the necessity of speaking to any one.

CHAPTER XVI

Cold, shaking, and miserable, Adèle, on reaching her chamber, wrapped a shawl about her head, and, without altering her dress, crept into bed. The sense of security and freedom from observation which this retreat produced, greatly contributed to tranquillise her; sufficiently indeed for a salutary flood of tears to take place of the less kindly agitation she had felt before: and worn out, as it seemed, by all she had done and all she had suffered, she happily sunk to sleep, and thus became better able to endure the scenes which immediately afterwards she had to pass through.

By the time Adèle had returned to the saloon through which she re-entered the house, several servants had already made their operations audible in the offices, and it was probably under the cover of this that she again passed by the library door unchallenged; for she no longer felt the power of measuring her tread as she had done when passing it before. But Mr Hargrave, if he heard her, noted her not; and her own maid, giving her credit for uninterrupted and most profound repose after the fatigues of the ball, carefully abstained from approaching her.

In order intelligibly to explain what now occurred, it will be necessary to go back to the time at which the three gentlemen who had been engaged at the whist-table with the unfortunate M Bertrand took their departure from Mr Hargrave's dwelling. The coachmen of two of these gentlemen had drawn up their carriages round the corner of the wall which surrounded the court-yard; the equipage of Lord Hartwell was in the court, and he immediately drove off, but the other two walked out together in the direction one of the servants of the house pointed out. Just as they came in sight of their carriages, but before they had well quitted the *porte-cochère*, they both perceived a man closely buttoned up in a great-coat who appeared to be approaching with intent to enter by a small *porte de service* at one corner of the courtyard. No sooner, however, did he perceive them and the servant who was still attending them from the house, than he suddenly turned about and retreated at a rapid pace, till he reached the opening of a narrow passage on the opposite side of the way, through which he disappeared.

'Who is that, I wonder?' said M de Soissons, addressing the domestic.

'I should have said it was our young ladies' favourite old footman, Roger,' replied the man, 'if I didn't know that it was quite unlikely.'

'Unlikely or not,' said M de Beauvet, 'it is perfectly necessary we should question him a little;' and, without waiting for any reply, he darted across the street, and immediately disappeared down the passage.

'But we must follow him, my friend,' said M de Soissons to the servant. 'You have heard what has happened, have you not? *Allons! C'est un brave homme ce Monsieur Beauvet*, and we must not let him be murdered all alone.'

Perfectly of the same opinion, the domestic of Mr Hargrave joined the chase, and in a very few moments they all overtook the person who was so evidently endeavouring to avoid them.

'Holla!' exclaimed M de Beauvet; 'whither so fast, and why so shy, good man?'

The hunted man gave a look over his shoulder, and apparently perceiving that there was no hope of escape, deliberately turned round, and, touching his hat, said very respectfully, 'Have you any business with me, gentlemen?'

'Business, my good friend? Oh dear, no; no business in the world!' returned M de Soissons; 'purely a matter of pleasure and amusement, to which so civil a gentleman as you seem to be cannot refuse to contribute. Have the kindness, monsieur, to tell us why you happened to take fright at the sight of us? And why you so disobligingly turned your back upon us and fled?'

'Fled, gentlemen!' said old Roger, for the fugitive was no other; 'I have no cause to fly from any one. What may be your pleasure with me?'

Now Roger, being a man of some talent and more ambition, with high wages and little work, had not passed twenty years in the capital of *la grande nation* without having learned its language; he *had* learned it much more thoroughly than men of his station generally do, and spoke it with facility and very tolerable correctness. But now he made sad work of it; and, in fact, shewed in all ways such unequivocal symptoms of agitation, that his fellow-servant stared at him with astonishment, and the two strangers with undisguised suspicion.

'There is little occasion, I suspect,' said M de Beauvet, 'to explain to you what has been going on to-night in the house we saw you entering when the sight of honest men made you take in such haste to your heels; it is enough to tell you that you are shrewdly suspected to have had a hand in it, and, therefore, by your leave, old gentleman, I thus make you my prisoner.'

The words were accompanied by the most appropriate action possible, for as he pronounced the last member of the sentence he laid violent hands on poor Roger's collar, and, by the help of M de Soissons, who at the same moment committed a like ungenteel assault upon his heels, lodged him in one of the carriages which had now drawn up to the spot where they stood.

Much less alarmed at this violent proceeding than he would have been by a few civil questions as to whence he came and wherefore he had gone, old Roger suffered himself to be deposited in the carriage of M le Comte de Beauvet without any resistance, his only symptom of contumacy being a rigorous silence.

'This fellow wears your master's livery,' said M de Beauvet, addressing the servant who attended them from the house. 'Has he a right to do so? or is it only put on for purposes of fraud?'

'He has a right to wear my master's livery,' replied the man, 'at least till such time as it is taken off his back; and that, as I take it, will be before he is much older. With such goings on as we have heard of to-night, it is not very easy to mistake as to what kept the old rogue out of his bed, or what made him run away in such a hurry when he caught sight of your honours.'

Short of the feeling which exasperated the Moor against the harmless Cassio, it was hardly possible that stronger hatred could exist in the heart of any uninjured man against a fellow-creature than that which animated the bosom of Louis Querin against Roger Humphries.

The causes which led to this were scarcely of sufficient dignity to be recorded; but the contemptible nature of the impulse did not render its effect less strong. Querin was a Frenchman, – young, tall, with black *favoris* that might have served for the mane of a pony; and black eyes, large, bright, and bold, which in his soul he believed were not only the finest eyes in Christendom, but of a beauty which might fairly entitle him to compete with the noblest heroes in court or camp as *un homme à bonnes fortunes*. He had, perhaps, amidst the shining vicissitudes of *la jeune France* encountered adventures which had served to nourish his prodigious vanity up to the enormous growth at which it now flourished; but, whatever the cause, it is certain that in his vocation of serving-man he never by any chance waited upon a lady, let her character and quality be what it might, without expecting to be treated in some way or other as a favourite. When impudent vanity is of as vigorous a stamina as that of M Louis Querin, every thing that can by possibility be converted into nourishment will act as such; and without intending the slightest reflection upon the discretion of any of the various ladies he had previously served, it is not to be denied that when he entered the service of Mr Hargrave he anticipated considerably more favour than he found. His appearance and deportment being exactly what Mr Hargrave himself approved in that portion of his establishment retained for show, he was permitted to continue in it, although both the young ladies of the family happened very particularly to dislike him. That such should be the case was a thing so difficult of belief to the mind of Louis Querin, that it is probable nothing would have made him receive it as true, but the marked favour and even familiarity of both Mademoiselle Hargrave and Mademoiselle de Cordillac towards Roger Humphries. That a fellow, old, ugly, and (stranger than all!) AN ENGLISHMAN, should be preferred as a personal attendant upon ladies (by the ladies themselves), had something so monstrous, preposterous, and unnatural in it, that the acute M Louis was driven to meditate very profoundly on the cause; and soon convinced himself that it arose from the *espionnage*, reports, and general ill offices of the said Roger, for the which he hated him with very cordial abhorrence.

So much is necessary to explain the conduct of this very worthless individual in the transactions which followed.

'*Ecoutez, mon enfant!*' said M de Beauvet, as he proposed to enter the carriage in which he had lodged his prisoner. 'Go back to the house and go to bed without saying a single syllable about our having caught this very suspicious-looking old fellow. Doubtless he has confederates, and the purpose of justice might be defeated by their being informed of his capture. You will be sure to hear of us in an hour or two, as we shall require your evidence respecting the manner in which we found and secured him.'

Louis received these instructions with an air of respectful deference, and punctually obeyed them.

* * *

It was nearly noon when Mademoiselle Agatha, the *femme de chambre* of Sabina, gently approached the bed of Adèle to reconnoitre whether she slept or not. But the noise she made, however slight, sufficed to awaken Mademoiselle de Cordillac, who, starting up, astonished the Abigail by shewing that, though found in bed and fast asleep, she was completely dressed.

'*Mais, mon Dieu!* Mademoiselle has been up already! and, it may be, has been waiting for her breakfast?'

'No, no, I have not wanted breakfast. Is my sister up?'

'*Mais oui*, mademoiselle, and dying to see you. Ah! such an adventure! And mademoiselle knows nothing of it?'

'I suppose Sabina is in the boudoir?' returned Adèle, leaving her bed and making some hasty reparation of her toilet.

'Shall I send Susanne, mademoiselle? or will you give me leave?' said the girl, offering to assist her.

'I am quite ready, thank you, Agatha;' and with a step lighter than her heart Adèle hurried to the boudoir.

'Oh, Adèle, how ill you look!' were the first words with which her sister greeted her. 'I had hoped, dearest, that your quiet and, comparatively speaking, long night, would have made you fitter to hear what I have got to tell than you now seem to be. Are you ill, dear Adèle?'

'No, Sabina, not ill; but most exceedingly curious to learn what it is Agatha has been talking about.'

'Then you have heard it?' said Sabina. 'Is it not dreadful?'

'I have heard nothing,' replied Adèle; 'excepting that you have something terrible to tell me. Let me know what it is, I beseech you.'

Sabina then related the scene which had taken place in the hall on the preceding night, and described in lively colours the agony of poor M Bertrand. 'I cannot help thinking,' she said, 'that they must have been mutually attached, his words and manner had so much the appearance of true affection.'

'And have no tidings been yet heard of her?' demanded the trembling Adèle.

'Nothing, as Agatha tells me, has been learned beyond the frightfully alarming fact of her disappearance, excepting that the canvass walls of the temporary rooms in the garden have been broken through, and the door on the east side of the garden, leading, you know, into the narrow passage that goes to the stables, was found open: both of which circumstances indicate with sufficient clearness the manner in which this dreadful deed was effected.'

'How?' cried Adèle, almost gasping; 'Were there any traces – any marks?'

'No traces, you know, could be more legible,' replied Sabina, 'than those furnished by the open passage through which she must have been carried. Never, surely, was so daring an attempt perpetrated. It must have been effected under cover of the noise and bustle of that horrible cotillon; yet papa says that he thinks he saw her dancing in it.'

'Where was papa during the cotillon?' demanded Adèle.

'Dancing,' replied Sabina. 'He danced the cotillon with Mademoiselle de Charmonte.'

'Did he dance the whole of it?' asked Adèle, remembering the long interval which had elapsed after the well-known notes of the cotillon first reached her, and before she saw the tall figure re-enter, whom at one period during the vacillating meditations of that eventful night she had believed to be Mr Hargrave.

'No, not the whole of it,' replied Sabina. 'I particularly remember seeing him come in from the garden-rooms after the first two or three figures were over. I remember it because I noticed that he looked exceedingly ill and tired. But, nevertheless, he immediately began dancing, and exerted himself wonderfully, for I observed afterwards that I never saw him appear in greater spirits. He positively seemed to be dancing with a dozen ladies, besides his own partner; and, therefore, I have no doubt that he really did see poor Madame Bertrand dancing – for he seemed too much on the *qui vive* not to know every body.'

Adèle pressed her hand to her forehead and remained silent.

'You should take some coffee, my dearest Adèle. The breakfast is getting cold while we talk, and I am sure you look as if you had need of it,' said Sabina, placing before her a cup of the fragrant beverage she recommended; and then setting her the example of applying to the breakfast-table for support under the anxiety that had fallen upon them.

Adèle endeavoured to follow it – she endeavoured to rally, she endeavoured to talk – but thoughts, wildly improbable, yet frightfully harassing, had taken possession of her mind; and though her judgment rejected them, it was totally beyond her power to shake them off. Why had Mr Hargrave said that he had seen Madame Bertrand dancing? Why was she still, in defiance of all probability, in defiance of her most ardent wishes – why was she still so strangely disposed to believe that the tall figure she had distinctly seen leaving the building and return to it some twenty minutes or half-hour afterwards (but still before there was light sufficient to distinguish him) – why did she, against her utmost efforts to prevent it, cling to the renewed belief that this tall figure and the one she had so perfectly distinguished go and return afterwards were the same? The coincidence of time; the fact that he had entered the ball-room considerably after the cotillon had begun; that he looked ill; that he had danced with such unusual vehemence of animation; and, lastly, that he had stated his belief of Madame Bertrand having been engaged in the same dance, although the cry she had heard so fearfully proved the contrary, all pressed together upon her memory, and made her feel as if her senses were leaving her.

But the more these hateful suspicions settled upon her mind, the more earnest became her wish to conceal them completely and for ever from Sabina. She knew the tender devotion of her attachment to this mysterious father, and she felt that either her life or her reason would probably be the sacrifice were she to know that such thoughts had ever been conceived concerning him. But Sabina's eye was upon her, and she feared that she should sink before it. There was one way, and one only that suggested itself, by which such a turn might be given to their conversation as might account for her own weakness without disclosing the real cause of it. Adèle related with as much distinctness as was in her power all that Count Romanhoff had said to her, and the sudden resolution of sending to Coventry, which had been its result.

Sabina listened to her with the most earnest attention, and evidently with more sympathy and emotion than the elopement of Madame Bertrand had caused her.

'My sweetest Adèle!' she said, 'is it this that makes your dear eyes look so unlike themselves? Believe me, Adèle, you have done nothing but what was perfectly right. Had any weak, feminine punctilio prevented your doing that excellent young man justice, I should never have forgiven you. But the answer, dearest? Old Roger, despite the deliberation of his movement, might have traversed the distance half-a-dozen times since I saw you creep out of the supper-room. What was the answer?'

'I do not know,' said Adèle.

'Not know? Do you mean that you have not seen your messenger? Adèle! this weakness is unworthy of you,' said Sabina, eagerly ringing the bell. 'To think of your permitting any scruples whatever to prevent your inquiring into circumstances on which the whole fate of your life depends!'

Adèle replied not, and her sister felt little wonder at seeing her lay her arms on the table and bury her face upon them. It was quite natural, she thought, that her emotions should overpower her at the moment of receiving an answer to such an embassy.

'Send Roger here!' she said to the servant who answered the bell.

'I do not think he is in the house, mademoiselle,' replied the man; 'for we could not find him when he was wanted for his breakfast.'

'At what hour was that?' inquired Sabina.

'At eight usually, mademoiselle; but at nine to-day.'

'Not at home at nine!' repeated Sabina, her fair brow contracting with a look of vexation. 'Go, Justin, and look for him again; and, as soon as he comes home, send him here.'

'How very strange this is!' exclaimed Sabina, as soon as they were again alone. 'The old man must know pretty nearly as well as I do, Adèle, that this errand was no common one. Coventry could not have detained him for seven or eight hours. I cannot understand it.'

'It is very strange that he should not be come back,' said Adèle, looking up at her, with an expression in her eyes which Sabina could not understand. Had it been possible that the person who had despatched such a note as her sister had repeated to her could be indifferent as to the answer to it, Sabina would have thought, from that glance, that Adèle was positively thinking of something else. But this was *not* possible; and the affectionate girl, feeling terrified at an expression in the dear familiar features which she was not able to interpret, got up, and seating herself close beside her, threw an arm about her neck, and kissed her fondly.

'I shall believe myself the wiser woman of the two, presently, Adèle,' she said; 'and that is an honour and glory that I do not want just now, for——'

'Hark!' cried Adèle. 'What noise was that?' and she started so violently, that the arm which embraced her fell, and the eyes of the two sisters met, as they had never met before, without a single spark of reciprocal feeling being exchanged. Adèle was not thinking of Sabina, – she was not thinking of Roger, or of his mission, – she was not thinking of Coventry: her shaken and bewildered spirit was wandering in the garden, – stealing into the retirement of her step-father's library, – prowling about the blood-stained hoard that lay buried in the earth, and all this, with such feverish intensity of imagination, that she was very nearly unconscious as to where she was or who was her companion.

'Surely, dearest love,' said the frightened Sabina, 'the mere circumstances of old Roger's delay ought not to effect you thus violently. May he not have been too late, and, finding that Coventry was gone, have set off in pursuit of him, rather than return without delivering your note? I assure you, Adèle, I should not be at all surprised: Roger Humphries is quite capable of this sort of *dénoûment.*'

'No, he is *not* capable of it!' returned poor Adèle, answering to her own thoughts, yet catching at the words which reached her ear. 'Why should I torment myself by believing it when I know it is impossible?'

Inexpressibly shocked at a tone and manner which evinced so much deeper suffering than she thought reasonable, Sabina remained silently gazing on the face of her sister, as if to find there an explanation of what was passing within. Adèle caught her eye thus fixed upon her, and winced under the examination. 'Why do you look at me so, Sabina?' she said: 'it is not kind of you.'

'Oh, Adèle! do not say that – do not say I am unkind, when I would give my right hand to tranquillise and comfort you!'

The accent in which this was uttered went straight to the heart of the agitated and bewildered girl, and did her a world of good, for it once more brought a flood of tears to her eyes; the strain upon her mind seemed relaxed, and recovering her self-command and awaking anew to the feeling that her first duty, let what would ensue, was to guard the peace of the innocent Sabina, she roused herself strenuously and effectually from the frightful reverie into which she had fallen, and gave herself sufficiently to the theme to which her dear companion again recurred (and which even then had some interest for her), to listen to her arguments concerning the non-appearance of her messenger, and at length to adopt the interpretation of it, believing, with as much concern as she could at that moment bestow on any subject (but one), that the intemperate zeal of the old man had really induced him to follow Mr Coventry from Paris.

No theme could be more favourable for the object which at that moment was the most important in the world to Adèle, namely, the keeping the mind of her sister from Madame Bertrand, and all the horrible circumstances which she too well knew had attended the '*elopement*,' of which she now spoke so lightly; and after this followed another, to which, for the same reason, as well as for many others, Adèle listened with deep attention, – for it concerned Prince Frederic, and the conversation which had passed between him and Sabina at the supper-table. This supper-conversation, had it not been for its conclusion, would, as the blushing girl frankly allowed, have appeared to her the most delightful she had ever listened to, for it was full of the most flattering, yet ingenious expressions of admiration, esteem, and warm regard. 'But it ended,' said Sabina, while a tear trembled on her eyelid, – 'it ended by his telling me, that he feared his *fête* upon the 1st of May would be the last and only one on which he should have the happiness of again seeing me, as it was his intention to leave Paris the day after. Do not think me foolishly vain, dear Adèle,' she added, with a glowing cheek and a smile that battled vainly with her falling tears; 'but I do think that, had he been something less than royal, he might have loved me.'

'And you, Sabina, what do you feel for him?' said her sister, anxiously.

'That had he been less than royal, I could have loved him too,' replied Sabina firmly, and as if she felt that she had no cause to blush for the sentiment she thus frankly expressed.

'Thank God he is leaving Paris!' exclaimed Adèle fervently, while her clasped hands and eyes raised to heaven seemed to shew that she was in truth deeply thankful for the news.

'Surely, surely, Adèle, this thankfulness for his departure is unnecessary,' said Sabina gravely. 'I think you do me less than justice, sister.'

Thankful that she was not understood, the trembling Adèle only shook her head, and for a moment Sabina interpreted the silence that followed unkindly. But in the next, her gentle, sweet, and reasonable nature told her that she too ought to be thankful for this wise departure, which might spare lengthened misery to more heads than one; and in this tone they chatted on, with no interruption from Madame de Hautrivage, who rarely left her own apartments till the first easy toilet of a Frenchwoman had been exchanged for that, less rapidly completed, in which she better liked to meet the 'garish eye of day.'

CHAPTER XVII

While this long conversation took place in the boudoir of the sisters, a very different scene was passing in a different part of the house.

Mr Hargrave, having shaved, dressed, and satisfied himself by consulting his glass, with even more attention than usual, that he looked very nearly as he wished to do, sat down to the solitary cup of coffee which constituted his first refreshment, *le grand déjeûné* at which he met the ladies of his family in the dining-room never being served before two o'clock.

Whilst thus engaged, the well-known knock of Mr Jenkyns was heard at the door, and upon the permission to enter being given, that important functionary made his appearance, followed by M Jules Marsan. As this visit was not unexpected, or unprepared for, it was graciously received; M Marsan was requested to sit down and Mr Jenkyns dismissed.

Whatever was the business transacted, it did not take long; the bell was rung, the well-pleased Jules committed to the hospitable care of the steward, and Mr Hargrave once more left alone.

Scarcely, however, had he tasted the enjoyment of the lounging leisure which he was preparing for himself upon the sofa, when he was again interrupted by a knocking at the door of the library, and again, but much more reluctantly than before, he pronounced, 'Come in.' It was not now his confidential tormentor, Mr Jenkyns, who appeared as the door opened, but the much more elegant and animated Louis Querin.

'*Pardon, monsieur,*' he began, '*mais il faut vous annoncer——*'

'Announce nothing now, Louis,' exclaimed Mr Hargrave, yawning, 'for I am tired to death.'

'*Pardon, monsieur!*' interrupted Louis, '*mais il faut——*' and ere he could finish the sentence, M de Beauvet and M de Soissons passed by him, entering the room with little of ceremony, but with an air of busy eagerness that considerably heightened the complexion of the gentleman they came to visit.

'We must beg ten thousand pardons for breaking in upon you so early, Mr Hargrave, after a night of so much harassing fatigue,' said M de Beauvet, 'but circumstances have occurred which make it absolutely necessary we should consult you. I am extremely sorry to say that it has become my painful duty to announce to you that suspicions of the most serious nature attach to an individual of this family respecting the lamentable occurrence of last night.'

'What do you mean, sir?' said Mr Hargrave, fiercely.

'*Mon cher monsieur,*' said M de Soissons, in the most conciliating tone possible, 'I trust that the endeavours we have used to throw light upon the terrible transactions of last night will not be misunderstood by you as shewing any wish to interfere with what does not concern us. Neither M de Beauvet nor myself would willingly lay ourselves open to such an imputation; but you must be aware that after witnessing the agony of the unfortunate M Bertrand, as displayed in your hall last night, it was impossible for any one possessed of common humanity not to feel interested in his sufferings and disposed to do every thing possible to discover the offenders. It so happens, I am sorry to say, that accident has led us to the discovery of circumstances which tend very strongly to criminate one of this family. But surely, my dear sir, you would rather wish to promote the inquiries which these circumstances have led to than to check them?'

'Of course, sir, – of course,' replied Mr Hargrave, whose complexion was now of the most leaden paleness. 'Pray be seated. I shall rejoice, – deeply rejoice, if any traces can be found which may lead to discovery. Have the kindness to tell me to what you allude?'

M de Soissons made a sign to indicate that he wished his companion to undertake the task of narration; and, accordingly, M de Beauvet gave a clear and succinct account of their meeting with Roger, and then proceeded as follows:–

'Having secured the old man, who persevered rigidly in maintaining the most obstinate and contumacious silence to all the questions addressed to him, we lodged him at the *corps de garde* till the hour at which the proper authorities should be ready to receive us. Monsieur de Soissons and myself attended the examination; and, I am sorry to tell you, that the authorities consider it necessary to detain your servant in custody till the premises have been completely examined, and till he has given such an account of himself as may be deemed satisfactory.'

'Roger Humphries!' said Mr Hargrave, when the narrative was finished: 'Roger Humphries!' These were the only words he uttered, and, as he repeated them, his tongue seemed to cleave to the roof of his mouth.

'I grieve to see that the heavy suspicions which rest upon him affect you so deeply,' said M de Beauvet; 'and, really, but for his obstinate and most unaccountable silence, I should say that he had the appearance of an honest and respectable old man. But his flight from the premises the moment he saw us, his pertinacious refusal to answer any questions that can be put to him respecting his object in concealing himself, or the manner in which he had been employed during the latter part of the night, render it almost impossible to doubt that he must have been engaged in the nefarious business into which it is our painful duty to examine.'

'I had really believed,' said Mr Hargrave, drawing a long breath, 'that old Roger Humphries had been an honest man. If your suspicions be correct, gentlemen, and it is impossible to deny that circumstances are strongly against him, he can only have been an agent for some one from without. I have, I think, before hinted to you my suspicions that this will turn out to be merely an affair of gallantry; and, bad as it is, that there is no reasonable ground for supposing that any violence has been used. Poor M Bertrand appears to suffer so severely for the loss of this young woman, that it will be very painful to open his eyes to the real state of the case. But take my word for it, gentlemen,' – and a vast deal of what appeared private and personal knowledge laughed in Mr Hargrave's eye as he spoke, – 'depend upon it, gentlemen, that when pretty Madame Bertrand came here last night, she had fully arranged the manner of her departure. Her magnificent *trousseau* contained more than one shawl – you cannot doubt it; and more than one cloak of ermine, also, perhaps. At any rate I neither feel now, nor did I last night, any very severe anxiety lest this *belle personne* should take cold during her drive. But, to speak seriously of a matter which is evidently felt seriously by one of the parties at least, I should strongly advise poor M Bertrand to make as little fuss about the matter as possible.'

'May I, without indiscretion, ask you, monsieur, if you have any particular reason for thinking Madame Bertrand a person likely to elope with such very scandalous publicity?' said M de Soissons.

'As to the discretion of such a question, my dear sir,' returned the gay Hargrave, laughing, 'I must leave you to pass judgment, yourself; and for my answer – has it not been given already?'

'And do you suppose the gallant to have been among the party assembled here last night?' inquired the same gentleman.

'Upon my word that is a point to which I have not yet turned my attention,' replied Mr Hargrave. 'But now you suggest it,' he continued, musingly, 'I should rather say not. The fact is, gentlemen, and I believe if you will inquire among any of the company present last night, they will tell you that the boast is not *cet d'un fat*, the lady in question was exceedingly gracious to me; and I am ready to own that, as far as dancing and flirting could go, I made the most of it. For, to say truth, I was inexpressibly amused by the unmitigated coquetry of this new little beauty, and did not consider myself called upon, in any way, to check it. I will confess, too, that I do not think the lover with whom I presume she has eloped could have been present; as I think she would have been more reserved in manner if he had.'

'This is most extraordinary,' said M de Soissons, who had listened to every word spoken with the most earnest attention. 'I have been told, by persons who knew her well in the humble station from which the wealthy Bertrand has raised her, that she was a model of modesty and discretion, – I cannot understand it.'

'*Hélas! cher ami!*' returned Mr Hargrave, shrugging his shoulders; 'I am grieved to say that such cases are not of very rare occurrence. But to return to this old man of whom you have made a prisoner, greatly, as I should suspect, to his astonishment. Do you really think it likely he should have been concerned in a business of this kind?'

'It does not appear to me that the nature of the business is quite so clearly ascertained as you seem to suppose, Monsieur Hargrave,' replied

M de Soissons, thoughtfully. 'It still strikes me as much more probable that this unfortunate young woman should have been forcibly carried off for the sake of the immense wealth she carried about her in jewels, than that she should have eloped, within a month of her marriage, in a style of such unprecedented audacity. The police, I can assure you, are clearly of this opinion; and though M de Beauvet, as he will tell you, suggested an interpretation of the adventure similar to your own, they paid little or no attention to it; saying that, let there be a lover in the case or not, the carrying away such an amount of property, whether by force or fraud, must be looked after. It was remarked, too, in reference to the mysterious conduct of your aged servant, that it was utterly impossible such an elopement could have taken place, let the object have been either love or plunder, without there having been a friend in the garrison to assist the *sortie*; and that, consequently, if this old man should be at last induced to speak and prove his innocence, a confederate with the guilty parties, whether the lady be one of them or not, must, of necessity, be looked for in your household.'

'Nay, then,' returned Mr Hargrave, sighing, while his deportment suddenly changed from gay to grave, – 'nay, then, if this be the case, I fear, indeed, that old Roger may have had a hand in it. The old man has often shewn himself avaricious; it is, as we all know, the vice of age – and I will not deny the having been long aware that it was his. But if robbery has been intended, gentlemen, depend upon it that it has been perpetrated under the mask of love; and that all the guilt which lies at the door of old Roger is that he has received a bribe, – a heavy one, I doubt not, to render the elopement easy.'

'If it prove so, if his share in the business be no worse than this, a frank confession would, of course, secure his release; as his rascality, presuming love to have been the ostensible object of the elopement, would appear to be of a nature of which the good-natured law takes no cognisance. But, of course, as long as the old fellow holds out, and continues to persevere in refusing us all information, he must be retained in custody; unless, indeed, we discover in the course of our investigations some other person or persons whose agency in the business may prove to have been sufficient, without any necessity of implicating him: for in that case, you know, neither evidence nor suspicion would lie against him.'

These words were uttered by M de Soissons with great eagerness and rapidity; while, as he spoke, the eyes of Mr Hargrave were fixed upon him with a look, the direction of which never varied, though the expression of it did repeatedly; and more than a minute elapsed after it was ended, before any word was uttered in reply; both the Frenchman remaining silently gazing at him, as if waiting for his opinion.

'I have been thinking,' said Mr Hargrave at length, 'and I am thinking still, gentlemen, what will be the best manner of proceeding in order to satisfy the ends of justice, in case any illegal act has been committed; or to obtain as much information as possible under the contrary supposition, in order to set the mind of poor M Bertrand at rest, by convincing him that the affair is merely one of gallantry. And it strikes me, that the best way will be to keep the old man in custody, and entirely alone, without stimulating his obstinacy by any further questions whatever. I know the nature and character of that old man well, and while I have little or perhaps no difficulty in believing that he may have been capable of receiving a bribe to assist the *escapade* of a pair of lovers, I consider it as absolutely impossible that he should have any thing to do in a more criminal undertaking. My knowledge of his character leads me also to the conviction that the silence which you very naturally denominate obstinate, but which he would consider honourable, is not likely to be shaken by any thing you could do or say to him. He is capable of being as firm as a rock − I know him to be so; and I therefore repeat that I strongly advise his being retained in custody, but without being questioned.'

'But what is to be hoped for as the final result of this?' demanded M de Beauvet. 'I confess I see not what can come of it, excepting that we shall be confining a man on our own responsibility, instead of placing the whole affair in the hands of the constituted authorities.'

'Pardon me, monsieur,' returned Mr Hargrave, while his lip trembled either from displeasure at hearing his opinion controverted, or from some other feeling, − 'pardon me, monsieur, that is not my meaning. If the old man be retained in custody, it should be only, I think, in my house, and with the understanding that I am greatly displeased by his refusing to answer the questions put to him. I would recommend that nobody should be admitted to see him but myself, and I have little doubt that I should soon gather from him all and every thing that he knows on the subject.'

'We shall hear what the magistrates say on the subject,' said M de Soissons, slightly knitting his brows. 'In a case of this kind, I should imagine that no private interference would be allowed.'

'Permit me to observe, gentlemen,' replied Mr Hargrave, mildly, 'that my interference has been wholly involuntary. It is my most earnest wish that justice should take its course; and rather than be suspected of interfering with it, I will, if it be thought advisable, withdraw from Paris for a few days, till all proceedings connected with the affair shall have been brought to a conclusion.'

Considerably shocked and surprised to perceive that their observations should have led their amiable host to conceive such a measure necessary, both the gentlemen hastened to assure him that he must have misunderstood the spirit in which they had spoken, and that so far from having any wish that he should absent himself, they had come, on the part of M Bertrand to request his presence at an examination of their prisoner which was about to take place.

Mr Hargrave coloured slightly, and bowed profoundly. 'No, gentlemen,' he replied, 'it is impossible. Had nothing been said during the present meeting to suggest the idea that any interference on my part would be objectionable, the delicacy of my own feelings would, I flatter myself, have led to the same conclusion. The fact that one of my own servants is suspected of being implicated in the affair is quite sufficient to prevent my taking any part whatever in the proceedings; and I will trust to you, gentlemen, to make my motives for holding back, understood and appreciated.'

There was so much mild dignity in Mr Hargrave's manner of saying this, that both his hearers were greatly struck by it. They were both of them good sort of men, and neither the one nor the other had any motive for the active part they appeared to be taking, beyond a feeling of compassion for the suffering they had witnessed in the unfortunate M Bertrand. The idea that a man, so every way superior as Mr Hargrave, should have reason for a moment to suppose that his conduct was, or could be, reflected upon as obtrusive or incorrect in any way, really distressed them; and they vied with each other in offering him the most earnest apologies for any thing they might have said to wound his feelings.

Mr Hargrave rose, and extending a hand to each, said, 'Apology, my dear friends, is wholly unnecessary. I am convinced that there is one common feeling between us all concerning this unfortunate occurrence, and it is quite impossible that we should mistake each other. But you will allow for the peculiarity of my position respecting the old man who is in custody. If any individual of my establishment can be suspected of having assisted, even by the mere withdrawal of a bolt, in this unfortunate business, it would be disagreeable to me to be obliged to interfere in it; but in the case of my old retainer, Roger Humphries, it, indeed, would be most peculiarly painful. I have confessed, with a degree of frankness which I am sure you must appreciate, that I do not consider the old man as likely to be proof against a bribe, but on all other points I have an excellent opinion of him; and were I to be examined as an evidence respecting his character, it is highly probable that I might be betrayed into expressing a warmth of kindly feeling and regard towards him which might be injurious, perhaps, both to him and me. I shall, therefore, steadily decline appearing in the business; and shall leave it to you, my good friends, to explain my motives for doing so, whenever you may hear the circumstances spoken of. I must also request you, if you please, to state both my refusal and the motive for it to the magistrate.'

This speech was concluded with a bow, which seemed to say, 'I dismiss you!' And the two gentlemen accordingly rose, uttered various obliging expressions of concern that his amiable hospitality should have involved him in so unpleasant an affair, and took their leave.

CHAPTER XVIII

The two sisters were still sitting *tête-à-tête* in their boudoir; Sabina opening all the thoughts of her heart to Adèle, and Adèle the while, most cautiously concealing the one overwhelming idea that had taken possession of hers, and which had swallowed up all the rest, when a well-known step was heard at the door, and a well-known knock followed it.

'Ah! there is papa!' exclaimed Sabina, springing to the door, and throwing it open.

Adèle felt as if her life depended upon the degree of power over herself which she should be able to exert during this interview; and the pressure of the moment rendered her, as it has done millions of others, an actress. During the interval occupied by the embrace, given and returned, between Sabina and her father, Adèle seized upon a cushion of the sofa, and laying it on the table before her, rested her head upon it. Could she have pressed it with her heart instead, there would have been no simulation in the act, for it throbbed in a manner that would have made the pressure welcome.

'You are suffering, my dear girl!' said Mr Hargrave, advancing gently, and leaning over her with a countenance of the most paternal kindness. 'Dearest Adèle! I feared your restless night would make you ill.'

'Has her night been restless?' cried Sabina. 'Why did you not tell me so, dearest? I thought you looked very pale when you first entered, but you have been letting me chatter so since, that I quite forgot it. It is I have made your head ache, dearest Adèle!'

'No, no; it is only because I got up so foolishly early,' replied Adèle, attempting to smile. But she had better not have made the attempt; for the effect produced by it was so greatly unlike all former smiles, that Mr Hargrave, whose eyes were fixed upon her, changed colour. Luckily she saw it not, or her discomfiture would have been complete. As it was, she rallied sufficiently, as Sabina bent over her, to say in a tone of very well affected languor, 'Dearest child! it seems cruel to tell you so; but if the truth must be spoken, I do think that our long gossipings have completely knocked me up; for I really do feel ill: and as you have now got papa to talk to, I think I shall positively go to bed again;' and pressing her hand to her forehead, Adèle rose, and walked towards the door.

'If you are ill, Adèle, I cannot stay from you, even to talk to papa. You must let me be your Abigail, and put you to bed,' said her sister.

'And shall we not begin talking again if you do?' returned Adèle, shaking her head. 'That will never do; you must let me go by myself, dearest.'

'She is quite right, Sabina,' said Mr Hargrave. 'I really will not let you go with her, because I am so very sure she will be better without you; while I, on the contrary, shall be vastly better if you will stay.'

This settled the business, and Adèle was suffered to depart.

'Did she not tell you, Sabina, that she had passed a restless night?' said Mr Hargrave, as soon as the door was closed upon them. 'Did she not tell you that I had heard her moving early this morning, and entered her room to inquire what occasioned it?'

'No, papa; she never said a word about it; and I am sure I wonder she did not, for that would have made me easy at once, as it would have explained her looking so very unwell and heavy-eyed. I taxed her with being ill, but she positively denied it, and said she only wanted to hear all the particulars about Madame Bertrand, which Agatha had begun telling her. But she knew nothing about that scene in the hall last night. You did not say any thing to her about it, papa, when you went in to her this morning?'

'No, indeed, I was only anxious for her to lie down and go to sleep again. But tell me, Sabina, was all the gossiping of which Adèle complained about Madame de Bertrand? – had you no other subject on which to talk to her?'

Sabina blushed, but made no other reply.

'I could not but remark, Sabina, that Prince Frederic paid you very great attention last night,' said Mr Hargrave; for the first time touching upon the subject which had been so long next his heart, and which his last night's observations, notwithstanding the many calls upon his attention from different quarters, had led him to think was in a state sufficiently advanced to justify paternal inquiry. 'It would be a great pleasure to me, dear love, if you would in this matter treat me rather as a friend than a father; and tell me candidly, and without reserve, the nature of the conversation which you and the Prince held together, particularly at the supper-table.'

Sabina felt that she ought to comply with this demand, and, despite some painful beating at the heart, she did so; telling her father, as she had before told Adèle, that the Prince had expressed the kindest and most flattering sentiments towards her. 'But what he said that was most important,' she added, with a sigh she could not check, 'was just when the supper was over, and he was going away. He told me then——' She stopped, for she felt her voice failing her; and not even the noble frankness of her most pure nature, nor the almost boundless confidence she had ever reposed in her father, made her feel it necessary that she should display all that those last words of the Prince had cost her. The pause she made sufficed to let loose the coursers of Mr Hargrave's imagination, and on they galloped even to the very utmost goal of his wishes. 'My darling, sweet Sabina!' he exclaimed, 'fear not to trust your father! Tell me what he said! – tell me all!'

'Nay, papa,' replied Sabina, gently, 'it was not much; only I have seen him so often lately that I was rather sorry for it. He only said that he was going to leave Paris immediately after his own ball, and that he should not be able to meet us to-night.'

'Leave Paris!' cried Mr Hargrave gasping, – 'leave Paris immediately! It is impossible, Sabina! You do not believe he was in earnest?'

'Oh yes, papa, he was quite in earnest,' said Sabina, quietly; her composure restored, as it seemed, by her father's want of it.

'Then he is——' vehemently ejaculated Mr Hargrave; but suddenly stopping himself, he added, in a tone as light as he could contrive to make it, 'a very capricious fellow.'

'Why so, papa?' said Sabina, looking in his face with some anxiety.

'Merely because he seems to have changed his mind without having any very good reason for it,' replied her father. 'But come, Sabina, be quite candid with me. Has not Prince Frederic given you reason to suppose that he wished to gain your affections?'

'NEVER!' answered his daughter, with great solemnity; all weaker emotions giving way before the honest and honourable wish of doing justice to the Prince. 'Never, papa, for a single moment; and if my vanity ever led me to suspect that I had touched his heart, it was when he told me that he was going: for I then thought it possible he might have felt for me what, in his station, it was his duty to overcome. If this be so, he is as noble-minded as he is amiable, and I shall never cease to remember him with equal gratitude and esteem.'

All traces of anger, and even of vexation, had passed from the countenance of Mr Hargrave. He sat for some short time in a sort of meditative silence, and then said, 'I agree with you, my dear child, in believing the Prince to be in every way estimable. Be very sure, Sabina, that he is a man whom you might trust under all circumstances. If, notwithstanding the admiration it is so very evident he feels for you, he should persevere in his intention of leaving Paris, it is because his attachment is less strong than his ambition; but should he change his purpose when he again sees you, and *remain*, be sure that he loves you better than all else. In all things I am convinced he may be trusted, for there is no falsehood in him.'

'Most surely he may be trusted!' replied Sabina, earnestly; 'and it is therefore that I know his departure is certain. God forbid I should think otherwise!'

'Why so, Sabina? Do you dislike Prince Frederic?'

'Dislike him? Oh! papa!'

'If not, my dear, why should you so fervently deprecate the idea of his remaining here?'

'Because I would not for the world believe that he could wish me to like him more than is consistent with my honour,' said Sabina, while a burning blush seemed to dry up the tear that trembled on her cheek.

Her father rose, and took her hand. 'I will leave you, my love,' he said, 'for I perceive this discussion agitates you. But, ere I go, let me say one word, lest the same noble mind which can so well understand Prince Frederic should unhappily misunderstand me. If the Prince feel for you the sentiments for which I have given him credit, his confessing it to you can lead to nothing but your honour. Sabina Hargrave may become a Princess of ——, but need not fear that any one will dare offend her by the utterance of a sentiment unfit for her to hear.'

Having said this, Mr Hargrave quitted the room, leaving his daughter, as he intended to do, in a state of the most violent agitation.

'So!' he exclaimed, as he once again enclosed himself in his library, 'the plot thickens upon me. Now or never! Glory, honour, and magnificence for life, or ruin, exposure, and death!'

* * *

On leaving Mr Hargrave, the two gentlemen, whom accident had thrown into so close a participation with the affairs of M Bertrand, as made his interest appear almost like their own, hastened to present themselves before the Correctional Police, accompanied by Louis Querin, who, according to agreement, stood ready at the door of his master's hall to attend them.

They found M Bertrand, with whom they had communicated more than once during the course of the morning, already there; and, immediately after their arrival, Roger Humphries was brought forward as a prisoner, and Louis Querin and themselves desired to appear as witnesses against him.

The facts deposed against him consisted of his having been seen at about half-past five o'clock in the morning, wrapped in a plain great-coat over a very sumptuous livery, approaching his master's house, apparently with the intention of entering it; and, on being perceived, turning suddenly away, and making off, with very evident desire of concealment.

But although these circumstances were stated with perfect correctness, it was not done without such a mixture of commentary and interpretation as gave to old Roger's movements a vast deal more meaning than met the eye. Louis Querin, in particular, contrived to render his gloss of considerable more importance than his text, the examination proceeding in this wise: —

'How long have you known the prisoner?'

'Not long enough to have known any good of him; but it may be about two years.'

'Has he ever before been the object of a criminal prosecution?'

'If he has not, he has been luckier than many a better man; but I never heard that he had.'

'What are your reasons, besides the fact of your having seen him endeavouring to conceal himself, for supposing it likely that he was engaged in the carrying away of Madame Bertrand?'

'First, because I know him to be a very wicked old fellow, that would be ready to sell his soul for a piece of twenty sous, — which, to speak honestly, is considerably more than it is worth. Secondly, because he has the true spirit of the devil for intrigue: and, thirdly, because it stands to reason that it is impossible that the lady could be carried off, clear and clean, out of the garden, unless some one who knew where the key of the door was kept, had lent a helping-hand.'

'That is quite true. But because a helping-hand was necessary, it does not follow, you know, that it must have been his?'

'Not at all,' returned Querin, with a graceful bow. 'Only if many circumstances tend to shew that he had something to do with it, and that all the rest of the household had not, the conclusion appears rather obvious.'

'Undoubtedly. But how does it so clearly appear that no other individual of the household (which is a large one) had any thing to do with it?'

'Because it would be easy to prove, by the evidence of many, that this old fellow was the only one of the whole set who was not seen in his proper place till the entertainment was completely over, even up to the time when these two gentlemen went out. Whereas Roger Humphries was called for, and not found, just after the supper was over; nor was he seen by any of us, till I had the honour of spying him attempting an *escapade* down the alley.'

'He must be certainly remanded for further examination,' said the magistrate; 'and to give time for further circumstances to become known. Meantime it will be necessary to examine the premises.' Then turning to the puzzled, but in no way agitated old man, he said, 'The charge against you is a very grave one. Have you any thing to say for yourself?'

'Not a word,' replied Roger.

'Would it not be proper to search him?' said the miserable-looking

M Bertrand, who, till now, had not uttered a syllable, and whose countenance shewed that a few hours of mental agony can bring a strong man low. 'Would it not be well,' he said, 'to examine if he has upon him any sum that may look like a bribe, or any trinket, such as my captured and perhaps murdered wife wore about her?'

That Roger Humphries was an Englishman certainly told much against him in the estimation of all the persons before whom he stood; nevertheless, there was a sort of decent dignity in his demeanour, which inspired something like a feeling of respect for him; and before M Bertrand's very natural proposal was agreed to, the magistrate used the ceremony of asking the venerable prisoner if he had any objection to it.

'None in the world, monsieur,' replied Roger, 'provided no very dirty hands handle my livery.'

This was said without the slightest appearance of a sneer on the part of Roger; but yet, notwithstanding the spotless purity of the full-dress white coat, and bright blue waistcoat, *et cetera*, the magistrate slightly knit his brows, for the hands of the officials present were certainly not in a state to abide the conditions suggested by Roger. The old man was probably aware of the embarrassment which his request was likely to produce, and accordingly set himself to perform the required examination, and that in such a way as fully to satisfy all present. First, the coat, heavy with crested buttons and broad silver lace, was drawn off, and, rather ostentatiously perhaps, held up to view, the pockets being turned inside out, and the pocket-handkerchief and fine damask napkin they contained, opened and shaken to the entire satisfaction of all parties. The waistcoat followed, and the spectators were introduced to an equally familiar acquaintance with that; and then Roger turned out for their edification the pockets of his sky-blue small clothes. One of these was entirely empty, but the other contained two sovereigns and a Spanish dollar. The old man laid these coins upon the desk of the magistrate, who, with the feeling, whatever it is, which often leads people to examine money that is placed before them, took them into his hand.

'Where did you get these from, my friend?' said the officer of Correctional Police, applying a glass to his eye as he examined them.

'From my master,' replied Roger. 'He paid me my wages a fortnight or three weeks ago, and that money is a part of it.'

'How did you happen to have it in your dress small-clothes?'

'Because it was in those I put off, and I did not choose to leave it there.'

'But you might have locked it up, you know?'

'I had no time, sir. I dressed myself in a hurry.'

'You are quite sure you had this money, – these very identical coins, from your master?'

'Yes, sir, – perfectly sure.'

'Does he always pay you in English gold?'

'No, sir, not quite always. But my master knows I like English money best, and always indulges me with sovereigns when he can get them.'

'Do you know how he got these?'

'No, sir, I do not.'

'Did he pay you the whole of your wages, on this occasion, in gold?'

'No, sir; a part was in silver.'

'Such silver as this?'

'Yes, sir.'

'Should you have any objection to letting me change this money for other coins of the same value? – It would oblige me.'

Roger made a civil bow, and replied, –

'No objection whatever, sir;' adding, with a slight shiver, 'May I put on my coat and waistcoat, sir?'

'By all means,' was the reply; and while Roger carefully replaced his garments, the magistrate counted out the amount of the money which the pockets had contained, with honourable and scrupulous attention to the rate of exchange.

'I presume, monsieur, that you doubt the fact of this money having been paid him by Mr Hargrave?' said M Beauvet, in a low voice, to the magistrate.

'For that . . . I don't know,' he replied; 'but I think it is as well.'

'Certainly – assuredly – beyond all doubt. Perhaps you suspect that the person who eloped with her is an Englishman?'

'For that . . . I don't know,' repeated the magistrate.

'Do you wish, gentlemen, that I should take off my boots?' demanded Roger, collecting the silver money which had been laid for him on the desk, and dividing it among all his pockets with scrupulous care, that the inconvenient metal might greatly injure none of them, – 'Shall I take off my boots and stockings, gentlemen? – or undo the lining of my hat?'

'No, it is not necessary,' replied the magistrate. If it had been, it would have been all one to Roger; for neither in his boots, nor his stockings, nor yet within the lining of his hat, was the note of Mademoiselle de Cordillac deposited, but, carefully enveloped in a morsel of silver paper, it lay enshrined in the folds of his muslin cravat, and had any hand sought it there, a struggle would have ensued which might have passed for the old man's care to protect his own throat from violence; for he would have fought to preserve that precious scroll with quite as much energy as to preserve his life; and rather, infinitely rather, would he have died, than betray the confidence, the flattering, the unbounded confidence, which had been placed in him.

'You still resolutely refuse to tell us where you had been when these gentlemen and your fellow-servant saw you yesterday?' resumed the magistrate.

'Yes, sir, I do,' replied Roger, again bowing with great civility.

'Neither will you tell us why you ran away, and endeavoured to escape the moment you saw them?'

'I have not the least objection to tell you that, sir,' said Roger, with great alacrity. 'It was only because I did not want to talk to them, and to be asked where I had been.'

'We might have contrived to guess as much as that, my friend,' said the magistrate, half smiling. 'However, I will trouble you, at present, with no more questions; and you may retire, under care of the *gensd'armes*, while I have some conversation with these gentlemen.'

Roger Humphries was then led out; after which Louis Querin was given to understand that, for the present, his attendance was no longer required: but, just as he was about to take advantage of this permission to retire, the principal officer present, and who had been the spokesman through the preceding scene, left his place behind a high desk at which he sat, and accompanying Querin to the door of the office, said to him in a whisper, as they both stood in the passage upon which it opened, –

'Observe, my good fellow, the eye of the police is upon you, – not on your own account, you have hitherto behaved perfectly well; but on that of people near you. This, however, may eventually prove greatly to your advantage; for you may be useful to us, and we never forget our friends. But if you wish to count yourself as one of them, you must scrupulously and absolutely – remember, *absolutely* – obey our injunctions; and the first of these is, that you breathe not a syllable of the arrest of this Englishman, nor of any thing important or unimportant which has passed during the examination, to any living being whatever; and, to avoid all mischief from listeners, or any other accident, observe, I include your master. You understand, – you are not to mention the arrest of this old man, or any circumstance connected with it, to your master, or any one else. If you attend to this, it shall be the better for you; neglect it, and it will be very considerably the worse! And now, farewell; our eye is over you.'

Louis Querin at once shewed himself worthy of receiving this confidential command, for he uttered no word in reply to it, but gave the intelligent agent of the Correctional Police a look which fully satisfied him. That gentleman then returned to his place, and addressing himself to M Bertrand, who sat supporting his head upon a huge interleaved copy of the Code Napoleon, he said, –

'Shall you wish, sir, to attend us to the mansion of Mr Hargrave? If you do, I will by no means refuse you the satisfaction of doing what you desire; but if you have no such wish, I shall be, on the whole, better satisfied: for to my judgment, founded, as you are probably aware, upon a good deal of experience, the fewer persons present on examinations of this kind the better.'

M Bertrand readily assured him that he should be perfectly satisfied to leave the investigation of this dreadful affair entirely in his hands; adding, that he was himself quite conscious that he was in no state to help the business.

'These gentlemen also, will, I hope, excuse me, if I beg to decline their attendance?' resumed M Collet, turning to MM De Beauvet and De Soissons. 'The result shall be communicated to them without delay.'

Both gentlemen expressed themselves entirely satisfied by this arrangement, and the party separated.

CHAPTER XIX

It was about three o'clock in the day, and the grand *déjeûné*, or luncheon, at which all the family assembled, was over. Mr Hargrave appeared at the table, with little or no alteration in his usual demeanour. When he addressed Sabina, indeed, there was, perhaps, a shade more of tenderness than usual in his look and manner; but in all other respects he was unchanged.

Madame de Hautrivage was in high spirits, and exceedingly eloquent on the brilliant party of the preceding night, which she had her own reasons for thinking one of the most agreeable of the season: for, in the first place, she had waltzed with two noblemen; and, secondly, had won three hundred and fifty-five francs at *écarté*.

Mademoiselle de Cordillac looked wretchedly ill, and confessed that she felt so; while Sabina, struggling vainly to recover the composure which the astounding nature of her father's parting speech in the boudoir had driven away, looked more beautiful than ever.

Exactly such conversation as might have been expected under the circumstances took place, and no other. Roger was inquired for in the most easy manner in the world by Mr Hargrave; whereupon the two girls coloured, and exchanged a furtive glance; but the servant's reply, 'I believe he is out, sir,' appearing perfectly satisfactory to his easy master, it elicited no remark. At the conclusion of the meal, Madame de Hautrivage drove out to make some trifling but indispensable purchases for the Prince's *fête*; and, *bon gré mal gré*, made the absent and half-dreaming Sabina go with her. Adèle retired to her room, declaring her intention of laying down till dinner; and Mr Hargrave mounted his unrivalled cob, in order, as usual, to shew himself *partout*, and to indulge in a few pleasant jestings with those he might meet on the singular elopement of the preceding night.

It was, then, about three o'clock, when, both carriages being fairly out of sight, M Collet, the principal officer of the Correctional Police in the *arrondissement*, together with two other persons belonging to the establishment, gave the *sessamé* knock on the *porte-cochère* of Mr Hargrave's residence, which, without question asked, causes the *cordon* to be drawn, and the entrance left free. The ready portress, however, stopped the party ere they had passed the archway which led into the court, informing them that both '*M Hargrave et les dames étoient en ville.*'

'*C'est égal,*' said M Collet, and passed on.

Having entered the open door of the mansion, and reached the ante-room, in which two or more idle retainers were ever lounging, sometimes gambling, sometimes reading the edifying romances of the day, and sometimes discussing the politics of both the household and the nation, the chief of the party inquired for M Louis Querin.

'*Mais il est ici,*' replied a liveried *élégant*, neither raising his head nor turning his eyes from the draught-board, by the aid of which he was beguiling his superfluous leisure into taking the form of occupation. And '*Ici, monsieur!*' cried the individual inquired for, starting from a corner in which he was enjoying, with an equality perfectly republican, the *Charivari* which his superiors in the establishment had enjoyed before. '*Je suis à vos ordres, messieurs.*'

'We are come,' said M Collet, quietly, 'to examine the door, or doors, by which it is supposed that Madame Bertrand was taken away last night.'

These words at once centralised the attention of the draught-playing footman and of his friend, – of the porter, who was frowning in his arm-chair over the exciting columns of the *Presse*, – and of a youthful individual who had ventured to steal from the precincts of the stable-yard, in the hope of being suffered, unnoticed, to swallow a few gulps of the delicious and intoxicating literature with which all the ante-rooms of *la jeune France* are sure to abound; – not to mention M Louis Querin himself, whose interest in the business, however, was rather marked by the look of stolid indifference which he immediately assumed, than by any symptom of the curiosity which animated his fellows.

They all started up, and seemed vehemently ready to assist in the proposed examination.

'*Mais oui, monsieur, certainement,*' said the porter, solemnly.

'*Par ici, messieurs!*' exclaimed the draught-player, hastening to open a side door.

'*Je connais la porte, moi,*' said the young helper.

'*Peut-être, je puis vous être serviable?*' hypothetically suggested the footman's friend.

To all which M Collet replied by shaking his head, and raising his hand with an action which seemed to say, 'Avaunt, gentlemen! if you please, for I want you not.' Upon which the four speakers drew back as if they had been shot. The citizens of *la jeune France*, taken individually, have the least possible inclination to meddle with her police; though, collectively, they like nothing better than for ever to set themselves in array against it, with their tongues and their pens, and occasionally, when sufficiently environed by their hopeful *gamins*, to give it battle with paving stones and rotten eggs.

'Louis Querin,' said M Collet, 'we have been given to understand that you were heard to speak of this affair as if you knew somewhat concerning it. It is you, therefore, who must accompany us into the garden.'

The individual thus addressed cast down his eyes, and bowed his head in silent and respectful humility, and then opened the side door from which his rebuffed fellow-servant had retreated.

Louis Querin led the way in silence, and in silence was followed by the officials of the Correctional Police, to the door in the garden-wall, which had been found open, and there he stopped; but after the pause of a moment made another step in advance, drew the bolts, and threw the door open.

'It was thus,' he said.

M Collet nodded, and stepped out, followed by his two attendants. They traversed the alley in the same order, a few yards to the right and a few yards to the left; but the alley was well paved, and there was no soil to indicate the recent passage either of men or horses. Immediately around the door, however, both within and without, the ground shewed traces of having been trodden; and the acute M Collet pointed out more than one foot-print to his companions, which had evidently been made by the delicately finished sole of a dancing *escarpin*.

'But there is no woman's foot-mark here?' said one of the assistants.

'I perceive it,' said M Collet, with another nod.

The trio then re-entered the door, which Querin still held open in his hand; but hardly had they done so, when the chief, and the one who followed next, simultaneously pointed to a portion of the path where the mixture of earth and gravel had the appearance of having been recently passed over by two female feet of very pretty dimensions; but both before and after the point at which these impressions were distinct were long and continuous tracks, as if the same small feet had been dragged along. Advancing farther into the garden, all traces of steps, or of dragging upon the walk, ceased; but the grass from that point to the corner of the temporary buildings had evidently been passed over, though in what manner, the nature of the surface rendered it difficult to decide.

M Collet, after carefully examining the whole line, dictated to the third individual of the party certain notes upon it, which were immediately committed to writing by the aid of materials produced from the breast-pocket of his coat. Having waited without uttering an additional word till this entry was completed, M Collet ran his eye over it, and then walked on to that *sortie* from the building which the still suspended canvass made visible. Here again he stopped, and very carefully examined every object, and particularly the ground. But here the grass had been so generally battered and bruised by the workmen employed upon the erection of the edifice, that it was impossible to trace any thing distinctly. M Collet and his companions entered, and Querin, at his command, removed the pole which supported the canvass, and by dropping it reduced them to nearly total darkness; all the light they had proceeding from the chinks and crevices which the imperfections of the construction had left in the walls and roofs.

'Go by the shortest path to the offices, and procure a light,' said M Collet, addressing Louis Querin, who started off, and returned, bearing a large lamp that threw forth a strong light, with a degree of promptitude which procured him another approving nod.

The canvass, after a skilful touch or two, was made to hang as it had done when the room was prepared for the reception of the company; and M Collet was as much struck, but more enlightened, perhaps, than Mademoiselle de Cordillac had been, by remarking the judicious position of the two large orange-trees, which so well assisted the effect of the arch between them.

'Exit not to be detected from within,' said the chief to the secretary; and the words so spoken were committed to paper.

'Now then, my friend,' said M Collet, addressing Querin, 'replace that pole as you found it.'

Louis set about obeying him with his former silent and docile obedience, but he failed in immediately discovering the point at which the fluted columns, which formed the painted arch, divided.

'It is cleverly painted,' observed M Collet to his brother officer; and as he spoke, he pointed out the division to Querin, and the continuation of the coloured columns upon the canvass which passed under it to his companion.

'Who built these temporary rooms?' said M Collet, again addressing Louis Querin.

'He is called Ponton,' was the reply.

'But the workmen – do you happen to know the workmen who did the job; not the *bourgeois* who employed them?'

'As it happens, monsieur,' replied Querin, 'the man who was always about the place while the work was going on, and who seemed to keep all the rest going, is at this moment in Mr Jenkyns' room (that is our *intendant*, monsieur), and he is waiting the return of Mr Hargrave, to know when he is to set about removing them; for sometimes, with us, this sort of thing is left standing from one *fête* to another, and it seems that Mr Jenkyns knows nothing about it, – and all the family are out.'

'All the family are out, are they? Do you think, my friend – do tell me what is your name. You seem to be a very intelligent fellow, and I shall like to be better acquainted with you.'

'Louis Querin, monsieur,' replied the accomplished domestic, bowing with an air of profound respect.

'*Eh bien*, Louis. Do you think you could contrive to get this man, this workman, out of the *intendant*'s room for five minutes? I should not want him longer, – but no one must know to whom you are bringing him.'

'*Rien de plus facile*,' replied Louis. 'I have only to tell him that our Madame de Hautrivage has left a commission for him.'

And in less time than it took M Collet and his subordinates to walk round the flowering *bocage* in which they found themselves, he had done his errand, and was seen returning through the now dismal, but lately bright arcades, followed by a man in the ordinary attire of a working mason.

'I want you to tell me, my good man,' said M Collet, 'under whose orders these very pretty rooms were erected?'

'I worked under the orders of M Ponton,' replied the mason.

'*Ah ça* – we have a wager about it. I say it was Mr Hargrave himself who gave the designs, and my friend here thinks it must have been a professional architect.'

'*Pas du tout, monsieur*,' replied the mason, perfectly satisfied by this explanation of the question; '*et vous avez gagné votre gageure*. It was Mr Hargrave,' he added, 'who composed the whole.'

'And he superintended the work himself; I'll answer for him?' said M Collet.

'*Rien de plus juste* – particularly this part of it. *M Hargrave est un homme de talent – mais tout-a-fait homme de talent, monsieur*. It was he who arranged this *sortie avec tout de finesse*.'

The wager thus satisfactorily settled, the mason was dismissed; and M Collet, after dictating another little note to his secretary, passed again under the uplifted canvass, and, followed by his attendants, returned into the garden.

Here again it was not difficult to trace footsteps round the corner of the building; but here again they appeared to be the result rather of the promiscuous treading of many workmen, than the distinct traces of footsteps. The examination, however, was not abandoned, and this perseverance was soon repaid by the marks of steps, turning off the grass, and leading to a thicket amidst the evergreens of the shrubbery, which promised more discoveries.

Precisely the same process which had been performed by Mademoiselle de Cordillac about nine hours before was now repeated by the agents of police, but with considerably less of trepidation and a more satisfactory result; for, whereas individuals of the species to which Adèle belonged never encounter any trace of crime without a pang of suffering, those of the Correctional Police are rather supposed to receive a throb of pleasure from the same, their sensations greatly resembling those of a sportsman who has succeeded in his pursuit of game.

In each of these examinations of the ground fate seemed to pay more than her ordinary attention to the feelings of the persons employed in them. What Mademoiselle de Cordillac found has been already related; but the discoveries of those who followed her went farther, for M Collet himself using the trowel found on the ground, with considerable strength and agility, perceived that the earth had been moved to a greater depth than that of the spot where the settings of the mutilated trinkets lay, and presently came to the corner of a delicate white silk pocket-handkerchief, which, having been seized and dragged from its dark receptacle, was perceived to be copiously stained with blood.

The professional gentlemen exchanged looks and shrugs, while the startled Louis Querin turned his eyes, first to one and then to another of them, to read in their faces, if possible, what they thought about it.

M Collet did not seem disposed to converse on the subject of the remarkable relic he had found; but silently displaying to his secretary, first the mass of settings, and then the blood-stained handkerchief, he said, '*trouvés ensembles*;' and then, with the assistance of his other attendant, carefully enveloped the whole in his own ample bandana, converting the packet into a tight roll, little calculated to attract attention. This packet he confided to the hands of his companion, and then prepared to leave the ground.

'We will go through the garden door,' said M Collet, addressing himself to Louis. 'You have behaved with acuteness, discretion, and propriety, and you have only to continue the same line of conduct, in order to ensure a degree of attention from us, which may be highly advantageous to you. You understand me, Louis Querin? You understand that I still expect from you the most rigid silence as to all you have witnessed in this business?'

'Yes, sir, I do,' returned Louis, and without adding another word he preceded the party to the garden door, which led into the alley, and opened it for them. M Collet, as he passed through, bestowed another of his favouring nods upon his conductor, and so they parted, the gentlemen of the police quietly pursuing their unobtrusive way through the streets, and the well-contented Querin returning to the ante-room with a very elegant air of unruffled composure.

'*Mais dit donc*,' cried two or three voices at once as he made his appearance. 'What do they say about it?'

'Very little,' replied Louis, yawning. 'These gentry are never communicative. But my own opinion is that they think the lady went off by her own free will – in short, that there is a lover in the *case*.'

'To be sure there is!' was replied in chorus, followed by *quelques bons mots de valets*, which produced a hearty laugh; and then, with that ever-changing variety for which French conversation is so justly admired, the subject was dropped, and another started.

And was this all the new light acquired by the family of Mr Hargrave from the visit of the police to his premises? Not quite. There was one other person to whom chance had made it known, and for that one it had not passed off so lightly as for the party in the ante-room.

When Mademoiselle de Cordillac told the family before they set off for their different airings that she intended to lie down in the hope of getting rid of her headache, she said nothing but the truth, for such was, indeed, her intention; but no sooner did she feel that, excepting the servants, she was absolutely alone in the house, than the most feverish restlessness took possession of her. The discovery of the morning, and all the doubtful, frightful circumstances attending it, never left her memory for an instant, and she felt as if something within her was for ever gnawing at her heart. Yet still she fancied – such ever is the false reasoning of anxiety – that if she could know the worst at once she should suffer less; and fearless as to whom she might meet, now that the eye of her step-father was removed, she suddenly determined to revisit the spot where she had made the discovery which so grievously tormented her.

Having taken this resolution, she made her way through the great saloon, now almost totally dark, from the erections before its windows, and along the intricate and equally dark arcades, which led to that part of the structure which contained the hidden opening into the garden. Despite the darkness and the intricacy, however, there was no great danger of her going wrong, for she had paced the passages, and conquered their seeming difficulties so frequently, that she now knew perfectly well in which direction lay the Chinese room and in which the Turkish tent. She had already reached the mimic bower, now fully lighted by the broad glare of day, which streamed through the opening from whence she intended to enter the garden, and was directing her steps towards the space between the two orange-trees, when she distinctly heard the sound of many steps without. Not doubting that they were those of servants coming to remove the plants, now languishing for more light and air, she turned aside into what had been a flowery passage of *treillage* from this bower of sweets to a room appropriated to ices, but did so rather to avoid the possibility of bandying words with any one than from any fear of being discovered there.

Both the obscurity and the form of the passage completely concealed her, and, ere she took her way by another entrance to this ice-room, which she knew would lead her back to the *sortie* from the saloon, she paused for a moment to learn if she were right in her conjecture about the plants, as, in that case, her project of returning to the buried gold must be abandoned for the remainder of the day, as the plants would all have to be ranged upon the lawn previous to their restoration to the conservatory, or to the gardens from which they had been hired.

A very short interval sufficed to shew her that she was mistaken. The party certainly did not exchange many words, but the broad daylight, let in upon them by the opening through which they passed, shewed that they were not gardeners, nor, excepting Louis, in any way belonging to the family. Though already perfectly concealed, she gently retreated another step or two, yet not so far but that she was able to hear distinctly every word that followed.

The replacing the canvass, the sending Louis for the light, the pithy remarks on the concealment of the opening, and, finally, the examination of the workman as to the contriver of the device, all reached her without the loss of a single syllable.

The trembling girl now felt that her concealment was indeed important, and hardly permitting herself to breathe, she remained motionless as a statue till the mason was dismissed, and M Collet and his party returned to the garden.

It was easy enough, from the nature of the structure, for the ear of Adèle to ascertain in which direction their steps were turned. The grotto-like wall of the ice-room, into which she immediately turned, formed the termination of the temporary buildings, and a small aperture of about two feet square had been left at one end of it for the purpose of bringing in the necessary relays of ices, without the inconvenience of conveying them through the house. This aperture was but imperfectly closed by a curtain, and here, without any risk of being seen, Mademoiselle de Cordillac placed herself.

It is not necessary again to go through the particulars of the objects disclosed by the operations of the police, nor can any be at a loss to imagine what must have been the feelings of Adèle as she saw them displayed. The dreadful evidence of violence, so much more decisive now than before, seemed, as she gazed upon it, almost to turn her to stone; and the strangers had departed, and all traces of their visit passed away, before she had sufficiently recovered herself to find her way back to her own room. But, being arrived there, she did indeed throw herself upon the bed; and grievously did she lament, during the first agonising moment of lying there, that she had not kept the promise so affectionately extorted by her sister, that she would try to sleep.

But as the first tumult of horror, terror, and confusion of intellect subsided, more settled, though not less miserable, thoughts took possession of her mind; and she began to examine herself as to what she ought to do under the extraordinary circumstances in which she was placed. It was impossible not to read aright the visit she had witnessed, – it was impossible that she could doubt having seen the agents of the police seek for, and discover, the traces of a fearful crime, or that they, too, as well as herself, felt a conviction that Mr Hargrave was implicated in it. But to her this idea came with a difficulty of belief, which made even the evidence of her senses appear doubtful. Far, too, from combating this incredulity, she cherished it; and most assuredly both her memory and her judgment furnished abundant arguments which seemed to prove that, despite all appearances to the contrary, it was impossible Mr Hargrave could have been guilty of the crimes which accident and the fatality of circumstances appeared to lay to his charge. With the resolute calmness which an urgent necessity is almost sure to inspire in such a mind as Adèle's, she once more set herself to examine all the facts which had come to her knowledge since this dreadful period of her existence began. She had heard Mr Hargrave engage an agent to assist him in obtaining possession of some female whom he professed to adore. He had paid a degree of attention to Madame Bertrand, which might easily enough be interpreted into making love to her. Madame Bertrand had subsequently disappeared, and Adèle had great reason to believe that Mr Hargrave had assisted in her abduction. This was bad enough, and sufficiently lamentable to cause her the deepest regret; but how immensely distant was such regret from the feelings which must follow upon believing that her step-father was guilty of the crimes which she could not doubt that the agents of the police were prepared to lay to his charge! But how was she to separate and divide events which were so closely woven together? How separate the abduction of Madame Bertrand from the horrible fate which had too evidently followed it?

Again and again did Adèle ponder over the possibility of so dividing into different events facts which seemed but part and parcel of one and the same, as to believe that her step-father had said the words which she heard him speak, and been in the places where she had seen him appear, and yet was neither an assassin nor a robber.

So strongly, indeed, did all she had ever seen and known of him plead against the possibility of his being guilty of the crimes which she felt certain would be laid to his charge, and so beyond measure improbable did it seem that a man in his worldly position, even if less averse to such acts by nature, should have committed them, that she finally brought herself to the conclusion that it was impossible, and that some turn in the labyrinth which she contemplated was concealed from her, which, if seen, would account for truth lying in one direction and the appearance of it in another.

To this belief she clung, and according to it she determined to act; and the first step towards putting this determination into practice was to seek Mr Hargrave the moment he should return to the house, and tell him of all she had witnessed in his absence. The resolution to do this, once taken, was a great relief to her; she should no longer have to groan under the weight of the oppressive secret, and whatever danger, whether just or unjust, real or imaginary, threatened the protector of her childhood, the husband of her mother, and the father of her beloved Sabina, she would have set him on his guard against it.

While these things were passing in the mansion of Mr Hargrave, that gentleman was enjoying an exhilarating drive up and down the Champs Elysées, and as far along the Boulevards as fashion would permit him to go. During the course of which drive he had met nine-tenths of the elegant idlers of Paris, to nearly all of whom he was known, and with many of whom he stopped to hear and to utter a light word or two upon the misfortune of the unlucky *millionnaire*, who had lost the pretty wife he had purchased, before he had got tired of her. To all of these Mr Hargrave related, with much humour, the tragic-comic scene which had been performed in his ball the preceding night, declaring, that though he could not but laugh at the recollection of poor M Bertrand's gesticulative despair, it had really affected him very differently at the time, and that, all jesting apart, he was very sorry for him.

All this lasted till nearly six o'clock, about which time he returned home, considerably fatigued by the exertions of both day and night, and throwing himself upon the sofa in the library, prepared to repose for a few moments before he dressed for dinner and for an evening engagement at the house of the —— Ambassador, which was to follow it.

Before he had lain there five minutes, his eyes closed and he dropped asleep; but ere this needed reprieve had lasted as many more, it was chased by the voice of Mademoiselle de Cordillac, who, having gently touched his shoulder with her finger, pronounced the word 'Papa!'

Mr Hargrave awoke with a violent start, and looked up with an eye that seemed to expect alarm: but the moment he saw Adèle, the expression of his countenance changed, and gaily taking her hand, he said, 'Sit down, my dear girl, I have something exceedingly amusing to tell you.'

Adèle, as we have seen, had managed to soothe herself into believing that it was as impossible, as it certainly was improbable, that her step-father could be guilty of the crimes which appearances seemed to lay to his charge; and though her knees trembled and her pulse kept no healthful time as she approached him, she was nerved for the task as much by the hope that naming the subject would lead to an explanation

of what was now so darkly difficult, as by that of preparing him for the
measures which the police were likely to take against him.

It may be thought, perhaps, that such an air of innocence on his part as
was displayed by the gay words he uttered upon seeing her, ought to have
increased her confidence and set her comparatively at ease; but it was not
so. On the contrary, there was something so revoltingly incongruous in
the tone to the actually known and acknowledged state of things, that she
felt as if the chill of death had seized upon her, and when she sat down it
was less for the purpose of listening to him than to prevent herself from
falling at his feet.

'I have taken a long drive,' resumed Mr Hargrave, 'and have
encountered half Paris, I believe; but to convey to you an idea of one half
of the comic stories that are afloat about little Madame Bertrand is, I am
afraid, impossible! Upon my honour, Adèle, I have laughed till I am as
weary as an old post-horse after his fourth stage, and it will be a proof of
immense affection and generosity if I rouse myself in order to
communicate a portion of it to you.'

'Do not, father!' said Adèle, in a voice that might have startled any
man, let his nerves have been in what state they would. Though speaking
to her, he had as yet hardly looked in her face, for he lay stretched with
apparent listlessness on his back, with his half-closed eyes fixed upon the
ceiling. But now he started up and gazed at her with orbs that seemed
starting from their sockets. All self-command was for the moment lost,
and fear and guilt looked out through every feature.

Adèle felt as if the dark curtain which concealed the truth had been
drawn up before her eyes, and that all which her soul shrunk from
looking on, was now disclosed. She, too, gazed both long and fixedly, and
the group might have served a copying sculptor well, for the two figures
sat as if they were already turned to stone.

Mr Hargrave attempted to speak; he would have asked her meaning,
but no sound proceeded from his dry and parted lips. But Adèle now
needed no questioning. Happily for all parties, the idea of Sabina seemed
suddenly to take entire possession of her; neither horror, indignation, nor
fear towards the miserable man before her, entered into her heart or
head. He must be saved! – Sabina's father must be snatched from the
horrible fate that was preparing for him, though all the *gensd'armerie* of
Paris were to rush forward to prevent her! When a woman of strong
feelings is placed in a situation sufficiently exciting to make her
thoroughly and entirely forget the weakness of her frame and the habitual
cowardice of her nature, she becomes as dauntless as an Alexander. Adèle
de Cordillac at that moment wholly lost sight of self, and this, together
with an important object to be achieved, suffices to make a hero.

No sooner had her mind received from the testimony of her eye the full conviction that Mr Hargrave was guilty, and consequently in the extreme of danger from the arrest which threatened him, than the conveying him instantly away seemed half accomplished; so completely, and without a second of interval, did it take possession of her thoughts.

'Father! there must be no questions asked, and I must manage for you,' she said, with a degree of sedate steadiness that did more towards bringing the unhappy man out of his seeming trance than any exclamations could have done.

'You know it all then, Adèle?' he replied, his fixed features relaxing and his pale lips trembling like those of a woman when in the agony that precedes the relief of tears.

'All, father, all! And you must leave Paris this night, and France with all the speed we may. The agents of police have been here, examined the garden, and found every thing! They think themselves secure of you, and we must make them think so still for a few hours. Dress instantly, command yourself during dinner, drink wine if you need it, leave the rest to me; but remember – *always* remember, that Sabina knows nothing, and NEVER shall! Beware of this, and take good care of her; should this fall on her, we all sink together. REMEMBER THIS! I ask no more of you, leave all the rest to me. Dress for the Ambassador's party, – dress instantly.'

With these words, Mademoiselle de Cordillac left the room, and felt, as she returned to her own, as if some unknown and supernatural power sustained her. She found her maid busily engaged in laying out the dress and the ornaments which she was to wear at the evening's *fête*, and walking to the bed and examining some of the finery which lay upon it, she said, in a voice perfectly steady though a little hoarse, – 'Go to my sister, Susanne. I was quite tired and ill when she went out, and greatly doubted if I should feel equal to this ball to-night; but tell her, – will you? – that I am so much better that I intend to dress and go.'

The maid left the room, and Adèle flew to ransack a shelf in her wardrobe, on which, among other preparations for the fancy-balls of the last carnival, was a pot of rouge. No disguise of wig, powder, or any thing else had ever so changed the appearance of Mademoiselle de Cordillac, as putting a large quantity of carmine upon her usually pale and delicate cheek; but, without intending to go the length of disguise, she applied it now, for she had caught sight of her almost ghastly face as she passed a mirror, and certainly did much towards restoring her usual appearance by the slight and cautious use of it. Thus prepared, she awaited the return of her maid, and then went through the business of dressing without the least appearance of agitation or even of indifference to the business that was going on.

'*Monsieur votre papa va en ville ce soir, avec ses demoiselles?*' said Susanne, interrogatively.

'*Mais, certainement,*' replied Adèle. 'What makes you doubt it, Susanne?'

'No, mademoiselle, it is not I that doubt it at all, for I know you never go out without him,' replied the girl; 'but it was Louis Querin who told me to inquire.'

'And what sets him thinking about it?' said Adèle, carelessly.

'That is more than I can say, mademoiselle. I don't know what he has got in his head altogether. There is nobody more *aimable* in general than Monsieur Louis, but to-day he has been so stiff and so silent that it was impossible to get a word or a look from him. The very first word I have had from his lips to-day – at least, since breakfast – was his asking me if *monsieur votre papa* was going to the ball to-night; and then when I answered, "Yes, to be sure he is," he began again about it, and in his old coaxing way of asking any thing, desired me to inquire particularly and to let him know before your dinner.'

'Satisfy him by all means, Susanne,' returned Adèle, with a familiar smile. 'We are all going to pass the night *chez M l'Ambassadeur de ——.*'

Mademoiselle de Cordillac was the first of the family who entered the drawing-room dressed for dinner, and to her great satisfaction her step-father was the next.

'This is well, papa,' she said, going up to him and speaking gravely, but kindly. 'I rejoice to see you alone for a moment without the appearance of seeking you.'

She then looked carefully round the noble drawing-room to ascertain that they were quite alone, and approaching nearer still, she whispered a few words in his ear which caused him to look at her with equal gratitude and surprise.

'Preserver!' he exclaimed; but if he wished to say more he was prevented by the entrance of Madame de Hautrivage, who, in full dress, swam up the room smiling in happy consciousness of the very peculiar elegance of her attire. Sabina followed the minute after, and began to challenge the looks of her sister, who in truth, despite her delicate touch of rouge, looked wan and hollow-eyed.

'You must not heed my looks, Sabina,' she replied aloud, as a servant entered to announce the dinner, 'I am perfectly worn out with these eternal *fêtes* and shall look no better till they are over.'

The dinner passed much as usual; for it Mr Hargrave and Sabina talked less, Madame de Hautrivage and her eldest niece talked more – the one from the joyous anticipation of an evening as successful as the last, and the other because she was steadfastly predetermined not to be silent.

Coffee followed them into the drawing-room as they re-entered it, and when this was dismissed and all the servants had left the room, Adèle rose from her seat, and going to the sofa where her aunt and sister were sitting together, she knelt upon a footstool at their feet, and taking a hand of each said with great solemnity, – 'Dear aunt! dear Sabina! I have heavy news to tell you; but if you have prudence and courage – if we have all of us prudence and courage – every thing may yet be well.'

'Heavy news!' was uttered by both the terrified females thus addressed in the same breath.

'What can you mean, Adèle?' almost shrieked Madame de Hautrivage.

'Speak, Adèle! speak!' muttered Sabina.

'I will speak,' returned the resolute girl, with astonishing firmness, 'and you must listen to me calmly and reasonably. My father – your father, dearest Sabina – has most rashly involved himself in a plot against the present Government, which, if he were taken at this moment, would probably endanger his life; but if he can contrive to escape from Paris to-night, will, it may be, produce no further ill consequences than the necessity of choosing for a time some other residence. But we must be both prudent and prompt in the aid we give him, or he is lost.'

'*Mais, mon Dieu! quelle aventure!*' exclaimed Madame de Hautrivage, turning her eyes to heaven. '*Cependant il faut faire l'impossible pour lui sauver.* for, after all, who can blame him! Thank God! there is nothing vulgar in the business! On the contrary, it is a romance of the highest interest, and if he succeeds, as we must all pray he may do, who shall say to what rank he and his family may not attain when the château next changes its inhabitants?'

While the prescient Madame de Hautrivage uttered this burst of prophetic wisdom, Sabina seemed struggling between life and death, and with one hand clasped by her father and the other by Adèle, was literally gasping for breath to speak. At length she said, – 'Father, I can do any thing! You shall find I am not weak; I will be strong as our glorious Adèle, who even now looks composed and self-possessed. Oh, happy Adèle! teach me, tell me what to do, and you shall find I am not unworthy of you.'

'Sit down, papa,' said Adèle, gently; '*et vous ma tante*, I pray you keep yourself from exclamations that may betray us. I am sorry to tell you that if papa is taken, perpetual imprisonment will be the consequence to us all: it is quite impossible that any of us should escape.'

'*Mais, Dieu m'en garde!*' exclaimed the terrified lady. 'In the name of the Virgin Mother, and all the blessed saints, her company, what am I to do? Tell me, Adèle! – tell me!'

'Endeavour to compose yourself, aunt, and decide at once whether it is your wish to share our exile, or whether you would deem it best, as, perhaps, it may be, to remain in Paris in your former apartments, and with every appearance of knowing nothing about the matter.'

'*Mais certainement, ma chère* – that, of course, is the only line of conduct for me to pursue. I will go to the ball, and my discretion shall be perfect.

I will return here to sleep, and in the morning pack up my little wardrobe and depart. *Heureusement ces choses là ne font pas de scandale — tout au contraire.* But you must tell me before we part, to what part of the world you are going during this little interval?'

'To England,' replied Adèle, — 'to London.'

'*Ah ça — c'est très-bien — mais parfaitement bien. Vous seriez tous, si bien là! Il ne faut pas m'écrire directement, vous savez, mais sans doute j'aurais bientôt de vos nouvelles.*'

Adèle nodded assent to this, and then turning to her sister, said, —

'Sabina, my dear love! I have the greatest confidence in your courage when called upon by such a crisis as this; and for the scheme I am about to propose to you, I shall require it all. Any other but yourself, dearest, might think that I imposed the heaviest task upon you, while taking a lighter myself; but you will not think so, Sabina, even when I tell you that I mean not to go to this ball to-night, although you must. Think you that you can bear this, and with such an aspect as may not do more harm than good?'

'Yes, Adèle, I do think so,' replied Sabina, fervently kissing the hand of her father, which still clasped hers, as if solemnly pledging herself to the task, and at the same time expressing the feeling which would enable her to perform it. 'And you, Adèle,' she added, with such a look of intense anxiety in her eyes as left no need of further speaking to express it, — 'what shall you do the while?'

'My purpose is to employ the interval that you are to pass at the ball, in *obtaining a carriage to convey us post to Calais, whence, if the starting of the packet favour us, we shall reach England in a few hours,*' said Adèle, with emphasis. 'Fear nothing,' she continued, 'about a change of dress — I will provide for that. Remember, father, that on leaving the carriage when you arrive at the Ambassador's, when the footman inquires at what hour you shall require it, you must reply, "*four;*" we are often later than that on these dancing occasions, and it can create no surprise. You will not object, aunt, to remaining till that hour, will you?'

'*Mais non, ma chère,*' replied the philosophical conspirator, '*quand on joue, on ne s'ennuie pas.*'

Madame de Hautrivage then rose, and offering her cheek to her brother-in-law, said that, her toilet not being yet '*absolument accompli,*' she was obliged to retire, and might not again find so favourable an opportunity of expressing her perfect esteem and admiration for his noble *dénouement* to the cause so near to her heart. She then embraced her two nieces, and charged them not to forget '*la pauvre tante*' in the gay scenes to which, of course, they would be immediately introduced at the court of England, where they were so well calculated to shine.

'You will, for this night, be profoundly silent, my sister, on all that concerns me?' said Mr Hargrave, earnestly.

'*Mais, mon Dieu, oui, mon frère!*' she replied, with some little appearance of displeasure. '*Est-ce que j'ai jamais de ma vie fait des imprudences? — et puis, croyez-vous enfin, que je désire être claquemurée tous mes jours pour l'amour de jaser?*'

And with these words she left them, to the great relief of the wretched man and the two innocent girls, who were now to sit in council upon all the details which concerned his liberty and life. The moment was an awful one to them all.

'Fear not her discretion, father,' said Adèle, answering to the anxious expression of Mr Hargrave's eye, as he watched his weak and heartless sister-in-law depart. 'Should she send all the *gens d'armerie* of Paris after us on the road to Calais, it would do us no harm, for we must travel by a route less likely to be thought of for us, even without the aid of our good aunt's tongue; and in a manner, too, as different as possible from what she has now heard me mention.'

'But who is there about us that you can venture to trust, Adèle?' said Mr Hargrave, almost in a whisper. 'If Roger, indeed — if Roger Humphries were returned —'

It was now Adèle's turn to change colour, and, alas! to feel also in some sort guilty. Had she not, in the feverish imprudence of her unauthorised feelings for Alfred Coventry, despatched this faithful servant on her own affairs, he would have been now at hand to give the aid so greatly needed, and which, most truly, they could look for, with perfect trust and confidence, from no other. She rested her aching head upon her hand, but said nothing.

'It is possible that he *may* be returned,' cried Sabina, thoughtlessly, starting from her seat, and seizing the bell.

Adèle shook her head, and almost groaned; while Sabina, now fully recollecting all the circumstances of his absence, heaved an unchecked sigh, and shook hers also. They both had but too good reason for fearing that this hopeful suggestion had no probability in it, yet still they both hung with deep anxiety on the reply of the servant who had answered the bell, to the question put by Mr Hargrave, — 'Is Roger returned yet?'

'No, sir, he is not,' replied Louis Querin, demurely, for it was he who had obeyed the summons; and after he had said it, he waited, with his large eyes in full activity, reconnoitring the group, as if expecting some order to follow.

'Tell him when he returns,' said Mr Hargrave, 'that I shall want another packet of the same crayons that he got for me last week, and that I shall desire to have them as soon as I am up.'

The handsome lip of Louis Querin curled into a smile, but he replied, with all observance, 'Yes, sir,' and retired.

'That man,' said Adèle, who had seen the smile, and perfectly understood it, — 'that man is under the orders of the police. The same chance that discovered the rest to me discovered that. Should he attend the carriage to-night, as I have no doubt he will, take care that he distinctly understands that it is your purpose to remain till four o'clock; he will hardly wait in the hall till that hour — he will go, probably, and return.'

'If he has it in charge to watch me, Adèle,' said Mr Hargrave, strongly agitated, 'I fear not — I fear not!'

Mademoiselle de Cordillac shuddered, and turned away her eyes from the troubled countenance that was directed towards her. All the horrid circumstances of the crime which the law was waiting to avenge recurred to her, and for a moment she doubted the rectitude of her own conduct. But the look averted from her step-father fell upon Sabina, and her fixed purpose returned in all its force.

'Perhaps this is what we have the greatest reason to fear,' she replied; 'but we must be prepared for it.'

She then explained briefly, but with perfect clearness, the plan she had arranged for meeting them in a *fiacre* at the corner of the street in which the Ambassador's hotel was situated; a white handkerchief, hanging from her hand out of the window, would shew them at what carriage they were to halt. Such a mode of taking their departure would have nothing uncommon in it, inasmuch as all persons (and there were many) who made use of a *fiacre* upon those occasions being obliged, by the regulations of the mounted patrol, to leave the vehicle at the end of the line.

'But should that man — that Louis stop us, Adèle, how are we to evade him?' demanded the trembling Hargrave.

'By in no degree appearing to evade him, sir,' replied his youthful counsellor. 'You must leave the rooms with Sabina, ready cloaked, on your arm, in the usual way, at about two. If you do *not* see Louis, pass out as if your carriage had been announced. The servants at the entrance, if they know you, will think that you are going to another party perhaps, or, at any rate, unwilling to wait till your people come up. Nor does it matter what they think. If, unfortunately, Louis is in the hall, and comes up to you, tell him that Sabina is suddenly taken ill, and that he must run with all speed for your carriage, declaring aloud your intention of waiting in the hall till he comes back. He will probably think you too safe there to make any difficulty of obeying you, and immediately after his departure let Sabina ask for the fresh air, and then lead her out. Should you recognise the carriage of a friend in the court, get into it, pleading Sabina's illness, and on reaching the end of the street, where I shall be stationed, get out, under pretence of having reached the dwelling of the medical man whom you wished she should immediately consult. You will see the handkerchief, and depend upon it I shall see you. You understand me – both of you?'

Both assured her that every word she had spoken was clearly understood, and would be well remembered.

Adèle then rang the bell, and desired her maid might be sent to her, for she felt unwell; and after swallowing a reasonable quantity of sal volatile, and so forth, she retired to her room, declaring herself too seriously ill to accompany the others to the ball.

The first proof given by Madame de Hautrivage of her perfect discretion was her exclaiming, pretty nearly aloud, to Sabina, after accompanying the invalid attentively to the bed-side, –

'*Comme elle joue bien la comédie, n'est pas?*'

Fortunately, however, this sally was not overheard, and the party set off, leaving the anxious Adèle to accomplish the task she had set herself.

During the short interval given by Madame de Hautrivage and Sabina to their attendance on Mademoiselle de Cordillac to her room, Mr Hargrave entered his library, as he keenly felt for the last time, and putting the moments as effectually to profit as if no such paralysing thought had occurred to him, he opened the secretary drawer, into which, for long years of reckless extravagance, he had been in the habit of throwing the large sums of ready money he kept for daily use, and drawing thence gold, and other valuables, to a very considerable amount, had the satisfaction of feeling that he carried away with him all the convertible treasure that was left from the wreck of his once ample fortune and many successful schemes; and the consideration tended to console him even in that moment of misery. He then hastily entered his own room, and threw together a few necessary articles of clothing for Adèle to convey, and then rejoined Sabina and her aunt.

CHAPTER XX

Susanne, the personal attendant of Mademoiselle de Cordillac, remained beside the bed of her mistress when Madame de Hautrivage and Miss Hargrave left her. As Adèle for a few moments lay perfectly still, the girl, who really loved her dearly, hoped that she had dropped to sleep, and was gently about to withdraw herself, when she was startled by her mistress's suddenly rising up from the pillow, and taking her hand.

'Susanne,' she said, 'am I right in believing that you love me?'

Earnestly and affectionately the girl replied that she should be the most ungrateful creature living if she did not.

'Then, Susanne, I will trust you, my good girl, with a secret dearer to me than my life;' and so saying, Adèle sprang from the bed, and began in all haste to disembarrass herself of her various ornaments.

So sudden a recovery, accompanied by such words, would probably have suggested to any waiting-maid in the world the idea of a love-affair; and, to a French one, any other interpretation was, of course, impossible.

'*Mais oui, mais oui!*' exclaimed the tender-hearted Susanne, with great unction; 'mademoiselle may confide in me as in her own heart. Ah! mademoiselle is too beautiful not to have many lovers!'

'That a lover is in the case, Susanne, I will not deny,' replied Mademoiselle de Cordillac, with a nod and a smile that in an instant awakened all the girl's sympathies in favour of whatever there was to be done or said in the business. 'But it is not *my* lover of whom I must speak to you, – it is the lover of the dearest friend I have in the world, or rather, Susanne, it is of herself. Have you courage enough to assist in saving her? For myself, Susanne, I give you my honour that I would die to do it!'

'*Que c'est beau!*' exclaimed the girl, raising her bright eyes to the ceiling, and then adding, with an accent of great enthusiasm, – '*Oui, mademoiselle* – anything and everything! There is nothing – no, nothing that I am not able and willing to do to serve so good a mistress in so good a cause.'

Adèle then explained to her that the friend in question, whom from delicacy, she said, she should forbear to name, had been most cruelly treated by her father, who had not only contrived to get the '*estimable jeune homme*' she adored sent to Africa, but insisted upon her marrying another immediately. 'This friend of her father's, Susanne, is the most odious creature that exists; old, ugly, jealous, and *si avare*, that he was never known to give away a franc in his life. – *Imaginez!*'

'Poor – poor young lady!' replied the waiting-maid, touched almost to tears. 'What is there we can do to help her?'

'Listen to me, Susanne, and you shall hear our plan. This hateful marriage is fixed for to-morrow; and to-night – this very night, Susanne – we must assist my friend to escape.'

'*Mais c'est tout naturel,*' replied Susanne.

'You must immediately contrive to bring into my room, unseen by every body, two of your own dresses, complete, – every thing, observe, from head to foot; and I will give you in exchange for them, – look here, Susanne, – these three silk dresses, and this favourite shawl that I have so often heard you admire. Will that content you?'

'Content me? Oh! mademoiselle, *c'est bien vous, ça!* And will you put on one of my dresses, mademoiselle? Ah! that is delightful!'

'Well, then, manage it all well for me, dear Susanne, and you shall be rewarded for it more hereafter. There will be no difficulty, I suppose, in your taking these dresses away? It will only appear that I have been giving them to you because I have done with them.'

'*Mais assurément*, mademoiselle! I should like to see anyone finding fault with me because it is your pleasure to give me a dress. There is nothing very new or surprising in that, mademoiselle. If you will be pleased to sit down and repose yourself for about five or ten minutes, I will be back again with all you want. *Mais tenez*, mademoiselle, – let me have some of your *collerettes* to put on the top of the basket in which I will bring the things for you and your friend; and then, if I chance to be met as I come back, it will pass for bringing your linen from the laundress.'

This clever proposal was readily agreed to, and the well-pleased Susanne set off upon her errand, thrice happy, – in obliging a mistress she loved, in making a splendid addition to her own wardrobe, and in being actively employed in a love-affair.

But the promised minutes of Susanne's absence were too precious to be spent in repose. No sooner had she left the room, than Adèle hastily collected, for herself and Sabina, a few needful articles of comfort, which she made into a parcel for Susanne to carry; while about her person she concealed a magnificent set of pearls, which her mother had received as a *cadeau de noces* from her father, and a few other valuable trinkets, which, with the small sum of ready money in her possession, would suffice to secure them from pecuniary distress during the interval which must necessarily elapse before she could hope to arrange her own affairs so as to ensure the regular receipt of her own income.

This necessary precaution taken, she ran to the apartment of Mr Hargrave, found the packet he had promised to leave, and then returning, so arranged her dress, as to be ready to assume in a moment the exterior garb which was to convert her into a *soubrette*. Before this was fully completed, the faithful Susanne returned, furnished so completely with all that was necessary for the double metamorphosis, that it would have been difficult to say whether she displayed therein most professional cleverness, affectionate attention, or masquerading readiness of invention.

The remainder of the dressing business was soon completed, and the suit intended for Adèle's '*friend*' being added to the small packet already prepared, nothing now remained but to get out of the house unseen, or, at least, unchallenged. And here the *savoir faire* of the waiting-maid was of essential service; and she assured her mistress, who trembled from head to foot when this critical moment arrived, '*Qu'il n'y avait rien au monde de si facile.*'

'But all the servants, Susanne?' said Adèle, as she cast a terrified look at the mirror, and shuddered at perceiving how very much less smart and *débonnaire* she looked in her new attire, than any individual she had ever seen of the class she was attempting to imitate. She fancied her awkwardness would bring all eyes upon her, and again repeated – 'Oh, Susanne! the servants! 'Twill be impossible they should not know me!'

'Why if mademoiselle presented herself in the midst of the *maisonnée,*' replied the girl, laughing, 'I would not undertake to answer for her passing unobserved, – Mademoiselle looks frightened, – *et nous autres, nous ne sommes pas comme ça*; but I am not *si bête* as to propose that mademoiselle should be seen, nor myself either. *Ciel!* going out at this hour! Not that there is danger in the streets either. We shall get a *fiacre* in a moment. *La place est tous près. Venez, mademoiselle! Ne craignez rien: je m'y connais si bien!'*

Adèle had no alternative but to trust entirely to her guidance; for in this part of the enterprise she felt as helpless as a child. But Susanne was no vain boaster, and it was soon evident that she knew perfectly well what she was about. The weary servants, too, had nearly all of them, long ago, retired to rest; and the obscure and, to Adèle, utterly unknown passages into which they turned, almost immediately after quitting her room, brought them, after many windings, both up and down, to a dirty little passage, leading from the offices into that corner of the garden from whence issued the *sortie* to the alley which has been already mentioned.

It has been said that the domestic architecture of France, and of southern Europe in general, if accurately examined by intelligent eyes, shews symptoms of a very remarkable degree of prescient attention to the probable wants and wishes of future inhabitants, in such articles as staircases, passages, and posterns, *à la dérobés*; and most certainly no ordinary English mansion could have afforded such facilities for escaping unseen as that through which poor Adèle had now followed her light-footed guide. Happily no sight or sound startled her in her progress; and it was probably another *nuance* of the same national amiability, which prevented the yawning *cocher*, when aroused by the voice and the touch of Susanne from the *dolce reposo* of his iron step, from testifying the very least possible degree of curiosity at the spectacle of two young girls, each carrying a bundle, desiring to be set down in front of the Chamber of Deputies at half-past one o'clock in the morning.

Having once mounted the rattling vehicle, Adèle felt that the most difficult part of her enterprise was accomplished, and throwing her arms around the neck of her humble, but most able assistant, she kissed her cheek, and thus addressed her, –

'Susanne! you have this night rendered me a service which, as long as I live, shall never be forgotten. The time I hope and believe will come, and at no very great distant period, when I shall be able to prove to you, by more than words, the gratitude I feel. But for the present, dear Susanne, we must part. I have promised my friend to go with her, and to go alone. I owe you two months' wages, Susanne, – here is the money; and here are a hundred francs more to take to your mother. If you will take my advice, you will remain with her till you hear from me, which you most assuredly shall do in some way or other ere long. Meanwhile, return to our hôtel, my dear Susanne. Pack up all that belongs to you, and leave Paris as soon as it is daylight. Will you promise me this?'

'I will promise, and I will do whatever you desire, my dear − dear mistress,' returned Susanne, bursting into tears; 'but I did not guess that our adventure was to end by our being separated.'

'It must be so, Susanne; I have pledged my word for it. But it is only for a time, my good girl. − Here we are! − God bless you, Susanne!' And again Adèle kissed her.

'My first duty is to obey you, mademoiselle, and that I will do, though it breaks my heart,' replied the girl; and silently complying with Adèle's whispered 'Go, dear Susanne, go!' uttered as the coachman opened the door precisely in the centre of the noble flight of steps which leads to the Gallic palace of wisdom, she sprang upon the pavement, and, after hastily pressing the hand of her mistress with her lips, she darted off towards the Rue de Lille without once turning her head to spy in what direction the *fiacre* proceeded after she left it. But Adèle followed her with her eyes as long as she was in sight, and registered in her heart this little trait of womanly feeling and true sympathy.

The coachman was then ordered to drive on to the spot at which she had promised to meet Sabina and her father; her hand rested on the window-frame next the pavement, and her white handkerchief reflected the glare of a gas-lamp that burnt before the still open door of a *café*. Nearly half-an-hour of agonising suspense followed, which, to Adèle's fevered nerves, appeared so long, that nothing but the evidence of her watch could have convinced her there might still be a chance of seeing those she so tremblingly watched for.

With what intensity of earnestness did she strain her sight in the direction from whence she hoped to see them come. The street was full of carriages of all ranks and degrees, waiting to convey the company from the ball; but on the *trottoir* there was scarcely a passenger to be seen.

At length it occurred to Adèle, that if they *did* come at last it would be a great relief to Sabina to find the door of the carriage open, that she might shroud herself at once within it; and to effect this, she let down the glass behind the sleeping coachman, and tugged at the cape of his ragged coat till he was sufficiently roused to understand that he was to get down and open the carriage-door for her.

Just as he had done this, and while Adèle was leaning forward from the carriage to make him comprehend that she wished it to remain open, with the steps down, two gentlemen, gaily laughing, lounged, arm in arm, out of the coffee-house, and stopping within the light of the lamp, to examine his watch, one of them exclaimed, – '*Trop tard? Mais non!* – *pas du tout.*' And so saying, he drew his friend away in the direction of the Ambassador's hôtel. It was Count Romanhoff who had thus spoke. Adèle knew his voice in an instant, and drew back, with a sudden movement, into the corner of the carriage. But it was too late, the Count had already caught sight of her face, and stood like one transfixed. But before Adèle could be conscious of this, he moved on, feeling that, as a gentleman, he was bound not to interfere with the incognito of a fair lady, but as thoroughly persuaded that he had seen Mademoiselle de Cordillac as if he had conversed with her for an hour.

At last, and when the almost gasping Adèle had nearly persuaded herself that all hope was past, and that Louis Querin had assuredly given Mr Hargrave into the hands of the police, her eye caught sight of the tall figure of her step-father, and of the muffled and hurrying Sabina at his side.

They had perceived, even before she had caught sight of them, the still extended handkerchief; and ere the lounging coachman, who was amusing himself by peering over the window-curtains of the coffee-room, could attend to the summon of Adèle, they were already in the carriage.

'Now, drive us to any hôtel near the Messagerie Royale that you think likely to be open, and you shall be well paid for your patience,' said Adèle to the coachman; to which order the man, now wide awake, replied with an expressive nod, which promised at once obedience and discretion. From the moment, indeed, that he had taken up the two young women, the man had felt quite satisfied that some one of those interesting little affairs were afoot which always ensure extra pay to the fortunate *cocher* engaged in them. What it might be he had not greatly troubled himself to guess. One of the bundles might contain a baby going to the Hôpital des Enfans Trouvés, or two suits of boys' clothes, in which the damsels were about to disguise themselves for a frolic. In either case he knew he should have a handsome *pour boire* for being patient, and therefore patient he had been; but, on getting sight of the stately figure of Hargrave, who was still pre-eminently handsome, and of the evidently youthful female on his arm, the coachman's imagination took a higher flight, – an elegant *escapade* appeared, written in silver characters, before his eyes, and the *fiacre* started off with a degree of velocity which, considering the hour, was truly astonishing.

As the distance was considerable, however, the agitated party within it had time to ask and answer many questions. Mr Hargrave and Sabina had walked through the crowd of servants assembled in the hall exactly as Adèle had directed, and had seen nothing of Louis Querin on their way. That clever personage was, indeed, at that very moment particularly engaged in receiving orders from M Collet, as to the manner in which he was to dispose of Mr Hargrave and the ladies upon their leaving the ball, it being decided that the suspected delinquent should be taken into custody before he re-entered his own house; and M Louis had just promised that he would make the coachman drive in the direction indicated, and, after the police had the gentleman in charge, that he would escort the ladies home, at the very moment that the fugitives were driving past the *corps de garde* where the consultation was being held.

The delay, which had appeared so interminably long to Adèle, had been occasioned solely by a lingering rubber of whist, in which Mr Hargrave had engaged, as a mode of escaping the innumerable questionings relative to Madame Bertrand, which met him on all sides.

Had any such assailed him, previous to his tremendous conversation with Adèle, he would have welcomed the occasion for the display of witty *innuendo*, and that sort of wordy fencing in which he delighted; perfectly preserved, by his matchless skill, from any hits himself, while thrusting right and left, with admirable grace and unfailing effect, against those he wished to attack. But now, the skull of Yorick was hardly in a worse plight than his own. 'Where were his gibes now? Not one left to mock his own grinning – quite chap-fallen!' In this state the card-table was a welcome refuge, of which he had eagerly availed himself; and notwithstanding his ticklish position, the twenty minutes of delay, which the last *partie* had caused, appeared less oppressive to him than to Adèle.

It is true he lost his money; and though the stakes were not high, he felt that the gold pieces he so gracefully delivered over to his adversary might soon be greatly needed by him; yet, nevertheless, he would rather have paid them ten times over than have been exposed to the '*Ah ça, mon cher Hargrave! dites moi,*' &c. &c. which he well knew he should encounter if seen wandering disengaged about the rooms.

Sabina, who behaved with a degree of firmness which she often remembered afterward with astonishment, had seated herself in the card-room, from which she never moved, pleading the over-fatigue of the preceding evening as a reason for refusing to dance.

The moment, therefore, that her father moved, she was at his side, and, wrapping herself, as she passed on, in the mantle which she had put off in the last room of the suite, they walked forth together, unchallenged, except by offers of service from the obsequious domestics, which were easily settled by '*Oui, oui, merci; mes gens sont là bas.*' This, together with the air of haste and *empressement* assumed by both father and daughter, sufficed to ensure their escape.

All this was explained as the *fiacre* rattled on, more rapidly than it has been done here; nor did it prevent Adèle from employing the interval in making Sabina exchange her white satin slippers for a more substantial *chaussure*, and exchanging the wreath upon her brow for a snug straw bonnet and veil. Her long, dark-coloured silk mantle did the rest, and, when they arrived at the hôtel which their intelligent *cocher* had selected for their accommodation, there was nothing in their appearance much unlike that of other travellers. The hat and large cloak of Mr Hargrave had, also, been selected with a view to his present use of them; and one of the parcels brought away by Adèle contained what was necessary to convert the very finest gentleman of a Parisian drawing-room into a tolerably unremarkable *voyageur*.

The timid 'Where are we to go, Adèle?' of Mr Hargrave, found place, also, before the carriage stopped, and was answered by his step-daughter thus, –

'Any where, sir, except to England. Fortunately, we may be very sure that Madame de Hautrivage will whisper our destination, such as she believes it to be, to so many of her dear friends, that, ere to-morrow night, half Paris will be ready to swear that we are on our road to London. This, of course, will send us in another direction, and either Germany or Italy might furnish a secure asylum. But, at the present moment, the finding three places unoccupied in the same diligence must, I think, decide the route by which we set off.'

'Adèle!' said Sabina, with sudden energy, 'you name Germany. Do you remember the half-dilapidated castle near the Mummelsee? The young man we saw there told us that some of the rooms were habitable, – do you remember, Adèle? – but that no one had the courage to inhabit them? Would not this place suit us well?'

'Indeed it might,' replied Adèle, thoughtfully, and endeavouring to recall all the circumstances of the happy morning in which they had together visited the spot to which her sister now alluded.

'Do you speak, Sabina, of the marvellous edifice of which you told me so much at Baden? – the castle that seems to vanish and return?' demanded her father, with a good deal of animation; and on receiving an answer in the affirmative, he added, 'Then let us go there, Adèle. The superstitious legends connected with it may be turned to good account in such a situation as ours – as mine.'

'Is not Baden-Baden too near and too public?' demanded Adèle, doubtingly.

'What need have we of Baden?' said Sabina. 'Is there not the remote and unfrequented little town of Gernsbach? This would be amply sufficient to supply all our wants. And who among the gay throngs of Baden-Baden will be likely to hear that a young peasant girl, speaking German but clumsily, goes now and then to purchase household commodities at Gernsbach?'

'Perhaps we cannot do better – at least for the moment,' replied Adèle.

Then it must be the Strasbourg diligence we inquire for,' she added; 'and Heaven grant we may find three places unsecured!'

This decision was arrived at within two minutes of their reaching the hôtel, and it enabled Mr Hargrave to inquire, with a tone of very desirable certainty as to whither he wished to go, whether they could have three places in the first diligence about to depart for Strasbourg. A certain *commissionaire* of the establishment, who had greatly the air of having been exempted by Providence from all necessity of sleep, answered 'Yes,' it being one of his multitudinous duties to ascertain the state of the way-bill at the neighbouring Messagerie before their office closed for the night.

While Mr Hargrave was thus engaged, Adèle dismissed her well-pleased *cocher*, and the harassed party then retired to their rooms, from whence they were to be summoned in time for breakfast before the departure of the diligence.

That the sisters asked for *one* room for their accommodation will be easily believed, and that then locking the door which secured them in it, and taking refuge in each other's arms, was the greatest relief – the greatest joy, that either of them was at that moment capable of receiving.

But who that had watched that cordial embrace could have guessed the total absence of confidential openness which wrung the bosom of poor Adèle as she fondly pressed her lips upon her sister's forehead? All, or very nearly all, that made the misery of the elder sister was as utterly unimagined by the younger as if the distance of the poles had divided them. Yet, there they sat, side by side, the hand of one clasped in that of the other, perusing, with looks of love, each other's face, to see how the rude adventure was borne. But all that was in common between them was their mutual love.

In almost any other imaginable case, such conscious delusion, such entire absence of sincerity in every word she spoke, would have greatly increased the suffering of the high-minded and truth-loving Adèle; but as it was, it afforded her the only stimulant and the only consolation which could have sustained her in her bold enterprise. The very agony she herself suffered, as her mind reverted to all she knew and all she guessed concerning Mr Hargrave, made the concealing it from Sabina a task that seemed to bring courage with it, despite all its terrible suffering; and when at length she saw her young sister drop asleep on the pillow beside her, she watched her slumbers as a mother might do those of a darling infant whom she had saved from violent and sudden death.

The miserable, dirty, comfortless vehicle, into which the delicately nurtured girls and their guilty protector were to make the tedious journey to Strasbourg, was announced as ready to start at a few minutes past seven o'clock. The eager step with which Mr Hargrave obeyed this summons made Adèle shudder; while Sabina, who also remarked it, felt her heart bound with a joyous emotion, as she thought that the danger, which the too chivalresque spirit of her beloved father had brought upon himself in support of the exiled family, was so nearly over, and her own bounding step sprung after him joyously.

The tedious, irksome, and most fatiguing journey was got over without interruption or alarm of any kind. At Strasbourg, the party furnished themselves with wearing apparel of very nearly the humblest description, differing little from that of the better sort of peasants or small farmers; and this needful business performed, they proceeded with a *voiturier*, hired for the whole distance, to Gernsbach, where they took up their quarters at a small *gasthaus*, which, though the best in the place, was by no means of an order to consider guests of their rustic appearance intruders.

Sabina being by far the best German scholar amongst them, undertook the task of explaining to the kind and simple-hearted good folks of the house the reasons why their father, who was an English farmer, had been obliged to leave his country from having

'Lost his little all in a lawsuit;' –

with various other interesting particulars of which her imagination formed a net-work for the protection of her father, which she deemed it not a sin to use.

It was agreed amongst them that, as this tale was received with the greatest sympathy and kindness, they should go on to state their wish of finding some little cottage in the neighbourhood which might furnish an unexpensive residence, reserving all mention of the castle till they had examined it, and ascertained whether it would serve them as a decent shelter; in which event their intention might be mentioned as the result of an accidental discovery.

The family at the little *gasthaus* consisted of an infirm old man, who, though the master of the establishment, had nothing to do with it, except bowing his head in salutation to the guests who in winter approached the chimney, and in summer the garden door, where his arm-chair was stationed. All the weight of the concern fell upon his widowed daughter, a stout, buxom, hard-working, light-hearted *frau* of fifty, and her fair-haired daughter, Gertrude.

The most superficial observer, in travelling through Germany, must have remarked the tendency there is in all ranks of the people with whom business, pleasure, or mere accident brings him in contact, to mix kind feeling in the intercourse. This is the case where there is much less to excite it than Gertrude and her mother found in the desolate girls who now asked for their friendly aid; and, accordingly, the sort of intimate intercourse which established itself between them was very speedily cemented on all sides by a strong sentiment of affection. Harsher natures, indeed, than those of the Frau Weiber and her daughter Gertrude might have been won by the looks and words of Adèle and her sister. There was in the manner in which they both entered upon the business before them so much gentle courage, yet so much innocent ignorance, that it would have been difficult for them to have been seen with indifference anywhere, and in Germany it was impossible. Before they had been three days at Gernsbach, Frau Weiber would have walked five miles barefoot to do them pleasure, and Gertrude would have run ten.

Little did either of these simple-hearted creatures guess, however, how precious was their kindness or how needful their aid. Little did they guess the miserable feelings made up of pity and abhorrence, with which Adèle regarded the lately loved protector of her youth, or the agony of tender alarm with which Sabina watched the prostrate spirit of her altered father. Had they known all, however, they could not have done more to comfort them; for all that genuine womanly kindness or active thoughtful attention could do, they did. Nor were their efforts vain; for, without their friendly support, it may reasonably be doubted if these fragile daughters of opulence and ease could have got through all the difficulties they had to encounter.

The first day or two after their arrival at Gernsbach, Mr Hargrave either was, or fancied himself to be, extremely ill; and any idea, either of leading him out upon an exploring expedition, or of leaving him alone, was equally out of the question. But this time was not altogether lost; for it enabled both the girls to establish themselves so firmly in the good graces of their hostess and her daughter, as to remove, in a degree which they wondered at themselves, the forlorn wretchedness of being among strangers. During this interval, both the mother and daughter mentioned so many little dwellings in Gernsbach and its neighbourhood, which were either wholly or in part untenanted, that Adèle felt strongly tempted to abandon this romantic search after the mystic castle, and content herself with such concealment as their remoteness offered. But never, on any former occasion, had she seen Sabina appear so resolute in purpose as on this. With tears in her eyes, she conjured her sister not to give up the project which had brought them there, till they had found reason to believe it was impracticable; and though the worn spirit of Adèle would have rejoiced at abandoning further enterprise, that tender pity which always arises in our hearts for misfortunes greater in extent than the sufferer to whom they attach is aware, led her to yield to pleadings in which she thought she saw more whim than reason.

CHAPTER XXI

A morning of the brightest German sunshine seemed in some degree to revive the wretched Hargrave, and he himself suggested the necessity of actively entering upon their search for the profound shelter which he had been taught to hope for. He declared himself, however, perfectly incapable of accompanying his daughters on the expedition which he wished them immediately to undertake, pleading continued illness as an excuse for remaining in his room; but Adèle read in one glance of his now-often averted eye the true feeling which thus made him a prisoner. Terror of discovery lurked in every line of his sunk and altered visage, and the glance he now gave her spoke an imploring petition that she would not urge him to shew himself.

This was more than enough to make her even entreat him to remain at home. Her intercourse with him was become acutely painful, and every accident which lessened it was a relief. To such a mind as hers, the crimes of which she knew him to be guilty made him an object of abhorrence; while care for the peace of Sabina, now become the only object for which she wished to live, forced her to assume feelings towards him so foreign to her heart, that it was most painfully difficult for her honest nature to assume them. On his side, too, the intercourse was terrible. It was no longer love and affection that he felt for her. Such feelings cannot exist without the belief, at least, that they are reciprocal; and did he not know that Adèle, whose admiration he had so dearly loved to win, must loathe him? No! it was no longer tender affection that he felt for her, but a sort of abject and dependent gratitude, strangely mixed with fear. She alone of all his former admiring friends knew of his guilt; and had it not been that he still clung to her with hopes of aid and protection, he would have given his right hand never to have beheld her more.

It might not have been very difficult, perhaps, for Adèle to guess as much, had she set herself either to watch or to divine his feelings. But she did neither. Sabina was the centre of every thought that employed her mind, – Sabina, so lately the idol of all the bright world in which she had lived – the beloved, the admired, the envied, the desired of so many hearts, now the exiled companion of a guilty felon – loving him in her ignorant innocence more fondly than ever, and even finding consolation under all her sorrows and privations from the fancied nobleness of the abject being who had destroyed her! All this formed a picture so full of woe, that the very soul of Adèle melted in pity as she thought of it; and her own share of the misery was often as completely forgotten as if she did not feel it.

It suited not with the manner in which this castle scheme was eventually to be made known to their friendly hosts, that they should previously make any inquiries of them concerning it. The two girls, therefore, set forth in search of it without venturing a single inquiry as to what direction they were to take. But the impression left upon the mind of Sabina concerning its locality was wonderfully clear, considering the manner in which she had seen it. She knew that though not on the road to Baden, it lay between Gernsbach and that place; – she knew, too, that it was neither on the level of the Mourg, the lovely stream on which the town was built, nor yet upon the summit of the bold hill above it. All this she explained to Adèle; and therefore, on quitting Gernsbach, which they took care to do on the mountain-side of the river, they turned their steps from the precipitous road which descended from it along the corn-fields which spread along the sides of the declivity.

Poor girls! their young feet stepped lightly over the undulating path, and their spirits were braced to great energy by the importance of the enterprise they had undertaken; but the hearts of both were sad. It was not the contrast of this rough walk with the luxury of the conveyance which had before brought them within sight of the object they were now so laboriously seeking; nor the coarse garments, in which they looked like pearls encompassed with a setting of iron; nor yet the absence of the admiring eyes in the presence of which they were wont to move, like stars of brightness along the unclouded vault of heaven; it was none of all this that made them sigh as they pressed each other's arms while they walked on in silent musing. Each had her separate and her different cause for sorrow; and though the elder was incomparably the most miserable of the two, the younger felt her spirit bent to the very earth as she remembered the sunken eye and languid smile with which her father had received the caress she bestowed upon him at parting.

For above two miles their path lay so plainly in the direction which Sabina wished to follow, that there was no need of consulting each other as they followed it; and during nearly the whole of that distance Adèle enjoyed the doubtful advantage of uninterrupted meditation on all her various sources of unhappiness. Had Coventry received her note? Did he at length know, or, at any rate, had he at length reason to believe, that she was not the heartless and capricious thing she had appeared to him? Where was the good and faithful Roger? What would be his feelings on returning from the too-zealous enterprise she still attributed to him, upon finding that they were gone, none knew where? And this concealment, so painful, indeed, in the case of their attached old servant, but so vitally necessary to their preservation, as to all others, could they be secure that it would continue? The thought that there might be a possibility of all their efforts being vain, – that the lynx-eyed police might find them even here, – that discovery, shame, conviction, and death, might dog their guilty companion, and find him, despite of all they had done or could do to conceal him, shot through the brain of the unhappy girl with such keen agony, that she groaned aloud.

'Alas, Adèle! my dearest, dearest sister! how grievously must you be suffering to utter such a sound as that! Are you wearied, Adèle? or are you frightened at our loneliness?'

'Forgive me, sweetest!' replied the conscience-struck Adèle, shocked to think how ill she was performing the task she had imposed upon herself: 'I was thinking of our dear old Roger and poor Coventry. But I will be so silly and so selfish no more. I am not in the least tired, Sabina. Which of those two paths, think you, should we follow now?'

'Perhaps, Adèle, you think the search for this remote shelter unnecessary, and even childish? Perhaps you think our better course would be to take steps that Roger may know where to find us? It may be, I do think, Adèle, that the terror of pursuit which first seized us, however reasonable it might be in France, ought greatly to be softened here. It is not very likely – is it? – that the government of Baden should be greatly on the *qui vive* to seek out persons suspected only of being hostile in their wishes to the present dynasty of France? If, indeed, we find this wild place capable of being converted into a tolerably comfortable residence, we may persuade my dear harassed father to inhabit it for a time; but if not, I am quite ready, Adèle, to give it up, and to persuade him to look out for something where you would feel less miserably forlorn.'

'No, no, Sabina! you are wrong, – quite wrong,' cried Adèle, earnestly, while a tremor ran through her whole frame. 'Believe me, dearest, we might be leading him into great danger were we for a single moment to relax our efforts to keep him concealed. It must not be thought of! Let us walk stoutly on, Sabina: and God grant that this strange castle that we used to jest about may speedily be visible to our eyes, but unseen, if possible, by all the world beside!'

Thus urged, Sabina again started forward in the path which she fancied the most likely to lead them right, for again she felt as eager as ever to secure the sort of almost supernatural protection which she fancied this lonely place would furnish. Fortunately for her sister, Sabina had never inquired as to the particulars of the political plot in which she believed her father to be entangled. She shrunk from the idea of knowing what even in her dreams she might betray. But her confidence in the judgment of Adèle was unbounded, and perceiving that she thought all possible precaution necessary, her fancy for the mysterious castle again returned upon her with all its first strength, and she would almost have thought herself guilty of all her father's danger had she relaxed in her efforts to obtain what she firmly believed would be the greatest security. But the nature of the ground they were upon almost baffled her determination to supply Adèle's avowed ignorance of their route, by the aid of her own

fanciful ideas concerning it; for the uneven surface they were passing over
was sometimes raised so high, and at others dipped so low, as to make her
change her opinion every five minutes as to whether they were right or
wrong. At length, however, they reached the top of one of these swelling
hillocks, which, to Sabina's great joy, was high enough to give them a
distinct view of the little lake known by the name of the Mummelsee.

'There it is! – there is the Mummelsee!' she exclaimed. 'Now, Adèle, I
know we are right. There (raising her right hand) is the mountain; and
there (pointing with her left) is the lake. Now then, observe, our castle
must be somewhere between the two. Do you see any object, Adèle, as
far as the lake extends, that looks at all like a castle?'

Had Adèle been in better spirits she would certainly have replied,
'Nothing! yet all that is I see;' but now she only shook her head, and
replied, 'I think you must be mistaken, my dear, about the place, there is
certainly no castle there.'

'And so you thought, Adèle, when you looked down from the rocks
above, now nearly a twelve-month ago. Do you not remember saying
then that you were sure there was no castle there? And yet, within a few
hours of your saying so I saw, as plainly as I see you now, a vast edifice of
stone, exactly upon the spot we had looked down upon.'

'The curly-haired young man told you so, my love,' returned Adèle,
with a faint smile. 'But I do not think it is very certain that you saw it
yourself. Do you?'

'Oh, Adèle! Do you really think I would have made you take this long
walk had I not been quite certain that there was neither fancy nor
delusion in the case? Be sure – be very sure, there is a castle somewhere
thereabouts,' said Sabina, pointing towards a spot at which nothing was
visible but one of the sudden little hills, of which they had already
climbed so many.

'Then let us go on, Sabina,' replied her sister, with renovated spirit:
'this is not an hour of such idle talk as that when last the existence of this
peep-bo edifice was discussed between us; and I feel as sure of your being
in earnest now, as I was doubtful of it then. I almost wish, Sabina, we
might see the curly hair again, he would tell us all about it directly.'

'You would pass by without knowing him if he stood here in the path
before you,' returned Sabina, with a melancholy smile and varying cheek.

'Oh, no! I should not,' returned Adèle, laughing. 'Though I will
confess that I believe you looked at him with more attention than I did.
But I declare that I think I should know him by the same sort of features
which the enamoured lady points out in the song:–

> "Oh! by his pilgrim hat and staff,
> And by his sandal shoon."'

'Ah! there it is,' said Sabina, in an accent of reproach; 'you saw his dress, and nothing else, and therefore, were he to appear before you in another dress, you would pass him by as one you had never seen before, or else——' But these last words were inaudible.

'I think it is very possible I might,' replied Adèle, with a sort of mock gravity that made poor Sabina sigh, by recalling the gay tone of other days. 'But there is a reason for that,' added Adèle; 'for his dress really was remarkable: it was something between a hunter of the Alps on the stage and a real *bonâ fide* German botanist in a forest. So no wonder I remember it.'

'Oh, dear no! I am not at all surprised that you should remember his dress,' returned Sabina; 'though I may be a little so at your remembering nothing else.'

Adèle turned suddenly round as she walked to look at her. It was the first time that she had thus openly avowed that on herself the impression made by the young stranger's appearance was deeper than ordinary; and the downcast eye and glowing cheek she encountered increased her surprise. She again answered gaily however, saying, 'Yes, but I did, Sabina. Have I not always remembered his curly hair?'

'Have you never seen anyone since whose hair was the same?' said Sabina. 'Have you never met anyone in Paris who struck you as very like him?'

'No, dearest, I cannot say that I ever did. But, by the question, you have, I presume. Who was it, Sabina?'

'Prince Frederic of ——,' replied Sabina, gravely.

'Prince Frederic of ——! Surely, dearest, you have lost your wits, or say this only to amuse me by its out-of-the-way incongruity. The one, saving your presence, having very much the air of a handsome peasant boy, and the other, that of the most accomplished prince in Europe!'

'Adèle,' returned her sister, 'I know not how it happened that I never told you of it, but do you remember when we stopped the carriage for the second time upon the mountain-road? – do you remember that when I got out, you refused to accompany me, and that I went to the rock alone?'

'Yes, dear, I remember it perfectly,' was the reply.

'Well, Adèle, I saw him again then.'

'Saw whom?' demanded Adèle, with one of her own smiles, 'Prince Frederic of ——?'

'I could almost think so,' said Sabina.

'There is certainly some very mysterious influence in yon lake of the Mummel folk,' replied Adèle; 'for I remember thinking that your head wandered a little when we were near it last, and now I am quite sure of it.'

'Yes,' said Sabina, sadly, 'my head wanders now, Adèle, from the present to the past: I cannot account for it. But the idea that Prince Frederic and the young man seen upon that rock are the same, returns upon me at this moment with a force that I can no way explain. It is very strange. Is it not very strange?'

'Strange, you mean, that such an idea should occur to you at all. It surely is, – *very strange*. But what do you mean, my dear, by talking of its returning upon you? You do not mean to say that such an idea ever seriously suggested itself to you at Paris?'

'It did once, Adèle, and then I asked the Prince if he had ever been at Baden. Upon which he shook his head, in token of denial as I thought; and immediately after his whole manner changed, and he spoke, and looked, and moved, so like the noble gentleman he is, and so unlike the humble swain I had dared to fancy him, that I felt quite ashamed of myself, and never again permitted my thoughts to take the same direction. But now, in spite of myself, it comes back upon me. I remember so freshly, as I look out upon that lake, and the hills beyond it, the countenance I saw when last I looked upon them, that I could almost fancy I saw it still, and that it was the same, and no other, as that of Prince Frederic.'

'And now, dear love, dismiss the idea again as fast as you can,' said Adèle, 'for trust me it is worthless and unsound. – But, mercy on me! What have we got here? A castle, sure enough, and, ruinous though it be, a most enormous one!'

For the last few minutes of the foregoing conversation the sisters had been toiling up the abrupt acclivity of one of the little hills before mentioned, and having reached its summit, perceived immediately before them, but at a much greater depth than that to which the ground sank on the side from whence they came, a widely extended edifice of stone, in a state of rapidly approaching dilapidation, but bearing every appearance of having once been a princely residence.

'That yon castle should be completely invisible from Gernsbach and its neighbourhood, is satisfactorily explained by this bold and lofty mass of rock,' said Adèle, gazing at the picturesque scene before her with equal surprise and pleasure. 'But why it should be concealed from the eyes of those who stand on the cliff above it on the other side, I can by no means conjecture. It seems impossible.'

'Yet you yourself, Adèle, stood on a projecting promontory of that cliff, and saw no castle,' said Sabina.

'Most true, I did so stand, and most true is it, also, that I saw no castle. But, Sabina, look down from hence, here, close to the very edge of this fine precipice, and I think you will be able to guess at the explanation of the mystery. Do you not perceive that a wild fosse runs entirely round this deserted château? Depend upon it, that the fairies who have driven the Grand Ducal mortals hence, and then thought proper occasionally to conceal the spot once honoured by their residence from ordinary eyes, haunt the place in the shape of vapour, mist, and fog, – all very poetic forms, you will allow, and exceedingly appropriate to this particular region. But, all jesting apart, can you not easily conceive that on a foggy day the evaporations from that stagnant water, finding it impossible to make their way into upper air through the already moisture-charged atmosphere near the lake, may settle down in the form of a heavy veil upon these turrets and domes in such a manner as to make them quite invisible?'

'I do, indeed,' replied Sabina. 'And though this explanation, with a power as strong as that which occasionally removes the mist, blows away a vast deal of shadowy poetry before it, I readily welcome it. And now that we understand all about it, let us try to get down to it – shall we, Adèle? It is quite evident that, though deplorably out of repair for a princely residence, there must be a multitude of rooms within its wide extent which would still afford a dwelling.'

'And it may be a very commodious one, too, particularly through the dry months of summer, which are now approaching,' replied Adèle. 'I really think that your notion may turn out at last to be very valuable, for if any superstitious prejudice really exist against this remote shelter, it would render it invaluable to us. But as to getting down to it from the spot where we now stand, I am afraid it is impossible.'

'There must have been some approach to it, and we must set about finding in what direction,' said Sabina, changing her position again and again, by springing actively from rock to rock. 'As to the approach that has been,' said Adèle, remaining stationary, and sheltering her eyes with her hand, so as to enable her to 'look out afar,' towards Baden-Baden, 'I fear that I perceive it very clearly in the very last direction where I would wish to find it, namely, approaching in very stately style, between two rows of poplars, from the bath of baths. My only hope is that, broad as the way looks, it may no longer be very practicable, and, moreover, that we may be able to find some humble and near access on the side of our quiet, friendly Gernsbach.'

'But which way will you turn to find it?' asked Sabina, by this time quite convinced that the château was impregnable by a direct descent from the rock on which they stood.

'My counsel is *reculer pour mieux sauter*,' said the elder sister. 'Let us walk back a little, and I think the chances are that we shall find we can get down to the level on which this huge building stands without breaking our necks by attempting to descend this unpromising rock.'

In pursuance of this opinion, the two girls, too much excited at this moment to remember their fatigue, turned back towards Gernsbach, but by means of seizing upon every opportunity which the ground afforded for getting lower and lower on the side of the hill which sloped towards the Mummelsee, they succeeded, in very satisfactory accordance with Adèle's prediction, in getting to the level of the lake; and having achieved this, a path that had evidently been once widely trod, but which was now but faintly visible, led them by the most direct line possible, from the shores of the little lake to a small postern entrance, where a rickety bridge for foot-passengers crossed the moat, and conducted them to the offices of the *ci-devant* Grand Ducal residence.

Short of absolute, total, and entire devastation, there is nothing which gives to an edifice that has once been the dwelling of man so complete an air of ruin and desolation as the creaking hinges of a long-unfastened door. It was by such a portal as this that the two daughters of the high-born Adèle de Tremouille found their way into the forsaken building wherein they hoped to hide that noble lady's much-loved husband; and such was the urgent necessity for concealment which pressed upon the hearts of the two motherless girls, that upon a look and word being exchanged on discovering this symptom of utter abandonment, they both as by one common impulse exclaimed, –

'Thank God! if we can but find a shelter, there is no-one who will disturb us here!'

Fortunately the sun was still high in the heavens; and the light breath of spring having dispersed the vapours which heavier seasons generated, the broken casements, as they passed along, let in upon them nothing but gentle warmth and invigorating freshness; so that their long passage from the inferior to the superior chambers rather augmented than diminished their earnest hope of finding a habitable shelter within the forsaken walls.

As they continued their progress, however, they naturally confessed to each other that there could be nothing to wonder at, in a land whose sovereign possessed residences innumerable, and boasting among them of almost every possible species of attraction, that the dwelling through which they were now passing should be left to desolation and decay.

'I suspect,' said Adèle, 'that in days of yore the now quiet little town of Gernsbach might have been a place of sufficient consequence to look for the inspiring effect of the sovereign's presence near it for a week or two in every year. But whether the little town fell into atrophy and weakness, and so let go its hold of the Grand Duke; or that the Grand Duke, finding that he could bear these dismal walls no longer, forsook the little town, and that it has faded and dwindled away in consequence, demands a more learned chronicler than I am to expound; but one or the other has been the case, depend upon it.'

'Then it must have been the decadence of the town that led its prince

to think his presence might be more beneficial elsewhere,' replied Sabina:
'for I never can believe the sovereign owner of this noble dwelling, with
its sublime air of solitary grandeur, would ever have forsaken it in mere
distaste. Look through that long line of open doors, Adèle. What a
splendid suite! Fancy them richly hung and brightly furnished, and then
say if they would not be a dwelling worthy of a prince! I think I know
one who fancied them so.'

Adèle smiled, and shook her head: 'You never knew any such person,
depend upon it. But, mayhap, it may amuse you, Sabina, so to people this
desert, if indeed we are to shelter ourselves within its citadel. But do you
think it will be possible?'

'Why not, Adèle?' returned the other, with some quickness. 'Here are
a multitude of rooms in perfectly good repair; and among that quantity of
dilapidated old furniture that we passed in the smaller rooms before we
entered upon this noble suite, I doubt not we should be able to find
chairs and tables, beds and boxes, and all other needful commodities for
our temporary hiding-place; unless, indeed, you think, my dearest Adèle,
that poor papa would find it painfully dismal for him.'

The fair brow of Adèle contracted by a sort of involuntary impulse,
and she answered with quickness, 'The difficulty will not lie there, I
imagine.' But immediately checking the feeling to which the idea of her
step-father's wish for a gayer residence had given rise, she added, 'But
how, Sabina, are we to obtain permission to occupy these rooms, and
make such free use, as you suggest, of the old furniture within them?'

'If what the – if what that young stranger said be true,' replied Sabina,
after a moment's meditation, 'there are superstitious terrors connected
with this place, which would render our entering it a matter of very light
trespass. Go where we will, Adèle, some human beings must be in our
confidence, or we must perish. May I not then speak to my friend
Gertrude on the subject? I believe that pretty girl loves us already, Adèle,
well enough to serve us more faithfully than so short an acquaintance
would make it reasonable to expect; and I confess I should not feel the
least afraid of trusting her, – should you?'

'No, I should not. Her circle of gossips must be so small, that I doubt
her power to harm us even had she the wish; and that her feelings are all
made up of truth and kindness to us, I am as sure as you are,' replied
Adèle. 'But alas!' she added, with a heavy sigh, 'how easy of achievement
do things appear at a distance, which when we draw near and set about
their accomplishment prove full of difficulty. Oh dearest Sabina! we have
much to do; and helpless fine ladies as we are, how shall we set about it?
Food, fire, beds, attendance – things that as yet have seemed to come to
us like the air of heaven, unsought for and yet found. God help us, my
poor Sabina! we have much to learn. As far as courage and enterprise,

and such ladylike qualities could carry us, we have done very well. Our being here, apparently in undisturbed possession of what I question not is a Grand Ducal residence, and haunted by fairies besides, is no bad proof of this. But for the detail of daily existence, alas! alas! where are we to begin?'

'Will you trust this to me, my darling Adèle?' cried Sabina, eagerly. 'Have you not done enough? Our marvellous escape – which even now seems like a dream – did *you* not do it all? Then is it not my turn? Besides, what seems difficult and irksome to you will be but delightful occupation to me. The idea of inhabiting this wild place has something in it which inspires me. I even doubt if on my own account I shall long be able to regret the monotonous routine of Paris. The Prince was not at *my last ball*, Adèle. He told me when we left the supper-table, on what was probably the last *very* happy evening of my life, that he should see me but once again before he left Paris: this was to have been at his own *fête*, you know. But Providence forbade that interview from which my poor father expected so much. But these dreams are all over now, Adèle; and what can be so likely to cure me of remembering them as making me your active *ménagère*?'

At the moment Sabina began speaking they had reached in their progress through the long suite of rooms on which they had entered one which had still various articles of faded furniture in it. Their progress through the perspective of open doors which Sabina had observed upon led them, *of course*, before a long line of windows, which looked out upon the Mummelsee lake, and the bold outline of lofty hills, dark in their 'Black Forest' clothing, beyond it. Here they paused as by tacit but mutual consent; and seating themselves upon a mighty sofa, which seemed to stretch out its massive arms to invite them to rest, Sabina was tempted to talk and Adèle to listen, till both had quite forgotten how strange was the place in which they thus reposed, and how strangely they had taken possession of it.

'What do you mean, Sabina?' said her sister when she ceased speaking: 'what was it your father expected from that meeting?'

'*Your* father!' repeated Sabina, reproachfully. 'Adèle! you never used that phrase before. Why do you not call him still papa? You do not feel that he is less your father because his exalted feelings have led him into danger? – that is impossible.'

'Quite – quite impossible!' replied Adèle. 'The phrase meant nothing, dearest, and was uttered totally without thought. What in truth occupied me was the question that I asked, Sabina; and that you do not answer. What was it that papa expected from that meeting with Prince Frederic?'

'If any other than papa had said it, or any other than you had asked me to repeat it, I should be ashamed to do so. But whatever papa says to me you have a right to hear, my own sweet sister, and you will not laugh at me when I repeat his words. He said, Adèle – papa said – that, did Prince Frederic ever speak to me of love, it could only be—— But mercy on me! I am telling you this as if I had some doubt of it, and Heaven knows I would rather – far rather die, than believe the contrary! But what I do *not* believe possible, Adèle, although my father did, was that Prince Frederic should ever speak to me of love at all!'

'But if he ever did, my father thought it could only be in the hope of making you his wife?' said Adèle, supplying the deficiencies of her sister's explanation. 'Of course there can be no second opinion on that point. But, dearest Sabina, though that point is not doubtful, another is. I own that I have often thought Prince Frederic did more than admire – I have thought that he loved you, Sabina. But, dearest, he is the son and brother of a king; and in that rank love has rarely anything to do with marriage. His never having breathed a word of love to you does him the highest honour. Royal and loyal heart! may he recover the peace which his visit to Paris has perhaps shaken! He deserves to be happy, and I trust will be so when time has healed the wound. But at the same time we have learned his honourable feeling, we have learned his purpose too; and when he told you that his purpose was to leave Paris, he told you also that you would meet no more.'

'I know it, dear, dear Adèle, – I know it! I repeat it to myself incessantly, night and day, that I may never forget it. And now, dear sister, having said so much, do you not feel that the best thing I can do is to employ myself? Will it not be wise and kind to let me be the active busy body? I do so wish it, Adèle!'

'Bless you, sweet love! I will not hinder you. But how will you set about it all, Sabina? I have brought my pearls, which, as you know, are worth some thousands sterling, and some other trinkets too; but I know not how we are to convert them into cash; and of money I have very little, not more than three or four hundred francs, and this will not go far, for you must hire assistance as well as purchase necessaries. Do you think it would be possible to employ Gertrude to sell some of the lesser baubles at Baden without danger of discovery?'

'I think we might venture to employ my friend Gertrude in any way, Adèle, and that, too, without any fear of discovery; for I believe her to be a very sensible girl, with as much discretion as kindness. But trouble not yourself about selling trinkets and other such heroine-like devices, sister mine, for it needs not. When you left me alone with papa yesterday, while you went to perform some notability upon our new wardrobe in our chamber, I, having my head full of my house-keeping projects, ventured to break in upon his political musings by asking if he had contrived to bring away any money with him from Paris; stating as my reason for this rather new sort of provident anxiety on my part, that I did not suppose it would be possible to render the shelter we hoped to find in this forsaken château habitable without some trifling expenditure.

'"Let not the want of that stop you, Sabina," he said with such earnestness of manner as plainly shewed his anxiety to get here, – "let not that stop or impede you in any way," he said; and then from beneath the pillows of his bed he drew forth two bags, such as bankers send, you know, with their five-franc pieces; one of them he put back again, so I know not what was in it; but the other he opened, and shewed me that it was full of gold. Is not this good news, dearest?'

The news could not certainly be called bad news, inasmuch as all the evil it brought with it had been guessed at and endured before: yet Adèle felt a cold tremor run through her frame at this mention of a 'bag of gold;' for it brought back to her memory a whole host of terrible thoughts, which through the last few wretched days had, one by one, come to torment her in the fearful twilight of doubt and dread that present circumstances seemed to shed upon others that had gone before. The quantity of gold coin she had seen in her stepfather's possession, while he so positively stated that he had it not, together with the sickening recollection of Count Romanhoff's narrative concerning the outrage committed on the successful players on their return from the salon de jeu, all rushed into her mind together, and she shuddered perceptibly from head to foot.

'You are taking cold, my dearest Adèle!' cried Sabina, suddenly starting up: 'these long-deserted rooms feel damp to you: let us leave them instantly.'

'Yes, I am cold, I believe,' said Adèle, drawing one deep breath, and struggling to recover herself, 'but it will go off as we walk home.'

'What a thoughtless trick it was to sit down and tell you such long stories here!' said Sabina, taking her sister's arm, and leading her away. 'Why did you not stop me, Adèle?'

'Because I listened to you with too much interest to remember where I was,' she replied. 'But we will go now, Sabina, for the place must be damp, I should think, till fires have been lighted and windows opened. But when this shall have been done, Sabina, I see nothing to prevent our being very safe here, if we can but obtain permission to seek a shelter in these forsaken rooms.'

'On that point we *must* consult Frau Weiber and her daughter,' replied Sabina, in a tone of more decision than she usually adopted on any subject. 'For it is clear to me, Adèle, that without the assistance of some trusty friends we cannot possibly avoid running into perpetual danger of discovery; but with such I shall fear nothing. I fancy that I see already exactly how we shall go on — somewhat roughly, perhaps, and in a style most new and strange to us. But if you, dearest Adèle, can bear it patiently for a while, and if our dear father be safe, and if you will let me make myself useful, and if I can find a way to climb up to that dear mysterious spot from whence I first beheld these friendly walls, – oh! I shall be so perfectly contented, and so much – so very much happier than I could possibly be anywhere else!'

'God bless you for saying so, dearest!' returned her sister, fondly pressing the arm she held. 'If this be so, I could soon school myself into wonderful resignation.'

In this comparatively happy frame of mind the two sisters set off on their return to Gernsbach, which they reached in perfect safety; the path seeming not half the length that it had done before. But they found Mr Hargrave waiting for them with a degree of feverish impatience that made Sabina again regret that they had lingered so long in the château. He listened, however, to her hopeful account of it with an eager intensity of interest which at least made her rejoice that she had seen enough of it to have so much to tell.

CHAPTER XXII

From that day Adèle, from many motives, and all of them wise and good, yielded to her young sister, Sabina, the helm of the little vessel in which they were embarked; not, however, sitting idly beside her, but giving her assistance only as an aid, and not as a general. In the first place, poor Adèle felt that the heart of Sabina was not sinking within her from any of the miserable feelings which paralysed her own. In every exertion, therefore, which she should make to establish a home with such an approach to comfort as their circumstances might permit, the effort would be calculated to sustain her own spirits, by the impulse of hope and the healthful discipline of activity. Whatever Sabina might do to increase the accommodation or pleasure of her father, would be like returning to the dearest feelings of other times; whilst to the unhappy Adèle every thought that drew her nearer to him, was but a misery the more. Adèle felt too, that while she, in actively employing herself to prepare the château of the lake, could only fancy herself an agent busied for the consolation of crime, Sabina would feel all the delightful consciousness of being occupied in the performance of her duty.

Besides all this, it was very evident to Adèle that there was for her sister a fanciful charm about the region they were preparing to inhabit that filled a void in her heart which otherwise might have pained her more. So, for all these reasons, Adèle, lately so boldly enterprising, permitted herself to sink almost into apathy; and, perhaps, found her best relief under the misery which seemed to have closed around her, in forgetting for brief intervals that herself, with her innocent and fondly-loved sister, were doomed to companionship with crime, by transporting herself in thought to the side of the lost Coventry, and listening in fancy to the voice that she never – never could hope to hear again.

All, however, that Adèle had lost in activity Sabina seemed to have gained; she became notable, active, and energetic; and it was evidently with pleasure that her father remarked the important share she was taking in the preparations for his removal.

What Adèle de Cordillac had done to save her sister from the agony of learning her father's guilt was as precious in effect to him as to his innocent daughter. Before his preserver, however, his spirit was bent to the very earth; and though he well knew that she had saved him, his gratitude bore no proportion to the suffering produced by the conscious degradation into which he had fallen. Perhaps he guessed also that his safety, and such delusive sort of credit as she had contrived to mix with the reports which must of necessity follow his departure, were valuable to her less for his sake than that of Sabina. In short, she had 'out-lived his liking,' and great was the relief when his own child, ignorant of his guilt, and loving him, if possible, more devotedly than ever, put herself forward as the one who was to manage every thing for his comfort, and consult with him on the means still remaining in his power to ensure it.

It was Sabina, then, who undertook the task of ascertaining from their friendly hostess how far it might be advisable to apply for permission to inhabit the rooms they had seen, or how far it might be possible to take temporary possession of them without it. All she asked of Adèle was that she should be present at the conversation on the subject.

As Mr Hargrave, still pleading illness, preferred taking his breakfast in bed, the two girls were left in possession of the 'upper chamber, swept and garnished,' which was allotted to them as their sitting-room at the little inn; and to this room Sabina (who was naturally the selected favourite of the Weiber family, on account of the great facility with which she spoke their language) contrived to bring both the good *frau* and her pretty daughter as soon as the breakfast was over.

'I do not think the house over the bridge will do for us, Frau Weiber,' began Sabina, 'because my father is never happy, and never will be, if he lives in very small rooms.'

'Now that is unlucky!' replied the good woman, in a tone of very friendly regret; 'for neither Gertrude nor I, for the life of us, can think of any other that would be, as you say the English like to have it, all to your own selves; and I don't believe there is such a place far or near.'

'Where do you think my sister and I got to yesterday, Frau Weiber?' said Sabina, with a smile.

'Nay, then, how should I guess, my pretty maiden? Maybe you walked away along the river-side – was that it?'

'No! that was not it. But will you not think us bold and courageous girls when I tell you that we got as far as the old château near the lake of the Mummelsee?'

'To the Château of the Lake!' said the good woman, crossing herself.

'To the Château of the Lake!' echoed Gertrude; 'not close, not very close I hope, my dear darling young lady?'

'Nay, but we did – we got into it, Gertrude!'

'Into the Château of the Lake!' screamed the mother and the daughter in the same instant.

'And why not, dear friends? the fairies love my sister and me – we know they would not be angry with us. There was no chance of our meeting any body else, was there?'

'No, no! I promise you, my dears, no chance of that whatever. Why the very priests are shy of walking near it even in broad daylight; and I don't believe there is one to be found, unless, perhaps, it was the Grand Duke himself, who would dare to go into the doors.'

'That is because the Grand Duke, perhaps, is the only person on good terms with the fairies. They are the kindest little people, you know, in the world to their friends.'

'That is true, mother,' said Gertrude, very gravely.

'And you went, young ladies, truly and really into the old residence?' said the mother. 'Why, it has not been entered by mortal foot, to the very best of my knowledge and belief, for nearly a score of years. It must have been an awful spectacle, *mein fraulein*! – What dust, what rubbish, what confusion!'

'But were you very sure the fairy folk were friendly?' demanded the kind Gertrude, timidly.

'You shall hear, Gertrude, and judge for yourself,' said Sabina. 'My sister and myself set out as you know upon a walk, and much did I wish at the very bottom of my heart that we might be lucky enough to find some place fit for a dwelling-place for our dear father! We walked on, and on, and on, a great long way, but never saw any thing the least bit in the world like a château or building of any kind.'

The mother and daughter clasped their hands, looked in each other's face, and exclaimed, 'Ay, ay! that is always their way.'

'But hear,' resumed Sabina, smiling, 'what happened at last. Just as we were beginning to be very tired, and both of us, I suppose, in our hearts thinking it would be as well to turn back, just at that very moment we saw before our eyes a large, stately building, with endless-looking rows of windows, and the terrace, and the wall, and the statues, and the fosse, all looking so grand and so great, that nobody living could think of going near, much less of going in, without very particular leave given by those who have a right to say yes or no!'

'Oh! – for certain!' exclaimed Frau Weiber, 'no reasonable body, – dear young ladies! Nobody quite and entirely in their right mind would ever have dreamed of doing such a thing, – nobody ever *does* do it.'

'But listen, *mein frau*; while we were standing, awe-struck as it were, and gazing as if the château before us were just fallen from the heavens, or risen out of the earth, we suddenly felt every kind of fear and terror go away, and a sort of kind and friendly feeling come into our hearts, just as if we had received an invitation to visit the good people who lived there. From that very moment we never had any more hesitation or difficulty about it. We found our way – Heaven and the fairies only know how – from the top of a very steep rock, where there was no more path than there is up and down the sides of your house, – we found our way, I tell you, as pleasantly as if it had been along a carpet, to the very door of the Grand Ducal residence! We neither of us, I dare say, knew very well how it had happened, but we just looked at each other, and in we walked.'

'You did!' ejaculated Frau Weiber, with uplifted hands.

'Mother! they were doomed and invited to do it,' said Gertrude; 'but oh! mother, mother, don't interrupt, – let us hear all! Was the door of the residence standing open for you, my young lady?'

'Yes, Gertrude,' replied Sabina, 'wide open; so in we went, as I told you. Just at first it did not seem as if any very great preparation had been made for us. In fact, things appeared to have been thrown about rather carelessly; exactly, indeed, as I have always heard in my own country that the fairy people do when they are in a sportive humour and feel frolicsome. But as we went on and got into the grand part of the building, it was quite different. Every thing almost seemed taken away, as if on purpose, not to make a litter. For my own part, I quite believe that the dear little people were afraid to trust themselves with too many playthings; and that, for the sake of good order, the furniture was most of it put away. However, we came at last to a beautiful room. Oh, Gertrude! so grand and so large! And there we found sofas and chairs put just on purpose for us to rest upon, because, at that time, we were both beginning to feel very tired. Was it not kind of them? I do so love the fairy people, and I certainly believe that they love me. Well, good friends, there we sat and talked, as quiet and comfortable as if we had been two young princesses of the house of Baden; till, by little and little, the thought came into our heads that we ought to make *that* our home, and no other house whatever; for that it was as plain as daylight that the little people had invited us. – Don't you think so, Frau Weiber?'

The good woman crossed herself for about the hundredth time since the conversation began, and said, 'This is a matter that without our priest we could never think to meddle with. I dare not say yea or nay without consulting him.'

Sabina looked disappointed, but somewhat awed, and remained silent for a minute or two, when Adèle ventured to remark to their pious hostess, that the very greatest secrecy was necessary in all dealings with the little people, for that their kindness often turned to enmity if their doings were too much talked about.

'No doubt of it,' replied the good woman, solemnly; 'and it shall be no tongue of mine, nor of Gertrude's either, that shall offend them that way. But it is one thing, dear ladies, to keep quiet about them, – to hear all and say nothing, that is one thing, – but to give my judgment as to your being invited, and my advice, it may be, as to your accepting the same, that is quite another thing, dear ladies; and I may not and must not do it without counsel from the priest.'

Adèle answered nothing, but looked at her young sister as if to watch how she intended to proceed. In truth, this allusion to asking counsel from a priest could not be made before the two sisters without both of them feeling conscious that it was one of the very few points on which they differed in opinion. Both had been brought up in the Roman Catholic faith by their mother, and both remembered to have seen their father abandon the creed in which he was born to adopt that of his wife. This lady, amidst her many high connexions, had the honour of counting a cardinal as her uncle; and as the conversion of Mr Hargrave took place during a visit to Rome, made about eight years before the death of his wife, it was ever supposed that the holy influence of this venerable relative had produced an effect so highly agreeable to his lady and all her distinguished race. At her death, therefore, she had the satisfaction of leaving her husband and daughters of one faith; and so it was supposed, by the generality of their friends and acquaintance, that they still remained – but Adèle knew, and Sabina guessed, that it was not so.

Fame, which, even in a Roman Catholic metropolis, can, in these happy days, venture to speak of Protestant eloquence, brought to the ears of Mademoiselle de Cordillac such an account of the extraordinary power of a preacher of the French Protestant Church, that her eager desire to hear him overcame all scruples, and, despite the gentle remonstrance of her sister, she left her chair in St Roch untenanted, and was conveyed to the quiet, modest fane of the Oratoire.

It is a wholesome saying, and, like its fellows, very pregnant with wisdom, that 'we cannot touch pitch and not be defiled.' But, with equal truth, it might be said also, that, except to those who are under the condemnation of hearing without being able to understand, it is impossible to be where 'light shineth in darkness,' and not to perceive its brightness.

Adèle de Cordillac was not under such condemnation, and as she listened to the voice of truth, uttering the counsels and precepts of GOD in a strain of eloquence rarely equalled among men, her ears were opened and her heart was changed. Again, and again, and again, she followed this mighty preacher from the Oratoire to Ste Marie's, – from Ste Marie's to the Battignolles, and then to the Oratoire again, – till it was no longer in her power to doubt whether it were the stately Popish temples of Paris, or the humble ones assigned to the reformed faith, which returned the purest echoes to the word of God.

Once convinced, it was not in the nature of Adèle to hesitate. She made herself known to the good and gifted man whose preaching had wrought this change in her; and as, although no seeker after converts, he never refused to listen to those who turned to him for help, and to give it with all the energetic devotion of his exalted character, she speedily became one of his flock, and a truly pious Protestant.*

All this was well known to Sabina, but fully proclaimed to none beside. Mr Hargrave, indeed, was aware that Adèle had ceased to attend the church to which the rest of his family resorted, and spoke to her with his accustomed gentle amiability on the subject; but when she would have frankly answered him, he stopped her, saying, –

'Excuse me, my dear love, I cannot hear you on this theme. I have alluded to it merely for the purpose of requesting that you will neither make your secession from the church of your ancestors a subject of conversation with our general friends, or of reasoning and conversion with my daughter. On this latter point I am very deeply interested, but must throw myself wholly on your good faith and honourable feeling that my earnest wishes on this subject shall not be violated. You know me too well, my dear Adèle, not to be aware that it would be inexpressibly painful to me, were I to find myself driven to any other mode of keeping Sabina from following your example. And now, my love, we will never recur to this subject again.'

Mr Hargrave then kissed the forehead of his step-daughter, and left her.

Adèle considered it her duty to obey him, and she did so, – a task which was rendered the more easy by the evident care taken by Sabina to avoid every thing that might be likely to lead them to the subject.

Such being the state of their religious feelings, and such the scrupulous avoidance of every thing on the subject, which was now become habitual to them, this reference of the good hostess to her priest could not fail of producing some feeling of embarrassment to them both. But a moment's

---

* Though the reverence felt for the name of M Coquerel must prevent its being introduced among the personages of a romance, it would be hardly fair to the reader not to state that this most eloquent preacher delivers a sermon on three successive Sundays of every month at the chapels named in the text.

thought decided Adèle on the course she ought to pursue. She approached her sister, and whispered in her ear, –

'You have promised, dearest Sabina, to settle every thing, therefore I shall leave you to settle this;' and without waiting for an answer, she quitted the room.

If any thing could have brought a lasting feeling of relief to the harassed spirit of Adèle, it would have been this power of leaving all details respecting their future proceedings in the hands of the innocent and unconscious Sabina; for so only could every needful step be taken with some mixture of hope and cheerfulness, and so only could she herself be permitted to find that species of quiescent inactivity which was the nearest approach to peace that she could hope for.

With the image of Alfred Coventry in her heart, and all other thoughts as much as possible banished from her head, Adèle wrapped herself in her homely coif and shawl, and strolled out for a solitary walk along the banks of the lovely Mourg. It is hardly possible to conceive a position of more painful contrast with all that had gone before it than that in which she now found herself. Nevertheless there was, at that moment, a species of enjoyment in it. The immediate and galling pressure from without was, for the time, removed. She had neither to look at the man whose presence made her shudder with an eye of feigned kindness, nor close up with unnatural violence every outlet to genuine feeling, lest the poor Sabina, for whose dear sake she endured it all, should catch the bitter truth, and become still more miserable than herself. For the first time since the storm had burst upon her she stood apart, under the shelter, as it were, of her own pure spirit, and wept and prayed alone.

The conversation, meanwhile, between Sabina and her two humble friends went on in a tone of the most perfect mutual confidence. Nothing could be farther from the wish, and, indeed, the very nature of Sabina, than treating lightly such scruples as they expressed; and though her feeling at encountering a difficulty which she had not expected was that of disappointment, a few moments' reflection brought to her mind the great need she had, and her dear father likewise, of spiritual advice and comfort.

'We should be very glad,' she said, 'to make acquaintance with your priest, Frau Weiber, and to ask for his advice and spiritual aid. Does he live with you?'

'Hard by the church, young lady, – and a good and holy man he is, and one, too, of high account in his sacred calling. He only comes to our poor town because his venerable mother, good lady, lives here. Father Mark was born here, and that is the reason he clings so to the old place, though there be bishops and archbishops, – nay, I believe, the very Pope himself, who would be glad to have him.'

'A good man is always likely to be a good son,' replied Sabina. 'I will speak to papa about Father Mark – I dare say he will like to see him; and when he comes to us we can consult him, you know, about the château.'

Sabina, who was really as good and pious a young lady as ever lived, was greatly comforted at hearing that she was likely, in this remote spot, to find the comfort of a friendly priest and confessor. The mention of his attachment to his old mother prepossessed her to see in him a man as likely to be valuable to them as a friend, as his holy profession rendered him precious as a guide and adviser, and her sweet face was beaming with pleasure and with hope as she presented herself at the bedside of her father.

'Dearest papa, I have good news for you!' she exclaimed. 'Frau Weiber says that their confessor, Father Mark, an excellent man and pious priest, lives close to us. Shall you not like to see him?'

At the first mention of a stranger whom it was expected he should see, Mr Hargrave's complexion underwent one of those violent changes to which the constitution both of his mind and body made him liable, and for a minute or two he made no reply. But it seemed that this interval was sufficiently long to permit the feeling of alarm with which he had first heard this news to give way before another, suggested by reflection; for when he spoke, it was to express his very cordial sympathy with Sabina's satisfaction.

'It will, indeed, be a comfort, my dear child,' he said, 'both for your sake, my Sabina, and my own too. As a holy and anointed priest, I can neither scruple to intrust all the circumstances of my position to him, nor think for a moment of seeing him without opening my heart to him in confession. You, dearest, of course, will do the same; and fear not to avow your knowledge that the sad necessity for our being here arises from my having, with more zeal than prudence, taken part in a plot, having for its object the restoration of Charles Dix to the throne of France. I am quite aware that, from the nature of the part I have taken in this business, my being given up, if discovered, would be made a matter of state, and would be hardly refused by any country actually at peace with France. For which reason the utmost caution respecting my name, and all other circumstances that might lead to my being identified with the once brilliant Hargrave of Paris, is vitally necessary. On such points as these, our holy religion commands not that we should make disclosures. Remember this, my Sabina, – remember that our only name is Smith, and that of Adèle, Leman. With this one restriction, which has in it, you will perceive, nothing whatever to do with the state of our souls and consciences, – with this one restriction, which my pledged faith to the good cause demands, I would wish you fully to open your heart to the pious man.'

Sabina, as usual, listened to him with most loving and dutiful attention, and having promised to conform most strictly to his wishes in all things, proceeded to inform him of the little *supercherie* she had practised, in the hope of overcoming the superstitious scruples of the Frau Weiber and her daughter respecting their wish to find shelter in the deserted Grand Ducal residence.

He listened to her, as if feeling that every word she spake was of the most vital importance, and could hardly afford a smile in return for the playful narrative she gave him of her bold assumption of fairy favour.

'Any thing — every thing, my Sabina,' he said, 'which may assist our getting shelter in a place as much guarded by superstition as by its desolate remoteness, it will be most wise to practise. You say right, dear love, it will be utterly impossible for us to live there, or any where, without trusting to *some one* for the needful supply of necessaries, as well as for domestic service. All you tell me of these good people leads me to hope that they may be safely trusted; and I have little fear that when I shall have seen this Father Mark, he will consent to assist our views by telling his humble penitents that you may venture to accept the fairies' civilities without danger either to body or soul.'

'If you can do that, papa, — if you can but contrive to convince these good Weibers that there is no sin in putting ourselves under the protection of the little people, I should not be at all surprised if I were to succeed in persuading my dear friend Gertrude to take service with us. Oh! you guess not how far our friendship is advanced already. She has confided to me all the particulars of a little love-affair; and, if you thought that we might prudently afford such an expense, I suspect that if Gertrude comes to live with us, her dearly beloved Hans would come too; and then we should have a hewer of wood and drawer of water without tasking the strength of our own little hands; not to mention that the said Hans could buy and bring home, with the help of his mother-in-law elect, all we should require, and that without drawing upon himself any observation at all.'

'Excellent! — admirable! my Sabina!' exclaimed Mr Hargrave, with reviving animation. 'And have no fears, dearest, about my being able to supply all the money you can possibly require. I have many valuable trinkets with me, — old family jewels that belonged to my mother — stones that I have kept by me because they were unset, — this Hans, if we find him trustworthy, might easily put us in a way to dispose of them, and might take a few at a time, perhaps, — or — the priest himself,' he added, musingly. 'In short, my love, there is no need whatever that you should fear expense in your arrangements; even my five hundred gold pieces will go a good way in such a country as this. Do you know, my love, whether your sister has brought any valuables with her?'

'Yes, papa; Adèle has brought her pearls, and some smaller trinkets — diamonds, I believe — that she, too, said might be easily disposed of.'

'That is all right; and I have no doubt that, between us, we shall do exceedingly well about money. But I would not wish you, my love, to say any thing to poor, dear Adèle about the unset stones that I told you of. If she knew they were my mother's, it would hurt her feelings should she learn that I was obliged to part with them. Poor, dear girl! though I have reason to believe, from the rank and opinions (as far as I know them) of her father's family, that her political feelings would lead her to approve the act which has driven me into exile, we cannot forget that the unhappy turn which her religious opinions have taken, must prevent her thinking me as fully justified as I think myself, for all I have wished to do for the cause in which I have embarked. You understand me, my dear child, and will abstain, dearest, – will you not? – from naming these old jewels to your sister.'

Sabina, delighted to find her beloved father sufficiently recovered in mind and body to enter into this discussion of his affairs, promised most scrupulously to follow his instructions in all things; and presently left him, at his own request, with a commission to their hostess for an immediate summons to Father Mark. 'Bid her tell him,' he said, 'that a penitent, ill at ease, both in mind and body, requests his spiritual assistance.'

Few circumstances could be of much rarer occurrence in the existence of Father Mark than the reception of such a message from a stranger. The Frau Weiber, moreover, delivered it with such commentaries on the good mien and gentle bearing of her guests as considerably augmented the curiosity which the novelty of the thing alone was quite sufficient to excite. The good priest, therefore, did but make some slight improvement in his dress; converting the loose black serge vestment, in which he was sitting at a book-lumbered table in his mother's little parlour, into a very respectable clerical frock, ere he set forth to obey the summons.

The account given by the hostess and her daughter to Sabina of the situation and character of this good man was perfectly correct. There was scarcely, perhaps, a religious society remaining in Europe, into the bosom of which he would not have been cordially welcomed; for he had produced more than one volume on the immutable authority of the Church, considered to be of merit in the very highest quarters; and had only to shew himself at Rome, in order to receive such reward as Rome alone can give. But solitary mystical speculation and his native Mourgthal had more charms for him than Rome and all its glories; and he loved his old mother better than a cardinal's hat, or even than the chair of the Pope itself. He was deeply and *strangely* learned; but, more fortunately for the cause which he espoused than for himself, the tenderness of his conscience interposed between the light his mind received from the many sources his reading opened and his faith; so that in proportion as his reason whispered doubts, his truly honest fear of heresy smothered them into silence. At one period of his life Father Mark had suffered greatly in spirit from the extreme terror into which he fell from the idea that his belief in the dogmas of the Roman Catholic Church was shaken. Having the tremendous syntax of his religion as completely by rote as that of his grammar, it never failed to recur to him every time he ventured to indulge in the perusal of the Gospels, and felt the cheering warmth of their universal charity at his heart. Such feelings, however, were in open revolt to the authority under which he had vowed to live and hoped to die; and literally almost shook his reason by their utter incompatibility with his faith.

That 'a little learning is a dangerous thing' was very well said, and truly; but a great deal is still more so, if it be received into the memory of one whose judgment does not keep pace with his powers of apprehension. To such a man every new thought his researches brings home to him becomes a stumbling block; for if two conflicting opinions be equally well argued in the pages he ventures to peruse, how is he to choose between them? Poor Father Mark reeled under the struggle that was going on within him, and for some months lived in a very harassing and painful condition; being about equally likely to turn Trappist one mood of mind, or altogether to renounce his religion in another. At length this vacillating state was put an end to, during the course of a long, solitary, and most delicious walk over hill and dale through miles and miles of the delicious region he inhabited,

> 'It was the pride, the manhood of the year,
> And every grove was dight in its most deft aumere;'

and as he looked from heaven to earth, and from earth to heaven, – as he marked every beast, every bird, every insect, yea, every reptile, luxuriating in the joys provided for them by Providence, and felt his own heart swell with joy and gladness at the sights and the sounds amidst which he was created to move, – such a full conviction of the gentle mercifulness of God's will came upon him, that his very soul seemed melting within him, and the whole scheme of the most holy Inquisition, and all its results, past, present, and to come, rushed upon his memory with all the majestic power of contrast. For one short moment the whole fabric was in very considerable danger of being trampled in the dust by natural piety and common sense; but in the next, the Popish priest stood still, his eyes cast upon the ground, the dew of terror bursting from every pore, and his limbs, poor man! trembling as if shaken by an ague.

'And against what is it that I thus dare to lift my impious thoughts in rebellion?' he cried aloud: and it seemed to him that the hills around echoed 'Rebellion!' 'Authority!' he exclaimed, again raising his voice in the deep solitude. 'AUTHORITY, against which the wavering reason of one weak man ought to bend and grovel in the dust. I bend – I bend,' continued the terrified priest, throwing himself upon the ground (without daring, however, to thank God for the sweet freshness of the herbs that received him), 'I bend – I bend,' he cried. 'I know nothing, understand nothing, judge nothing; but believe all that the most holy authority of the Church of Rome commands and teaches. On every theme but one I will indulge in the use of such faculties as God has given me. But on this, AUTHORITY shall be my sole and only guide!'

A vow thus taken in the maturity of manhood, and with such deep conviction of the sacredness of the duty which enforces its being kept, is seldom broken; and Father Mark lived and died in the odour of Popish sanctity, without ever again torturing his brain by meditating on the subject, but comfortably reposing every doubt and every fear upon the soft cushion of AUTHORITY. This vicarial sort of faith suits well for those who, with tender consciences, still love their ease; and for such, is as much preferable to the process of inquiry as the swallowing one pill is to imbibing a dose of rhubarb by single grains. For the rest, Father Mark was a truly charitable and kind-hearted man; ever ready to lend a helping hand to all who needed it; pure in his life, regular in his devotions, and ready at a moment's warning to strip off both cloak and coat for the honour and service of the Church.

Considerably within an hour from the time Mr Hargrave had expressed a wish to see him, Father Mark stood beside his bed, whereon he still lay, though suffering from no other malady than a rather feverish inclination for more self-indulgence than the uncarpeted stone floor of the little parlour could afford. The appearance of the room where he lay, and of every thing in it, was of too humble a character to suggest any ideas of rank or wealth in its occupant; the consequence of which was that the manner of the good priest became particularly kind and respectful, all his partialities being in favour of those on whom he thought he could bestow assistance, rather than for the more powerful from whom he might hope to receive it.

To those high in the Church, indeed, his feelings were, of course, altogether different. To them, his deference, observance, humility, veneration, and obedience, were all part and parcel of his religious worship.

Exactly as a burnt child dreads the fire, did Father Mark tremble at the thought of separating in his mind the visible Church of Rome from HIM in whose bosom it professes to be instituted. He had suffered terror to a degree that amounted to agony, from believing, for a few short moments, that he had rebelled against the power of God as manifested in the authority of his Church, and he would gladly have died rather than repeat the sin.

* * *

Were it not at this moment my business to go on with my story, instead
of stopping to preach a little by the way, I might be tempted to say a page
or two on the nice distinctions which, in some cases, divide right from
wrong. If I believe in any earthly means of improving the moral and
social condition of man, while in his mortal state, it is in the influence of
a pious and pains-taking Anglo-Catholic priesthood; each clergyman
being the centre of a small circle, the circumference of which should be
within easy reach of his pastoral eye. But one single step taken in a wrong
direction at setting out from this rational, pure, and natural principle,
suffices to lead the wanderer into superstition, hypocrisy, blasphemy, and
the most fearful abuse of power that human annals record.

* * *

But let us return to Mr Hargrave.

Father Mark stood before his humble-looking couch the very picture
of charity and gentle kindness. Mr Hargrave begged him to be seated,
thanked him for his prompt attendance, and expressed a vast deal of
sorrow at not being able to rise in order to receive him. To all which
Father Mark replied with the most unaffected good-humour, but a little
as if he thought so much ceremony unnecessary. His new penitent, the
while, kept his eye steadily fixed upon him, his whole soul being intent
upon discovering what manner of man he had to deal with.

Mr Hargrave had ever piqued himself upon his power of looking into
the hearts of men, and it was no light object with him at the present
moment to get a peep into that of Father Mark. As far as he could judge,
however, there was little upon which to exercise his ingenuity; plain,
quiet, simple friendliness being the unmistakable characteristic of the
man before him.

It is not impossible that Mr Hargrave might have better liked a more
complicated map of mind. He was more skilled in threading a labyrinth
than in finding his way over plain ground, and might, perhaps, have
fancied it easier to produce effect in recesses of the heart but seldom
reached, than on thoughts and feelings open to all men.

By the time Father Mark had answered a gentle word or two to all the
respectful civility bestowed upon him, and seated himself in the arm-
chair set for him by Gertrude, Mr Hargrave had decided that upon
ordinary men ordinary influences were likely to be most effectual, and
therefore determined to expatiate a good deal upon his great personal
intimacy with the exiled monarch. He accordingly took care to inform
the good father that he had been driven from a splendid home, and all

the joys Parisian life could give, in consequence of his loyal and devoted attachment to Charles the Tenth of France. He dilated largely on the high rewards that of a certainty would await those of any country who should befriend him now, declaring the success of the plot in which he was engaged certain, provided the party in general, and himself in particular, were shielded from discovery and pursuit.

Mr Hargrave was very richly gifted with powers for talking with effect. He had handsome features, expressive eyes, a pleasing and flexible voice, and a store of words inexhaustible. So, on he went, dignified, pathetic, and conciliatory, prophetic of high events, and abounding in promises of all kinds.

To the whole of this long harangue Father Mark listened with unfailing patience, never interrupting him for a moment, either by word, or cough, or yawn; but his mild countenance reflected too little of the matter he heard for the orator to consider him as a good listener. He was, in fact, at that moment thinking of a little particular spot by the river-side, where, when the sun shone, as it did then, he was wont to find shelter and shade, calm and coolness, for a dearly loved hour of reading or repose, as chance decided.

'Surely the man is a fool,' thought the puzzled man of the world. 'But he is a priest too,' added his sagacity, as his eye fell on the carefully close cut of his bright brown hair. And thereupon –

'He changed his hand, and checked his pride,'

as far as his own earthly honours were concerned, and suddenly sounded a deep and thrilling appeal to the interests of the Church of Rome, as being vitally implicated in the decision of this great political question.

Like as a rock, round which storms and tempest, winds and waves, bellow and rush in vain, rendering nothing but enduring silence in reply, is yet found to return an echo, quick, distinct, and clear, if but the gentlest sound addresses it from one mysteriously right direction; so Father Mark, imperturbable before all else, answered to the mention of the Church of Rome in a tone that at once told his wily watcher from what point he might address him with success.

From this moment the most perfectly good understanding was established between this most incongruous pair, as far, at least, as that understanding can be called good, which on one side is all truth, and all falsehood on the other. If the usually acute Hargrave had erred in deeming the tranquil-seeming Father Mark a fool, his perspicuity now atoned for it by the rapidity with which he dived into the master secret of his character.

Had he known as much as the reader does, concerning the good man's by-gone struggles and appalling fears, he could not have managed him more ably. Before the interview ended, Father Mark felt himself bound, body and soul, to aid, assist, abet, and support Mr Hargrave, under evil report and good report, in dangers and in difficulties, openly and in secret, to the very utmost stretch of his power and influence, and in utter defiance of all human obstacles of any nature or degree whatever.

CHAPTER XXIII

It can hardly be doubted that after this all things went easily with the well-protected strangers. Mr Hargrave was an actor by nature; and as a squirrel can never be well or happy without climbing (even if it be, *faute de mieux*, a tread-mill), Mr Hargrave, from a like activity of instinctive impulse, could only thrive, either in mind or body, when he was performing a part. Sabina was delighted, though she could by no means understand the benign influence produced on her father by his intercourse with this gentle Father Mark; while Adèle, who truly believed his conscience to be in a state to torture him into still deeper despondency than he had yet exhibited, began to give him credit for more sincerity in his Romish creed than she had ever done before, and to believe, in good earnest, that the ceremony of absolution had set him at peace with himself.

It was hardly possible that the good Weibers could become more kindly civil and attentive than they had been before; but something of reverence now mixed with this, particularly towards Mr Hargrave himself, which, like applause to all performers, increased the spirit of his acting, till, instead of the accomplished Parisian man of *ton*, he became, to all outward seeming, a dignified, sedate, apostolic sort of nuncio-like personage, his credentials known to his confessor only, but the sacred nature of his mission suspected by all.

As to the Grand Duke's dilapidated 'residences' (as all his numberless palaces, inhabited and uninhabited, are called), all doubts concerning it were finally settled in the course of the second private conversation held between Father Mark and his new penitent, some passages of which may as well be given as a specimen of the confidential terms they were upon.

'One word from you, my reverend father, will, of course, suffice to remove all the silly scruples of these poor people respecting the fairies and their supposed authority,' said Mr Hargrave; 'and when this has been accomplished, I shall wish to shelter myself, and the holy work committed to my charge, within the remote walls of that forsaken dwelling as speedily as possible. No place, certainly, could have been found so admirably calculated to ensure the concealment upon which the success of this great business ultimately depends.' And in pronouncing the words 'great business,' Mr Hargrave crossed himself with more than usual solemnity.

This action was repeated by Father Mark, with less of pontifical grace, perhaps, but with equal reverence.

'I will take care,' he replied, 'that nothing shall be left on the consciences of these excellent people likely, in any way, to militate against your pious wishes, my son. But respecting the Castle of the Lake, would not the manner of your abiding in it be more satisfactory if you were to apply to the Grand Duke himself? – Even I, honoured sir, humble as I am, could undertake to get this request handed to him if you approve.'

'Hush! hush! hush! – my father!' exclaimed Mr Hargrave in an agitated whisper, and extending his hand so near to the lips of the good priest as nearly to touch them, and so enforce the discretion commanded. 'You know not what you propose – you know not what you do! Those, Father Mark, whose names I hold as too sacred to mention, have given me to understand that no temptation, however great – no accommodation, however much required – no false, idle, and merely secular ideas concerning frankness, sincerity, and that species of weakness commonly called plain dealing, must for a single moment be permitted to affect the profound secrecy in which I am commanded to envelope myself. To the Church, and to the Church only, I have permission to open my heart; and were the deserted mansion in question the property of some bishop or archbishop, or even of the most obscure individual who held office as a priest, of any rank whatever, from the very highest to the very lowest, I would, without an hour's delay, fly to him, as I have done to you, holy father, and open to him at once the secret upon which the safety of the Papal see depends. But as it is I may not do it, for those who alone have the right to bind or to loose my tongue in this matter have forbidden it.'

'No more – no more, my son!' returned Father Mark: 'I will never again alarm your faithful ear or tender conscience by any proposal of the kind.'

Mr Hargrave received this assurance with a look of thankfulness; but still he appeared greatly agitated, and for some moments no word was uttered on either side. At length, suddenly dropping on his knees, he said, –

'Father! – Father Mark! – it may be that now, even now, in the very act of enforcing caution upon you, I may have sinned against the Church of God. Father! you are an anointed priest, while I am but a poor wretched worldling, sanctified in no way, save in having been chosen by God's vicegerent here on earth, and by one of the holiest of earth's mortal beings, as an humble agent in the mighty work they have in hand. Absolve me from my sin! – I have confessed, and do repent it!'

'*Absolvo te*, my son!' replied the priest, spreading his open palms above the head of his meek penitent. 'And thou art absolved,' he added, assisting him to rise from the kneeling position into which he had thrown himself.

'How healing are such words from the lips of one authorised to speak them!' said Mr Hargrave, reseating himself, and speaking in the tone of one enjoying relief from oppressive suffering. 'Is there,' he asked, while a charming smile seemed to illumine his whole countenance, — 'is there, among the wide multitude of the good God's favours to men, one that can compare to the joy of absolution! I feel like a being newly created to life, and fear not what all the powers of the earth can do to injure me!'

There was something so very touching in the holy fervour with which Mr Hargrave uttered these words, that Father Mark's eyes filled with tears as he looked at him.

'I shall ever consider it as one of the most blessed events of my life,' said the good man earnestly, 'that I have met with one honoured by the sacred commission which you bear. And blessed — thrice blessed shall I hold myself, if it fall within the compass of my poor power to aid or comfort you.'

'Both, both, holy father,' replied the humble and grateful Hargrave. 'It is by your assistance only that I can hope to find the needful shelter I seek. As we are even commanded — for so I have been taught — to turn the weaknesses of sinful and ignorant men to the service of our most holy religion, I should apprehend, Father Mark, that we could do nothing but righteousness in availing ourselves of the childish superstition of these rustic people, by leading them to suppose that my residing at the Castle of the Lake for some short time was permitted by the especial favour of the little people who are believed to hold sway over it; and it will be as well to make them understand, holy father, that those whom either I or you may intrust with the secret are, in like manner, distinguished by their protecting favour, but that great and terrible will be the vengeance taken if they divulge the secret! Will you, good Father Mark, undertake the task of making the Frau Weiber and her daughter understand this?'

Father Mark rubbed the fingers of each hand against the palm that belonged to them with rather a nervous and uneasy action. He was, in fact, in no way pleased by the task thus assigned him. Throughout the battle which had been fought within him between common sense and the authority of the Popish Church, and in which common sense had been overcome, by reason of the good man's frightened conscience having taken part against her — throughout the whole of this memorable struggle he had gradually, and one by one, submitted to receive as truths a most enormous quantity of falsehoods; but never, at any period, had he as yet set himself to invent any new lies, by way of proving his own piety or testing that of others, and having, by nature, as little propensity as any man living to this sort of mental exercise, he looked disconcerted at this proposal of bamboozling his worthy friends and pious penitents in the manner proposed.

With his accustomed tact, Mr Hargrave immediately perceived this, and exclaimed, with accent and emphasis admirably calculated to give his words effect, –

'How I reverence the feeling that I now see struggling at your heart, holy father! Truth, pure and undefiled, is your bosom's friend, and the habitual companion of your pious life. Think not, I beseech you, that though a man of the world, a political agent, and, I may proudly add,' he continued crossing himself, 'a religious agent also, – think not that truth is less dear to me than it is to you. I may not even hint to you, holy father, whose sacred profession places you at such an immeasurable height of wisdom above me, – I may not hint to you how often in human affairs one sacred virtue runs counter to another; and that we are permitted by the blessing and the license of our most holy Church, so to manage and arrange these conflicting principles as to derive from them the greatest portion of good; and above all things, to display thereby the strongest demonstrations of obedience to the will of the Church.'

Father Mark sighed deeply, and seemed as if intending to say something; but stopped short, looked frightened, crossed himself, and then turned away his head and muttered inwardly some words in prayer.

'But mistake me not, holy father,' resumed Mr Hargrave. 'Think not that I shall persevere in any measure that my confessor for the time being shall oppose. It will – it must be sufficient when I give account to those I have ventured to name to you, of my various efforts to obey their commands, that I shall plead the averseness of my spiritual guide in extenuation of the failure of this project, which – why should I conceal it from you? – was suggested by no less a counsellor than the Pope himself!'

A perfect shower of crosses fell from the trembling fingers of Father Mark upon his brow and breast, as he listened to these tremendous words.

'Not so, my son, – not so!' he exclaimed, almost gasping for breath to utter his obedience. 'It is enough for me ever, and always enough, to know the will of the Church, in order to make me perform it. I am an obscure and very ignorant man – ignorant of all things save the one great saving law of obedience, and to this I bow; even to the laying myself, and all the thoughts and reasonings of my sinful heart, in the dust. I will not fail to tell these simple women, my son, that it is their duty to aid and assist you in secreting yourself within the walls of the Castle of the Lake.'

*   *   *

Father Mark faithfully kept his word; and though he did no more – though his simple word of guarantee to the Frau Weiber and her daughter, that it was their duty, and no sin, to assist the Graf Schmidt in taking up his abode at the château, was as unlike as possible to the dramatic sort of eloquence with which Mr Hargrave himself would have dilated on the fairy favours his two daughters had received, it sufficed to obtain all the assistance wanted in order to effect the project that Sabina had conceived.

The first feeling in the least degree approaching to agreeable which Mr Hargrave had experienced since the full conviction of the discovery of his secret proceedings, arose from the perfect success of the scene he had thus acted before Father Mark.

'What is there I could not do?' he murmured to himself in the silence of his little chamber as soon as the pious man had left him. 'If drawing-rooms be closed against me, there are other walks which men gifted with talents, equal perhaps to my own, have not disdained to tread. I must think further on this subject. – Admirable Adèle! Though her presence makes my blood creep through my veins, till I shudder as I might do at the approach of some dreaded reptile, I cannot but admire the sort of intuitive talent which enabled her to throw so amiable, – so impenetrable a cloak over me! Will it not be received, in spite of all assertions or surmises to the contrary, that the version of Madame de Hautrivage – which she will spread unsparingly – is the true one? Who dare receive it other?' Mr Hargrave smiled complacently. 'There is more yet that may be made of this; and what matters it under what form commanding talent shews itself? The name of a monk may ring as loudly beneath vaulted roofs at that of the graceful Amphytrion of Paris. I must think of this.'

* * *

The task of Sabina now became little short of delightful; and though poor Adèle, for a thousand reasons, could not share her pleasure, she exerted herself to the very utmost to increase it. She shuddered anew, indeed, as she perceived, though not a word was said about it even by the open-hearted Sabina, that store of money was not wanting to put in action the various little schemes which the affectionate daughter had conceived for the accommodation of her father; and truly Sabina shewed a talent for business in her proceedings which no one had ever given her credit for before.

There was one duty which Father Mark was speedily called upon to perform, which he did with hearty good will, and with no mixture whatever of the repugnance which his spiritual advice concerning the little people of the lake had cost him. He joined the honest hands of

Hans Klopmann and Gertrude Weiber in holy matrimony, thereby making a very loving man and wife, and furnishing Mr Hargrave and his daughters with all they wanted in the way of domestic assistance in the abode preparing for them.

Gertrude would greatly have preferred gaining her living by taking service with Sabina and Adèle to any other mode whatever, and Hans best liked whatever was preferred by Gertrude; but Mr Hargrave was by no means disposed to rest his hopes of their fidelity upon these grounds, and failed not to seek and to find opportunities of conversing with them both, and impressing upon their minds the extraordinary good fortune which had attended their nuptials, in their having taken service on the very day they received the priest's blessing with a family to whom so much supernatural favour had been shewn. 'You will be long-lived, happy, and rich,' said Mr Hargrave in very good and intelligible German, 'IF – remember this important IF, my good children, – you will be rich, happy, and long-lived, if you keep faithfully the secret that the spirits of the Mummelsee and good Father Mark have permitted me to intrust to you. But should you fail in this, – should you betray this trust, or even tell to the people with whom you may occasionally converse or have dealings, why it is that you live near the Mummelsee, your punishment will be very terrible.'

Much less than this would have done to keep the young couple from amusing their neighbours with accounts of what they saw, and of the very little which they understood, respecting their new master; but it requires considerable knowledge of the perfect faith which is given by the simple people of that romantic region to the local legends amidst which they have been reared, in order to comprehend the degree of influence which such words produced upon Hans Klopmann and his pretty bride. Fondly as they loved – and German peasants can love very heartily as well as their betters, – they would each of them infinitely have preferred burning pretty severely the right hand of the other, rather than have incurred for both the far greater danger of neglecting the warning thus given.

There was, in fact, but little danger that any eye not particularly interested in finding him should be directed to the retreat of Mr Hargrave. On further and more deliberate examination of the innumerable chambers of the forsaken residence, it became evident that of one sort or another, there was a vast deal more furniture than the small knot of interlopers who intended to take possession of it could possibly require. For the most part this was of a nature which it required not the aid of superstition to preserve from the depredations of the rustic neighbourhood; being of a rich, lumbering, heavy character, that would have made it at once difficult of removal, useless when obtained, and bearing most unmistakable evidence of the station of the parties to whom it must have originally belonged; thus challenging a degree of curious inquiry by no means convenient in cases of violent abduction.

It appeared probable, indeed, from the great abundance of these fading remnants of former splendour, that the abandonment of this very unattractive residence had been gradual, and more silent and unproclaimed than could have been the case had its still-life inhabitants been made to follow the steps of their errant owners.

Not, however, that Mr Hargrave, his daughters, or even their faithful attendants, could have taken up their abode, even for a single night, at the château without many essential, though not very bulky, additions to its furniture. But such of these as were purchased either by Hans Klopmann or the Frau Weiber, in the town, were conveyed to the little *gasthaus* either without any remark at all, or such as signified an opinion that the business of the little establishment there was going on prosperously. From thence it was easily removed under the shelter of night to the château; and in this manner everything thought to be absolutely necessary to a moderate degree of comfort, was provided for the family, before they took their first night's sleep in their strangely new quarters.

There was one circumstance, and that of considerable importance to their comfort, which furnished the observing eye of Mr Hargrave with doubly important evidence of the assured security of the position. This was the finding an underground cellar of considerable extent, pretty nearly filled from the pavement to the roof with pine-wood from the neighbouring forest, ready cut into commodious logs for burning. This not only gave the strongest evidence that no intruding eyes had ever ventured to spy out the secrets of this stronghold of superstition, even with a view to plunder, while it gave him an opportunity of pointing out to his two followers the obvious patronage of the tiny race, who were celebrated throughout the region for doing the household work of their favourites.

At length the day came when Sabina and her assistants ventured to announce that all was ready for 'the flitting.' Herself, her sad but ever-aidant sister, and Gertrude, removed themselves to their new abode exactly at the hour of noon, when no eye save that of the bright sun was likely to be fixed upon them; all the world being, for a certainty, engaged in eating their *mittagbrod*. Mr Hargrave and Hans Klopmann were to follow them by star-light; Hans being by this time sufficiently acquainted with the route to undertake the office of guide without any other.

If Adèle de Cordillac had wanted any reward for the devoted affection she had manifested towards her young sister, she would have found it in the brightness of Sabina's eye and the glow upon her cheek during the whole of this busy day; for she read therein that her painful efforts had not been in vain, but that, in spite of the wreck of all the ordinary materials of happiness in the midst of which they stood, the peace of mind which she had so dearly cared for had not been wholly destroyed.

Nor was Adèle herself idle. Under the orders of her notable sister, she contributed greatly to the result which was the great object of all Sabina's exertions; namely, the giving an air of comfort to the wide and lofty saloon which had been selected for their sitting apartment, and arranging a sleeping-room for her father that should not revolt his delicate *impressionability*, by any of the wants he had complained of at the little *gasthaus*.

Notwithstanding all this useful activity, however, Sabina, without counting as a cause of woe her abrupt transition from a state of wealth, in which the utmost power of human ingenuity was set in action to contrive luxuries, to one in which equal ability was called for to supply the want of them, – poor Sabina, without counting this, had a thorn in her heart, which, to a less high-minded creature, would have sufficed to destroy activity, health, and usefulness for ever. We rarely, perhaps, know *how* dearly we love any thing till we have lost it; and it is certain that Sabina, in the midst of the varied gaiety of Paris, her heart fortified by the conscious necessity of checking every feeling approaching to woman's love in her intercourse with Prince Frederic, was very far from being aware how infinitely little in her eyes was the proportion his rank held in the general sum of his perfections, or how widely different were her own feelings towards him to those of the smiling crowds that fluttered round his greatness, wishing for nothing but such a portion of his attention, bestowed before the eyes of all men, as might add another feather to their well-plumed caps.

It was only when she felt that she had lost sight of the young man for ever that she knew, from the pang this thought cost her, how dear – how very dear, he had become to her. But never did an innocent young heart struggle more honestly with its weakness than did that of Sabina when she made this discovery. With as much good sense as right principle, she abstained rigorously from indulging herself by talking of him to Adèle; and the only feeling in which he had part that she did not resolutely seek to smother, was that which made her so eagerly cling to the desolate Castle of the Lake, as the place of refuge for her father. It is true that she did, indeed, believe it to be the safest and the best; but it is true, also, that the persuasion of having seen and conversed with Prince Frederic on the rock above it, had grown, by degrees, into the most assured conviction; and the idea that it was *he* who had told her of its existence while it was still invisible to her eye, gave a vague but delightful feeling that she owed her father's safety to him, which was the source of such fanciful gratification to her.

It was certainly, as young ladies go, no very trifling or very ordinary degree of right and noble feeling which, in the midst of so much devotedness to the recollection of this young man, could enable her to shake off all that was morally objectionable in the feeling, and remain still not only the fond, but the active and useful child of her unfortunate father.

But not even Adèle knew how much credit she deserved for this; for by no means giving her credit for the gentle but steadfast courage which enabled her to abstain from talking of him, her sister flattered herself that he had left no impression on her mind sufficiently profound to affect her peace, or add in any way to the heavy load of misfortune which had fallen on her half-unconscious head, and which it was the chief study of her own existence to make fall lightly on her.

But though quite unconscious of all the merit due to the gay-looking little manager for her well-sustained efforts to be both cheerful and useful, Adèle loved her, as she thought, a thousand times more dearly than ever for her practical piety, in thus receiving on her young head the pelting of so pitiless a storm without uttering a single murmur of complaint, or even suffering a shade of sorrow to rest upon her lovely brow. Yet, while contemplating her thus, with a heart overflowing with love and admiration, she groaned inwardly as she remembered *what* that father was for whose sake this dear Sabina was thus ready and contented to bear all things.

CHAPTER XXIV

Nothing could better prove the sagacity of Mademoiselle de Cordillac than the use made by her aunt of the communication she had deemed it prudent to make to her respecting the departure of Mr Hargrave.

As long as that gentleman and his daughter remained in the *salons* of the —— embassy, the good lady had held her peace, though beyond all question it was pain and grief to her; but no sooner had she watched him lead his daughter off, and received from Sabina a soft parting glance, which the gentle-hearted girl could not withhold from her mother's sister, than she began – as she sorted the hand of cards just dealt to her – to sigh very pathetically, and to murmur odds and ends of the secret of which she believed herself to be the repository.

'*Eh, mon Dieu! – c'est à vous, monsieur, à jouer – que c'est affligeant d'entendre des choses semblables!*'

'Of what do you speak, madame?' said her partner.

'*Hélas! – j'ai tort – j'ai tort d'en parler – jouez, monsieur, s'il vous plaît.*'

Then, finding that, notwithstanding her sighs, the game seemed to create more interest than her sorrows, she went on, –

'Of course you all know – I believe (looking round) that I may speak with safety – of course you all know that there has been another most unexpected political combination discovered – the knave was mine.'

But, when requested to explain herself, she went no further than to say that one deservedly dear to her in all ways had most imprudently demonstrated his strong personal attachment to a certain illustrious individual who should be nameless.

'*Mais qui donc?*' was demanded with more eagerness than discretion by one of the party.

'*Excusez moi, je n'ose pas poursuivre;*' and presently added in a whisper, 'You will hear enough of it ere long, depend upon it. For my part, I say nothing; I am not incapable of putting a just value upon noble sentiments, and yet I lament, and perhaps do not altogether approve, any attempt to disturb the *aimable* tranquillity in which we have of late been permitted to live. But I can never lose sight of the fact that my illustrious *beau-frère* is the most noble-hearted of men, and, as an Englishman, decidedly *sans pareil. Ah! mon Dieu!* Paris will find reason to mourn his loss!'

To all the questionings naturally elicited by these words, and many others of similar tendency, she would, however, accord little more satisfaction than might be found from the repetition of '*Excusez moi, messieurs; j n'ose pas.*' Yet, as soon as they let her alone, she again recurred to it; and before the party was finally broken up and her carriage announced, no inconsiderable portion of the company had become fully aware that Mr Hargrave was discovered to have been implicated in some political intrigue which rendered it necessary for him to leave Paris, in order to preserve his personal freedom.

Any story thus circulated through half-a-dozen *salons*, from mouth to mouth, must inevitably be subject to great variations in its progress, even when the original has been fully and clearly stated. But, in repeating the obscure hints and innuendos of Madame de Hautrivage, there was hardly a possible addition or interpretation which was not added. Some had been given clearly to understand that Mr Hargrave was in close alliance with Prince Louis Buonaparte, and had received his promise that he should be made Minister of Public Instruction as soon as the Prince found himself firmly established on his immortal uncle's throne. Others were as satisfactorily convinced that Mr Hargrave had killed a political adversary of the old *régime* in a duel, and that the new *régime* intended to have made an example of him; while others as confidently declared that France had nothing to do with the business, and that the departure of the elegant Englishman was solely occasioned by his having received an intimation from the Spanish *chargé d'affaires* that the French government would be called upon to interfere in order to put a stop to certain proceedings which were understood to be going on by and with the connivance of Mr Hargrave, to produce an immediate restoration of the exiled king of Spain to his throne.

The place held by Mr Hargrave and his beautiful daughters in Paris society rendered all these statements, and any others that could have been circulated respecting him, of the greatest interest, which feeling was, of course, brought to its acme by a loud disturbance which arose in the hall, when Madame de Hautrivage, having, at four o'clock, inquired for Mr Hargrave's carriage, and been told that it was *avancée*, walked through the crowd of servants *alone*, or at least attended only by the gentleman who gave her his arm.

Louis Querin, who, by way of being particularly vigilant, had been for the last two hours seated among the servants, with one of the *gendarmerie* beside him, enveloped in his own livery great-coat, started forward the instant he heard Mr Hargrave's carriage called for, with his official companion at his side, and, with his eyes on the alert, stood ready to watch his doomed master into the equipage, the driver of which had already received orders, from a quarter whence no orders are questioned, to drive the party to a place indicated; when, after lodging him there, he was to proceed with the ladies of the party to their home.

All this had been admirably arranged, – nothing could be better, – nothing more certain of success; and Louis Querin had spent a considerable portion of his two hours' watch in calculating the comparative advantages of continuing his present profession of show-servant, or changing it for 'a place under the government,' in other words, becoming an agent of the police, which he felt little, or rather no doubt, would be at his disposal, as a reward for his important services on the present occasion.

When this very clever fellow first caught sight of the splendid turban which completed the dress of Madame de Hautrivage, he gave his companion a nudge with his elbow, and both started together to their feet.

'Is that the man?' whispered the agent of police, glancing at the gentleman who had the honour of giving Madame de Hautrivage his arm.

'Not at all, *mon cher*,' was the reply; 'that old lady is our sister-in-law; he will follow in a moment with his daughter, and you will see a beauty, I promise you, – proud little minx as she is. The other, who is prouder and handsomer still, is not here to-night.'

'Never mind about their beauty, my good fellow,' said the other. 'Where the devil is your man? I see no sign of any body belonging to your old lady, – and here she comes, looking about for you, no doubt. Put yourself forward, man, and let us hear where her brother is.'

Querin did as he was directed; and no sooner did Madame de Hautrivage get sight of him than she exclaimed, with great satisfaction, '*Tout va bien donc!*' and then added, '*Ah ça, Louis, ton maître n'est plus ici. Je m'en vais retourner seule. Va voir si la voiture est prête.*'

Querin bit his lip, and instead of obeying the command, turned short round to his companion, demanding, in no very happy tone of voice, '*Qu'est-ce qu'il faut faire?*'

'*Faire!*' repeated the official, muttering in smothered anger, '*nous nous sommes joliment arrangés, n'est-ce pas?*' Then, raising his voice to the proper tone of authority, he proclaimed to all who chose to listen that his business there was to arrest a gentleman who was probably concealing himself, but that the individual with whom his business lay would do much more wisely by giving himself up quietly; that he was too well known in all ways to leave the slightest possibility of escape; that his name was Hargrave; and that it was highly advisable that no person should assist in concealing him.

The rapidity with which the purport of such an harangue spread through the *salons* of the —— embassy may be easily imagined; and then it was that the colour which Adèle had given to the affair achieved its object with the *beau monde* of Paris. The shapes in which the story was carried forth, and spread, were as various, indeed, as the tongues which gave them birth; but the substituting treason for felony was uniform and universal; and the illusion thus produced was sufficient to counteract, with an immense majority of listeners, particularly of the higher class, the effect of the true version of the story, even when afterwards told with the most faithful accuracy; for to such the first crime seemed possible, but the last not; and then it was so natural that every pains should be taken by the authorities to keep secret what, beyond all doubt, was an important state matter, that the sharpest eyes listened with a knowing wish, and the wisest heads with an incredulous shake, when vulgar hints of the truth were hazarded.

'*Oui, oui, oui, c'est très-bien – très-bien. C'est mieux que la chose va comme ça. N'en parlons pas. Nous savons, nous savons,*' was the style and tone in which the mysterious subject was canvassed from one end of Paris to the other. Nay, there were not wanting some, endowed with peculiarly keen political sagacity, who broadly hinted that the whole affair of Madame Bertrand's disappearance had been got up by the government in order to conceal the progress which certain principles were making in certain circles.

The buzzing whispers, therefore, which went round and along, and up and down the throng of liveried lacqueys, and in which the truth, if not quite the whole truth, was soundly stated (thanks to the friendly feeling existing between M Louis Querin and most of the set), was entirely, and altogether, for their own vulgar use, and even if heard distinctly by the noble phalanx of their masters and mistresses, would have been listened to with dignified contempt.

To do Madame de Hautrivage justice, she behaved during the scene in the hall with the most consummate judgment and propriety; for though, of course, she naturally availed herself of so brilliant an occasion for a slight touch of faintness and fine feeling, she did not lose sight of the dignity which attaches to a trusted friend in a political affair of first-rate importance, and after having received *flacons* from half-a-dozen hands, and made eloquent appeals with her accomplished eyes to all the most distinguished of the friends and acquaintance who crowded round her, she walked forward to the carriage of Mr Hargrave, now attending her for the last time, with a step which would not have disgraced a royal heroine when about to yield her neck to the stroke of the headsman.

Among the persons present at this scene, was Coventry's friend, Count Romanhoff. The eyes of Adèle had not deceived her; it was the Count, and none other, whom she had seen before the door of the coffee-house during the terrible interval employed in waiting in the *fiacre* for Mr Hargrave and Sabina.

This young man, – who though he had not himself altogether escaped the taint of Parisian dissipation, loved and valued, as it deserved, the exalted character of Alfred Coventry, – had exerted, not in vain, the power of his eloquence upon the galled spirit of his unhappy friend, during the first few miles of their drive out of Paris, at five o'clock in the morning of this same eventful day. The result of this eloquence was the obtaining a promise from Alfred, that he would give up the solitary distant wanderings he had meditated, and consent to accompany the Count in a long-projected tour through England, Wales, Scotland, and Ireland. This promise once obtained, the Count left his friend's travelling carriage as abruptly as he had entered it, and returned to Paris about five hours after he had quitted it, exceedingly well satisfied with the result of his short expedition, and greatly pleased at having secured for his longer one a companion so greatly to his liking.

Having occupied several very busy hours after his return in setting all things *en train* for leaving the abode which he had enjoyed perhaps too keenly and too long, he dined at the Hôtel de l'Europe with a friend, then dressed, and beguiled away another hour or two, and at the moment Adèle recognised him, was in the act of proceeding with his friend to the ball at the —— embassy.

Fortunately for the fugitives, Mr Hargrave, in quitting the Ambassador's hôtel with his daughter, took the precaution of crossing the

street in which it was situated, for the express purpose of escaping exactly
such rencontres as would infallibly have occurred, with Count
Romanhoff, had he not done so. Such a meeting, after his detection of
Mademoiselle de Cordillac, hiding herself within the shelter of a
hackney-coach, would have sent him into the ball-room with materials
for gossip, which would have fallen in well with the scraps of information
which Madame de Hautrivage had set in circulation. But as it was, he
entered it believing, and well contented to believe, that the fair coquet,
who had given so severe a heartache to his admired friend, was engaged
in some abominable imprudence (probably an elopement), which would
go far towards curing Coventry of his love. So far, indeed, was he from
suspecting that her sister or Mr Hargrave were in her counsels, that on
entering the dancing-room, where the orchestra with its echo of 'many
twinkling feet' were in full activity, he looked round it for Sabina. He
was not, perhaps, the less inclined to join in the dance from perceiving
that there was no chance of his meeting her in it, and immediately did so
with a fair lady, whom he perfectly well knew would have enjoyed it the
more, and liked him all the better, had he amused her with an account of
the mysterious glimpse he had caught of one who had ranked as fairest of
the fair in that set; but, to his immortal honour be it said, he did no such
thing. When, however, he caught the name of Hargrave, as he was
making his exit through the ball, and heard it coupled on all sides with
rumours of his political enterprise, the recollection of Adèle's strange
position recurred to him, and with an interpretation wholly different
from what he had attached to it before.

It was quite impossible that the two circumstances could be
unconnected; and, as he listened to the statement of Mr Hargrave's
having been seen playing at cards till near two o'clock, and having then
made his exit with his daughter, as it now appeared, without using his
carriage, the obvious fact suggested itself, that Mademoiselle was waiting
for her plotting step-father and his daughter to join her.

At the first moment this solution satisfied him perfectly, being, indeed,
almost too palpably evident to admit of a doubt; but as he still stood
listening to the various versions of the tale Madame de Hautrivage had
circulated, it struck him as exceedingly strange, that a young lady so
perfectly independent in all ways as Mademoiselle de Cordillac should
think it necessary to identify herself thus in a political intrigue, which
could not be likely to have any consequences more serious than Mr
Hargrave's absenting himself from the French capital. Why was it
necessary for her to disguise herself in the manner he had seen? Why
should not she follow this step-father, if it was her pleasure to do so,
without descending to any such objectionable manoeuvres?

Count Romanhoff at first started these questions (which, by the way,

were propounded to himself alone) solely from his predisposition to find
every thing that Mademoiselle de Cordillac did 'wrong and ill done;' but
it chanced, that after listening for some time to the hubbub which the
officer's demand for Mr Hargrave's person produced, he was, at length,
once more making his way towards the door, when his ear caught a
gibing phrase about the cunning trick of the *les grands messieurs,*' in
pretending to believe that the *vaurien*, who had so cleverly slipped
through the hands of justice, had only been plotting a little against King
Philippe; when the fact was, that he had been discovered to be the
greatest thief in Paris, and, as some said, a cruel murderer into the
bargain.

This might have been sufficient to arouse the curiosity of a quieter
spirit, and one less interested in the business, than was Count
Romanhoff; but upon him it acted like fire upon tow, he was instantly in
a blaze of eagerness to know what this might mean. That the *vaurien* thus
mentioned indicated Mr Hargrave, he was not permitted to doubt, as the
name of that gentleman was audibly bandied from mouth to mouth,
among the group to whom the speaker of these exciting words addressed
himself. But how was he to learn more? Could the proud Russian noble
join himself to the liveried throng and question them? Impossible! No,
not even for the sake of having to tell Coventry how exceedingly
thankful he ought to feel at escaping so terrible a connexion, – no! not
even for this, could he so degrade himself.

The extreme difficulty, not to say impossibility, of finding any one at
that hour, except the lackeys, who would be able to give him the
information he was dying to obtain, sent him, by the absolute force of
necessity, home to bed for the remainder of that night; but most faithfully
did he promise himself not to see another till he had made out to his own
satisfaction the origin of this discrepancy between the version given of
Mr Hargrave's disappearance by the valets and that put in circulation by
their masters.

In consequence of this excellent resolution, Count Romanhoff rose on
the following morning full ten minutes earlier than usual; but, while
submitting himself to the inevitable delay of eating his breakfast, it
occurred to him that he was without any clue whatever by which to
guide his researches, and that, unless he stood at the corners of the streets
to question the passengers, he had no means of learning more upon the
subject which so piqued his curiosity than he knew already.

Considerably vexed and disconcerted by this result of his clear-headed
morning meditation, his breakfast, begun in haste, was finished at leisure,
and he even set himself tranquilly to the perusal of half-a-dozen
newspapers, when he recollected that, as Madame de Hautrivage had
evidently not accompanied the fugitives from Paris, nothing could be

more natural, necessary, and polite, than the paying her a friendly visit at the mansion, which he still presumed to be her home. No sooner had this bright idea occurred than it completely engrossed him. If he could but get a sight of that most *bavarde* and silliest of middle-aged gentlewomen, he should be certain of learning every thing he wished to know; and a stronger proof of the interest which he took in the business could hardly be given than his inwardly resolving rather to make love to her outright than fail in his purpose of obtaining all the information she had to bestow.

He waited, however, with becoming patience till the hour arrived at which such a visit might be made without the certainty of receiving an assurance at the door that Madame was not '*encore visible;*' but his carriage was peremptorily ordered to the door punctually at the time fixed upon, and when it was announced, he sprang into it as eagerly as if it were about to convey him to the presence of the most charming woman in Paris, instead of taking him to that of the person whom he happened to think most pre-eminently the reverse.

In the hurried conversation between Mr Hargrave and his family on the preceding evening, Madame de Hautrivage had almost anticipated the proposal made for her remaining in Paris; and, in fact, would almost as willingly have consented to mount her funeral pile in order to be burnt alive, as have abandoned that only scene of imaginable enjoyment. '*Paris sa grande ville,*' was all her world; and at that moment she had certainly no other idea than that of returning as promptly as possible to the perhaps equally agreeable, though less splendid, mode of life which she had established for herself before she had been invited to become the chaperone of her two nieces.

But, on awaking on the following morning, and passing in review, as she sipped her early coffee, all the circumstances which had so suddenly occurred, it appeared to her far more proper that she should remain where she was, till it was finally decided whether the conduct of her noble-minded *beau-frère* had been such as to render his permanent absence from the French capital necessary; or whether the affair would prove only one of those passing sparks of political excitement which render the position of *la belle France* so inexpressibly interesting.

There was much that she felt to be particularly agreeable in thus remaining alone in Mr Hargrave's mansion. She was certain that by doing so she should play the part of a political heroine, *à très bon marché,* in every sense of the phrase, and that nobody worth seeing in Paris would fail to pay their compliments to her under the circumstances. The fear, therefore, which had tormented Count Romanhoff, as he drove along, that the lady might altogether refuse to receive visitors, was quite unfounded; for the first order of the day, given by Madame de

Hautrivage to her *femme de chambre*, was, that she should make it known to 'the people of the anti-chamber' that whoever called was to be admitted.

If Count Romanhoff particularly wished for a *tête-à-tête* he was disappointed, for when he entered the spacious drawing-room selected by Madame de Hautrivage as that in which she should best like to receive her inquiring friends, he found it already half full. But whatever his previous wishes on the subject might have been, he was soon reconciled to the actual state of things, by perceiving that the process of examination and cross-examination was going on in the most satisfactory manner possible, whilst Madame de Hautrivage appeared as desirous of answering, as her friends of asking, questions; and thus, while he obtained all the information she was able to give, he escaped the necessity of paying for it, by such expressions of lively interest in her own share of the business, as those who questioned her felt it necessary to express.

'Ah! but it is you I think of in the midst of all this!' said a peer of France, in a tone of the deepest sentiment. 'My charming friend, I dread a nervous attack for you!'

'Alas! yes – I must expect it,' replied Madame de Hautrivage, applying a golden *flacon* to her nose, and a richly embroidered pocket-handkerchief to her temples. '*Mais le moyen de l'éviter?*'

'The only *moyen* is to be found in your own noble heart,' said another gentleman, who, seated close beside her, with his thin person bent forward, so as to enable him to turn and regard her, *en face*, as she spoke, seemed determined to endure no ignorance which questions either of eyes or lips could remove.

'*La cause est si belle!*' he continued, 'that it becomes a glory to take part in it, *coute qui coute*. But tell me, I implore you, where is your noble relative gone? There are none here but trustworthy friends, be sure of it; *et puis*, if he is out of the kingdom, you know, there can be no danger in gratifying our affectionate curiosity, for all danger must then be over.'

'Eh, bien, bons amis,' replied Madame de Hautrivage, looking gratefully round her, 'that is perfectly true, and it is precisely for that reason that I may indulge in an *épouchement de coeur*, which the frankness of my temper renders so necessary to me. *Mais prenons garde!* And never let us forget that the fate of kings may hang upon our breath! *Ah, quelle idée superbe!*' And here the golden *flacon* was of the greatest service, for it was evident, from the closing of the eyes and the general agitation of her person, that Madame de Hautrivage must have fainted without it.

'*Mais, au nom de Dieu, poursuivez, chère, donc!* Where is our estimable friend? Where are M Hargrave and his charming daughters?' fervently demanded the gentleman by her side.

'At this moment,' replied Madame de Hautrivage solemnly, raising her prodigious eyes to Heaven, while her hands, *flacon*, and handkerchief, admirably grouped together, were elevated before her to the level of her nose, but several inches in advance of it, – 'at this moment, by the blessing of the *bon Dieu*, I flatter myself they are at the foot of the English throne, and enjoying the benign protection of a race remarkable for their love of noble deeds!'

'*Mais déjà!*' exclaimed the peer, raising his flexible eyebrows nearly to the top of his forehead; '*ma chère amie*, I saw him last night, and his beautiful daughter also, *à l'Ambassade d'*——'

'*Mais oui, certainement, monsieur, il y était – cependant*——' And here Madame de Hautrivage stopped, as if there was something of mystery in the explanation she wished to give; upon which her thin neighbour exclaimed, –

'*Expliquez-vous, madame! Au nom de grace!* How can this be? Remember M Hargrave counts among our dearest friends, and affection so devoted demands confidence.'

'*Mais certainement,*' replied Madame de Hautrivage, with a very graceful action betokening thanks, 'the heart should be of marble that could refuse you! My noble-minded *beau-frère*, then, and both his lovely daughters, immediately upon leaving the Ambassador's last night, threw themselves into a *berline*, with four, or, I believe, five post horses attached to it, and set off, *ventre à terre*, for Calais. *Mon beau-frère est énormément riche*, and all the world knows what gold can do.'

'*Mais c'est vrai, c'est bien vrai!*' returned the thin gentleman. 'It is to Calais, then, that our *cher* M Hargrave is gone?'

'*Mais oui, monsieur, à Calais,*' was the reply.

This statement was so point blank, and it seemed so very little probable that the dwelling of Mr Hargrave, the lady who presided over his family, his servants, and every thing else belonging to the mansion, should be thus completely *in statu quo*, had the words uttered by the attendants in the Ambassador's hall contained any mixture of truth, that Count Romanhoff, satisfied that in this case the more general report was the true one, rose to go as soon as the decisive words '*à Calais*' reached his ears. Just as he reached the door, another gentleman, released from his attendance, as it seemed, by the same conclusive assertion, reached it also, and as he civilly retreated a step for the Count to pass, that gentleman looked in his face to ascertain whether this mark of respect proceeded from an acquaintance.

He at once saw that this was not the case, for though the individual was exceedingly well dressed, even to precision, the quick eye of Romanhoff perceived, in an instant, that he was not, as he would have expressed it, *de nous autres*. This was the result of the first glance; but after he had withdrawn his eyes, an idea struck him that he had seen the face before, and that recently, but where, or exactly when, he could not recall.

The feeling inevitably consequent upon this sort of puzzle is the wish
to get another look at the features which have produced it; and Count
Romanhoff, after descending the stairs with the rapid step of an active
young man, paused at the bottom of them to indulge this wish.

The stranger was close behind him, and, as the Count turned to look
at him, a classic sort of an Italian profile, very remarkable for its outline,
recalled, in an instant, that of the person whom he had seen conversing
with Mr Hargrave on the night of the ball, when he was escorting
Mademoiselle de Cordillac to the supper-table.

Under any other cirumstances the sight of this man, and the
recollections of the words which he had heard addressed to him, which,
at the time they were spoken, made but the slight impression which the
private manoeuvres of one dissipated man might be expected to do upon
another, – under any other circumstances, this recognition, and the
recollections which accompanied it, would have only produced a desire
to get out of the way; but now it suddenly occurred to Romanhoff that
neither of the versions which had reached him concerning the absence of
Mr Hargrave were in any way consistent with the adventure of which he
had been himself in some sort the witness.

Was it possible that the strange appearance of Mademoiselle de
Cordillac had, in reality, nothing to do with the evasion of her stepfather
and her sister?

Was it possible that he had, after all, mistaken a stranger, bearing
resemblance to the beloved of his friend, for the young lady herself?

Was it possible that this full-dressed melodramatic-looking personage
could throw any light upon the circumstances that so tormentingly
puzzled him? The torment, by the way, being, to do the Count justice,
produced less by baffled curiosity than by a fear of reporting to his friend
Coventry any thing that was not strictly true concerning Mr Hargrave or
any of his family, well aware that what might fall harmless, as mere idle
words, elsewhere, would to Alfred appear matters of deepest
consequence.

It is a mightily tedious process to write down the thoughts of a man;
for long and long before one phasis of the varying surface be described,
another succeeds, and another, and another, setting the recording pen at
utter defiance. In much less time than it has taken to write a single word
of the above sketch of Count Romanhoff's meditations, they had all
passed through his mind, and, moreover, he had formed the resolution of
addressing the Italian behind him, in the hope of obtaining something
from him which might throw a light upon the subject.

'I beg your pardon, sir,' he said, civilly touching his hat, 'but I should
be excessively obliged if you could explain to me a little more clearly
than our good friend Madame de Hautrivage has done, what it is which

has induced Mr Hargrave so suddenly to leave the French capital? I am much interested about him, and it would be a great kindness if you could give me any information on the subject.'

Now, though the person of Signor Ruperto was only known to Count Romanhoff in the very slight degree that has been described, and that his name was not known to him at all, the Signor was perfectly well-acquainted with both the name and person of Count Romanhoff, and was perfectly aware that he was a young nobleman, possessed of great wealth, and a free hand wherewithal to scatter it. This was precisely the class and order of man with whom the active and serviceable Italian liked to make acquaintance, and taking off his hat with much respect, he said, with a very graceful bow, that nothing could give him more pleasure than conversing on any subject with the celebrated and highly esteemed Count Romanhoff.

'You are very obliging, sir,' replied the young man, looking earnestly at him. 'May I take the liberty of asking to whom I have the honour of addressing myself?'

The Italian for a moment seemed to hesitate, and then, with the air of one who has *pris son parti*, he said, –

'My name, Count Romanhoff, will probably not convey much information to you; nevertheless, I have no inclination to withhold it. My name is Julio Ruperto, and in most of the capitals of Europe I have been fortunate enough to make, sooner or later, the acquaintance of nearly all the men of fashion to be found in them. I am not, however, noble; I pretend to nothing which does not belong to me. A certain knowledge of the world, rather more general – I believe I might say universal – than often seems to fall to the lot of an individual, has made me, I am proud to say it, useful to many of them. Should I ever be able to add the name of Count Romanhoff to the list of those to whom I have been fortunate enough to render service, I shall esteem the chance which has now brought me acquainted with him as a most happy one. Perhaps, Count, I might not at so very early a stage of our intercourse have spoken to you so explicitly as I am now doing, were it not that a considerable degree of confidential openness is necessary before I can have the honour of answering, with any degree of sincerity, the questions you have put to me with such amiable frankness respecting M Hargrave.'

Here Signor Julio Ruperto paused, and again bowing to the Count, seemed to await his reply.

Count Romanhoff would have been better pleased if the confidential information hinted at had been given without his again addressing himself to the equivocal personage beside him. The Count's carriage had set him down outside the gates of the large court in which Mr Hargrave's hôtel stood, and was waiting for him when he left it. The above conversation, therefore, had taken place between the door of the mansion and the *porte-cochère* in front of it, and they now stood together beside the carriage.

Count Romanhoff paused and felt that he had put himself into a dilemma. He must now either submit to ask Signor Julio Ruperto to mount his carriage, or walk forward with him, ordering his equipage to follow. There was, indeed, one way by which he might have escaped from between these threatening horns: he might have bowed himself off, on the score of being too much occupied at the present moment to listen to the communication which the Signor was so obligingly ready to make. He longed to do this, for he had taken the Italian in utter aversion; but then he must, in all likelihood, remain hopelessly endeavouring to look through the atmosphere of darkness visible that surrounded Mr Hargrave and his affairs.

The Count was decidedly very curious upon the subject for his own sake, and seriously anxious for that of his friend; so, at length, he replied, but somewhat coldly, 'You are very obliging, sir. If you will do me the favour to drive with me as far as the end of the Italian Boulevard, where I have a visit to pay, I shall be able to profit by the communication you have promised to make. Will this be taking you out of your way, sir?'

'Not the least in the world, Monsieur le Comte,' replied the Italian, lightly springing into the ready equipage. 'Le Boulevard des Italiens can never be considered as out of the way by a man of the world of any nation, and assuredly not by one of mine; its nature, as well as its name, belongs to us. Sunny, bright, brilliant, and beautiful, it well deserves the inviting name it has received. And now,' he continued, taking off his hat and placing himself much at his ease in the corner of the carriage, – 'now I will confidentially hint what I have no doubt, M le Comte, will very considerably surprise you. But observe, M le Comte, I give you my honour,' and Signor Julio Ruperto pressed his hand upon his heart, – 'I give you my honour, Count Romanhoff, that had Mr Hargrave kept his engagements to me, I would not have broken mine to him; but it is desirable – highly desirable, that all gentlemen should be taught to understand that the promises and the faith of men of honour are reciprocal. When an engagement is broken, Count Romanhoff, it is broken. It cannot hold on one side and be loose on the other. It is contrary to the nature of things, – it is impossible!'

Again the Italian seemed to expect that Count Romanhoff would speak, but he did not.

'My motive in calling at the house to-day,' resumed the Italian, 'was to ascertain where the gay Englishman had betaken himself. I have no acquaintance whatever with any of the ladies of the family, but when I was about to question the domestics I observed such multitudes of

visitors admitted that I thought I might without difficulty pass in with
the rest; and though it rarely happens that so much can be learned on any
domestic subject in the *salon* as in the ante-room, I still wished to hear
what account the family themselves might give of the absent gentleman.
And you heard, sir, as well as I did, I presume, that he is gone to Calais?'

'Yes, sir, I did,' replied Count Romanhoff, 'and therefore it is not on
that point that I ventured to ask you for information. I confess, I wish, if
possible, to know what reason could have induced Mr Hargrave to leave
Paris in the manner he has done?'

Signor Julio Ruperto laughed slightly. 'Be not impatient, noble Count,'
he said, 'I shall reach that division of the subject immediately; and I
suspect that you will be a good deal surprised at what I shall have to tell
you, for already two distinct romances have been invented both equally
foreign from the truth. It is not improbable that you have heard both.
One we had both of us the advantage of hearing freely discussed in the
salon we have just quitted. You heard it roundly stated – did you not? –
that Mr Hargrave had been obliged to leave Paris recently in order to
escape from the hands of the police who are in search of him, on account
of a political intrigue into which he is said to have deeply entered. You
heard this, Count Romanhoff, did you not?'

'I did, sir,' replied Romanhoff stiffly.

'And perhaps, also, you have heard the other story; more likely, for any
thing I know, to be true, and nevertheless most absurdly false. Have you
heard this second version, Count?'

'I have heard nothing distinctly,' replied the Count, evasively,
'excepting what you heard also in the *salon* of Madame de Hautrivage.'

'Nay, then, *sans façon*, I will tell you that the other story which has got
into circulation is of a much more disgraceful character, and if true would
render our friend liable to the galleys for life, or to the guillotine itself, if
the worst parts of the history were proved. In short, it has been broadly
asserted, particularly among the lower classes, that Mr Hargrave carried
off Madame Bertrand, the rich banker's wife, from his own hall, robbed
her of her diamonds, and then murdered her. I give you my honour that
such a story is in circulation.'

'It is a consolation in hearing such horrors stated,' replied Count
Romanhoff, 'to hear at the same time the positive contradiction of them
which you seem disposed to give. If I rightly understand what you have
said, you mean to declare on your own knowledge, sir, that this frightful
statement has no foundation in truth?'

'Why really, sir, though I have no particular reason to think well of Mr
Hargrave, inasmuch as he has very grossly defrauded me of a sum of
money that was justly my due, I nevertheless am rather peculiarly well
able to assure you that there is not a single word of truth in this story

from beginning to end. As a gay and gallant young gentleman, Count, you will find the true version of the romance considerably less difficult to believe; and I have no scruple in the world to confess that I was myself a party in the business, and therefore have some right to understand it.'

'I shall be obliged by your letting me hear it from you,' said the Count, perceiving that his companion again appeared to expect that he should say something.

'That is enough, sir,' replied the Italian, with *empressement*. 'It is my wish to oblige the noble Count Romanhoff, and my history of this matter shall be equally unreserved and true. Mr Hargrave and I have known each other for some time; that, however, is not to the purpose. A day or two before the grand ball which took place last night, he called upon me at my lodgings – here is my address, Count' (presenting a card) – 'and with his usual frank and easy manner told me that he had conceived a violent passion for Madame Bertrand, that he had no great reason for thinking that he was disagreeable to her, but that such was the watchfulness of her husband, and such her extreme terror of him, that he was quite convinced an elopement was the only means by which he could hope to obtain her. To this decisive step he confessed that he should not venture to ask her consent, though he feared not her ultimate resentment. To make my story short, suffice it to say that I agreed to assist him in this enterprise. I promised to have a carriage at a certain door of the garden, which, opening upon a passage that led only to the stables, was as retired as the business required. No servant was to be in attendance, and the driver had orders to set off with all speed to a certain dwelling which I indicated to him, as soon as he perceived by the shutting of the carriage-door that the party to be conveyed was in it, but that no word was to be spoken, nor was he to wait for or expect any further orders. *Eh, bien!* M le Comte, I executed my part of the business to perfection. I hung about the premises, easy enough of access at a moment when all the world was coming in, and contrived to receive my last instructions from Mr Hargrave a few moments before he led the lady into supper. He assured me in his gay way that he had every reason to be certain he was not going to offend her beyond forgiveness, and then instructed me as to the exact spot where I was to receive her from his hands at a moment when he should lift the canvass of his temporary buildings in order to refresh her with a little air after the dance; he was then to retreat into the room that he might be seen again amidst the crowd by any who had marked his manoeuvring with the canvass, though of course his object was to choose, if possible, a moment when the spot he had selected was free from observation. All this was accomplished very successfully. Provided with a cloak in which to envelope her, I held her very snugly *empaquetée* till her adorer again joined us, and then I placed my charming *fardeau* in his arms, making my escape again into the house, where if, *par malheur*, any alarm concerning the lady was given, I was to volunteer an account of having seen her in a way to delude all inquiries as much as possible. All this I faithfully performed: and you will allow, Count, that it was a service of danger and well deserving some reward. Will you then believe me when I tell you that I have received none – that I am positively cheated – *joué* – by this gallant gentleman? But if I am not revenged, may every man I meet laugh me to scorn! At ten o'clock this morning I was ordered to call at a particular place where I should find a sealed packet addressed to me. Since that hour, I have called six times, and found nothing, and doubtless *il se moque de moi*, and thinks that I dare not repeat such a tale as this. *Mais il se trompe joliment*, I have learned where I can find him, and find him I will! And now, M le Comte, I will wish you good morning, and beg you to believe that there is nothing which I should not be ready to do *avec la plus grande fidélité* for any gentleman of honour who did not abuse my generous confidence.'

Count Romanhoff, by this time desiring nothing so much as to get rid of his companion, pulled the check-string. The carriage stopped, the step was taken down, and in another moment he had the satisfaction of finding himself alone.

CHAPTER XXV

Nothing could be much farther from a satisfactory explanation than that which, after all his care and pains, Count Romanhoff had contrived to obtain concerning the cause of Mr Hargrave's mysterious departure from Paris. Though by no means an ill-tempered man, he was vexed, out of sorts, and, worse than all, exceedingly angry with himself. He had, in fact, done no less than three things of which he was heartily ashamed, – he had, undeniably, listened to the cabals of a set of serving-men, while he was not known to be an auditor; he had condescended to pay a visit to a woman he detested, solely in the hope of picking up news; and, lastly, he had made acquaintance with a consummate scoundrel, and driven through the streets of Paris with him in his carriage, for the same purpose. His pride, of which he had enough, underwent a very severe penance as he submitted himself to this close self-examination; and he heartily wished that the conceited Englishman had been lodged at the bottom of the Red Sea before he had ever plagued himself about him

Had this eager search after truth been successful – had he obtained intelligence of some well-established fact, which might have sufficed to cure his friend Alfred's love-fit for ever, he might have judged himself more leniently. But what had he learned by all this quidnunc gossiping? Only that all the people in Paris, from the highest to the lowest, were busily engaged in talking about Mr Hargrave, but evidently without knowing positively any single fact concerning him.

There was one statement, and one only which rested upon Count Romanhoff's mind with the full weight of truth. Madame de Hautrivage had positively asserted that Mr Hargrave and his two daughters were gone to England. This was a matter of fact concerning which that much-detested lady could hardly be supposed to be misinformed or mistaken; and he therefore fully believed it.

As to the three conflicting histories which had reached him, he certainly could not be said completely to believe either; but of the three, the one which he had received on the vilest authority was that which appeared to him most likely to be true. Against it, indeed, was the fact of the two young ladies having departed with the hero of it; but it seemed not improbable that he might have taken them off under pretence of an ordinary excursion to his own country, in order to masque his real purpose for making it; and the hints of Madame de Hautrivage, concerning political motives, might have been left her by the gallant Lothario as a gossiping stalking-horse, with which she might amuse herself and her acquaintance till he came back again. The words he had himself heard pass between Hargrave and his vile accomplice were, in short, so strong a confirmation of his story, as nearly to outweigh all that might have been urged against it; and almost sufficiently to convince him that he must have been mistaken when he fancied he saw Mademoiselle de Cordillac in a hackney-coach, when there was such very good reason to believe that she might have absented herself from the Ambassador's for the purpose of preparing for her expedition to England.

The only statement of the three, however, to which he paid absolutely no attention, was the true one. The circumstance of the police being in search of the gentleman never, for one instant, suggested the possibility that it might be true, for there was no difficulty whatever in believing that the outraged husband would take this means of redress, the moment he learned who it was that was suspected of having robbed him of his wife. A secret not at all likely to have been safer yesterday in the keeping of Signor Julio Ruperto than it had been to-day.

The result of all this was a determination on the part of Count Romanhoff to write to his friend Coventry, to state to him, with one exception, all he had heard, to confess that he could not make up his mind to leave Paris till this singular mystery was explained; and, finally, begging him very earnestly to return to his old quarters for a few weeks, to watch with him how the business would end. After which he should

be ready to renew their delightful plan of travelling together; and knew
of nothing to prevent the whole of the coming summer from being thus
agreeably employed. The *one* circumstance which he omitted to mention
was Mademoiselle de Cordillac's reported journey to England, – a
precaution which shewed that the young man felt by no means certain of
having produced any very permanent effect on the state of his friend's
heart by the spirited and graphic description he had given him of the
unfeeling levity with which the fair but false Adèle had listened to the
mention of his name.

The letter thus decided upon was immediately written and sent off;
after which, a desire of ascertaining how Prince Frederic of ———
received the rumours of the day, respecting a family for whom he had
shewn so marked a degree of respect, induced Count Romanhoff to pay
his Royal Highness a visit, at an hour of the evening when it was usual to
find him at home. He was not disappointed in his expectation of finding
him. The Prince was at home, and surrounded by a larger circle of
gentlemen than usual. Count Romanhoff had not joined them above half
a minute before he perceived that the same subject which had engrossed
him during the whole day was that which was now being discussed with
considerable animation before the Prince.

The arrival of Romanhoff was not likely to interrupt it, as his vivacious
manner of entering into discussion on all subjects was well known; and
more than one voice was raised to welcome him.

'*Mon Prince! écoutons Romanhoff; soyez sur qu'il sait tout,*' said a young
man who was standing near his Royal Highness, and who was
advocating, half in jest and half in earnest, the *felonious* interpretation of
the mystery, declaring that Mr Hargrave's notorious passion for show
amounted to monomania, and might account very satisfactorily for the
history of the stolen jewels, murder, and all.

'I shall be happy to hear Count Romanhoff's account of this singular
affair,' said the Prince, gravely; 'and I shall be greatly surprised, M le
Chevalier, if he gives the same interpretation to it that you do. If every
gentleman who entertains his friends with elegance and unbounded
hospitality is to be considered as a madman and a thief, I fear that every
individual will feel inclined to be his own entertainer for the future.'

Had the theory and belief of the Count accorded in all respects with
that of the Chevalier de Beaumont, he would hardly have had the
hardiesse to state it after listening to so very pointed a reprimand. He
rejoiced exceedingly, however, that his honesty was not to pay toll to his
politeness, and answered promptly, '*Dieu m'en garde, monseigneur*; for if I
believed it, I would turn hermit or Trappist without an hour's delay, for
assuredly the world would not be fit to live in.'

'Indeed it would not,' said the Prince; 'I quite agree with you, Count

Romanhoff. And now, sir, you will do me a pleasure if you will let me hear to what conclusion you have been induced to come, by such sifting of truth from slander as it has been in your power to achieve. You are every where, Count, and must, of course, have heard the report, which at this moment we can do Mr Hargrave no injury by repeating, concerning the more zealous than prudent part which our good friend has taken in politics. Do you apprehend that Mr Hargrave has committed himself very deeply with the present government of France?'

'Will you permit me, *mon Prince*,' replied Count Romanhoff, 'to relate to you an adventure which happened to me this morning? I shall feel singularly obliged if your Royal Highness will permit me to do so, without uttering a single word of comment or opinion of my own, as it would be an honour I should greatly desire, might I hope to hear your Highness's opinion upon the truth or falsehood of what I have heard?'

'Go on, Count, I shall be extremely glad to listen to your narrative, even if you refuse me the advantage of your own judgment upon it.'

Count Romanhoff then related, with very scrupulous exactness, every thing that had passed between Mr Julio Ruperto and himself in their drive from the Rue de Lille to the Italian Boulevard; and when he had finished, he bowed profoundly, but in silence, to the Prince, and seemed to expect that his Royal Highness should perform his part of the compact, to which he had seemed tacitly to have acceded.

Prince Frederic, who had listened to the narrative with deep attention, remained silent for a minute or two after it was finished, − a silence which was imitated by the whole party. At length the Prince said, 'I will certainly give you my opinion, Count Romanhoff, as you have asked for it; but you must remember that I shall speak of the tale, not as coming from you, but from the self-acknowledged villain from whom you received it. I consider it to be from beginning to end a most vile and atrocious falsehood, invented for the purpose of bringing forward the scoundrel who related it, in a manner which he thought might make himself advantageously known. Be very sure, Count Romanhoff, that there is no single word of truth in it. It is an invention altogether clumsy, contradictory, and improbable; and if there were nothing else in it to discredit its truth, is not the fact, that the young ladies, his daughters, are gone with him, amply sufficient to prove that not only this story is impossible, but every other in which there is the slightest tincture of dishonour? In believing Mr Hargrave to have been indiscreetly zealous in his wish to revive a fallen dynasty, we may impeach his wisdom, but not his honour. This only can render his being accompanied by his daughters intelligible; and this only do I feel it possible to believe.'

When princes condescend to form a decided opinion, and to utter it, those who have the advantage of listening rarely feel disposed to dispute

it. A murmur, sufficiently distinct for its meaning to be caught, ran round
the circle, by which it was made manifest that every gentleman there,
whatever his opinion might have been before, *now* entirely agreed in the
view of the case which Prince Frederic of —— had taken.

Now there was one point in the chain of events which had come to
the knowledge of Count Romanhoff, that had greatly contributed to his
forming the judgment he had himself come to on the subject under
discussion, but of which none but himself and one other had the
advantage. This was derived from the having involuntarily overheard the
words which had passed between Mr Hargrave and the infamous
Ruperto. Had he been *tête-à-tête* with the Prince, it is possible that he
might have been tempted to repeat them in defence of his own theory;
but as it was, an invincible repugnance to declaring to all the party
present, that he had obtained his information by listening to what was
not intended for him to hear, restrained him, and he suffered the Prince's
opinion to pass, by default of shewing any further arguments against it.

⋆   ⋆   ⋆

It may be that Prince Frederic of —— was himself surprised to find how
completely all the interest he had felt in the *fête* he was about to give had
vanished. He had steadily kept his wise resolution of not meeting Sabina
at the ball at the —— Embassy, but he had not even attempted to conceal
from himself that the hours which he was to pass with her at his own
entertainment, and which he was determined should be the last, would
be among the most interesting, though certainly the saddest of his life.
But now that both the bitter and the sweet of this meeting was put out of
his reach, he would have been exceedingly glad, could his ball have been
given by deputy, and been accepted, nevertheless, by the *élite* of Paris as a
suitable return for all the elegant hospitality he had received from them.

But as this could not be, he screwed his courage to the task before him,
and performed it, too, in princely and right royal style; but not without
feeling, from the beginning to the end of it, that he would far rather have
laid his head upon his pillow, whence his thoughts might have wandered
without interruption to England, whither the fair Sabina was gone – as
Madame de Hautrivage had confidentially given all Paris to understand.

But if this direction of the young man's thoughts shewed weakness, the
conduct which was the result of that night's meditation gave proof of
excellent strength, and of a sincerity of honourable purpose which
deserved to be accompanied with happier feelings than at that moment
accompanied it. Sabina was gone to England, and therefore Prince
Frederic determined that he would *not* go there. This resolution
proceeded less from a wish to spare himself from further struggles

between the inclinations of his heart and the duties of his station, than from the fear that any of those who had witnessed his admiration might suppose he had followed her. The thought that the slightest whisper from the lips of slander should be breathed against this innocent and lovely creature on his account was dreadful to him; and he at once resolved, that, cost him what anguish it might, he would see that beautiful face no more.

But, although Prince Frederic's entertainment, brilliant as it was, was a wearisome and heavy business to the young host, it was far otherwise to the rest of the company; for, besides the enjoyment of fine rooms, brilliant light, good music, sumptuous supper, magnificent dresses, and magnificent people, the company possessed the additional advantage of having a great deal to talk about.

The 'elopement,' as it was called, of the unfortunate Madame Bertrand (now universally spoken of as an affair of gallantry), had, however, almost entirely given place to the more recent, and infinitely more interesting departure of Hargrave, '*le magnifique, et ses deux charmantes demoiselles.*' On this theme no tongue had, as yet, found it possible to weary; and many years had passed over the head of Madame de Hautrivage since she had been an object of so much flattering attention as she was that night.

Endless were the romances in circulation. Some scrupled not to declare that they had excellent good reason for believing that one, at least, of the exiled royal family had been for weeks living concealed in Mr Hargrave's hôtel, and that the safety of these illustrious persons had been the only consideration which had rendered the secret departure of the Hargrave family necessary. Other seemed to know a great deal more than *that* about it; but although they permitted this fact to be guessed at, they resolutely abstained from entering into any particulars. Others, again, were sorry to say that it was but too certain that Mr Hargrave had lent enormous sums of money to the parties in question; so much, indeed, as absolutely to have distressed himself, notwithstanding his prodigious wealth. Another party – of the quiet, sentimental loyalist class – professed to know that the motives which had actuated Mr Hargrave in this business were of the most disinterested and noble kind, having their source and origin in national gratitude. No honourable Englishman, they said, could ever forget the court which had once been held at St Germains; and the noble-minded Hargrave had given '*l'assurance la plus sublime,*' that he remembered it!

All this, and a great deal more like it, was doubtless pronounced in accents more distinct, *da capos* more frequent, from the evident concurrence of the royal host in all such statements and in all such feelings; and both from the example set by him, and the eager hope of obtaining further particulars to weave into still longer romances, there was scarcely an individual in the room who did not in the course of the evening find an opportunity of offering a little flattering and affectionate homage to the interesting position of Madame de Hautrivage.

The finding herself thus suddenly grown into a heroine was sufficient to make her feel this remarkable evening to be a most delightful one, even though the week or ten days which had elapsed since the departure of the devoted legitimist had sufficed to enlighten her on one or two points concerning him, whereon she would have been better pleased to continue in darkness.

Her notion, that it would be equally agreeable, convenient, and unobjectionable in all ways for her to remain at her snug quarters in the Rue de Lille till her sublime *beau-frère* should find it convenient to return, had received some considerable checks since the time when it was first conceived. And, just before she retired to dress for Prince Frederic's party, the care-worn visage of Mr Jenkyns had presented itself at the drawing-room door, requesting permission to enter; which permission being given, the following conversation took place, Madame de Hautrivage replying to the melancholy steward's statement in the best English she could command.

'I beg your ladyship's pardon,' said Mr Jenkyns, who, though he saw a prodigious difference between a French countess and an English one, could never bring himself to believe that any of the species extant, let the clime in which they were found be what it might, could be properly addressed in any other manner,– 'I beg your ladyship's pardon, but I am sadly afraid that your ladyship cannot have been made acquainted with the real state of the case, respecting the reason of my master's going away; and I have just made bold to step up-stairs to inquire if your ladyship knows that my honoured master is so deep in debt as to render his return home very improbable, not to say very unsafe.'

'Vat is dat mann vat you dar to say *à propos de mon beau-frère?* mon broder-in-lowe?'

'I say nothing, my lady, that it is not terribly easy to prove; only that I should be sorry do any such a thing in the presence of your ladyship. It has been said in the servants' hall, that your ladyship has made up your ladyship's mind to remain where you are, till such time as my master shall return; and no sooner did I hear these words spoke, than I made up *my* mind upon what it was my duty to do. It would be great sin and wickedness in me, my lady, to let your ladyship stay on here till such time as there was neither board nor bed left for your ladyship's use.'

'I am *horriblement mystifiée!*' cried Madame de Hautrivage, literally trembling from head to foot. 'It is one *diabolique* slander! Vat! de finest fortune *de tout Paris? Ah! ça.* I understand de English of de aristocrasie, *mais parfaitement, parfaitement*; but for you, my friend, no, – I comprehend not a single vord of all you please to say.'

'Indeed, my lady, you must try to understand me,' replied poor Jenkyns, who was really in distress. 'I am sure if I knew how to speak any plainer, I would do it with all my heart and soul. But I don't know how; and as to trying my hand at French, I am quite positive it would not answer. Do pray, my lady, try to listen to me; because it is as clear as daylight, that if I cannot compass the making your ladyship understand, something very disagreeable will come of it. There will, indeed, my lady.'

'*Eh, bien! monsieur l'intendant*. I understand you quite veal enough. It is, then, that *mon beau-frère* is a ruined man? Dat is vat you vish me to know?' said Madame de Hautrivage.

'Yes, my lady,' replied Jenkyns, with a very pitying expression of face; for, in spite of her rouge, it was easy to see that the poor woman had turned as pale as death; 'and the best and safest thing that you can do will be just to put together all that belongs to you, my lady, and get it out of the house as fast as you can; for I have had a hint that to-morrow those who think they have the best right will be here without asking any body's leave, and take all they can lay their hands on without ceremony.'

It was astonishing to remark how perfectly this last impressive speech of Mr Jenkyns appeared to be understood by the lady. Fortunately, she was at no loss for an asylum; for the strikingly pretty apartment *au troisième* in the Rue de Rivoli, which she had furnished and occupied for several years before her sister's death, was still in her hands, she having originally taken a long lease of it; and from the pretty, fanciful style of its fitting up, it had never remained long without a tenant. It was now, however, fortunately unoccupied; and the recollection of this and of the interesting effect which her present position would give to her return to it, consoled her with a degree of rapidity very delightfully French.

The old steward, himself exceedingly well off in the world, though by no means a dishonest man, seemed greatly relieved by the active air of business which had succeeded to the lady's difficulty of comprehension, and being, like all the rest of his old servants, exceedingly attached to his improvident master, he zealously exerted himself to assist the only one of the family who seemed likely to suffer from the embarrassments into which he had fallen.

Not a syllable had as yet transpired among the household concerning the suspicion that their master was concerned in the disappearance of Madame Bertrand, – a concealment entirely due to the rigorous obedience of Louis Querin to the orders he had received from M Collet, and from which he had hoped to derive substantial benefit. Mr Jenkyns, therefore, was exceedingly well disposed to believe, with undoubting faith, the confidential hints with which Madame de Hautrivage favoured him in return for his assistance in collecting together all that she thought it advisable to claim as her property; and before she had arranged with him all that she wished him to do for her, she had made him fully comprehend that, great as Mr Hargrave's expenditure had been, his property would have been fully equal to it, had he not expended vast sums upon the different members of THE FAMILY to whom his heart was so legitimately devoted.

To this statement Jenkyns listened with the most perfect confidence in its truth; for Mr Hargrave's habits of lavish personal expense were such as often to have swallowed up sums upon which his steward had reckoned as the means of paying up arrears, which by degrees had overpowered him. Here, therefore, was another version of the course which had driven the generous Englishman from Paris; and Madame de Hautrivage failed not, on arriving amidst the crowd at Prince Frederic's, to whisper these self-devoted imprudences to the five hundred dear friends she found among them.

How was it possible that, amidst such a number of dazzling fables, the dim, dark, little spot of truth should be discerned by the *beau monde* of Paris? The easy and rapid propagation of a lie is notorious; but many a meditative looker-on, who may be perfectly aware of this, may, nevertheless, overlook the fact that was side by side with it, namely, that in a thousand unsuspected instances, truth is as easily doomed to death as falsehood to life.

CHAPTER XXVI

A run of very great good luck, which Mr Hargrave would have elegantly called 'the influence of his protecting star,' had thus far so multiplied the effect which had hastily struck Mademoiselle de Cordillac as possible when she first conceived the idea of hinting that his *délit* was political, that had the fugitive presented himself in any fashionable saloon in Paris, he would have been welcomed as a most interesting personage and most noble gentleman. By some, indeed, he might have been hailed as a hero; while, on the other hand, there would certainly have been some, who, though ready to confess the generous nature of his devotion, might have thought he would have employed his noble fortune better by listening to the universal prayer –

'Oh! may he give parties as long as he stays,'

than by attempting to shake the foundations of a popular and well-ordered government. But as to any suspicion against him, in the slightest degree bordering upon the truth, he must have dived almost to the very cellars of Paris before he would have found it.

Nor did the benignity of the 'starry influence' end here, but found its way, by degrees, even to a region where the sifting of facts is in general better understood than the influence of opinion, – even to the *bureau* of the *préfecture de la police*.

The first reception given to M Louis Querin by M Collet and his colleagues, upon his arriving with the news that Mr Hargrave was not to be found, had a good deal of *morgue* and severity in it, and for a few moments the handsome *laquais* wished heartily that he had stuck to his former profession, and left the affairs of justice to take care of themselves, without the benefit of his advice or assistance. But it seemed as if the professional gentleman thought more highly of Louis Querin in this line than he thought of himself (a circumstance rather new in the history of his life and adventures); and, when he was bowing himself off, gave him to understand that they by no means doubted his fidelity in the business, though displeased at his want of address, and that they by no means either intended to lose the advantage of his knowledge concerning the suspected party.

M Collet, indeed, had at this time more reasons than one for wishing to secure Mr Hargrave; for, though the matter had been kept very profoundly secret, that active and intelligent functionary had good reason to believe that he had at length got a clue to the discovery of the culprit in the mysterious affair of the robbed gamester when leaving the *salon* of Riccordo with his winnings.

Within twenty-four hours of the last of these robberies, an English gentleman had called at the *préfecture de la police* where M Collet presided, and desiring to speak to him alone, stated that he was the person from whom the gentleman attacked on his way home from the *salon* had the money taken from him; and that, having marked every coin of a considerable sum which he had brought in sovereigns with him to Paris, and of which he had never parted with any, except at the gaming-table, thought it right, on hearing what had happened, to state the facts to the *chefs de bureau* in the hope of assisting to bring the criminal to punishment. The Englishman then produced a coin bearing the same private mark as those he had lost at play, and left it with the magistrate.

On this mark M Collet looked long enough to become perfectly well acquainted with it; and when the money found upon the person of Roger Humphries was put into his hands, he immediately perceived that every coin was marked in the same manner.

A clearer chain of evidence could scarely be desired; and there was, perhaps, something of sportsman-like eagerness in the zeal with which M Collet prepared to follow the scent. The vexation, therefore, of finding the quarry escaped at the very moment when he had appeared so nearly secure, may be easily imagined.

But the disappointment, after the first moment of dismay, only gave fresh ardour to the pursuit; and, in truth, the very circumstance of Mr Hargrave's having thus absconded furnished another proof of his guilt.

So few hours had elapsed since Querin had lost sight of his master, and so short must be the distance to which the fugitive could have reached, that the police of Paris were not likely to feel any great doubt respecting their chance of recovering the scent thus lost; and here M Collet had again recourse to Louis Querin. Had it appeared necessary, pursuit would have immediately been made through every *barrière* leading from Paris; but this sort of wide-and-wild chase was of course not resorted to as long as there was any chance of shortening the pursuit by finding out the direction in which it could most successfully be made. Querin was, therefore, desired to take his place as usual in the establishment, over which, as we know, Madame de Hautrivage for one delighful week fancied she might continue to preside, and to take all possible means to discover, either from his sister-in-law or the domestics, in which direction it had been his master's intention to travel.

The *habile* and intelligent M Collet was in no way mistaken when he gave Louis Querin credit for being wholly and heartily interested in the business upon which they were engaged together. There were many motives and feelings which contributed to this; but none, perhaps, more powerful than the desire of redeeming his credit as a 'very clever fellow' after the lamentable blunder which had afforded Hargrave time to escape.

He accordingly set about the new task confided to him with equal zeal and discretion, and had little or no difficulty in discovering, through some of the minor channels of intelligence, which took their rise from the well-head of Madame's confidental communications to her favourite maid, that Mr Hargrave, on leaving the —— embassy, had started with post horses for Calais.

Nor was this all the information which Louis Querin carried with him to the *bureau* of the Correctional Police. During the hours employed by Madame de Hautrivage in receiving the visits of her dear friends on the morning after the Ambassador's ball, Querin, fresh returned from his interview with M Collet, and eagerly bent on losing no possible opportunity of collecting intelligence, stationed himself in the ante-room that he might note those who entered, and, perhaps, catch something from the words that should fall from them during their entrances and exits.

Just at the moment when the influx was the greatest, Querin observed a highly dressed personage mount the stairs whom his experienced eye (and few eyes are keener in such matters than those of a long-practised *laquais*) immediately discovered belonged not, by the prescriptive right of custom, to any such circle as that he was now about to enter. No sooner did he perceive this, than the man of course became an object of particular attention to him; and, ere he had fixed his eyes upon his hirsute and strongly marked countenance for half-a-dozen seconds, he recollected that his name was Ruperto, and that he had more than once shewn him into Mr Hargrave's library as a confidential agent of some sort or other, a conclusion which he had come to from hearing the door fastened within as soon as he was admitted.

Never, however, had this fellow before attempted to obtrude himself into the presence of the ladies of the family; and Querin, therefore, stepped forward, partly from curiosity, and partly from a sort of official habit, of deeming it necessary to know who it was he admitted, and said, 'There is some mistake, sir, I think: Mr Hargrave is not in the drawing-room.'

'And pray, my friend, can you tell me where he is?' returned Ruperto, putting a five-franc piece into the hands of Querin.

'May I ask, sir, what your particular reason is for wishing to know?' demanded Louis, pocketing the gratuity.

'Yes, faith, may you, *mon cher*,' returned the other, 'and I will tell you, too, with all my heart and soul. I have no taste for secrets, except in the way of duty and business, where honourable confidence is given and expected on both sides, – and, by the Holy Madonna, that is not the case here. I will tell you why I want to find your *scelerato* of a master, if you will tell me in return all that you know about him, and give you a cup of wine into the bargain. But you must let me in here, though, without making any fuss about it; and you must not trouble yourself about giving in the name.'

'*That* you have paid for,' said Querin, tapping the pocket wherein he had deposited the five francs, 'and I will stand to my share of the bargain; and for the rest, I will meet you at nine o'clock to-night at the *Café Napoléon, au coin de la Rue St Jacques*.' To this appointment Signor Julio Ruperto nodded assent; the drawing-room door was then thrown open, and he entered. Here he had the good fortune to find Madame de Hautrivage so agitated and excited by all the affectionate interest expressed for her, that she never perceived his entrance.

The positive assurance which he there obtained of Mr Hargrave's departure for England made his promised interview with Querin a matter of much less importance than it had been; but he kept the appointment nevertheless, not doubting that he might learn some particulars respecting his faithless debtor which might in a greater or less degree be useful to him.

The consequences of this meeting were manifold. MM Querin and Ruperto became mutually convinced before the conclusion of it, that they were very fine fellows, and might become essentially useful to each

other. Querin, in return for his companion's passionate repetition of his
injuries, and deep vows of revenge against '*l'infame Hargrave,*' hinted to
him that the police would be the safest agents he could employ to ensure
the desirable end; and they parted with an agreement to meet again on
the following evening.

'All this shall to *M Collet's* ears,'

or words to the same effect, were murmured by the intelligent Louis, as
he returned to the quarters he still inhabited in the Rue de Lille; and at
rather an early hour on the following morning he stood before this very
respectable *chef,* and informed him of the very lucky accident which had
thrown in his way a fellow who had not only been an active agent in the
abduction of Madame Bertrand, but so deep in the confidence of Mr
Hargrave as to give good hopes of being an important witness against
him.

This valuable communication sufficed to seal the peace of Louis
Querin, and he again felt himself to be an approved and trusted agent of
that august power, which in all countries (sufficiently advanced in the
social process, up and down, to require and use its aid) is found, like the
purveyor of wild ducks, to seek its agents and objects from the same class.
In a word, Louis Querin had every reason to be satisfied with the
reception of his news, and no time was lost in requesting the presence of
Signor Julio Ruperto in the private cabinet of the Correctional Police.

All suspicion of Mr Hargrave's being concerned in the disappearance of
Madame Bertrand had till now rested entirely upon circumstantial
evidence; but in the statement of this man, delivered on oath, and with
an accurate exactness which left no doubt of its truth on the
professionally acute mind of his skilful examiner, there appeared the most
positive and direct testimony against him up to a certain period, *but no
farther.*

Ruperto, who appeared to have known him for several years, persisted
in declaring that he was perfectly certain the object of the abduction was
the lady's person; and that, if in truth she had been robbed, it must have
been during her solitary drive to the place whither Mr Hargrave had
ordered her to be conveyed. That gay gentleman's purpose having been,
as he avowed to his accomplice, to remove all suspicion, by returning to
the ball-room the instant after he had placed Madame Bertrand in the
carriage.

During that part of Ruperto's statement which described the interview
between himself and Hargrave previous to the abduction, as well as the
precise manner in which he, Ruperto, had made his way into the garden,
and received, exactly at the appointed spot, the full-dressed lady from the

hand of his employer, the *chef* listened without betraying any symptom of doubt or distrust; but, upon his repeating his conviction that robbed or not Madame Bertrand had been conveyed to the lodging provided for her, M Collet shook his head, and said that he feared he would find upon inquiry that he was mistaken.

'Mistaken! your Excellency?' exclaimed the Italian. 'How is it possible I could be mistaken? Depend upon it, if the postilion lads had been bilked of their fare, I should have heard of it by this time. They know well enough where to find me. It is not the first time that they were ever hired by me.'

'To what place was it that you told these boys to drive?' demanded M Collet.

'Your Excellency has asked me a question which I am not able to answer,' replied Ruperto, looking exceeding ashamed of himself. 'Signor Hargrave gave me the address very distinctly written on a card, telling me to give it to one of the post boys, to prevent all mistakes, as he should not dare raise his voice to give them orders. And though I know that I looked at the card before I gave it to the lad, and remember something about the distance, which the boy said, as I think, was about three leagues, I have no more idea where it was than your Excellency's horse.'

'That was rather a singular want of curiosity, was it not, Signor Ruperto?' said M Collet.

'Singular, your Excellency! oh, no, not the least singular, – not the least in the world. No men can be less troubled with curiosity in such matters than·I am. I consider myself as having been very particularly ill-used by the Signor Hargrave; and, therefore, have no reason or motive whatever for wishing to conceal any thing I know about him. But as to the identical spot to which he carried the lady, and from whence, as I learned from the old dowager his sister, he has set off for England (probably taking his fair friend along with him), I know it not.'

'Are you aware, Signor Ruperto,' said M Collet, 'that the suspicions against M Hargrave go a great deal farther than merely running off with a fair lady?'

'Yes, your Excellency; M Louis Querin has told me so. But I do not believe a word of it.'

'Indeed! and why so?'

'Because I know the man, your Excellency. I know him well. If ever there was a worshipper of pleasure, it it this Englishman. But as to murder, or robbery either, I must have better authority than any that has come up yet, before I shall believe it.'

'Then how would you account for what, as I dare say you may have heard from your friend Querin, – how would you account for what has been found in the garden?'

'My friend Querin, as your Excellency is pleased to call him, only told me that a robbery, and probably a murder, had been committed on the person of the unfortunate lady with whom the Signor Hargrave eloped. But he gave me no particulars; saying that he had bound himself not to do so. No, your Excellency, I have heard of nothing having been found in the garden.'

'Querin was right, and has behaved well in not telling you. But you have had so much to do with this transaction, that I would wish you to know the whole of it. It is by no means improbable that you may be able to assist us.'

M Collet then detailed the discovery that had been made in the garden of the golden *débris* of Madame Bertrand's magnificent jewels; not forgetting the handkerchief (recognised by Louis as belonging to his master) which was found stained with blood. Having concluded this narrative, during the course of which M Collet kept his eyes fixed on the countenance of Ruperto, he said, 'And now, Signor Ruperto, tell me what you think of this?'

'I can but repeat what I have said before, your Excellency,' replied the man, with the utmost *sang froid*. 'I feel still perfectly convinced that the motive the Signor assigned when planning this adventure with me, was the real one. I have no faith whatever in his having committed robbery and murder. My intercourse with mankind has taught me to know them better than that.'

'Are you aware, my good friend, that if M Hargrave did not commit the outrage, there appears every possible reason to suppose that you must have committed it yourself?'

'*Diavolo!*' exclaimed the Signor, laughing; 'I cannot say that this ever occurred to me. But, now you mention it, your Excellency, I must confess that it looks very probable. However, the suggestion can only be productive of a short inconvenience to me; as just half-a-dozen gentlemen of high distinction, who did me the honour of using my *petit billard* during all the later part of that night, will be able to prove to your Excellency's entire satisfaction that I was engaged in marking for them very nearly the whole time.'

'Very nearly!' repeated M Collet, with a rather sinister emphasis.

'*Oi, Diavolo!*' again exclaimed the Italian. 'That is true, your Excellency, – perfectly true. And if I had no better defence to offer it might go hard with me; inasmuch as it would be easy to prove that murder and robbery both might be committed within the space of time which this "very nearly" may cover. Nevertheless, your Excellency, I cannot pretend to say that I am greatly alarmed. Very few innocent men, I suspect, get sent to the galleys, or to the guillotine either. I have generally remarked in all countries, let the government be what they will, that robbery and murder is greatly objected to, and sharply looked after; and that being the case, it cannot often happen that the wrong man is taken instead of the right one.'

'Your observation is *supérieurement juste*, my friend,' replied M Collet. 'I have, myself, the greatest faith in it. But you must be aware that this admirable result can only be obtained by strict attention not to let the guilty escape; for without this, it would be nearly impossible to avoid occasionally condemning the innocent. In the present instance, for example, how is it possible to avoid the danger of believing either M Hargrave or yourself to be guilty of the terrible outrage, which it is but too certain has been committed, if no other person can be found on whom suspicion can rest?'

'I beg your Excellency's pardon ten thousand times,' said the Italian; 'but it strikes me that the same argument might constrain gentlemen of your honourable and most important profession, occasionally to seize upon the first comer, – *faute de mieux*.'

'Pushed to extremity, it might,' replied M Collet, half smiling at the man's audacity. 'But on the present occasion you will hardly think we are driven so far, even if we take the liberty of detaining Signor Ruperto till we see more satisfactory reasons for dismissing him than any he has yet stated.'

'*Eh, bien, donc, M le Chef*,' returned Ruperto, with the same imperturbable composure, 'if your deficiency of information lays you under the necessity of asking assistance from so very useless an individual as myself, I will suggest that, in the first place, you should despatch trustworthy and properly qualified persons to England, *viâ* Calais, by which means there is but little doubt of your being able to trace this fugitive gentleman, – a business in which I am certainly not a little interested myself. Secondly, I should recommend your taking the two postilions into custody; and, thirdly, I would advise you to satisfy yourself as to the recent occupation of that resolute elderly personage, who, as I understand from M Louis Querin, was found under circumstances very highly suspicious, near the supposed *locale* of the crime.'

'Had you been attached to my *bureau* for a score of years, Signor, you could hardly have displayed more correct views of the subject before us. I really honour you,' returned M Collet. 'For the first of your suggestions, permit me to assure you that it has not been overlooked. I have little fear of failing to discover by what exit your friend, M Hargrave, left Paris. For the second, I thank you; and shall request your assistance in pointing out the individuals you have named, when it shall immediately be put in execution. For the third, I declare to you that I have already done every thing in my power to put it in practice, but in vain. I think I never had so impracticable a personage in my hands as the stately old fellow you mention; but as you appear to be a person of very brilliant capacity, I shall have no objection whatever to your assisting at another examination of this obstinate old man.'

'May I hope to have your Excellency's leave to question him?' demanded Ruperto, with a leer.

'Unquestionably; my general habit is certainly to permit nothing of the kind, but the conduct of this man obliges me to vary my mode of proceeding,' replied M Collet. 'I shall, also,' he continued, 'wish to have Louis Querin present at this examination, for it is evident to me that he knows more against the man's general character than he has yet thought proper to state.'

Before this interview ended, it was settled that the renewed examination of old Roger should take place before Signor Ruperto left the *bureau*; and a message was accordingly despatched to the Rue de Lille to summon Querin.

As soon as he made his appearance, M Collet informed him that the present object of his being sent for was that he might be present at a renewed examination of Roger Humphries, adding, 'I shall to-day, Querin, make no objection to your asking him any questions which may suggest themselves to you. You evidently know more of the man than you have yet avowed; and it now becomes your duty to make use of that knowledge in order to assist the purposes of justice, and elicit the truth which he is so obstinately determined to conceal.'

Querin's heart leaped with joy. His hatred to old Roger was by no means appeased by the fact, which appeared clearly evident from his obstinate silence, that this favoured domestic was in the secret counsels of his master.

'A pretty fellow, truly,' thought this French Leporello, — 'a pretty fellow to select from a household, of which I made one, for an agent in an elopement. It shall go hard with me but I will make both master and man repent of their clumsy alliance!'

When Roger appeared before the party assembled in M Collet's cabinet, consisting of himself, one of his *confrères*, a clerk to take down whatever facts or observations might be obtained, and M Ruperto and Querin, he looked as nearly like a man made of iron, as it was possible for a living thing to do. The impassible rigidity of his countenance seemed to preclude the expression of any feeling whatever; and each and all of the sharp-witted party present felt that nothing in the way of information could be hoped from him. Nevertheless, the attempt was made, and M Collet once more attacked him upon the point of his having turned so suddenly away upon discovering that he was watched.

'Do you still,' said he, 'refuse to answer me when I ask you where you had been on the morning after the ball given at your master's house? Do you still refuse to explain the reason for your stealing away and hiding yourself in the manner you did?'

'You must have the goodness, gentlemen, to excuse my being an Englishman,' returned Roger, in his perfectly intelligible, but somewhat comical French.

'I do not comprehend you, old man. What do you mean by our excusing you for being an Englishman?' said M Collet.

'I mean, sir,' replied Roger, 'that being an Englishman makes me so used to go and come without giving account to any one, that I cannot fall into the way of answering such sort of curious questions as you put to me, especially without knowing why they are asked. It seemed to me that I met a party of mad folks at the time you mention; and one would think, gentlemen, that you must be as mad as they to lock up a peaceable man in the manner you have locked up me at their bidding!'

'I do not believe that you are quite so silly a fellow as you would have me think you,' returned the *chef*; 'whether English or French, I suspect you know better than really to think it extraordinary or unjust, that, when a great and mysterious crime has been committed, the officers of justice should make prisoner of a person found nearly on the spot, and under the very suspicious circumstances which you so obstinately refuse to explain.'

'Will you be so kind, gentlemen, as to tell me what this mysterious crime was?' said Roger, demurely.

'*Ce coquin joue bien la comédie,*' said Querin, giving a look of very malicious intelligence to M Collet.

'Will you have the kindness, M Roger Omfries,' he added, turning with an air of mock humility to the prisoner, – 'will you have the kindness to inform these gentlemen when it was that you changed your pumps and silk stockings for these gaiters and thick shoes? Come now, M Roger; that is a question which it cannot hurt the dignity of an Englishman to answer.'

'I changed them, M Louis,' replied Roger, 'when I went out of the drawing-room into the open air.'

'And that was as soon as supper was over, M Roger, if I mistake not,' rejoined the Frenchman; 'so that you must have had rather a long job to do, before we had the honour of meeting you, and putting your English mettle to the proof by making you scamper away from us.'

'After supper was it?' said Roger, quietly.

'Pray, may I be so bold as to ask, M Roger Omfries, where it was you got all that rather remarkable quantity of gold coin which I had the accident of seeing you counting one day, when I caught you sitting down before your *coffre-fort* in your bed-room?'

'I do not know, M Louis, what right you had to spy me then, nor what right you have to question me now; but, as it happens, I have not the least objection whatever to answer you. I got that gold, as well as every thing else that I possess on earth, from my noble and generous master, Mr Hargrave.'

The officers of the police exchanged a glance as he said this; and the superior said, addressing Roger, 'Should you have any objection to our having that *coffre-fort* brought hither in order to be examined?'

'Objection!' reiterated the old man, while a momentary flash of indignation crossed his features; 'I should have a very great objection to it.'

'*Je le crois bien*,' muttered Querin, with a sneer.

'I am sorry for it,' returned M Collet, quietly, 'because it appears to me absolutely necessary that we should examine it. Do you know, Louis Querin, where to find it?'

'In the sleeping apartment of the old gentleman, I conceive,' returned the malicious Louis, endeavouring to suppress the glee that was chuckling in his throat; 'for it was there I caught sight of him, counting his treasure when he fancied that he was all alone.'

'Go, then, to that place and seek for it, and bring it here,' said M Collet.

'By your leave, I must have help then, *M le Chef*,' returned Querin, laughing; 'the *coffre-fort* of M Roger Omfries is no such light matter.'

'Have you ever tried its weight, M Louis?' said Roger, in an accent of great civility.

'*Scélérat!*' muttered Querin through his closed teeth, and with a glance that spoke a great deal, but not of love.

'See for a man to go with the witness in search of this *coffre-fort*,' said M Collet, addressing the officer who sat near him; 'and send in a *gendarme* to watch the prisoner till he returns. I am wanted elsewhere.'

'May it please your Excellency that I should ask this old fellow a question or two, in the absence of his fellow-servant?' demanded Ruperto, in a whisper.

M Collet nodded, and reseated himself.

'That is a queer chap, that Louis Querin,' said the Italian, as soon as the door was closed upon the individual he named. 'I dare say, good friend, you could tell us whether he was greatly in the confidence of his master before the gentleman set off? Do you think now, that if Mr Hargrave had any little secret mischief to carry on, that gay fellow would have been applied to, in order to help him in it?'

'My master!' said Roger, fixing his eyes eagerly upon Ruperto, while the rigid obstinacy of his features seemed suddenly to relax: 'has my master any thing to do with all the questions you have been asking me?' Then, without waiting for a reply, he added, respectfully addressing the *chef*, 'It is no good, sir, wasting your time any longer in this matter; I am tired of it, and had rather stand the punishment, and have it over at once. I don't see any reason in the common course of things why a man should give evidence against himself; and that is the reason, as of course you guessed before, why I would give no answer. Nor do I mean now to tell you one bit more about the matter than your own cleverness can find out; and I must bear the penalty and punishment of all the harm that you can prove against me. But it is one thing to keep silence about one's self, and another to go on with it, till suspicion falls upon an honourable gentleman like my master; so I am willing to confess, once for all, that all that has been done wrong has been done by me; and that my master knows no more about it than the child unborn. Now, do your worst with me; I can bear it.'

'But in order to make this confession of use in exonerating your master,' said M Collet, fixing a scrutinising eye upon the harsh features of the old man, 'it will be necessary for you to do more than merely confess that you are guilty. You must render all particulars of this singular transaction, especially as to the place you came from when you were seen by the gentlemen who brought you hither.'

'And that is what I will not do,' said Roger, resuming his former look of obstinacy. 'I may be a very wicked man, and yet not bad enough, either to see an innocent gentleman like my master brought into trouble on my account, nor yet to 'peach against my confederates. Of course, you suspect I have got confederates by what that dark-coloured gentleman said just now about a fellow being wanted to help. And I sh'n't say a single word about them, so don't trouble yourselves with asking me.'

'But of what do you confess yourself guilty? It is nonsense to affect all this generosity, and then stop short, and leave us still in the dark. That, of course, is the way to make us suspect the innocent. Of what do you confess yourself guilty?' repeated M Collet.

'And so put all particulars into your hands?' said Roger, shaking his head. 'No, no, I will not do that. Besides, I may blunder in my speech, being a foreigner, if I go on telling too much. Justice to my master has forced me to confess that I am guilty, and not he, in this matter that seems to lie between us two: but I shall not tell you a single word more about it. It is your business, and not mine, to sift out all the particulars. When you bring me to my trial, I have no fear but what justice will be done; and that what I deserve I shall get, and no more.'

'May I speak to your Excellency in private for a moment?' demanded the Italian, addressing M Collet.

Willing, as it seemed, to listen to any thing that might enlighten a business which appeared more mysterious than ever, the chief of the *bureau* ordered the venerable prisoner to be removed, but kept within call, till Querin should return: and when left alone with Ruperto and the secretary, desired the former to proceed with what he wished to say.

'May it please your Excellency,' resumed the Italian, 'I have my own reasons for believing that what the old fellow says is true. Of course your Excellency knows your honourable duty better than to take any thing for granted because I say it; and so all inquiry will go on, as it ought to do, till your Excellency is perfectly satisfied. Only, as it would be both honour and pleasure for me to help your Excellency to learn the truth, concerning a business in which I certainly had some hand, I cannot but wish to tell you that I have known the Signor Hargrave very nearly twenty years; that he is a man of pleasure, neither more nor less, neither better nor worse; that if you pursue him for robbery and murder, you will be sure to get wrong; and that if murder or robbery, one or both, have been committed, it is not by him; so that you had better keep both eyes open, your Excellency, in order to discover the real criminal. My own firm belief is, that the Signor Hargrave has set off with his new flame for England; and that it is likely enough that the jewels of the lady, who certainly could not travel covered over with diamonds, as she was when I gave her into his arms, were deposited somewhere or other where this very suspicious old fellow got access to them, stripped off the settings, and buried them; and was probably returning from the place where he left the more valuable portion of his plunder, when Querin and the two gentlemen got hold of him; and if I prove to be right, your Excellency, I hope you will deem my services worthy of some reward; for not only shall I have helped you to find the right man, but saved you from the disagreeable accident of seizing upon a wrong one.'

'If events prove you to have been right, Signor Ruperto, you shall not find me ungrateful; but if Madame Bertrand, as you imagine, is at this time on her way to England, how do you account for this blood?' And as he spoke, M Collet opened a drawer with a key which hung from his watch-chain, and shewed him the stained handkerchief.

Ruperto took it in his hand, and extended it between himself and the light for a moment; then rolled it up again, and laughed slightly as he restored it to the commissioner of police. Collet looked at him earnestly, but neither of them spoke. At length the officer ejaculated, 'Well!'

'Well!' returned the Italian, with a profound bow. 'If it were not that I feared to appear presumptuous, by venturing to give your Excellency a hint on such a subject as this, I should recommend that you should not accuse any man of murder upon the evidence of that handkerchief. The lifeblood of a chicken would make a better show.'

'I suspect that you may be right in that matter, Signor; for, on examination, I have found the settings, which have evidently been torn off with much violence, are in many parts stained likewise; and I confess I have before suspected that these stains proceeded rather from the robber than the robbed. So far, Signor,' continued the *chef* with a smile, 'you perceive that our ideas are the same. It remains to be proved which of us is right on the points whereon we differ. I do not agree with you in your acquittal of M Hargrave from the suspicion of having turned his gallant freak into a source of profit. You will perceive my reasons for this pertinacity in maintaining my own opinion, ere long.'

Louis Querin was no loiterer when employed in business which gave him pleasure; and, as it seemed, he found no difficulty in discovering where old Roger's huge box might be found, for he arrived in a *fiacre*, containing what he was pleased to call the *coffre-fort*, considerably before he was expected.

The clumsy wooden box, painted of a deep blue colour, and with as little appearance of strength about it as any thing with a lock could have, was then brought into an apartment kept for private examinations, and old Roger Humphries was again led in before the same party as before.

At sight of this receptacle of the memorials, personal whims, and solid treasures, of forty years of service (for so long had the good man served Hargrave and Hargrave's father), Roger knit his brows, and looked infinitely more ill at ease than he had yet done.

Roger Humphries was a bachelor, and had all the morose-like sensibility concerning his own little personalities which may generally be remarked in individuals of both sexes, when they have lived to a certain age without having been tempted to give to any one the privilege of setting to rights their peculiar belongings. The grave but passionless composure of countenance in which his hard features had hitherto reposed (save at the moment that his master's name was first mentioned), was now changed for a very nervous and uneasy twitching; and it was hardly possible for any man to look much less at his ease than did Roger when Louis Querin, at a sign from M Collet, knelt down beside the box, and extending his hand towards him, pronounced authoritatively, –

'*La clef!*'

To have given up the key of all his petted and secret treasures to any man, would have been exceeding painful to poor Roger; but to the gibing and insolent Querin, who had never, since the hapless hour in which they first met, omitted an opportunity of treating him with ridicule and insult, it was dreadful, and every working feature shewed that it was so.

The eyes of M Collet and Ruperto met. There was at this moment something like a trial of skill between them; and each desired to see the effect which this remarkable alteration in the demeanour of the prisoner produced. The Italian smiled, and perhaps the Frenchman returned it; but if he did, the dignity of office prevented his permitting it to be visible, for his hand gravely enveloped the lower part of his face.

Meanwhile, Roger Humphries did not deliver the key. After hesitating for a minute or two, he folded his arms tightly across his breast, planted himself firmly where he stood, and shut up his eyes, as if to avoid seeing any of M Louis Querin's signs and grimaces.

'*Donnez la clef, mon ami!*' said M Collet, in a tone of quiet authority.

Considering the diminutive nature of the reasons for his averseness to comply with this command, the look of misery which accompanied his obedience to it certainly appeared exceedingly suspicious; and those who were so keenly watching him could hardly fail of being deluded in their interpretation of it. But though –

'A very foolish, fond old man,'

in regard to some of the secret memorials to be found in his box, Roger was not so overpowered by his feelings as to be insensible to the necessity of complying with this strictly official command; and after a short delay in finding it, he stepped forward, and deposited the old-fashioned little key in the hands of M Collet.

Could Roger have been aware how perfectly unintelligible to the lookers-on were the treasured articles which constituted the chief contents of this sacred repository, his sufferings would have been entirely removed; for concerning that weighty portion of them contained in a leather-bag, with a red-tape string twisted round it, which, like its master, had performed the same duties faithfully for the better part of half-a-century, concerning this, he thought no more than if it had contained three hundred bits of pasteboard instead of three hundred golden sovereigns.

The little pocket-book, on which Master Charles Hargrave had spent half-a-crown out of his seventh birthday *largesse* from his papa, as a present for his 'dearly-beloved Roger;' the old black-coat and crape hatband in which he had attended the funeral of Mr Hargrave's father; six carefully preserved silk pocket-handkerchiefs, hemmed by the delicate fingers of his late mistress, and presented to him as a mark of particular esteem; numberless little presents in books, writing-desks, queer snuff-boxes, and Heaven-knows-what, received from Adèle and Sabina, beginning from the time when they were almost babies, and continuing in regular, and not unfrequent succession, till within a few weeks of this terrible amd most unlooked-for day; and, strongest of all, a lock of youthful-looking, feminine, long hair, folded up in a morsel of paper, which tempted examination from the careful manner of its envelopement, and on which was written '*Sally!*' with a hand trembling, perhaps, with emotion as tender as that which dictated the beautiful '*Eheu, Evelina!*' traced by the pen of 'the Antiquary.' All these dearly-loved pledges of favour and affection were freshly remembered by the tortured old man, and he would willingly have given all his sovereigns to redeem them from the profanation of the ribald eyes before which they were now to be displayed. They were passed over, however, without observation or notice of any sort, except an occasional sneer and wink from the facetious Louis. But not so the bag of gold. No sooner did this meet the eyes of M Collet, than he stretched out his hand to receive it, and having thrown out the contents upon a table before him, drew from his pocket a magnifying glass, with which he began carefully to examine each separate coin.

This was an operation which evidently puzzled every individual present as much as it did Roger. M Collet, however, did not seem to be at all communicative on this point, freely as he had conversed with Ruperto and Querin respecting all the other circumstances connected with the prisoner. But having finished the operation, counted the money, and withdrawn five gold pieces from the scattered contents of the bag, he collected the remainder, replaced it in its leathern receptacle, restored the old string to its duty, exactly in the manner in which he had found it; and then, having seen the bag lodged in the blue box, turned the lock of it himself, and deposited the key, together with the abstracted coins, in the drawer, to which the only means of access hung from his own watch-chain.

During all this time he spoke not a single word to any one; but as he returned the chain to its place, he once more addressed the prisoner, and said, 'Have you any objection, my friend, to inform me from whence you obtained that large sum in gold?'

Roger paused to consider for a moment whether any species of harm to his master could arise from his declaring the truth, and not conceiving the possibility of this, he replied, 'I had it from my master.'

'You received three hundred louis d'or − sovereigns, I should say, − from Mr Hargrave?' demanded M Collet, once more fixing his suspicious eyes full upon the face of the prisoner.

'Yes, sir, I did,' replied Roger, with recovered composure; the safe custody of his little key in M Collet's keeping being a real comfort to him.

'Have you any objection to telling me for what reason your master intrusted you with so large a sum?' demanded the commissioner.

'Intrusted, sir!' repeated Roger, really puzzled by the phrase, and, for that reason, at a loss how to answer it.

'You will do better, my friend, by answering my questions directly than by repeating them. You cannot seriously hope to obtain any advantage by delay thus obtained?'

'I do not understand what you mean, sir,' replied Roger, without any rudeness of manner; for now that they had ceased to question him concerning the errand upon which he had been engaged when taken into custody, he felt little or no reluctance to replying to any questions that could possibly be asked, in which he alone was concerned; but the words that had been spoken concerning his master, and which led him to fear that he must have got into some gay scrape or other, rendered him cautious, when the inquiries made were such as to leave him in doubt concerning their object.

'Then first, or last, we must teach you,' replied M Collet, testifying more impatience at this evasive reply than he had yet shewn. 'I have other business to attend to, and can waste no more time on you. This affair must go before the proper tribunals. Remove him!' he added, calling in two of the *gendarmerie* in waiting without. 'He shall be removed into closer confinement to-morrow. Meanwhile, take care of him. The case is of considerable importance.'

Poor Roger, about equally shocked and puzzled by such of these words as reached him, was then led away; and M Collet turned to the witnesses, if such they might be called, telling them that they would receive notice when and where they were to appear to give evidence upon more than one point on which they would probably have to be examined. But before Querin left the *bureau*, the commissioner asked him if he too had been accustomed to receive his wages from Mr Hargrave in gold.

'No, sir, always in five-franc pieces,' was the reply.

'Do you think it probable that Mr Hargrave ever gave that old man the sum you have just seen displayed before you? Do you think it likely that he should ever have received seven thousand five hundred francs from his master?'

'No, sir, never!' replied Querin, with great earnestness. 'I am quite certain it is impossible. And you had a thief in your hands this day, if ever you saw one in your life.'

'*Allons, mon ami*,' said Signor Ruperto, bowing profoundly to the *chef*. 'There is not the least chance that his Excellency should blunder upon a fact so very clearly established. An eye less acute than that of Monsieur would have been able to detect the rogue in less than half the time that this old fellow has stood before him.'

Left to himself, M Collet, notwithstanding the pressure of business, gave a few minutes of meditation to all the circumstances of the two singular cases of robbery which had come before him. A few hours before, he had felt convinced that he had discovered the perpetrator of both in the same person; and now he was of the same opinion still, but with this difference, that the individual was changed.

That an old serving-man should have seven thousand five hundred francs in gold lodged snugly in the corner of his box, and yet be an honest man, seemed to him so improbable, that he should have felt ashamed to confess he had ever wasted a thought on its being possible. No! That Roger Humphries was a thief was established in his mind as a fact beyond the reach of doubt; and this being the case, the probability of his master's innocence strengthened in his mind with every moment's consideration of the subject.

The unimpeachable testimony he had received that the man he had in custody had most strenuously endeavoured to evade pursuit; his steadfast refusal to confess where he had passed the interval between the hour of supper at Mr Hargrave's entertainment, and that at which he had been seen skulking back to his home; the accordance of this with the period of Madame Bertrand's disappearance – various persons having deposed that she had been seen only for a few moments in a waltz after that time; the man's positive, though undefined, confession of guilt; and, finally, the discovery of this extraordinary sum of gold in his possession, of which he had given an account which appeared to the Frenchman so grossly false, as very greatly to increase the suspicion against him: all this together formed a chain of evidence perfectly irresistible; while the circumstance of many pieces of money having been found in his possession, both on his person and in his box, known to have been stolen from the gentleman who had been robbed on his return from Riccordo's, connected him with that atrocious crime also, in a manner the most clear and decisive.

Many other circumstances, also, seemed to suggest arguments in favour of Mr Hargrave's innocence. His immense wealth, *believed*, or, as enough people were ready to swear, *known*, by all the world; his character as a man of gallantry and pleasure; his intimate connexion with all the most distinguished personages in Paris; all this, in M Collet's estimation, rendered his having any thing to do with either crime as improbable, as the facts connected with his servant made the old man's participation, if not sole commission of them, the reverse.

When the mind of a judicial inquirer is fully made up on any subject, it is not easy to shake it: so it was with M Collet. It would have required much clearer evidence than he was at all likely to get, to have convinced him that Mr Hargrave was a rogue, and his servant Roger an honest man.

CHAPTER XXVII

The satisfactory firmness of decision to which the mind of M Collet had arrived on the respective merits of Mr Hargrave and Roger Humphries did not, however, cause any relaxation of his endeavours to obtain facts of all kinds on the subject; and ere the day appointed for the trial of the old man arrived, a considerable degree of new light had been thrown upon the matter.

It is not necessary to follow step by step every movement of this intelligent person towards the object which he had in view; nor is it intended to give any detailed account of the subsequent examinations or of the trial which followed, beyond what is necessary for making the final result known to the reader.

The advice of Signor Julio Ruperto respecting the postilions was followed, and their testimony confirmed that of Ruperto in every particular to which their evidence went. The next step, of course, was to repair to the spot to which these men had conveyed the lady; and what followed from this must be related rather at length, because the consequences of it were of sufficient importance to render all minor details concerning the evidence brought forward against Roger, unnecessary.

On entering the house pointed out to him as that to which the lady carried from Mr Hargrave's garden had been conveyed, M Collet had every reason to believe, that whatever attention might have been shewn her in other respects, the character of the inmates had not been considered as a matter of much importance. In fact, he perceived at once by an official glance of his experienced eye, that though the mansion (at the distance of about half a league from Paris) was exceedingly well *montée*, handsome, and even elegant in its furniture and fitting up, and having about it (almost) every appearance of being the dwelling *de gens comme il faut*, – the inmates were very unmistakably infamous.

In answer to his first inquiries respecting a lady who had been brought there early in the morning of the 24th April, he was told, in an accent of saucy indifference, that he had blundered, for that no such person was or ever had been there.

With quiet and patient perseverance he went on for a considerable time endeavouring to convince the lady who appeared to be the mistress of the house, that she would save herself a considerable degree of trouble by rendering easy the task he had undertaken of finding this lady dead or alive. But the more he endeavoured to make his inquiries in a tone gentle and conciliatory, the more did the insolence of that in which he was answered increase, till at length he found it necessary to cut the matter short, by informing the person he addressed that he found himself under the disagreeable necessity of calling for the assistance of a few official individuals who awaited his orders without in order to search her dwelling from the garret to the cellar in hope of finding some trace of the person he inquired for.

In saying this, however, the gentleman's manner did not by many degrees change so greatly as did that of the lady who answered him. From a jeering, gibing insolence, which had more than once given him to understand that if he became too troublesome, his ejectment would be a process neither long nor difficult, her tone became that of the most gentle, penitent, helpless, and obedient of human beings.

Without any further difficulty Madame Renny, for so she called herself, confessed that her husband had consented to receive a lady, who, from the exact coincidence of time, she concluded must be the person M Collet inquired for. This lady, she said, had been represented to them as a young person about to elope from her family with a lover every way unworthy of her; and that, in consequence of this information, they had agreed to receive and keep her in close custody for a month; one half of the charges for this service being very handsomely paid in advance, and the other half stipulated for at the end of that time, when her friends would, it was said, come forward and remove her.

M Collet gave himself not much trouble in sifting this statement in order to discover what portion of it might be true and what false; but testifying some little impatience that it might speedily be brought to a close, demanded to be instantly led into the presence of the lady.

There was exactly that sort of authority in the accent with which this demand was made that was calculated to ensure obedience in the quarter to which it was addressed; and with no further reply than '*Certainement, mais certainement, monsieur!*' Madame Renny led the way to a door on the third floor, the key of which she drew from her pocket; and, throwing it open, exclaimed, '*Mais entrez, monsieur, je vous prie!*'

The melancholy and completely dispirited look of the pretty young woman, whom he found in solitary possession of the handsome apartment to which he was thus admitted, really touched the feelings of the commissaire, and it was in a voice of great kindness that he said, 'Forgive my intrusion, madame, but I entreat you to tell me if you are the wife of M Bertrand?'

The question seemed to act like the infusion of new life into the pale and dejected being to whom it was addressed. She sprung towards the commissaire with extended arms, that looked as if they intended to envelope him in a close embrace; but, stopping short before she had fully reached him, she clasped her hands together, and exclaimed with a look of ecstasy, '*Mais oui, monsieur! — Mais oui, je suis sa femme! — Je suis Madame Bertrand!*'

The interval which elapsed between this moment and that which restored her to the arms of her husband was as short as possible; and that worthy man must have been as prone to receive, harbour, and nourish suspicion as Othello himself, could he for a single instant have doubted the truth of the statement which he then received from his restored and most happy little wife.

When the first raptures which followed their meeting were over, and Madame Bertrand had time to answer the inquiries addressed to her

officially and extra-officially respecting the abduction and the robbery
which followed, she gave the most clear and distinct account of the
whole affair; but positively denied that Mr Hargrave had any thing
whatever to do with it beyond the having led her into what she called the
'Serre,' and opening 'a door, or a window, or a curtain, or something, to
let in a little air, because it was so very hot.' She then went on to state
that Mr Hargrave, who had always behaved to her in the most polite
manner possible, had taken her by the hand and led her forward towards
the opening for a step or two, when he suddenly turned round just as
they had reached it, and she believed that somebody had called him,
though she did not see any person near them at the time. But she
distinctly remembered hearing Mr Hargrave say, 'Oui, monseigneur,' and
then he dropped her hand, and the very next moment, and before she
could step back to see if it was the Prince of ———, as she supposed, an
arm from without seized hold of her, dragged her forward into the cold
open air, and in the next instant she found herself almost stifled in the
folds of an enormously thick cloak that was thrown over her. In spite of
this, however, she stated that she attempted to scream; but, for what
seemed to her a very long time, though, perhaps, it might not have been
above a quarter of an hour, she was kept pinioned down with the most
cruel violence, while the cloak was held so closely round her head as
quite to stifle all the cries she endeavoured to utter, and very nearly to
prevent her breathing at all. During this time she was dragged along the
ground, and one time lifted off it, and carried for a short distance. And
then she fancied that there were two or more men near her, for she heard
voices whispering; but this was only for a moment, and almost directly
after she was again lifted for a little way and then set down again, and the
cloak was then thrown open and all her diamonds torn away from her in
the most quick and violent manner possible. And at that moment she again
tried to scream, but having taken the diamonds from her head, the robber
again almost stifled her in the cloak, while all the time he kept on tearing
the jewels from her dress; till, at last, when all were removed, she was again
half dragged, half carried along, for what appeared a much longer way than
she had yet gone, and then she was suddenly thrust forward into a carriage,
the door of which was instantly closed, and she was driven off at full speed
till she reached the house where M Collet had found her. Nothing she
could say, from the time she entered it, had ever been listened to with the
slightest attention any more than if the people had been deaf and dumb. All
she wanted, both of food and clothes, were brought her, but always
without a word being said. Her door was constantly kept locked, and she
had never been permitted to leave the two rooms assigned for her use, from
the moment she had first entered them till M Collet handed her down-
stairs and into that carriage that had brought him there.

Often as the little lady had to repeat this story, she never varied in it, but seemed perfectly to have retained her recollection during the whole of her very terrible adventure.

On being asked whether she had, at any moment, sufficiently seen the person of the robber to identify him, she replied that she feared not, for that during the time that the jewels were snatched from her head, which was the only moment in which it was possible to see him, the darkness was such as would have made it very difficult to distinguish one person from another; besides which, she thought that the man had a mask on, for when she tried to look in his face she saw nothing but blackness. She stated the man to have been very tall, and this was the only circumstance in his appearance concerning which she appeared to be at all certain.

It will readily be imagined that the return of Madame Bertrand under such circumstances, and with such a tale to tell, again made her a personage of great interest and notoriety, even though her diamonds did not return with her. In fact, all Paris talked of nothing else; the papers were full of it, and considerably before poor Roger Humphries (now universally recognised as the culprit) was brought to trial, there was scarcely a journal which did not venture to declare, upon exceedingly sure grounds, that it was well known he would be sent to the galleys for life.

When made acquainted, indeed, with the monstrous crimes charged against him, for he stood accused of the robbery near Riccordo's as well as that of Madame Bertrand, the poor man, convinced that he had blundered in supposing that his master's honoured name had ever been implicated in such atrocities, rescinded his confession, and declared that he knew not what he had been understood to confess when he had owned himself guilty.

Unfortunately, however, this contradiction of his own words produced an effect as far as possible from being favourable to him; for, not only did it appear as an incontrovertible proof of falsehood, but by changing the object of those employed to question him from endeavouring to make him declare the circumstances of the crime of which he had avowed himself to be guilty back again, as it were, to the making him confess that he was guilty at all, he lost the very important advantage which was likely to accrue to him in a court of justice from the inconsistencies which were sure to be detected in a statement so vague as that which he had previously made.

In fact, had he continued to declare himself guilty, while still perfectly ignorant, poor fellow, of the crime committed, it is impossible but that the truth, as far as related to himself at least, must have been discovered; and however guilty of bearing false witness against himself, he might have been shewn thereby, he must have been acquitted of acts, of which, even while he confessed them, he was sure to prove himself so profoundly ignorant.

As it was, however, every thing turned against him. Madame Bertrand having been requested to look at his tall gaunt figure, declared that such was exactly the height of the man who had torn her jewels from her, though the manner in which he was wrapped in a cloak prevented her judging further of his appearance. The white-handled hammer found buried with the mutilated settings, was sworn to by many of Mr Hargrave's servants as the property of Roger Humphries, who had a turn for nick-nack carpentry, which had led him to become master of many tools. These, and various accidental circumstances besides, either discovered or invented by the malicious Querin, and all turned to the best account in the many private interviews with which he was favoured by the official authorities, whose duty it was to seek for evidence, sufficed to make up a case against Roger too strong to admit a particle of doubt in the minds of any who listened to it; and never did less doubt remain on the minds of the public respecting the result of a trial than on this memorable occasion.

For, was there a single individual in all Paris who did not listen to all that was said on the subject? Were there any so high or so low as not to be interested in an affair, the details of which involved the names of so many well-known individuals?

Prince Frederic of —— delayed his departure from Paris till the trial was over.

Count Romanhoff confessed that, despite his passionate love of travel, there was no expedition which could possibly be proposed, even with Alfred Coventry for a companion, which could induce him to stir an inch till he had enjoyed the satisfaction of seeing that most superlative old villain condemned to labour in chains for the remainder of his life. And Alfred Coventry, far from urging a departure from which he expected no pleasure, felt more interest in the fate of the old man, rogue as he was, who had been one in the establishment which waited upon Mademoiselle de Cordillac, than he would have done in that of almost any other individual. The subject was, at least, a blessing to the newspapers, both French and English; and very ingenious, on both sides of the water, were the arguments by which the whole train of Roger Humphries' iniquities were made clear. As a confidential servant of Mr Hargrave's he had, doubtless, been in the habit of attending him to his club, which perfectly well accounted for the old villain's knowing when and where to pounce upon his victims in that quarter; while the same confidential familiarity with all that was going on in the premises of his gay master might naturally have suggested the possibility for effecting the robbery of Madame Bertrand.

Another circumstance greatly against old Roger was the disappearance of Ruperto. This man, upon the discovery of Madame Bertrand, began to suspect that his share in the business was likely enough to bring him into trouble. He was, in truth, greatly astonished at learning that she was still near Paris, as he firmly believed her to be, as he had said, in England, under the protection of his faithless employer; but her having been robbed and then violently detained as a prisoner in the lodgings which, by his own confession, he had provided for her, converted the gallant adventure into a sort of job, with which he by no means wished to mix himself. Being a remarkably clever person, all cities, as he was wont to boast, were alike to him, and rather than run the risk of being involved in the inquiry about to take place, he abandoned his hope of Mr Hargrave's debt and the fair city of Paris together; so that, when his much-esteemed new acquaintance, M Collet, waited upon him at the lodgings to which he had given him the address, the bird was flown, nor did any subsequent efforts of that repentant official gentleman enable him to atone for the negligence which had permitted such a man's leaving his *bureau* after he had once entered it, for, considerably before any search was set on foot for him by the police, he had embarked on board a vessel at Havre, intending to proceed, *vià* Archangel, to the real metropolis of all the Russias; and by this fellow's evasion, which at once threw doubts upon his evidence respecting Mr Hargrave, while it clearly identified himself with the crime actually committed, another material chance for eliciting the truth was removed, and the fate of the innocent old man apparently sealed past hope.

CHAPTER XXVIII

While these busy scenes were going on in Paris, every thing seemed to wear a very peaceable aspect at the Castle of the Lake. Though it might be that the tranquillity of its inmates was not quite so heartfelt as it appeared to the few simple souls who were its only witnesses.

Hans Klopmann and Gertrude Weiber, now become, by the blessing of Father Mark, man and wife, were both too busy and too happy to be likely to look deeper than the surface, or to discover that the folks who had got Mummel leave to inhabit one of the Grossberzag's own residences, who had plenty and plenty of money, with nothing to do but to amuse themselves, with the favour and good company of Father Mark into the bargain, could be otherwise than the very happiest people in the world, save and except their own happy selves.

Neither did Father Mark, though almost their daily visitor, suspect that there was any cause for anxiety among them beyond what met his pastoral ear from his two penitents. As for the heretic Adèle, he would have trembled, good man, had he found himself paying much heed to her in any way. But the confessions of Sabina shewed no inquietude, except for the safety and comfort of her father, and her gentle-hearted confessor failed not to assure her that the cause of his concealment was such, as not only to ensure the protection of those who ('praised be the saints!') were still the first and the most powerful among the sons of men, but, also, to draw upon him the especial blessing of the Virgin Mary and all the heavenly host, making it plain to all who saw with the eye of faith, that whatever he had lost and abandoned of earthly joys and earthly honours would be made up to him ten thousand-fold by the holier joys and higher honours which still awaited him, and that, probably, on earth as well as in heaven!

All this was, of course, a great comfort to her. But, perhaps, it only left her heart more at liberty to ponder over tender thoughts that now, as she perpetually told herself, brought no danger with them.

Sabina was at this time a whole year older than when she had loved to lend her imagination, and almost her belief, to the popular superstitions of the region which was now so strangely become her home; and she no longer tried to persuade herself that Goethe and Walter Scott believed in the lifelike fables with which their magic wands *poetised* the earth. Yet still the best, and, perhaps, the only atonement she found on the borders of the fairy lake for all the brilliant gaiety of Paris, lay in the visionary connexion which her fancy persisted in tracing between the hunter of the rock and the royal prince who had left his never-to-be-forgotten image on her heart. So far, indeed, did this fanciful connexion go, that there were moments (especially if she climbed to the well-remembered rock alone) when a wish would arise that she might once more see that hunter youth, and so satisfy her mind that he either was or was not the same, and no other, as he with whom had begun and ended all of earthly love to which she could ever open her heart. And then wild thoughts, nearly approaching to doubts, as to whether there might not be powers and influences floating about us, which ruled our destiny by means of which philosophy knows nothing, would steal upon her, and so interest her spirit in their soft and shadowy folds, that for hours together she would forget every thing except the dear delight of idle speculation. But she dared not breathe a word to her sister of these solitary musings, for she felt that they would not bear the test of discussion, and dreaded a light jest on themes that seemed to her little less than sacred. It would, perhaps, have been better if she had; for, in truth, any thought upon which she could have framed a jest would have been a relief to poor Adèle, whose melancholy musings on her own sad position, and that of the dear sister she so tenderly loved, and for whose sake she had endured so much (all of which, but for her, she could have turned from and escaped for ever), grew sadder and sadder with every passing day.

Had there been no crime, no vice, mixed in the cloud which overshadowed them, the high-minded girl would have borne it with the unshrinking courage of a martyr, whose very sufferings are a source of pride and glory. But now, the loss of caste, the loss of friends, the loss of the man she loved, and who she had so lately learned loved her, was accompanied by the ever-present and tormenting doubt of whether she had acted rightly in thus linking herself to crime and dishonour. On this point her ideas fluctuated with painful uncertainty. There were moments when she thought of her father and of the long-descended, noble race from whom he sprung, till her burning cheeks tingled with shame as she remembered the position in which she stood, and the nature of the association to which she submitted herself. And then, had her mind been constituted like that of Sabina, it is by no means improbable that she would have seen shadowy phantoms flitting round her, armed *cap-à-pié*, and raising before her eyes their burnished shields, quartered with *fleur-de-lis*, and bearing for device 'Sans peur et sans reproche.' But even as it was, she was sufficiently miserable, and it often required an exertion of all that remained of her former energy of character in order to preserve before Sabina such an appearance of tranquillity as might save her young sister from the misery of perceiving how utterly every hope of happiness was destroyed within her.

Meanwhile, the health and spirits of Mr Hargrave seemed daily to improve; the fits of gloomy silence into which, upon their first arrival at Gernsbach, he used to sink, for hours together, to the inexpressible grief of Sabina, but by no means to the surprise of Adèle, returned no more. He was not, indeed, so gaily talkative as he had been in the days of his Parisian splendour, but even when he was quite silent there was no trace of gloom about him: he ate well, walked actively, and was sometimes in the company of Father Mark, for hours together, on the borders of the little lake; and in answer to his anxious daughter's inquiries respecting his nights, assured her that he had never slept better.

Different as was the state of mind of the two girls respecting Mr Hargrave, they were, perhaps, equally surprised at the manner in which he bore this banishment from all the objects which had hitherto occupied and embellished his life, and the profound stillness of the existence which had taken their place.

Adèle wondered that a man so loaded with disgrace and sin could wear such an air of peace, and apparently self-satisfied composure; while Sabina marvelled that the gay, light, social spirit of her beloved father could endure with such admirable serenity a change so very violent and so very sad. To her eyes his character rose into something little short of sublime as she contemplated this admirable resignation; but to the unhappy Adèle the effect of it was most painfully the reverse. Had she wanted any additional argument to strengthen her in her new faith, she would have found it in contemplating the ease with which her Roman Catholic step-father seemed to shield himself from every feeling of remorse by drawing closer and closer the intercourse between himself and his confessor.

But in the inferences which followed her observations, she did Father Mark injustice. It is possible, indeed, that had she been fully acquainted with all the Church of Rome had to do in the matter, her reflections upon its influence might not have been more favourable than at present; nevertheless, as far as Father Mark was concerned, she was unjust. For neither did he, in the very slightest degree, value or desire the intimate sort of intercourse into which circumstances had led him with Mr Hargrave; nor were the dainty little dinners (which that gentleman's accurate acquaintance with the art of cookery, combined with the *gasthaus* ability of Gertrude, enabled him to offer, and which, compared with the frugal meal at his mother's table, were perfectly luxurious) any atonement to him for the loss of his wonted colloquial intercourse with the birds who inhabit his favourite thickets, or the flowers, from whom he ventured to receive incense, without tormenting his conscience with fears that he was defrauding the Church. Still less was there any possibility that his pure and simple spirit could have been won by the wealth of all the mines that ever man ransacked, as Adèle would have known could she have seen the innocent look of unfeigned indifference with which he laid upon the table a magnificent diamond which Mr Hargrave had presented to him with these coaxing words, –

'Let me, Father Mark, enjoy the supreme satisfaction of knowing that one of the gems which in my younger and more thoughtless days ministered to my vanity, has become sacred and holy by passing into the possession of a minister of the one only holy Catholic and Apostolic Church! So shall my worldly sin, in having worn it proudly, be absolved, washed out, atoned for, and forgiven!'

And, having laid the sparkling treasure on the good man's hand, which he had seized upon and turned palm-upwards to receive it, Mr Hargrave crossed himself on brow and breast, knit his fingers together in the true orthodox Popish clasp, and, dropping his eyes, appeared by the rapid movement of his compressed lips to be uttering a prayer.

Father Mark immediately crossed himself too, and remained not only respectfully but reverentially silent, till Mr Hargrave's muttered orison was concluded, and then said, having with the greatest difficulty mastered a yawn, –

'Not for much, my son, would I reject an offering which might tend to bring peace to your soul, especially when intended, as this evidently is, as a pious propitiation to the Holy Church. But if your purpose hold of presenting yourself at Rome as a candidate for the sacrament of ordination, and as a professed monk of the most holy order of St Dominic, I would suggest that whatever wealth you have to bestow should reach our holy and blessed mother the Church then amd there. It will be far easier for those with whom you will be brought into contact at that time to bring your oblation to the pious uses for which it is designed, than for me; and it is for this reason, and for this reason only,' continued the sincere and honest bigot, 'that I venture to reject it.'

Then calculating the time he had that morning given to Mr Hargrave, with as much conscientious exactitude as if the hours had been passed in the Roman Catholic exercise called '*meditation*', he rose to take his leave, having the sweet freshness of the neighbouring forest, and the delicious quiet he was going to find there, so strongly in his thoughts, that he almost felt the luxury of the change before he had made it.

'Nay, do not leave me, Father Mark!' said Mr Hargrave, reluctantly taking up the rejected stone, and concealing it in his purse, – 'do not leave me! I have displayed the whole map of my once worldly soul before you, and hang upon every breath uttered by one anointed and received by the blessed Church as her priest and servant, in the humble hope of becoming myself one day like unto him, and set apart sacred and sworn to her service.'

This of course could not be spoken without a good deal of crossing, in which the weary but observant priest thought himself obliged to join; while his spirit, still as volant as that of a schoolboy, was bearing him away up hill and down hill, faster – alas! much faster – than he dared to follow it. Father Mark had still to disengage himself from his fervent penitent, and that too without giving his priest-ridden conscience any cause to reproach him with indifference to the interests of the Church; and this was no easy task for him, poor man! Not only had Mr Hargrave given him to understand, as hinted above, that his purpose was to dedicate himself to the service of the Church, and to offer that service at Rome, but had informed him also that, notwithstanding the enormous sacrifices he had made of his hereditary wealth to the cause of the pious monarch whose interest he espoused, he still possessed, in diamonds and other precious stones, a sufficient treasure to make him feel that, by dedicating it and himself to the one and only Church, he might make an acceptable offering.

To the mimosa-like sensitiveness of Father Mark's feelings on all subjects connected with the authority under which he had determined to live, this was enough to make Mr Hargrave an object of great and conscientious importance, though (for some reason or other, which the good father sought not to inquire into) he could not manage to make him one of respect. Not, however, that he had the remotest suspicion that his new penitent had ever been guilty of any act or deed to justify his dislike; but, nevertheless, he could not for the life of him feel any sincere and genuine interest in any single thing he said. The more conscious the good priest became of this, the more impossible he felt it to be that he should ever conquer it; so much the more a great deal did he labour to do every thing, and neglect nothing, which his duty as a churchman required.

There was scarcely one of the seven deadly sins which Father Mark would not as willingly have committed, as permit his mind to examine why it was that the pope, cardinals, abbots, bishops, &c. &c. should, one and all, be so anxious to obtain the handling and management of that vile dross, which their vows had rendered so useless to them. All that he knew on the subject being that *so it was*, all he had to do was, of course, to forward their views and wishes whenever it fell in his way; and as this had rarely happened in the course of his quiet life to an extent so great as that which seemed to offer itself at present, his eagerness to do nothing that might check the pious purpose of the neophyte was very exactly in proportion to his own utter indifference on the subject. So that his days, for the most part, passed in a constant combat between his desire to get away from Mr Hargrave's pompous humility and loudly professing piety, and his terrors lest by doing so he should betray his vowed duty to the Church.

Had Mr Hargrave understood Father Mark only as well as Father Mark, with all his ignorance of past events and all his inclinations to be deceived, knew him, a great deal of very useless annoyance would have been spared. For Mr Hargrave having read Father Mark's work 'On the Authority of the Church,' as the majority of fashionable gentlemen brought up at Eton would read a Latin treatise on such a subject, he had picked out enough of it to persuade him that the good father was one of those who conceived persons of his profession could not be made too great a fuss with. Alas! for the painful hours which this blunder caused the poor priest to spend in listening to Mr Hargrave's long-winded homilies, when he might have been hearkening to the music of a waterfall, or inhaling the pure breath of nature, instead of the nauseous suspirations of hypocrisy!

But the wish to do his ill-understood duty was very strong within him, and Father Mark reseated himself now, as he had often done before, to endure the vain man's exhibition of himself in a new character, and to encourage his declared and oft-repeated intention to bestow all he possessed upon the Church; without yielding to the strong temptation of telling him, that if he bestowed himself too he would mix so much dross with his ore as would make the advantage, in the estimation of some at least, very doubtful. But upon the present, as upon all former occasions, the repentant philosopher consoled himself with the hope that the restraint and distaste which he thus compelled himself to endure would be accepted as penance for the involuntary flashes of unfettered thought with which he was conscious that he was still occasionally visited.

To a mind of such moderate-sized dimensions as that of Mr Hargrave, personal vanity will often become a sort of defence (though puffy and unsubstantial) against the vicissitudes of fortune. The tremendous downfall he had met; the overthrow of all his hopes; the deprivation of all best liked and most valued, would have been almost too bitter to bear, had he not been so cased in the cotton of self-conceit as to have the vital warmth of vanity still kept alive within him.

Feeling pretty tolerably well convinced that the world, commonly so called, was no longer a theatre upon which he could advantageously display himself, this same vital warmth gave him energy to turn his thoughts towards another; and the cloister, the consistory, the conclave of pope and cardinals, – nay, the very papal throne itself, all pressed forward upon his imagination as the scenery and decorations of a new one.

And very splendid decorations, and a very brilliant scene, they afforded. The long and graceful vestments; the scarlet, the violet, and the ermine – even the white satin slipper, attracting eyes to the Apollo-like foot, – were all remembered; and Mr Hargrave was quite aware that Apollo himself, had fifty *mortal* winters passed over him, could hardly assume a more graceful costume than that worn by the dignitaries of the Church of Rome. And then Mr Hargrave had read the enchanting papal biography of Roscoe, and really thought – a little induced thereto, perhaps, by his actual position – that after the first flush of youthful comeliness was past, it was hardly possible for a man to display himself to greater advantage than in the magnificent arena offered by the Church of Rome, or to settle down upon a cushion more delightfully soft than those prepared for her favourites.

Fortunately, most fortunately, as he now felt, he had never, from the time he visited Rome with his highly connected lady, lost any opportunity of recalling himself favourably to the noble cardinal, her uncle. A great variety of graceful Parisian presents had crossed the Alps, chiefly for the sake of receiving in return (which could be so advantageously shewn to his confessor) a nepotive-paternal benediction from a member of the sacred college.

Here, then, was one assured friend at Rome. And might not the cause for which he fled from Paris, and with which his uncle cardinal was already slightly acquainted – might not this cause win more?

There were moments when the fumes of Mr Hargrave's new and strongly fermenting piety so intoxicated his brain, that he was tempted to believe a ray of direct inspiration had fallen upon Mademoiselle de Cordillac when she suggested a plot for the restoration of Charles X as the cause of his running away from the police.

CHAPTER XXIX

Though Sabina still continued to be the active *ménagère* of the establishment at the Castle of the Lake, her sister readily and willingly aided her in every thing wherein her exertions could avail towards the comfort and well-being of the little household. Clothed in the ordinary dress of Alsatian peasant girls, carefully rejecting every trace of former luxury which might attract attention, they began to find that they might walk about with a basket on the arm, and the steady air of busy occupation in their gait, without attracting any very alarming degree of attention. A good deal of mystery was still preserved respecting their having become actually inmates and dwellers in 'the residence.' Some few asserted this to be the case, but many more denied it; and as Frau Weiber purchased all they wanted in her own name, and assisted, with considerable skill, to keep up mystification and doubt upon the subject among all those who frequented her house, the result was exactly such a degree of uncertainty as was most favourable for lengthened concealment; for if any, upon good authority, stated that they KNEW the château to be inhabited, there were ever enough to laugh the fanciful believer to scorn; and the more vehement his assertions, the less he was believed.

> 'Use lessens marvel,'

and it lessens fear too. Expeditions and undertakings, which at their first arrival would have appeared wild and impossible to both the sisters, speedily became things of daily occurrence; till at length, feeling a longing desire for a book or two beyond what their good priest could lend them, and hearing that many which would be now accounted most precious treasures could be procured at Baden-Baden, they resolutely determined to set off upon a walk to that place; braving, under the shelter of their peasant dresses and Sabina's excellent colloquial German, all danger of being unpleasantly noticed.

How well, as they set off together upon this expedition, did they both remember the time when they had traversed the same beautiful road amidst all the luxurious contrivances which wealth invents to make fatigue unknown! Had a voice direct from heaven told them then, that before the earth had completed her daily journey three hundred and sixty-five times, they should be pacing the lengthened way on foot in the garb of peasants, and with no hope, no wish, beyond being received and greeted as such by all whom they might encounter, would they not have said that the idle prophecy suited well with the neighbourhood of fibbing fairies, whose fitting delight it might be to persuade folks that

'All that is, is not?'

Yet that long walk was not without its pleasures. The day was one of pure, bright, spring-tide sunshine, but tempered, at least on the lofty ridge they had to traverse, by a delicious breeze, which made the very act of drawing breath, a luxury. They reached the well-remembered and beautiful little town, therefore, without any painful feeling of fatigue, having, before they descended the Herrnwiesse Hill, had recourse, each to her own basket, for refreshment, carefully stowed there by the neat-handed Gertrude. Like all wise travellers, they chose their place of rest beside a rapid rill of bright clear water, which completed the repast; and when they rose from the grassy sod on which they had seated themselves, they certainly looked not at all the worse for their long walk.

They perfectly well knew where to find the shop most likely to furnish what they wanted; and with looks demure, and eyes which, though not 'leaden,' certainly seemed to 'love the ground,' they took their way thither. Nothing in the least degree startling or alarming occurred to them. Adèle bought an English Bible, which she could not get at Gernsbach, and the delighted Sabina made herself mistress of Shakespeare, in one huge volume of ill-printed columns. Various other purchases were added to these, and, their business being ended, Sabina paid for them, and desired that they might be sent by a certain weekly carrier, of whom she spake with a proper degree of positive information, giving as the address 'Frau Weiber, at the Black Eagle, Gernsbach.' The only question by which she was troubled in return was uttered by the quiet, civil master of the shop, as he took down this address. 'Are all these books for the Frau Weiber?' said he. But Sabina's short but gentle answer, 'No, sir, they are for my master,' seemed perfectly to satisfy him, and he made no further inquiries.

As soon as Adèle had chosen her Bible, she took the liberty to seat herself in a distant corner of the shop, beside a table covered with newspapers, leaving Sabina, who was now, as usual, the spokeswoman, to transact all the other business herself.

The idea of obtaining a newspaper had often occurred to Adèle, as a means of looking back upon the world they had left, which she longed for, yet dared not venture to seek; but now, as they lay before her in tempting abundance and sufficient confusion, her quick eye caught sight of 'Galignani's Messenger', and, well knowing the satisfactory universality of its *multum in parvo* columns, she eagerly stretched out her hand and seized it. The leading article, the *party-coloured* extracts from the English papers, the well-digested mass of all the news of Europe, was all passed by with more than indifference – with an impatience that, still and silent as she was, seemed to stop her breath as she turned to the paragraphs headed 'PARIS.'

Poor Adèle! what did she hope to see there? The name of Coventry? It was not likely. The history of her step-father's acts, and her own and Sabina's departure in his company? She felt, as this last thought suggested itself, that she doubted if she could see it, and not betray her agony to all who looked on her. Yet still she read on, of this, and of that, and Heaven knows what, with such eagerness of attention, that it may be doubted if a cannon let off beside her could have disturbed it.

At length she came to the following paragraph: — 'The interest excited by the approaching trial of the old Englishman, Roger Humphries, is greater than any merely private trial has produced for years. It is now generally known, beyond the possibility of doubt, that this desperate ruffian, who still preserves the same obstinate silence, was not only the robber, and, as many thought, the assassin of Madame Bertrand, but also the perpetrator of the daring and atrocious robbery committed some weeks ago on a gentleman returning to his lodgings from the *salons* of Riccordo. No proof has yet appeared against him respecting the two former attacks of the same nature made against persons leaving the same establishment, an accurate account of which appeared in this paper; but it is very strongly suspected that the three robberies, so similar in object, time, and place, must have been planned and executed by the same bold hand. But whether these former crimes be brought home to the prisoner or not, the sentence expected to be passed upon him is condemnation to hard labour in the galleys for life.'

★ ★ ★

The miserable Adèle contrived to read this terrible statement twice, from beginning to end, without either screaming or fainting; but she was heart-struck, and felt as if she had never known real suffering till that hour.

The faithful old domestic, who had loved her from a child with such affectionate devotion — who would have done, and had done, any thing and every thing she had asked of him — what was his reward? Alone, unfriended, in a foreign land, and brought to condemnation for the crimes of one whom she had withdrawn from the hands of justice, and even, as it seemed, from all suspicion!

Did she rejoice at finding how successful had been her efforts for this precious step-father? Even for Sabina's sake did she rejoice at it? Alas, no! She only felt that she had made herself the participator of crime, and that, by sheltering the guilty, she had destroyed the innocent!

The paper was still in her hand; her fixed eye still rested on the half-read column; and in the next moment she discovered that the anguish it was her portion to endure was not yet complete; for further on she found another paragraph, referring at considerable length to the manner in which the old man had been apprehended, while stealing back to his master's house after committing the robbery, and commenting upon the singular chance which had thus thrown him into the hands of justice, by means of a delay in the departure of some of the guests, which, naturally enough, the old villain had not expected. Reference was again made to the contumacious silence uniformly preserved by the prisoner, accompanied by a remark, 'that his singular obstinacy in this respect had been far from beneficial to him, for it was that which, in the first instance, fixed suspicion upon him, the mere circumstance of his being seen about to enter his master's house at half-past five in the morning being by no means sufficient grounds even for his being apprehended. But, happily for the interests of justice, his attempt to retreat out of sight, and his subsequent stubborn refusal to state where he had been or how employed, had sufficiently indicated his guilt, and led by degrees to the discovery of all the circumstances which proved it.'

Here, then, was the full history of the faithful fellow's misfortune. It was in order to keep HER secret that he had given reason to suspect he had one of his own. And for this he was calumniated, outraged, imprisoned, and about to suffer what would be, perhaps, worse to him than the extremest penalty of the law!

Could the generous-hearted Adèle de Cordillac bear this? Could she remain in quiet security beside the real culprit whom she had snatched from danger, while the steadfast-hearted and devoted old man endured for her sake – for her HONOUR'S sake – this frightful accumulation of misery?

*   *   *

The business upon which Sabina had been engaged was completed; she turned to her sister to say so, and they left the shop. Sabina made some remark on the acquisitions they had made, but Adèle made no reply, and they walked on in silence, which was supposed by the 'ungalled' Sabina to arise from prudence, as they were still among the haunts of men, which was now always a signal for silence between them. But when they were again mounting the steep Herrnwiesse, and had nearly reached the sylvan solitudes which stretched away before them, on arriving at its summit Sabina said, 'I fear you are tired, Adèle?'

'Oh, very tired!' she replied; 'too tired to talk, dearest! Let us get home as fast as we can, and without exhausting our strength by speaking.'

After this they walked on in silence. Sabina, a little anxious about this over-fatigue for her sister, but with good hope that one of the old sofas, and a supper such as Gertrude's solicitude for them would be sure to prepare, might set all right again; and then, as usual, she gave the rein to her wandering fancy, and was speedily lost in a visionary world of her own, wherein the two figures which were ever her companions when she thus indulged herself sometimes careered on either side of her, and sometimes were mysteriously blended into one.

It was, perhaps, hardly possible for two minds to be in a state more perfectly dissimilar than were those of the two sisters as they thus walked on, side by side together. While the one was enjoying with unchecked freedom the wanton vagaries of her young imagination, the other was sternly bending all the strength and power of her mind upon the tremendous task that lay before her. That Roger Humphries should be saved, let who would perish by it, was a point already settled in her mind, as firmly as faith and truth could settle it, and that almost before she was conscious that she had formed the resolution. It was, in fact, an impulse which decided this, more sudden and powerful in its action than any deliberate process of judgment and volition could have been; but it was an impulse that every after-thought strengthened, and Adèle would rather have relinquished her life than have attempted to combat it.

There was something terrible in the distinctness and intensity with which she contemplated the mode and manner of achieving this. She saw all that lay before her as plainly as if a pictured chart was spread palpably before her eyes, on which was marked every rock and every quicksand through which she must steer her terrible way. Ay, and she heard, too, plainly as if a 'chisel' had been found to 'cut breath,' and bring its simulated likeness to the sense, all the questions that must follow her declaration of the old man's innocence. Must it not be proved by her avowal of her interview with him and of the errand on which he had been sent by her? But this shook her not. She saw it, she heard it, she knew it all; but it weighed not a single feather against the overruling motive that kept her purpose steady.

Had she known, too, as certainly that the release of Roger, which she was to purchase with all this agony, would of necessity be followed by the conviction of the real culprit, it would still have made no difference in that moment of stern, unshrinking justice. Nevertheless, Adèle did remember, even then, that in all that concerned Mr Hargrave she might imitate the steadfast silence of her faithful messenger, who, rather than betray *her* secret, had permitted himself to be condemned to the fate of the most desperate felon.

Such was the state of mind in which Adèle re-entered her strange home, and prepared to meet the greetings of her step-father.

There was one circumstance in the terrible intelligence she had acquired which was a comfort to her. After well weighing the question, she convinced herself that she might open her whole heart to Sabina concerning the expedition she meditated without any danger of being obliged to enlighten her upon the subject on which she hoped to keep her for ever ignorant. It did not follow of necessity, that because Roger was innocent her father was guilty; and truly rejoiced was poor Adèle at not being obliged to part with one she so dearly loved with mystery or dissimulation, – a rejoicing the more deeply felt, perhaps, from the consciousness that something very like a hope, fluttered at her heart, of not living to return after her task was accomplished.

But although she thus contemplated the speaking openly to Sabina on the subject of her intended departure for Paris, she resolved to delay doing so till she had communicated to her step-father the astounding intelligence she brought; and accordingly, as soon as the meal which awaited their return was over, she desired permission to accompany him for a few moments to a sitting-room peculiarly his own, and in which he always received his punctual but most unwilling confessor.

By well-understood but tacit agreement between the parties, no word had ever been exchanged between Mademoiselle de Cordillac and Mr Hargrave, relative to the cause of their leaving Paris, since the one short decisive moment in which she gave him to understand that she was acquainted with all the facts that rendered it necessary. How she had obtained her information was still a mystery to him; but though by no means without very acute feelings of curiosity on the subject, he would rather have 'burst in ignorance' than have given a look or a word which might lead to the return of a confidence which it was little short of agony to think of. It was, therefore, with no very agreeable feelings that he listened to this request from his step-daughter, but to refuse it was wholly out of the question; and, forcing one of his benignant smiles, he rose with every appearance of alacrity, and presented his arm for her acceptance. This act of politeness, however, Adèle either did not or would not see; but proceeding with rapid step the way she had invited him to go, she reached the room before him.

'Will you sit down, my love?' said Mr Hargrave.

'No, sir, I thank you; I would rather not. I shall not, I mean, detain you long enough to make it necessary. What I have to tell will be soon said. I have avoided, – very carefully avoided, any allusion to the cause which brought us here; and nothing but a very terrible necessity leads me to do otherwise now.'

It had been her intention to let one speech suffice, and to have told him, with all possible brevity, the facts which she wished him to know; but he trembled so violently on hearing these opening words that she felt compelled to stop, and recommended him to sit down.

'Am I suspected? Am I followed?' he said in a voice that plainly enough confessed the extremity of the terror that shook his limbs like a fit of the ague.

'No, sir; neither the one nor the other,' replied Adèle, coldly. 'What I have to say does not immediately concern yourself. I have seen a newspaper at Baden, which informs me——' Adèle's voice failed her for a moment, but the next she went on — 'which informs me that our old and valued servant, Roger Humphries, has been taken up on suspicion of having robbed Madame Bertrand; and the evidence against him has been such as to render condemnation to hard labour in the galleys for life, certain.'

'God bless my soul! How can this be possible?' said Mr Hargrave, with a countenance and manner intended to express a vast deal of sorrow and concern, but in the midst of which the very heart of Adèle seemed to read triumph and joy. 'I really think, my dearest love, that you must be mistaken.'

'No, sir, I am not mistaken,' she replied, with a stronger feeling of indignation and dislike than she had ever before been conscious of; 'and as a proof that I have neither read nor received this news lightly, I am here expressly to inform you that it is my purpose to set off for Paris immediately, in order to exculpate this innocent and greatly wronged old man.'

'Impossible!' exclaimed Mr Hargrave, in violent agitation. 'Impossible, Mademoiselle de Cordillac, – you cannot think of it! Would you really plunge me – would you plunge your sister into the abyss of shame and misery, to save us from which you have so nobly exerted yourself? I will not believe that such is your intention.'

'It is not my intention, Mr Hargrave,' replied Adèle, sedately, 'to plunge either my sister or yourself into danger or difficulty of any kind. I fully anticipate the being able to achieve the object I have in view without running any risk of doing so. But in this you must trust me.'

'I cannot trust you, rash girl!' exclaimed the terrified man. 'What power have you to prove this old man innocent except – the being able to prove another guilty?'

'I can prove an *alibi*, Mr Hargrave: I can prove that I myself sent Roger upon an errand from which he was returning at the time he was arrested,' said Adèle.

'Absurd! Who will believe the story? Who will believe that you sent the old man off upon an errand between four and five o'clock in the morning? The device is too shallow, Adèle, – too preposterously absurd. If you present yourself before a court of justice for the purpose of proving Roger Humphries innocent, my doom is sealed! I am lost, destroyed for ever, and Sabina with me; and when you have seen your sister perish at your feet, then turn to old Roger Humphries for consolation. But do the thing thoroughly, Mademoiselle de Cordillac. Say at once that it is your step-father – the husband of your mother, who has committed this deed.

Bring not the sneers of all Paris upon you by saying you knew who it was *not*, but for particular reasons beg to decline telling who it was; and then apostrophise the shade of your mother, and say that you have done much to save her child from shame!'

'Be not disturbed, sir, by any fears for the result,' replied Adèle, in that quiet tone which shews so plainly that contempt overpowers indignation. 'I shall take care to state nothing which I am not able to prove respecting Roger Humphries, and that without putting it in any one's power to infer that what he did not do, Mr Hargrave did.'

'Let me ask you, Mademoiselle de Cordillac – I have a right to ask you, for more than my life depends upon it – what proofs do you possess that this old man was not employed in the manner suspected at the time the – the robbery was committed?' demanded Mr Hargrave, almost fiercely.

'This is no moment,' replied his step-daughter, 'for settling or disputing our respective rights. But I feel no wish to withhold from you the facts I must soon proclaim to all who choose to listen. I sent Roger Humphries with a note to Mr Coventry at his hôtel; and he left my presence about ten minutes after four o'clock on the morning in question.'

No young Englishwoman, twenty-two years of age and perfectly independent, can be a fair judge of what Adèle de Cordillac felt in making this avowal now, and resolving to make it afterwards in public. Her lips trembled, and tears of great suffering started to her eyes. Mr Hargrave perceived this, and instantly endeavoured to take advantage of it.

'Do I hear rightly?' he said. 'Do I hear Adèle de Cordillac, the descendant of so long a line of noble ancestors, calmly declare that it is her intention to proclaim in Paris, before a public tribunal, that in the dead of night she bribed one of her step-father's serving-men to carry love-notes to a young Englishman at his hôtel? This is madness, – absolute madness! And it becomes my bounden duty to prevent it.' Then, rushing to the door, he turned with violence the clumsy key that for years had remained stationary in the lock, and put it in his pocket.

'You stir not from this room, young lady, till I have your solemn promise upon oath, not to quit this dwelling without my permission, and not to hold any communication, direct or indirect, with any persons out of it, without my concurrence and consent. As the husband of your high-born mother, Mademoiselle de Cordillac, and the representative of your equally noble father, it is my duty to prevent this disgraceful degradation. And I will do it!'

Whatever composure of manner Adèle had lost in naming Mr Coventry, she more than recovered now; and replied in a tone which shewed no consciousness of having degenerated from the noble stocks to which her step-father referred, – 'You must permit me to think, Mr Hargrave, that the honour of my ancestors is as safe in my keeping as in yours. *Au reste*, I shall certainly not do battle with you for the key of this apartment, nor for that of the château either. You will not fail to remember, long before the freedom you restrain becomes important to me, that it will be for your interest to let me go free, where and when I will. But I have no objection whatever that this door should remain closed against all intruders while I put both myself and you to pain by asking one question, suggested by a phrase I saw in the paper yesterday in reference to Madame Bertrand, and which phrase gave me hope that one very horrible idea which has vaguely, and without any continuous belief in its truth, tormented my imagination, is without foundation. Roger Humphries is said to have been *at one time* suspected of having murdered that unfortunate lady. Say, sir, did she leave your hands in safety?'

Nothing that Mademoiselle de Cordillac could have said to her step-father, short of assuring him that Roger Humphries had been tried, condemned, and hanged, could have given him so much satisfaction as the expressive doubt which this question indicated.

The eloquent burst of injured innocence which followed was perfectly sublime, and flowed on so long sometimes in touching pathos, sometimes in indignant rage, and sometimes in tender reproaches to the 'dear Adèle,' who might have known that whatever faults imperious distress had generated, cruelty to woman was not likely to be one of them; that his prisoner began to fear that her boast respecting her fearlessness as to the length of her detention was likely to prove a vain one. However, she had the satisfaction of hearing him explain as he went on, the manner in which he had shed the blood, the traces of which had so greatly shocked her, and was thus relieved from the sickening consciousness as she remembered it that *nothing* could be much more difficult of belief than what she already too well knew to be true – a thought that had haunted her at intervals, despite all the really well-founded reasons she had for hoping that this crowning horror was impossible. But, being fully satisfied on this point, she began to wish herself in her own room, arranging matters for her departure in the morning, and explaining to the still unconscious Sabina all the terrible reasons which rendered it necessary. Seeing, however, that the reproaches of the much-wronged and falsely suspected Hargrave did not appear likely to arrive at their conclusion for a good while to come, she felt it was becoming necessary to find a way to escape from it, and therefore said, – 'I am ready, Mr Hargrave, to apologise for all the wrong I have ever done you by unfounded suspicions, and am happy to find such satisfactory reason for doing so; but,' looking at the little watch she wore within her waist-riband, 'it is now seven o'clock, Father Mark will be here immediately, and I would not wish his wonder and attention to be excited by so unusual a sight as your heretic step-daughter locked up with you. The circumstance would probably not tend to increase his respect for you, and might lead to his addressing some inconvenient questions to me. Pray open the door, Mr Hargrave.'

'Father Mark! You are always right, Adèle! You are a most extraordinary girl, indeed; but tell me, my dear, when do you think of setting off upon this perilous expedition? Now I think of it, I have no doubt that you will manage it so as to do no harm. Your original suggestion, my dear, respecting the exiled royal family must strictly be kept to whenever there is occasion to speak of me – any alteration there would be very injurious to Sabina. You understand me, my love? Now go; we are both of us warm, Adèle, and have mutual need of each other's forgiveness. I accept your apology most willingly, my dear. Now go – go directly, will you, for I think I hear the voice of Father Mark speaking with Gertrude.'

He held the door open for her as he spoke, and she walked through it, rejoicing at having discovered so ready a means of frightening her contemptible step-father out of his contemplated opposition. She was little aware, however, how powerful was the spell she had put in action. The name of Father Mark suggested a new train of thought, and Adèle was not more anxious to quit his presence than he was to see her depart.

CHAPTER XXX

Mr Hargrave's ears had not deceived him: it was the voice of Father Mark which he had heard, and the good man stood before him within two minutes after Adèle had disappeared. The interview began by Mr Hargrave stating that he had much to say to him, and *that* upon a subject which he was sure his reverence to the Church would lead him to consider as highly important. Father Mark breathed one unobtrusive little sigh, and sat himself down with very meek resignation, and such a feeling of true martyr-like submission to penance at his heart, as might have atoned for many a wandering way-side speculation upon the species of intercourse which may exist between the creature and the Creator in regions not blessed with the over-shadowing presence of the Roman Catholic Apostolic Church – speculations by which he had been a good deal tormented during the whole of that bright breezy day, passed in solitary rambling amidst some of the loveliest scenes of the Mourgthal. As this penitent feeling was both true and lasting, this private interview between the priest and Mr Hargrave endured for several hours, and Adèle and Sabina passed the remainder of the evening alone.

Then it was that Mademoiselle de Cordillac, for the first time since their sorrows had fallen upon them, spoke with perfect and entire truth and confidence to her young sister, and even in the midst of the miserable intelligence she had to communicate, there was a feeling strongly approaching to pleasure in this return to confidence. The whole history of Roger's arrest, when seen returning to his master's house soon after five o'clock in the morning, exactly as it was related in the papers, might all be safely repeated to Sabina without the slightest allusion to her father. The commentary upon this terrible statement was made with equal quickness by both. It could not be doubted that he was in the act of returning from the errand upon which Adèle had sent him, and it was equally easy to guess that the obstinate silence which the reporter dwelt upon with so much severity was caused by the faithful old man's determination not to betray the delicate secret which had been confided to him.

There could be no second opinion between the sisters as to the course to be pursued. Adèle, who had sent the noble-spirited prisoner upon the business that caused him to be encountered at that suspicious hour, – Adèle, who knew where to apply for corroboration of her own statement by the evidence of the persons he must have seen at the place to which he was sent, – Adèle, who alone of all the world could exonerate the faithful agent from the promise of secrecy which he had pledged to her, – Adèle, in short, notwithstanding all the fearful reasons which made them both tremble as they contemplated the expedition, and all the exposure and humiliation which it involved, was urged as strenuously by Sabina as by her own generous heart to set off on the morrow upon her return to Paris.

It was now that the affectionate Sabina unconsciously repaid the pity with which Adèle's heart had been wrung for her. It would be difficult to find words to describe the pang she felt as she pictured to herself the scene through which her sister must pass, in presence of the tribunal which had arraigned Roger Humphries, before it could be made aware of his innocence. It was good for Adèle, perhaps, that she felt called upon to soothe the agony she saw produced by this. It obliged her to call forth all the excellent reasons which she had for feeling that the act was one of paramount duty, and that the shrinking from it would condemn her to remorse, ten thousand times more lasting and more bitter to endure than any thing she should feel, even when confessing before all Paris that she had privately despatched a letter in the dead of night to Mr Coventry. 'Oh, true, – most true!' cried Sabina, throwing her arms around her. 'Go, noblest, dearest Adèle! Could I but go with you – could I but believe that I might quit my father at this moment without committing thereby a most deadly sin, I should mind nothing! But to see you set off on this tremendous expedition alone will be very terrible!'

'Not if you remember that it would be a sin for me to stay,' returned Adèle, calmly. 'Sabina! we ought to consider the chance which enables me to do this "great right" as one of the greatest blessings that ever befell me. You have only to consider what my condition would have been had I not heard of this till it was too late to save him, – you have only to think of this, Sabina, in order to forget all present inconvenience. And now assist me, dearest, to make my preparations. I must walk to Baden, and go thence by a diligence; and I am in doubt whether I had better resume my Paris garb here or *en route*.'

'Here,' replied Sabina, – 'here, beyond all doubt, we have nothing to fear from the remarks of Hans and Gertrude – they love us, both of them, I am quite sure of that; but they must already consider us as beings enveloped in mystery, and a little more or a little less of it cannot signify here. Whereas *en route*, Adèle, your appearing at one moment in the character of your faithful Susanne, and the next in that of your faithful Gertrude, could hardly fail of producing disagreeable results.' This was too reasonable to leave any further doubt on the subject, and the two girls set themselves to make such preparations as were required, or rather such as were in their power, for Adèle's adventurous journey.

'Have you asked papa for money for your expedition, Adèle? Be sure that you take enough. It would be dreadful indeed, were you to want money in Paris!'

'Fear not! I shall not want money,' replied Adèle, shrinking as she ever did, from all allusion to her step-father's unrighteous hoards. But Sabina was not to be so satisfied; and with a movement of that filial fondness which ever seemed ready to shew itself, she said, 'Dearest papa! – I understand you, Adèle. You mean that he pressed upon you more than you thought necessary – that is so like him, – but he is quite right. I hope you did not make any difficulties about it, Adèle; but that you took whatever he thought necessary?'

The dissimulation which such sallies as this required was the hardest task of poor Adèle's daily life, and would often have been beyond her power to perform, had she not for ever kept in mind the object for which she had already done and endured so much. 'Shall I spoil all to save myself one struggle more?' thought she; and then replied in an accent as foreign from her feelings as it was possible for her to assume, 'There was no need to trouble papa about it at all, my dear: I have more – much more than I shall require for the journey; and when I get to Paris, my aunt will go with me to our good friend, M de Servac, who, you know, manages all her money matters, as well as mine; and then I shall not only be able to get whatever money I want, but shall have the advantage of being able to arrange with him the manner in which I am to receive my income in future.'

'Will there be no danger in this? – no danger of discovery to papa?' demanded Sabina.

'Not as I shall manage it, my love,' returned her sister. 'I shall only request him to pay in the money to my account at Lafitte's; and by means of any banker we may choose to fix upon at Strasburg, Francfort, or any where else, I can draw for it.'

Sabina sighed. She felt, with that sort of indescribable certainty which seems more like instinct than reason, that Adèle did not lean upon her father as she used to do. In short, it is pretty nearly a moral impossibility for a very honest heart to go on for ever feigning, and for ever with success; and had not this sudden interruption of their daily intercourse arisen, it may be, that, despite all the painfully sustained acting of Mademoiselle de Cordillac, some suspicion that she did not wholly approve her loyal step-father's noble conduct, might have crept in to sully the perfect love which had hitherto united the sisters.

As it was, however, all was still right between them; for ever as the thought of Adèle's increased independence suggested itself, Sabina remembered gratefully how successfully the newly awakened power had been employed in her dear father's service, and she blessed the change which half a moment before had cost her a heavy sigh. A good portion of that night was spent in talking, and the theme was Adèle's journey and all the possible results that might follow from it; there was no danger that any difference of feeling should arise between them: and when at last they agreed for health's sake they would talk no more, the kiss given and returned was as full of unmixed and unchanged love, as if Adèle had not known that their thoughts were no longer in common, and as if Sabina had not guessed it.

This was remembered afterwards by both of them with thankfulness.

*   *   *

At an early hour on the following morning, Adèle, once more dressed in the garments of her maid Susanne, and carrying a small bundle in her hand, sallied forth from her strangely acquired home upon a business still more strangely belonging to her. This *sortie* from one of the Grand Ducal residences of Baden by a descendant of maréchals, constables, and Heaven knows how many generals – the heroes, through successive generations, of the *oriflamme* and the lily – was one of those freaks of fortune which converts some scenes of human life into more whimsical melodrama than any dramatic romancer ever invented. Some thought of this kind seemed to pass through the mind of Adèle de Cordillac as she passed out; for a stifled sigh, a melancholy smile, and an unexplained shake of the head, which seemed as pregnant with meaning as that of my Lord Burleigh, shewed her mind to be full of matter. But to Sabina she spoke cheeringly, declaring that the object of her expedition rendered it impossible that she could be conscious either of fatigue or inconvenience; and that if the success which she confidently hoped for, rewarded her efforts, she should ever consider this pilgrimage as the proudest boast of her life.

Sabina knew her too well not to feel that this was no vain bravado; and the words produced exactly the effect which the speaker intended, – they withdrew the poor girl's attention from the miserable circumstances of their present parting, and made her feel not only the necessity for it, but the happiness which would reward the enterprise should it prove successful.

'But, dearest Adèle,' she said, 'you will not set off without seeing papa? I am afraid he is seriously unwell by his not getting up for breakfast on such a day as this; and to say the truth, dearest, I thought you would have proposed going to speak to him!'

Perhaps, of all the many miseries which had fallen upon Adèle de Cordillac, the continual necessity of not only concealing what she did feel, but of feigning what she did not, was that which she felt the most bitterly. A truer heart never beat in human breast; a temper of more noble, fearless honesty was never bestowed by nature, than her own; and yet, circumstances so forced her to be a hypocrite, that she scarely dared to speak without cautiously preparing herself to utter falsehoods.

Sabina's peace, Sabina's existence, seemed to hang upon the success of her dissimulation; and in most cases the thought of this had kept her so steady to her object, that it was very rarely she lost sight of it, even for an instant. Yet still there were some things which she felt she could not do; and the taking an affectionate leave of Mr Hargrave on the present occasion was one of them. The manner in which he had betrayed on the previous evening – the deliberate wish that his old and faithful servant should be left a victim to his heroic fidelity, in the hope of sheltering his own guilt, had gone farther to make her shudder at the sound of his voice, and turn with abhorrence from encountering his eye, than all which had preceded it. It was for this reason that she had roused Sabina at an earlier hour than was needful, in the hope that her dreaded step-father would take advantage of so obvious an excuse for avoiding a meeting not likely to be much more agreeable to him than to herself. Nor was she disappointed in this: but once again she was driven to have recourse to the equivocation she hated, in order to escape the importunity of her sister, and forced herself to reply that she would not take leave of Mr Hargrave; because she felt that it would be unwise to do or say any thing which might excite her feelings in any way.

Sabina said no more. She saw there was agitation and suffering in the manner of her sister; and though thinking that a few words from her dear father could do nothing but good, she urged it no farther.

The moment of parting between the two girls was one of great agony on both sides. Sabina felt as if all the terror for Adèle's safety during the long and dreary journey which lay before her, had never come upon her heart till that moment; and she strained her to her bosom, as if such restraint could alone ensure her safety: while poor Adèle herself felt as if, indeed, those dear arms removed, there would be nothing left to shield her from the world of exposure and desolation into which she was about to plunge.

Mr Hargrave had made Sabina promise to tell Adèle that no letter must be ventured upon from Gernsbach to Paris, lest their retreat might be traced by means of it; but Adèle, on her part, promised to write under cover to Frau Weiber, without signature, without date, and with no names mentioned which could throw any light on the correspondence, if examined at every post-office between them.

And thus they parted, in tears and in terror, and only supported by the feeling that it was a great and sacred duty which separated them.

★ ★ ★

It happened on this occasion, as it has often happened before, that no misadventure of any kind occurred to justify the dread which the idea of this solitary expedition had occasioned. Adèle quietly mounted the diligence which was to convey her from Baden to Strasbourg, in which her only companions were a French pastry-cook and his wife, who had been visiting Baden for the purpose of reconnoitring its eligibilities as a place for carrying on their trade on a more extended scale than they had been able to attain at Strasbourg; and so completely engrossed were they by their own projects, that if all the beautiful young ladies in the world had successively appeared before them in the disguise of *soubrettes*, they would neither of them have been capable of bestowing a thought upon them, or their mysteries.

At Strasbourg the poor pilgrim's inquiries at the coach-office enabled her to perceive that her purse was sufficiently well stored to permit her securing the *coupé* to herself, which she did on the plea of being very ill, and requiring to lay her feet on the seat of the carriage. Having done this, she retreated to a quiet little bed-room at the inn from which the diligence was to start; and again pleading illness as the cause of her retreat, obtained from a sympathising *fille de l'auberge* a *bouillon* instead of a dinner, and a cup of coffee by way of supper, – a scheme which not only saved her from what she most dreaded, the stare of idle curiosity, but gave her more opportunity than she had yet had for deliberately reviewing the business before her, strengthening her mind for the scenes she had to go through, and arranging in detail the steps it would be necessary for her to take on arriving in Paris.

Political economists tell us that supply always follows demand, and moralists may very safely assert the same law respecting the call which the pressure of circumstances makes upon the powers of the mind. An absolute dearth must in either case render the law of none effect; but where dearth is not, the human intellect will be found in a wonderful degree to answer the demands made upon it. Adèle de Cordillac, alone in her little chamber at Strasbourg, felt that she had undertaken a task which could neither be ill executed nor abandoned without the dereliction of a duty which her heart and conscience recognised as imperative. This conviction, deliberately reviewed and firmly established, left no room for weakness or vacillation; and the young, forlorn, and unprotected girl felt perfectly capable of performing her bold and righteous purpose.

Notwithstanding the strangely complicated tissue of misfortunes which had lately seemed to wrap her more and more closely round and round, as in a fatal web that separated her from all the bright and happy circumstances of her former life, – notwithstanding this seemingly persevering hostility of fortune, Adèle had no cause to complain of ill-luck on the journey, for never was an equal distance traversed with less of event or adventure of any sort; and on the evening of the next day but one after leaving Baden, she found herself, almost to her own astonishment, unscathed in limb, and rather strengthened than impaired in spirit, before the entrance door of her aunt's elegant little apartment *au troisième étage* in the Rue de Rivoli.

Her most anxious thought as she rung the bell was concerning the chances for and against her being known by the servant who should answer it; but here again fortune favoured her, for the man who opened the door was a perfect stranger to her.

Notwithstanding the beauty of the pale face that appeared under Susanne's cap, and the little straw bonnet worn over it, the Parisian footman of Madame de Hautrivage accorded her no very respectful greeting. '*Que voulez-vous, ma fille?*' were the words which welcomed her. Far, however, from repining at this want of respect, Adèle felt inexpressibly relieved at not encountering the astonished stare of an old acquaintance; and replied to the question by desiring that Madame de Hautrivage might be told '*Mademoiselle Adèle*' desired to speak to her.

As this was precisely the style and title of those important personages who act as accredited ambassadors between the important *modiste* and her deeply-interested customers, Mademoiselle de Cordillac justly thought that she could adopt none so likely to ensure her speedy admittance, as no individual holding service under Madame de Hautrivage would be likely to dismiss any one coming in 'such a questionable shape.' Could she have provided herself with a wicker-basket lined with oil-skin, she would have felt assured that no woman in Paris would have denied her right of *entrée*; but as she could not do this, she did what was next best to it, and her excellent tact and judgment were rewarded by being told that Madame would see her directly.

In fact, the interval she had to pass in the ante-room was a very short one; for her aunt's *femme de chambre* immediately appeared, uttering the careless '*Entrez, mademoiselle*,' usual on such occasions, without condescending to look sufficiently at the humble individual she addressed to discover the well-known features of Mademoiselle de Cordillac.

For half a moment, the glance of Madame de Hautrivage at the supposed milliner was equally careless and undiscerning; but then she caught a look from the matchless eyes of the pale and overworn Adèle, which caused her to exclaim in considerable agitation, '*Eh! mais, mon Dieu, donc! qu'est que cela veut dire? Non! ce n'est pas possible! – Mais oui! – Grand Dieu! c'est toi, ma niece?*'

Poor Adèle seated herself before she attempted to reply, and truly it was quite time she should do so; for the struggle to preserve such a quiet and composed aspect as might ensure her passing unnoticed, while her anxious and harrassed spirits were as far as well could be from the condition she laboured to assume, had lasted long enough; and the power of sitting down and crying heartily, without incurring any particular danger thereby, was a great comfort.

But the perceiving that her niece was incapable of returning any answers was no reason, in the opinion of Madame de Hautrivage, for not persevering in her questions; and accordingly, while Adèle went on weeping, her aunt went on interrogating, with a vehemence of curiosity which soon broke through all reserve, leading her to inquire, without even a shadow of caution, 'How they had been received by the royal family of England; whether Charles Dix had testified all the gratitude they had a right to expect; and whether it was really true that the ladies in London wore such very ridiculously large *collerettes* as they were reported to do?'

Whether Adèle's persevering indulgence in the comfort of weeping would have lasted so long had the theme of her aunt's questionings been less elegant and more alarming, may be doubted. But as it was, she did not stint; and was by no means insensible to the womanly gentleness with which her old acquaintance, the *femme de chambre*, stood silently beside her, with a large *flacon* of very refreshing *eau de Cologne*; so that the first few minutes of her dreaded interview with Madame de Hautrivage passed away in as desirable a manner, all things considered, as could have been hoped for. But Adèle had a conscience; and though it is very probable she would have preferred continuing her tearful silence a while longer, she yielded not to the temptation, but, the few minutes over, prepared to answer all the questions put to her in as satisfactory a manner as it was in her power to do, without absolutely defeating the purpose for which she had already made such tremendous sacrifices.

Of the Court of St James's, or of Windsor Castle, she modestly confessed she knew not enough to describe either with confidence. Of Charles Dix, she said, they had received no very recent news; and of the ladies' *collerettes*, she owned she knew but little, having been more occupied in comparing notes with her sister on their great and sudden change, than in making any on the various novel objects by which they had found themselves surrounded. And then, having completely convinced her aunt that there never had been so stupid a traveller, or one so utterly incapable of profiting by what she saw, Adèle was permitted to seek the repose she asked for, on the neat little couch of the amiable *soubrette:* the striking elegance of Madame's *joli logement* being chiefly confined to what met the eye, or, at any rate, not extending to a guest-chamber. While making a thousand apologies, however, for the *malheur* of a Cordillac's being obliged to lay down on the bed of Mademoiselle Josephine, she promised that a more fitting couch should be *loué* before night, and placed for her accommodation in a little cabinet which occasionally served her as a *boudoir*.

The agitation, embarrassment, and difficulties of all kinds which, of necessity, she had to encounter, both during her journey and immediately at the conclusion of it, being thus well over, Adèle enjoyed an hour or two of sound and restoring sleep, and when she awoke from it, felt herself able to prosecute her task without fearing that either her strength or courage would fail her.

Madame de Hautrivage, as a matter of course, was engaged to pass the *soirée* in society; but she took a cup of coffee with her niece before she set out, and, in the course of their conversation during the time thus occupied, learned from her that one part of the business which brought her to Paris was the new arrangement which their change of circumstances rendered necessary respecting the manner in which she should wish for the future to receive her income.

This, though true, was, as we well know, merely incidental; for poor Adèle would for years have dispensed with the necessity of receiving any money at all rather than have set out upon the journey she had achieved; but it served excellently well as a reason, in the estimation of Madame de Hautrivage, for all she had done, and enabled her niece to pass very lightly over the '*other things*' which made it absolutely necessary that she should return to Paris for a few days.

Adèle de Cordillac nourished no hope that her real business could be got through without publicity; but even while she felt this to be impossible, her anxiety to keep her aunt as long ignorant of it as might be, was very great, and she omitted nothing that could aid her in attaining this very desirable object. After some little difficulty, she at length convinced the good lady that she was in earnest in declaring that she did not intend to see any of her relations, friends, or acquaintance, during her short stay, – a statement which appeared utterly incredible, till she stated the fact of her having no dresses whatever, nor, for the present, any money to buy them. A proper garb in which to go out for the purpose of executing the business she had to do, she said that Josephine should procure for her, but beyond this she should purchase nothing; and this statement, so made as to ensure belief, effectually stopped any further attempt to convince the poor shipwrecked Adèle that it would be advisable to renew all her brillant associations, and blaze again in the *salons* of Paris as fairest of the fair. So ably, indeed, did she contrive to bring before her aunt the tremendous danger of being seen in a *toilette absolument honteuse*, if any of her acquaintance were let into the secret of her arrival, that Madame de Hautrivage left her, not only with a promise of keeping her being in Paris unknown to all the world, but with a wish of doing so hardly less strong than her own.

Fortunately for Adèle, her aunt's first engagement for the evening was joining a party at the Grand Opera, which took her off early enough to leave her an hour or two of very valuable time. Her first use of it was to despatch a note by the porter to an estimable old friend, who, besides having known her from infancy, had the advantage of being an *avocat* in great practice. She knew the *manière d'être* of this gentleman well enough to be pretty certain as to where her summons would be likely to find him: nor did this confidence deceive her; M de Servac came to her in even less time than she had dared to calculate as the least possible.

Highly as she esteemed, and perfectly as she was willing to trust him on the agitating and painful business which concerned herself, she had, however, no intention of betraying either the residence of Mr Hargrave or any thing which she still hoped might remain in mystery, concerning the cause of his leaving Paris; nor were the cross-questionings of her old friend in any way embarrassing. M de Servac, in common with the majority of Mr Hargrave's acquaintance, had received the history of his having been discovered in a plot against the government without in the least degree doubting its truth, and being himself a staunch supporter of the existing government, a feeling of honour would have prevented his seeking any information on the subject from Adèle, even if he had been urged thereto by a much stronger impulse of curiosity than he really felt. As to any grave fear that the plottings of an Englishman of such gay and graceful notoriety as Mr Hargrave could affect the stability of the reigning dynasty, he felt it not; and was, therefore, very easily led from a subject which he was rather inclined to treat as a jest, to one in which it was speedily evident to him that his admired young friend was most seriously and painfully interested.

'This is, indeed, a most distressing business for you, *ma chère enfant*,' said he, knitting his brows, and looking very grave. 'I have heard this old man's guilt spoken of in the profession as a matter of absolute certainty. Are you, indeed, sufficiently convinced of his innocence to justify your coming thus publicly forward to assert it?'

'I am, M de Servac!' replied Adèle, with an earnestness and almost solemnity of tone that gave great force to her words. 'You have known me long enough, and, as I think, well enough, to believe that I would not, on light or insufficient grounds, have thus come forward, and undertaken to do what you may well guess must be so painful to me.'

'You say truly, Mademoiselle de Cordillac,' replied the old gentleman. 'I ought not – I cannot doubt your deep persuasion of his innocence. But in the eyes of the court, my young friend, this will not be enough. You must be prepared to prove his innocence as well as believe in it. Do you come with power to do this?'

'I hope and believe that I do,' she replied. And then, blushing to her very temples, she added, 'But it cannot be done without my avowing what, were my own fate alone concerned, I think I would rather die than divulge. But I do not hesitate, – nothing shall or can make me hesitate as to the task that lies before me! If what I have to divulge impugns my good name while it exonerates his, I ought only to rejoice and be thankful that the power is still left me to do so much justice.'

'I am sorry to hear that any such sacrifice is necessary,' replied M de Servac, gravely; 'nor would I have believed, on any worse authority, that your mother's daughter, Mademoiselle de Cordillac, could have any such disclosure to make.'

'The agony it gives me to avow what I have done,' said poor Adèle, vainly endeavouring not to weep, 'convinces me that an act which, a few short weeks ago, I thought not only innocent, but just and righteous, must in itself have been far otherwise, or I could not thus tremble at the thought of revealing it.'

'Proceed – proceed, young lady,' said the *avocat*, again knitting his brows, with an air of severity. 'If it be your purpose to communicate the circumstances you speak of to me, you can gain nothing by delay or circumlocution.'

'True, sir, true,' returned Adèle, rather strengthened than shaken by this harshness. 'I have no wish to delay the communication. Madame Bertrand has, I believe, herself stated that the robbery committed on her person, on the night when she was violently carried off from Mr

Hargrave's house, was perpetrated between the hours of four and five?' said Mademoiselle de Cordillac, with recovered composure.

'So I understand,' returned the lawyer. 'But may I ask you,' he continued, 'why it is that you name with so much ceremony the gentleman whom you have always been accustomed to call your father?'

'Because to my feelings this business is a very solemn one, and I would wish to express myself less with familiarity than correctness,' she replied, colouring slightly; and then continuing her statement with steady composure: 'I am ready to depose on oath, M de Servac, that one quarter of an hour before four o'clock on that unfortunate night, or rather morning, I myself despatched Roger Humphries on a message, from which I know that he could not have returned till after five. Will not this evidence be sufficient to prove his innocence – to prove an *alibi*, as I believe it is called?'

'It would be evidence towards constituting such proof, but could not, I fear, suffice if entirely unsupported. It would prove most satisfactorily that *you* had sent him, Mademoiselle, but not that he went on your errand. How know you that he did not take advantage of your sending him from the house, in order to commit, or assist in, the robbery of which he stands accused?'

'I know it to be impossible,' replied Adèle, 'from my long acquaintance with the man; but I can, of course, understand that this is not an argument to be listened to by his judges. We must, therefore, seek for what may prove more convincing. Since I heard of this terrible arrest, I have had no means of inquiring; but I feel no doubt that the servants of the hôtel in the Rue de Rivoli will be able to prove his having been there within the time I have mentioned.'

'In that case I think the *alibi* would be established; for the distance could not have been traversed twice by an old man within the time specified, leaving sufficient interval for the spoliation and abduction, as sworn to, of Madame Bertrand; and, of course, if you intrust the commission to me, I will take care to gather all the information to be collected at the hôtel you mention. But there is one point which you seem to overlook, *chère* Mademoiselle Adèle, which, I confess, leaves me with very little hope of our obtaining the evidence you expect. The prisoner has never attempted to prove an *alibi*.'

'I know it, sir – I know it!' said Adèle, her steady composure of manner again giving way before the feelings this observation aroused. 'I know from the newspapers that the old man has preserved, throughout every examination to which he has been exposed, a silence invincible, either by threats or arguments; and it is this which has brought me hither to say for him what his fidelity to me has prevented his saying for himself. Roger Humphries could not have stated his having been at the hôtel without stating also who sent him there, and to whom the message he carried was addressed; as least I cannot but suppose that such questions would have been asked, and that his refusal to answer them would have invalidated any statement he could have made.'

'Most unquestionably it would,' replied M de Servac. 'But may I ask you what possible reason could prevent his replying to questions at once so obvious and so necessary? I really cannot imagine any rational motive strong enough to induce a man, in the very ticklish situation of this Roger Humphries, to refuse giving such information as you speak of; his fate entirely depending upon it, as it certainly would do, if he could prove thereby that he really went upon the expedition you mention.'

'His motive, M de Servac,' said Adèle, blushing very painfully, 'would have been to preserve from exposure and injurious suspicion the name of one who is determined to prove herself not wholly unworthy his generous fidelity. The letter which I commissioned him to carry to the Hôtel ——— was addressed by me to Mr Alfred Coventry, a young Englishman, well known in the fashionable circles of Paris.'

'If you do not deceive yourself, − if this old servant has really maintained the silence which has so strongly confirmed every suspicion against him from the motive you assign, he does indeed deserve all you can do, and every sacrifice you can make, for him. And gladly, Mademoiselle Adèle, should I set about any inquiries which might be likely to end in doing justice to one who so richly deserves it. And yet I shall be sorry, too, to be the means———' and here the worthy lawyer stopped short, took out his snuff-box, and inhaled an enormous quantity of snuff.

'To be the means of exposing me, you would say,' rejoined Adèle, with a melancholy smile. 'But if you please, my dear sir, we must neither of us at this moment bestow a thought on a subject of so very little comparative importance. Succeed in proving the *alibi* of Roger Humphries when this crime was committed, and I will bless you to the last hour I have to live, even if you were to find my unfortunate letter in your researches, and read it aloud in open court.'

'I think, then,' said the old advocate, rising, and kissing her hand as he bowed his farewell, − 'I think, Mademoiselle Adèle, that you can go no farther in giving me instructions as to sparing *nothing* to obtain success; and I shall certainly obey you with the less scruple, because I cannot for the life of me help doubting your having ever done any thing that could really disgrace the noble name you bear.'

Poor Adèle gently pressed the venerable hand which still held hers, and uttered a fervent 'God bless you!' − a word and an act that was very rightly interpreted by the long-esteemed friend of her family. The good man then left her, very greatly cheered and comforted by the interview.

CHAPTER XXXI

When Adèle on the following morning met her aunt at breakfast, she made no secret of having sought and obtained an interview with M de Servac on the preceding evening. It would by no means have suited, indeed, with her plan of operations to have enlightened Madame de Hautrivage upon the nature of the business she had intrusted to their old legal friend, and she deemed it not a sin to leave her in the persuasion (of her own spontaneous adoption, however) that the interview had related wholly to her financial affairs.

There had been no difficulty in making M de Servac understand that it would be better for the interest of all parties, as well as for her own tranquillity, that *Madame la tante* should not be made acquainted with what was going on, – a pretty long knowledge of her character enabling him to guess what sort of assistance they should be likely to derive from her co-operation.

Whatever the worthy lawyer might have thought of the business when his young client first stated to him her part in it, he had become cordially interested in it before he left her, and lost no time in making personal requisitions at the hôtel to which he was referred in the Rue de Rivoli, in order to discover what sort of a case he had to manage.

The three first gentlemen in the napkin, boot-jack, and scout line, who submitted themselves to his interrogatories, could afford him no information whatever; and the kind-hearted old gentleman began to fear that poor Adèle's firm and noble confidence in her old servant's honour and honesty was altogether ill-placed and fallacious.

He was not, however, one to be easily turned aside from any quest in which he was engaged, and his perseverance was in this instance rewarded by finding, in a manner the most full and satisfactory, the information he sought. He was indebted to his pertinacity for this success, in more ways than one; for not only was it by dint of reiterated inquiries that he obtained that for which he was seeking, but the resolute style in which he continued on the premises long after the *chef* of the waiters had assured him with a shrug, that at the hour he mentioned it was *absolument impossible* that any person belonging to the establishment could have been stirring, attracted the attention of the humble individual whose chief occupation was pumping water in a back-court for the use of waiters, chambermaids, horse-boys, or whoever else belonging to the Hôtel ⸺ might chance to desire a bucket-full of that commodity.

'On what day was it?' demanded the water-pumper, stepping forward during a moment of rare leisure, which he employed doubly, by asking the above question, and at the same time very ingeniously repairing the broken button-hole of his over-fatigued braces.

M de Servac answered the question with the most accurate exactness.

'*Ah ça*, that was the day, was it?' said the pumper. 'But now you must tell me what it was that happened on that day, or how shall I be able to give you any information about it?'

Though there was no very clear evidence on the face of this demand that its being complied with would produce the information desired, M de Servac scrupled not to do it, and that too with as much fulness and precision as if he were answering the Procureur du Roi.

'*Mais oui, mais oui, – oui, oui, oui, vous dis-je*,' he exclaimed in return. 'I remember the old fellow,' he continued, 'as well as if he was my father – a tall, lanky, long-legged monsieur, wrapped up in a *redingote* as if he was packed up for Africa. It was I, monsieur, – I myself, who told him that the *milor* he inquired for was set off with four horses as fast as they could gallop, just about ten minutes before he made his appearance; and if my word is not enough for you, any more than it was for him, why I will – for love and a *petit pour-boire*, – call out Desiré for you, as I did for him, when he did not seem willing to believe the news I told him.'

The *petit pour-boire* was not long in making its appearance, and as its amount was exceedingly satisfactory to the pumper, he ventured to disregard the begging buckets of two chambermaids stationed on either side the pump, while he galloped off in search of an individual who, like himself, had witnessed the despair of the unfortunate Roger on hearing that Mr Coventry was gone. This person was a respectable-looking man, who was employed as book-keeper, and who, being up for the purpose of seeing Mr Coventry off, perfectly well remembered the old man's coming to inquire for him, as well as the very great disappointment he seemed to suffer on learning that he had set off before his arrival.

'Is your recollection of this old man such as would enable you to swear to his person?' demanded M de Servac.

'Yes,' was the reply; 'I think I could safely swear to him.'

'I am exceedingly glad to hear it,' returned the lawyer; 'and I must beg that you will hold yourself in readiness to attend the trial of this poor fellow, who may be saved from the galleys by your testimony: for it is perfectly clear that if he was here at the hour I have named, he could not possibly have been guilty of the crime of which he stands accused.'

'I certainly remember the old man who came hither to inquire for Mr Coventry the morning that he left Paris,' said Desiré, 'and cannot think that I should feel any scruple about identifying his person upon oath. But if there is any doubt upon the subject, I can refer you, monsieur, to a young man who I know to be still in Paris, and who was jeering the poor old fellow for not having walked a trifle faster, which might have brought him in time. This young man, whose name is Oliff, is servant to the Count Romanhoff, and was here with his master, who came to take leave of Mr Coventry, but instead of that, set off with him, leaving his servant to follow, – a fancy which seemed to astonish Monsieur Oliff extremely, and he was still here chattering to me about it when the old man you inquire about, arrived.'

Though exceedingly well satisfied with the evidence thus acquired, M de Servac had no sort of objection to strengthen it; and having taken the address to Count Romanhoff's lodgings, repaired thither with all speed, and had again the good fortune to find a witness ready to swear to the person of an old man, wearing a livery great-coat, who came to the Hôtel —— on the day, and at the hour named, to inquire for Mr Coventry.

M de Servac, on receiving from the Sieur Oliff this welcome intelligence, gave him to understand that he would be required, in the course of the following week or ten days, to give this evidence in court.

'Willingly, sir,' replied Oliff, 'if my master, the Count Romanhoff, has no objection.'

'Objection! What objection can he possibly have, my good friend, to your obeying the summons of a court of law?' said the lawyer.

'None whatever, I dare say, sir,' returned the punctilious valet; 'but I would wish to have him made acquainted with the business.'

'Can I see him?' demanded the persevering M de Servac.

'I cannot doubt it, sir,' said the observant Russe. 'But if you will give me leave, I will inquire.'

He did so, and immediately returned with his master's request that the gentleman would be pleased to walk in.

Count Romanhoff received him with politeness; but when he proceeded to explain his business, and to speak of his anxiety to procure witnesses who might be able to identify an old servant of Mr Hargrave's, in order to save him, by proving an *alibi*, from being condemned to the galleys for a crime of which there was every reason to believe him innocent, his manner, which had been that of perfectly civil indifference, suddenly changed to great animation and the most lively interest.

'Is it possible,' he exclaimed, – 'is it possible that the atrocious old man, of whose contumacious insolence to the court, all Paris is talking – is it possible that he should be innocent?'

'I firmly believe, Count,' returned M de Servac, 'that this atrocious old man, as you call him, will turn out to be one of the most noble-minded and faithful servants on record; and I cannot doubt, therefore, that you will willingly permit your servant to attend the trial. It is true that I have other evidence, but in such cases it is scarcely possible to have too much.'

'Evidence of what, sir?' demanded the Count, with his usual eagerness. 'My servant is entirely at your orders: but have the kindness to tell me what is the point which his testimony is intended to prove?'

'His testimony, Count Romanhoff, is asked for to prove that a certain old man——'

At this moment an inner door of the apartment opened, and Alfred Coventry entered the room, not, however, with the air of a visitor, but of an inmate.

'I interrupt you, Count,' he said, perceiving a stranger, and also that his friend was listening very eagerly to the words which ceased as he entered.

'Pray come in, Coventry; this business will interest you as much as it does me. This gentleman, sir,' turning to M de Servac, 'was intimate in the family of M Hargrave, and will therefore, as well as myself, be grateful to you for any information respecting the trial of his servant. Alfred, this gentleman – M de Servac, if I heard the name aright, – is here to ask for the testimony of Oliff, in order to prove the innocence of the man about to be tried for the Bertrand robbery.'

'Alfred Coventry!' said the lawyer, repeating the name with an air of singular satisfaction. 'If you are M Alfred Coventry, this meeting is a singularly lucky one. Of all men living, sir, you are the most bound to interest yourself in this matter; for I have every reason to believe that you have been the involuntary cause of bringing a very honest man into jeopardy. Permit me to ask you, if you left the Hôtel ——, in the Rue de Rivoli, rather before five o'clock on the morning of the 24th April?'

'I did, sir,' replied Coventry; 'and may I in return request to know your reason for making the inquiry?'

'Were it not quite certain, M Coventry, that the whole of this business must of necessity be explained at full length in a few days, and that in the most public manner possible, – namely, in open court, – I might, from delicacy to a very admirable young lady, so frame my answer as to leave you still in the dark: but as this caution would be perfectly useless, as, most unhappily, nothing can be done for my poor client without exposing, very painfully, the little indiscretion of my charming young friend, Mademoiselle de Cordillac ——'

'*Ecoutez donc!*' cried the well-pleased Romanhoff, who had of late been a good deal troubled by symptoms of lingering attachment in the heart of his friend, and by finding his history of the *fiacre* treated as a blundering romance, – '*Ecoutez donc, mon cher*. Forgive this interruption, M de Servac,' he continued; 'but I wish my friend to hear this, and his thoughts seemed to be wandering.'

'The young gentleman, on the contrary, appears to be listening very attentively,' returned the lawyer; 'and I cannot but say that it would be strange if he did not, seeing the part he has in the affair. My motive, M Alfred Coventry, for wishing to know if you left Paris at the hour I have mentioned on the morning of the 24th ultimo, is, that your testimony may confirm that of others in proving the correctness of the statement I have received from Mademoiselle de Cordillac, on which statement the fate of my client, Roger Humphries, appears to depend.'

'As you have volunteered a promise to be explicit, sir,' said Coventry, 'I presume that I may, without indiscretion, inquire how it happens that the name of the young lady you have mentioned and my own have been brought together?'

'I would not tell you, sir,' replied M de Servac, shaking his head with an air of much vexation, 'if, by refusing to do so, i could keep you in ignorance of the facts, but, unhappily, this is impossible. I presume you have read in the papers all the proceedings that have taken place relative to the great diamond robbery, and are aware that suspicion, in most people's opinion amounting to proof, rests against this Roger Humphries, who, at the time of the robbery, was in the service of Mr Hargrave?'

Mr Coventry bowed his assent.

'And you are aware that one of the strongest circumstances against him is the obstinate silence which he has opposed to all the inquiries made as to where he had been, and how employed at the time he was arrested, which was about six o'clock on the same morning?'

'Yes, sir, I have read the whole account of the examinations,' said Coventry.

'Now then, sir, you shall judge of our *alibi*. Instead of being engaged in robbing Madame Bertrand of her diamonds, this poor old man was employed, precisely at the time this outrage was perpetrated, in conveying a letter from his young mistress, Mademoiselle Adèle de Cordillac, to you.'

'To me, sir?' exclaimed the young man, changing colour. 'If the safety of your client depends upon the establishment of this fact, I fear that there is little chance for him.'

'Because you did not happen to receive the letter, young gentleman? I wish it were possible to save this brave fellow without being able to prove that it was sent. The disagreeable part of the business is our having to shew, before the eyes of all men, that this nobly born, and till now most irreproachable young lady, did actually despatch, at that mysterious and unwonted hour, a letter addressed to M Alfred Coventry, at the Hôtel ——, Rue de Rivoli.'

Coventry was greatly agitated; he got up and walked hastily towards the window without speaking.

'Then the old man has broken through his silence at last?' said Count Romanhoff; 'and has, of course, told you, sir, as his advocate, all the facts of the case?'

'Indeed he has not, Count Romanhoff,' returned M de Servac; 'nor have I any reason to suppose that the truth would ever have been known if Roger Humphries had been the only person privy to the secret. It is clear that this stout-hearted and faithful old fellow has made up his mind to endure all that the law can make him suffer, rather than betray the secret intrusted to him. But, luckily for him, the nature of the person he has so loyally served is as noble as his own. Mademoiselle de Cordillac has come to Paris, perfectly alone, her step-father having so involved himself in some political intrigue as to render his entering France impossible. This beautiful young girl has taken this lonely journey, having before her eyes the exposure, which she evidently dreads worse than death, of the imprudence she has committed, for the holy and righteous object of saving the faithful servant whose silence was intended to save *her*. It is nobly done; and though I grieve that a daughter of so honourable a race should have been guilty of an indiscretion, the avowing it for such a motive, and despite such bitter suffering, is a glorious atonement; and so her family will think if they are worthy of her.' The old gentleman blew his nose lustily as he concluded, and not without reason, for his eyes were full of tears, which might have betrayed more weakness than he would have wished to exhibit before his two gay young auditors, had he not managed to conceal them by this device.

But he wronged them – wronged them both if he fancied that they had listened to his statement unmoved. Coventry, indeed, gave no audible sign of what he felt; but Romanhoff started to his feet, exclaiming, 'God forgive me! – How cruelly have I wronged that lovely girl! – Noble, noble creature! – I see it – I understand it all. It is I who have been the cause of all her suffering. Bear with me, Coventry. Listen to me, I entreat you, in order that you may understand this matter as well as I do.'

The agitated Count laid his hand on the shoulder of Coventry as he spoke, and but for the expression of deep and sincere suffering which was legible on his features, it might have been difficult to obtain a patient hearing from his friend; for at that moment Mr Coventry recollected, with more distinctness than was at all desirable, who it was who had exaggerated every seeming fault of the generous Adèle, and by whose influence he had been goaded to leave Paris in such desperate haste, when the delay of a few minutes only might have made him the happiest instead of being, as he now felt, the most miserable of men. He turned firmly round as the hand of Romanhoff touched his shoulder; but the sight of the altered countenance and working features of his unlucky friend disarmed him, and, instead of uttering the rough words which were upon his lips, he bent his head upon his hands, and cried, 'Oh, Romanhoff! what have you done?'

'I will tell you what I have done,' replied the young man, speaking with great rapidity; 'but it may be remedied. It is not too late yet, Alfred. Tell me, sir,' he added, suddenly turning towards M de Servac, 'where is Mademoiselle de Cordillac to be found?'

'She is at the residence of her aunt, Madame de Hautrivage,' replied the judicious old gentleman, choosing to give his fair client the advantage of the old lady's protection in the eyes of the young men. 'But you will have little chance of seeing her there, young gentleman. Mademoiselle de Cordillac does not mean to see any one.'

'*Pour cela*———' but the Count concluded the sentence thus begun with a slight cough. He scrupled not, however, notwithstanding the presence of the lawyer, to continue his explanation to his suffering friend.

'I perfectly understand all that has happened, Coventry. I went to that confounded ball, for the sole purpose of finding out what that girl was made of before I utterly condemned her. I well remember being at one moment inclined to think that I had wronged her when I fancied her indifferent to you. I well remember symptoms, in manner rather than in words, as I continued to talk of you, which made me suspect that the theme touched her nearly; but then her tone seemed suddenly to change; I thought she was trifling with me as well as with you; and having watched her escape from the room, as if on purpose to get rid of me, I flew back to you with the determination of using all the influence my friendship for you gave me, in turning your thoughts for ever from one whom I conceived to be unworthy of you. I must have left the house between three and four. This old man reached your hôtel before five. Is it not plain that, though her delicacy shrunk from making me her confidant, she could not go to rest till she had explained the conduct of which I had accused her, by writing to you? And well did she choose her mesenger, poor lady! and well would his errand have sped had I not so urged you to instant departure. Coventry! can you forgive me?'

'At this moment, Count, I cannot easily forgive either of us,' replied Coventry, actually trembling from excessive agitation; 'but this is no time to settle which has been the most to blame.' Then turning to M de Servac, he said, 'Believe me, sir, on the honour of a gentleman, — a pledge that I have never lightly given, — that my feelings in this matter are such as may safely be permitted to act, side by side, with your own. I have no strength, no power, at this moment, to explain myself further; but I implore you, by the interest you feel for — for your client, M de Servac, — to give me immediately the means of seeing the old man. You, as his counsel, will surely be admitted to him; take me with you instantly — instantly; an hour — an instant of delay, may be of importance!'

M de Servac looked at the young man with interest, surprise, and curiosity. The unmistakable sincerity of the emotions which shook his frame commanded attention, and justified the confidence which he felt disposed to place in him; but a remnant of professional caution induced him to say, 'If M Alfred Coventry would do me the honour to communicate to me the object of his visit to the prisoner, I should, professionally speaking, be more capable of judging of its utility.'

'No man can judge of its utility but myself, sir,' replied Coventry, endeavouring to speak with calmness. 'If you doubt me – if you doubt my being worthy of a degree of trust so little likely to be dangerous, let the fact of my having been deemed worthy by Mademoiselle de Cordillac of receiving a written communication from her, plead for me. Besides, sir, I have no wish whatever to converse with the prisoner, excepting in your hearing.'

'You have no need of any one to plead for you, M Alfred,' returned the old man, smiling kindly on him. 'I did but speak as lawyers always should speak, when the interest of a client is concerned, and that is cautiously. But come along, young gentleman. I am well inclined, I promise you, to bless the chance which has made you my *collaborateur* in this business. How shall we go? On foot, as I came here; or, for speed's sake, in a *fiacre?*'

'Will not my own carriage convey us more quickly?' said Coventry, laying his hand on the bell.

'It might, perhaps, if it were ready at the door; but even if it were there, I should *advise*, – professional again, you see, – that we should take the shelter of the *fiacre*. I don't love liveries. We never mount colours till the moment of action.'

Little or no answer was returned to this, except what was conveyed by the act of seizing upon a hat, and running down the stairs with more rapidity than the old lawyer could imitate; but the now friendly pair were soon stepping hastily side by side towards a *place de fiacre*, and, without an instant of unnecessary delay, found themselves seated in one of those matchless vehicles, which, despite the animated rivalry of London, beat the world in noise.

This, perhaps, might have been one reason for the profound silence of Coventry during their drive to the prison where old Roger was immured. He sat without uttering a word; his cheeks flushed, his eyes closed, and his temples throbbing, as if a pair of fulling mills had been at work within them. Nor was his companion in any degree more conversable, though it is possible that this was, in his case, less a matter of inclination than necessity.

On reaching the place of their destination, they presented themselves before the proper authorities for the purpose of obtaining admission, – a privilege immediately granted upon M de Servac's giving his name, and declaring himself counsel for the prisoner, Roger Humphries.

A turnkey preceded them to the cell of the poor old man, which, on being opened for their reception, presented to his wondering eyes the persons of two perfect strangers. He looked up and quietly examined the faces of both, but perceiving that he knew neither, dropped his eyes again upon a small book that he held in his hand.

'How long does Monsieur desire to be left with the prisoner?' demanded the turnkey, addressing M de Servac.

'Five minutes, my friend,' replied the lawyer; adding in a whisper, as the man bowed and prepared to close the door, 'But my assistant here will require to be left longer. My time is precious, – so take care to return at the end of five minutes precisely.'

While this passed, Coventry addressed the old man in a voice of extreme emotion, 'You are the servant of Mademoiselle de Cordillac – of Mr Hargrave, I mean? Do you know me? – do you remember me?'

'No, sir,' replied Roger. 'I may have seen you before; but I do not know your name.'

'One moment, my young friend, – one moment,' said M de Servac, laying his hand upon that of Coventry. 'Does this old man understand our language? if not, you must serve me as an interpreter.'

'I can both understand and speak it,' said Roger in French.

'That is well, my man, we shall get on all the better. I have allowed myself but five minutes, and must therefore waste no time; so listen attentively, my good friend, to what I say, and if you do not fully understand me ask this gentleman to help you. But, first let me ask you, do you know who this gentleman is?'

'No, sir, I do not. I have some thought that I have seen him before, – most likely among company at my master's house; but if I ever heard his name, I have forgotten it.'

'Cannot you recollect having heard the name of Alfred Coventry, – Monsieur Alfred Coventry?'

Roger started a little, a very little; but only shook his head in reply, and applied himself again very assiduously to the perusal of his book.

The lawyer spent at the very least one of his five minutes in studying the harsh, rigid features of the old man whose defence he had undertaken; and felt that if accident had not befriended him, in throwing a little light upon the matter, he should have had tough work to get out of him any fact which it was his will and pleasure to conceal.

'My five minutes must be nearly gone,' said M de Servac, having caught a furtive glance thrown by the prisoner upon his companion; 'and I shall leave you to make acquaintance with this young gentleman – who is your countryman you know – as fast as you can; first telling you, however, that I have been engaged to plead in your defence at your approaching trial, by your good friend, Mademoiselle Adèle de Cordillac, and that this gentleman is M Alfred Coventry: and there comes our turnkey, – there goes his key into the lock, – make the best use of your time both of you, and make my work next week as easy as you can, by treating each other as friends and countrymen ought to do, – that is, with perfect confidence.'

The door opened as he concluded these words, and the turnkey entered.

'How long will it be necessary for this young man to remain with the prisoner?' demanded the official. 'He must name the time, and be ready to keep it too when I come back for him.'

'A moment — a single moment will suffice!' cried Coventry, impetuously.

'Say ten minutes, if you please,' returned the lawyer, in a voice of authority. 'What I have left for you to do will not take less. *Allons, donc!* I am ready to go,' he added, addressing the man of locks, 'and come back to let out my companion in about a quarter of an hour.'

'That is longer than necessary!' interposed Coventry. 'For mercy's sake do not keep me here!'

The official gave him a grim smile. 'If your business is to lie in the correctional line,' said he, 'you must learn to look less frightened at the sight of a cell. But never fear, young sir, I'll fetch you out again before you can take any harm.' He then motioned to M de Servac to pass on, and the door was again closed, leaving Roger Humphries and Alfred Coventry *tête-à-tête*.

CHAPTER XXXII

'Is it true, Roger Humphries, — is it true that Mademoiselle de Cordillac intrusted you with a letter for me on the night of Mr Hargrave's ball, between the 23rd and 24th of April?' said Coventry, seizing on the old man's hand, and grasping it strongly.

'Is it true, sir, that you are Mr Alfred Coventry?' returned Roger, answering one very cogent question by another.

Coventry thrust his hands into his pockets, and pulled forth two or three letters bearing his address, 'Will not these satisfy you?' said he.

'These and your looks together, sir, do satisfy me,' replied the old man; 'and come what will, I humbly thank God for granting me an opportunity of doing my errand before I die.'

Then carefully untying his neck-cloth, he laid it across his knees, and deliberately untwisted fold after fold till he arrived at the little letter of poor Adèle carefully enveloped in a bit of soft paper, and very little worse for the wear.

'There!' said Roger, taking it gingerly between his fore-finger and thumb, and yielding it to the eager grasp of Coventry. 'There it is, sir; where those others went it can't be wrong to let this go too. And I won't say but I'm glad to get quit of it, for the job has been a troublesome one altogether, and that I can't deny.'

Did Alfred Coventry listen to this; or was he engaged in reading the words that he held before his dim and dazzled eyes?

'If Mr Coventry will let me see him for ten minutes before he leaves Paris (for Africa!), I shall be able to convince him that I am all that he believed me to be before our last miserable meeting, at which time I was led to suppose that he was exactly all which he has since thought me.

'ADELE DE CORDILLAC.

> '*Rue de Lille, half-past three, A.M.*
> *23 April, 1835.*'

'And this you have kept sacred and secret from every eye!' cried the young man, seizing the hand of the old servant in both his own with that cordial hold which hand takes of hand when the heart propels it. 'When I forget this, Roger Humphries, may every good man forget me!'

'A young man must not be surprised because an old man is honest,' said Roger, smiling through something very like tears. 'Miss Adèle, now, would not be surprised at it, because, for certain sure, she never would have trusted me had she not known pretty well that I deserved it.'

'Deserved it! – Excellent old friend! – She is giving proof of it this very moment, Roger, that she does know what you deserve. The family have left Paris, – gone far away, I know not where; and this young lady, your angel mistress, Roger, has returned hither alone and unprotected, because she discovered by accident that you had fallen into trouble upon her account. I have not time, – why does not that villanous gaoler come back again? – I do not wish at this moment to have time, Roger, to explain all she has done – all she was going to do in order to restore your liberty; I can only say – Oh! why does not that fellow return! – I can only say that mistress and servant are worthy of each other.'

'God bless her!' said the old man fervently; 'she deserves a better friend to serve her than ever I can hope to be. But, Mr Alfred Coventry! – excuse me, sir, if I take the liberty to say, that I hope the secret I have gone joyfully into prison to keep, will not be spoken to those who have no business to hear it in order to get me out again. Don't let that be, young gentleman! I can never forget, – no never, how beautiful and innocent her face looked, dyed all over with blushes, when she gave me that bit of a letter to carry to your honour. "Take care of my secret, dear Roger!" Those were her very words; and then she went on and said, "I feel as if I could not live if I did not send this letter; but as if I must die, Roger, if any but the one for whom it is intended should see it!" Did not that shew confidence, your honour? Did not that shew trust? Did not that prove that she held me worthy to be her friend, as I may say, as well as her servant? And where is the prison, or the halter either, that would have frightened me into betraying her?'

These last words were uttered with a burst of emotion that shewed itself on the face of the old man very like

'Iron tears down Pluto's cheek.'

Nor was the manhood of Coventry proof against the spectacle; but while the sympathetic drop still trembled in his eye, he once more started up, exclaiming, 'Why does he stay so long? Roger! Roger! every thing will go well, if I can but get to her. All the confounded parcel of nonsense and falsehood with which they have been endeavouring to overwhelm you will all be cleared away, like mist before the sun, if they will but let me out!'

Roger was quite persuaded that, now Miss Adèle's letter had been properly delivered, no further harm could come of it; and when Coventry again interrupted his own lamentations at the turnkey's delay, in order to assure his companion that the fact of his having been elsewhere when the crime of which he stood accused was committed, would now be proved without injury to any one, the patient prisoner was not only perfectly satisfied for himself, but did his best to convince his impatient new friend that the interval during which they had been left together was not quite so long as it seemed.

Roger was not believed; but, nevertheless, he was right, and the surly-looking gaoler faithful: for he came with great exactness at the appointed moment.

'Thank Heaven!' exclaimed Coventry, as he heard the welcome footstep. 'Now then, farewell, Roger! Dear, excellent old friend, many minutes shall not pass before I shall hear your name uttered with the praises and blessings it deserves by the lips of Adèle de Cordillac. For a few days longer, Roger, she must endure the pain of knowing that her brave and faithful friend is thus vilely lodged; but after the trial, and when your noble fidelity shall have been acknowledged, I need hardly tell you that your home and hers will be the same. Meanwhile, all the comforts which the law permits, shall be yours in the interval. There goes the key! God bless you!'

The rapidity with which Mr Coventry made his exit the instant the door was opened, so startled the slow and very unvolatile functionary, that for a moment he looked as much dismayed as if he had seen a prisoner escape, and the first expressive movement of feature that he had ever seen Roger Humphries exhibit was at that moment, when the old man burst into a hearty laugh.

'You shall grin in the galleys before you are a fortnight older!' growled the turnkey, as he once more closed the door, and locked it upon the solitary but well-contented old man.

*   *   *

Madame de Hautrivage appeared to be, and perhaps really was, more deeply wounded by seeing her niece, the daughter of a Cordillac, dressed in the humblest garb with which the stores of her waiting-maid had been able to supply her, than by all the misfortunes which seemed to encompass her *aimable beau-frère*. When Adèle met her at breakfast on the morning after her arrival she was greeted by a cry that very nearly approached a scream, and then followed such a storm of lady-like expletives, that it took some minutes before the young lady's quiet assurances that this evil should be remedied without delay, could be heard. And even when, at length, the words which were intended to pacify her reached her understanding, they failed totally in producing the desired effect; for the want of sufficient interest in the subject which they betrayed rendered the affectionate aunt as miserable concerning the moral condition of her niece, as she had before been for the disgraceful deficiencies of her wardrobe.

'*Est-ce vous! − Grand Dieu! − est-ce bien la fille de ma soeur qui parle sur ce ton, garnie d'un vêtement semblable? Mais c'est incroyable! c'est inouï!*'

Poor Adèle did her very best to persuade her aunt that she considered her cotton gown and its appurtenances as very serious calamities; and as Madame de Hautrivage had the satisfaction of perceiving, upon more minute examination, that her offending relative did certainly look very ill and very miserable, she suffered herself by degrees to be appeased; and, on receiving exactly all that remained in the little purse of Adèle, declared herself ready, for the honour of the noble houses of Tremouille and Cordillac, to set forth in person to purchase all that was necessary for her decent equipment; 'till such time as she should have received her rents, when she would willingly,' she said, 'charge herself (for the love she bore her ever-lamented sister) with the troublesome task of making her in all respects fit to be seen'

As Adèle dreaded nothing so much as having the strength she was hoarding for the terrible day of Roger's trial wasted and worn out by the file-like process of scolding and complaining, she yielded her full and entire consent to all these plans for her embellishment, and had, moreover, sufficient presence of mind to add, that if Madame took all that trouble for her, she hoped she would not refuse to take a little more of the same kind for herself; as it would be her particular wish to present her with a dress if she would do her the great favour of choosing it.

This made all things smooth between them; and, as soon as it was possible for Madame to get out of her *déshabillé de matin*, she sallied forth, almost as well pleased to go as Adèle was to get rid of her.

For the first few moments after she was thus left, Adèle felt her solitude a relief; but, as all the circumstances of the dreadful task before her recurred to her memory, her heart seemed to faint and die within her. For a high-born young girl of any land to come forward in open court and disclose herself guilty of having carried on a secret, midnight communication with a young man, a stranger to her blood and her country, may well be allowed to be a painful – a tremendous undertaking. But for Adèle de Cordillac, a young and noble French girl, known in every fashionable circle in Paris – for her to come forward thus, alone and unsupported by the protecting presence of any single relation or friend, was almost equivalent to an open declaration of infamy; and tears of mingled shame and terror ran down her cheeks as she thought of it.

It was at this moment that an altercation at the outer door of Madame's ante-room made itself heard in the *salon*; but it was little heeded by Adèle, who knew that both the man and woman servant had received orders from their mistress to admit no one till her return. Yet still the noise increased, and a sound, like the effect of positive violence, startled her; but, before she had time to be frightened, or to ask herself what it might mean, the door of the *salon* was thrown open, and Alfred Coventry stood before her.

Adèle did not scream – she did not even speak; but she rose up, her tear-bedewed cheeks, which for an instant were as pale as death, becoming 'celestial rosy red,' her hands clasped, and her eyes fixed upon the face of the intruder with an expression that seemed to have more doubt of his identity than fear of his presence.

The footman stood with the handle of the door in his hand, while the head, or at any rate the eyes, of Madame's *femme de chambre* were visible over his shoulder.

Before Coventry uttered a word, he turned round; and the first accents of the voice so often wished for which reached the ears of Adèle were, –

'Have the kindness to tell them, Mademoiselle de Cordillac, that you do not require their presence.'

'Go, good friends!' said Adèle gently, but strongly pressing her clasped hands upon her heart in the hope of stilling the palpitation which seemed threatening to choke her. 'Go, Josephine, – go, Edward – I do not want you.'

The door was immediately closed, and Mademoiselle de Cordillac and Mr Coventry left alone.

Adèle reseated herself, which she was quite right to do, being by no means in a condition to stand; and Alfred, drawing a paper from his bosom, approached her. For half a moment he stood gazing on her lovely but averted face, and then dropping on one knee before her, he extended the hand which held open the little billet that had caused her so much woe, and said, 'Adèle! was this note intended for me?'

She glanced her eye upon the paper, and stretched out her hand to seize it. He let her take it from him; but as, instead of answering his question, she seemed about to crush the precious paper with very injurious disregard to its frail texture, he boldly ventured to assert his right to it by catching it, together with the trembling fingers that held it, in both his hands, exclaiming, –

'I would aid Mademoiselle de Cordillac, at the hazard of my life, in destroying all that she wished destroyed, save this! While I live, Adèle, this lives too,' he added, carefully replacing the paper in his bosom; 'and when I die, if I have any one near loving me well enough to fulfil my last wish, it shall be buried with me.'

As one of Alfred's hands was sufficient to replace the precious scroll in its sanctuary, the other still clasped that which had traced the characters upon it; nor did Adèle seek to withdraw it. Oh! she had suffered too much to play any part at that moment, – not even that prettiest and most forgivable of female wiles which teaches a young girl, as by a radical instinct of her nature, to hide the first deep joy of knowing that where she loves she is beloved – not even that was in her power now. She turned her eyes upon him, and, in the midst of her solitary desolation, seemed to see a friend on whose affection, though as yet scarcely avowed, her soul trusted with undoubting faith. And her heart, as if laid bare by the rude work it had encountered since she had seen him last, uttered audibly by her lips, 'Thank God!'

'My precious Adèle! my first – my only love! Let me now owe the joy those dear words gave me only, only to the misery which I too well know this blessed paper has cost you! Tell me, tell me, if only by one glance of that speaking eye, whose language has for months been my only study; – tell me, Adèle, that you do not repent having written that letter, – tell me but this, and all – all will be well!'

'All!' repeated Adèle, with a sigh. 'Alas! that cannot be. Yet I will tell you, Mr Coventry, that much as I must for ever, and for ever, regret the consequences which it has brought upon my faithful messenger, and, through him, on me, I neither do nor can repent it; if it be the means of convincing you that I am not the unworthy creature you had so much reason to think me.'

It was now Alfred Coventry's turn to cry 'Thank God!' which he did with an emphasis that left no doubt of his sincerity on the mind of his auditor. And beyond this there is no need that the pen of the historian should follow them; for who is there who could be so 'earthly dull' as not to guess the full and perfect explanation which followed? But dear as these remarks were to both, both felt the cruel necessity of cutting them short. For, even after each had been made most satisfactorily acquainted with the feelings of the other, there was still much that required discussion before the return of Madame de Hautrivage; and it was Adèle who, first recollecting this, disturbed the smooth stream of happiness on which they were so delightfully embarked, by exclaiming, 'But oh! this trial, Coventry! – this dreadful, dreadful trial. This cannot be prevented, nor even delayed; for though the *alibi* will now be proved by no less than three testimonies besides my own, I know that as the poor fellow has been committed to take his trial, nothing but the judgment of the court can release him.'

'It is but too true, dearest!' returned the lover, looking at her with eyes that, while they seemed intending to express the concern which such an avowal called for, had nevertheless an expression of happiness in them which Adèle could not understand. This was very strange, considering how terrible for her was the necessity which he allowed to exist. But there was no room for displeasure in her heart, and she only said, –

'Would I could look forward to its being over, as you seem to do, Coventry, "and leap the gulf between,"' fancying that the look which had puzzled her was produced by the hope that when the dreadful business was over, happiness might yet be in store for them. 'But I cannot,' she continued, – 'I cannot forget, even while you are with me, the agony of avowing that I sent him on this secret embassy. Would it be possible, – oh, Alfred! would it be possible to get him acquitted, without shewing that his silence was for my sake, – without confessing, in short, that I sent him? And that all his reprobate obstinacy arose from being ashamed of betraying an indiscretion which I was not ashamed to commit?'

Alfred Coventry paused a little before he answered, and then said, 'Need I tell you, my beloved Adèle, that had I the power I would save you not only from this, but from every painful feeling that could assail you from any quarter? But I will not attempt to deceive you in this matter. It is impossible to suppose that any tribunal, charged with the trial of an individual for a crime so important as that of which old Roger stands accused, will pronounce his acquittal without having thoroughly sifted every circumstance connected with the testimony given, both as to his guilt and his innocence. This *alibi* that you have so generously come forward to establish, dearest Adèle, and in proof of which you have been fortunate enough to find such very competent witnesses, – this *alibi* cannot be canvassed without leading, of necessity, to the discovery of the parties between whom this guiltless old man was the messenger. For will not every one of the individuals whom your active friend, M de Servac, so triumphantly boasts of finding, – will they not, every one of them, set forth the fact as a necessary link in their chain of evidence, that Roger Humphries came at a certain hour to the Hôtel ——, in the Rue de Rivoli, for the purpose of delivering a letter, or a message, to me; and then will M de Servac, beyond all question, summon me; he cannot do otherwise consistently with his duty to the client whose cause you have intrusted to him. And how will the matter stand then, Adèle? Will it not appear, – let me answer as cautiously and as vaguely as I will, – that a domestic of your house was employed at a very unusual hour to convey a letter, or message, to me? It is dreadful to torture you thus, my best beloved,' added Coventry, as the poor girl dropped her head on the table, and hid her face in her hands; 'but to deceive you would be more dreadful still. I cannot hope to escape questioning as to the nature of the communication; remember that nothing could be said or done in your family at a moment so very near the time when the crime was perpetrated, which it is the object of the tribunal to punish, that would not be examined into with the most pertinacious exactness. It were folly to doubt it, Adèle. The fact of your having sent Roger to me must be stated, and must be proved. So only can you hope to extricate this poor man from the danger in which he stands.'

A stifled groan from Mademoiselle de Cordillac was the only answer to this too convincing statement, and the countenance of her lover would have proved to her, could she have seen it, that she did not suffer alone.

An interval of silence followed, which was one of very strong emotion to them both, though not exactly from the same cause; for the lady was suffering from a feeling nearly approaching to despair, while every pulse of the gentleman was throbbing with hope.

This silence was at length broken by Coventry, who said in a voice which he vainly endeavoured to render firm and composed, 'Adèle, there is but one means by which we can escape all suffering from the consequences of your generous exertion for this poor man; but one, Adèle, – one alone, and that I almost fear to propose to you.'

'Fear nothing, Mr Coventry,' said Adèle, with sudden animation. 'Speak, I entreat you! Tell me what you mean; and be very sure there is no exertion, no sacrifice, which I should deem too great, could I but thereby escape the killing exposure you speak of.'

'No sacrifice, Adèle, – not even the sacrifice of punctilio?' replied Coventry.

'Punctilio, Alfred! what can you mean? Gracious Heaven! is this a moment to think of punctilio? Do not jest with me, dear friend; but if, indeed, you can devise any mode, any possible plan, by which I might avoid what I so greatly dread, be very sure I will adopt it, and that most thankfully.'

'Only promise me forgiveness, if what I say should offend you, Adèle, and I will indeed point out a mode by which the necessity of your appearing will be entirely avoided.'

'Offended! Surely you are trifling with me,' she replied, still too eagerly occupied by the one terrible idea of avowing in open court what she had so often blushed in secret to remember, to attempt discovering what hidden meaning his words might have. '*Nothing* can offend that can be planned or plotted with such an object in view. But do not keep me in suspense! I feel as if I should be the very happiest creature that lives and breathes, could I but believe it possible that Roger Humphries could be set at liberty without my facing all the eyes that may be congregated to look upon me, while I proclaim aloud the having commissioned him to convey to you that most imprudent note.'

'Imprudent! Oh, Adèle! – But it is not that point which we must now discuss. I trust the time may come when you may feel disposed to describe it by another epithet. But, dearest – dearest Adèle! hear me with patience on another theme; for it is most necessary that, before your aunt returns, I should receive your answer upon a point that I feel to be the most important; no less so, indeed, than the decision as to whether you shall appear personally at the trial of Roger Humphries or not.'

'Nay, Coventry, on that point you may receive my answer without any discussion at all. I will agree to any thing rather than appear in court.'

Coventry smiled, but shook his head doubtingly.

'I dare not take you at your word, Adèle, lest you should reproach me afterwards, and say that I took an unfair advantage of your terror. But tell me, love, before I go on to state the remedy, – tell me what it is that you chiefly fear in answering to the summons you expect.'

'Alas!' returned Adèle, 'I fear every thing *chiefly*, – and, alas! too, I fear that your boasted remedy is only to consist of a little wordy eloquence, intended to prove that the thing itself is less terrible than my dread of it. But even you, Coventry, will only speak in vain if this be your object. The terror with which I anticipate this scene is too real, and too well-founded also, to be charmed away, even by you.'

'Nor, had I the power, Adèle, would I use it,' replied the young man, gravely. 'Could I wish, think you, that you should meet the gaze, the comments, and the ribald jests of an open court, and meet it unmoved? Oh! no, no, no; that is not it, Adèle, – you are wide, very wide, of the mark. But if you will not tell me what you chiefly fear, let me tell you. You fear to hear it said, – you fear to hear it proved, that Mademoiselle Adèle de Cordillac wrote secretly to Alfred Coventry. Is it not so?'

'Mr Coventry, there is no need of this, – I feel it quite sufficiently,' she replied, the tingling blood again mounting to her very temples.

'Then hear me, Adèle. This must never be! It would kill you, – it would drive me mad. But yet *thus* it would be, Adèle. M de Servac, whom you have engaged as advocate for the accused, will rise after all the evidence has been heard against the prisoner, and declare to the court that he is prepared to prove an *alibi*. If he does his duty by his client, YOU will be the first witness he will call. You would be able to prove having written the letter; then would follow the evidence of the three men who are ready to swear that they saw and spoke to Roger Humphries before five o'clock; and, lastly, they would have to question me, as to the fact of my having been, a short time before, at the place to which the letter was addressed, and so forth. But, instead of this, hear *what it must be.* When M de Servac rises for the defence, he must be instructed to say that there is a gentleman in court prepared to prove not only that the prisoner was elsewhere when the Bertrand diamonds were stolen, but also to shew what was the nature of the business upon which he was engaged, and its utter incompatibility with any partnership or participation with the adventures of Madame Bertrand in the interval between her having been seen in the ball-room and that at which, by her own account, the outrage was committed. And then, Adèle, I, the gentleman thus alluded to, would come forward, and testify on oath to the following facts: – That Roger Humphries was despatched from the Rue de Lille at four o'clock on the morning of the 24th of April (half an hour earlier than the time at which three or four gentlemen are ready to swear they saw Madame Bertrand in the ball-room), and that Roger Humphries was despatched at that hour by MY WIFE, Madame Coventry, with a letter addressed to me at the Hôtel ――, Rue de Rivoli.'

Adèle started, – and in the burning blush that dyed her beautiful face as she involuntarily raised her eyes to those of her lover, Alfred saw at once the almost terrified emotion which the sudden hearing of such words naturally produced, and the ingenuous avowal that he had indeed discovered a way to deprive her courageous testimony of all its bitterness. This would certainly have been, in some degree, the case any where; but in France, the remedy to her embarrassment which this change of name and title offered was greatly more perfect and complete than can fully be understood by any one unacquainted with the peculiarly *sacred* value attached to marriage in that country.

Adèle saw at once that the labyrinth-like coil of misery which seemed to have been twisting and twisting itself round her from the hour in which she had listened to her gay aunt's pleasant jest about Coventry, was now cut asunder as by the hand of an enchanter, and that she stood free and unscathed, with power to aid and support her poor Sabina more effectually than she had ever dared to hope; with means as unfettered as her will to set the faithful Roger free; and – and . . . In short, and despite all and every thing that the abruptness of the business could conjure up to frighten her, she did feel at that moment that she was the very happiest creature in the world.

Did she tell Mr Coventry so? Of course she did not. To feel all she felt, was as right as it was natural, and as delightful as it was both. But to mention it to the man who stood gazing at her as if his life depended on the first word that she should deign to utter, was totally out of the question, – was, in fact, totally impossible, and contrary to the nature of things as arranged by the Master-hand that framed us. It is, doubtless, for this reason that man is endowed with a power, whenever occasion requires it, of finding out with such wonderful rapidity and correctness, and in defiance of the most obstinate silence, and the most averted eyes, pretty nearly all that the fair statues before which he bends take such exceeding pains to conceal. So it was with Mr Coventry. Mademoiselle de Cordillac spoke not, – she moved not; and the first proof she gave that she was not actually marble, was the shedding (Miranda-like) a few bright tears, which shewed upon her cheeks most wonderfully like dew-drops upon the petals of a new-blown rose. But, somehow or other, the gentleman very soon became as well assured of the agreeable fact, that all he wished on earth was his as the lady; and then, for a few short moments, they were so improvident as to forget that any such person as Madame de Hautrivage existed in the world. Most properly were they punished for this indiscretion; for at a very tender moment, and when nobody in the world could have desired the entrance of any aunt in existence, good, bad, or indifferent, Madame de Hautrivage stood before them.

Fortunately, however, – if, indeed, the insular audacity of the young Englishman had led him to attempt snatching a kiss from the blushing descendant of such an immense line of de Cordillacs and de Tremouilles, – the deed was not actually witnessed by Madame; for the chenille fringe of her black velvet mantilla having been caught by some obstruction in the doorway, she had turned to extricate it, and thereby afforded time for both parties to seat themselves, with a becoming interval of space between, and as much appearance of composure as could have been reasonably hoped for.

Madame de Hautrivage had gone out in good-humour, and having spent the interval in the presence of materials for wearing apparel, of which she hoped ere long to appropriate a part, she returned in the same amiable state of mind. Nevertheless she was a good deal startled at the sight of this *tête-à-tête* in her drawing-room, and her first emotion was decidedly aunt-like and disapproving. But Madame de Hautrivage was, as the intelligent reader must be already aware, a woman of a quick and ready capacity. She certainly made Mr Coventry a courtesy, in which there appeared more of ceremony than affection; but before it was finished – before she had fully recovered the upright dignity of her usual attitude, she remembered more than one important fact. She remembered, first, that the young man before her was an excellent *parti* in every way; next, that a little blunder of her own had seemed for a long time to have robbed her niece of all chance of obtaining it; and lastly, she recollected, with a good deal of distinctness, that her elegant brother-in-law, though the most noble-minded man in the world, had been declared by his *intendant* to be ruined, and that it was therefore probable the young ladies, her nieces, would not in future have such favourable opportunities for forming splendid alliances as they had heretofore enjoyed. All this together brought a charming smile to her lips, as she repeated her favourite phrase, — 'Mais, c'est une éternité!' &c. &c. In short, it was immediately evident that Adèle's *futur* had nothing to fear from the severity of her aunt; but Alfred Coventry was almost as quick-witted a person as Madame de Hautrivage herself, and being aware that a great deal of business was to be done with very little time to do it in, he suffered himself not to be beguiled into any of the thousand and one *aimable* discussions upon which Madame was evidently so willing to enter, but manfully plunged into the very pith and marrow of what he had to say to her at once.

'Madame de Hautrivage,' he began, 'it is impossible, when hearing you converse, not to regret that times are not with us what they used to be in the Rue de Lille, when no serious affairs obliged us to sacrifice pleasure to business. The fact is, that at this moment a cruel necessity constrains me to say that I have but few minutes in which to enjoy the gratification ever afforded by your society; and even that time, short as it is, must be employed in confiding to you a matter which is to me of the greatest importance, and which the *aimable* kindness with which you have ever treated me, leads me to hope will be neither uninteresting nor displeasing to you.'

During this opening harangue Adèle had stolen out of the room, leaving the charming Clementina and Mr Coventry considerably more likely to understand one another than when they had last found themselves *tête-à-tête*.

No sooner had the door now closed upon Adèle than the good lady uttered half-a-dozen pretty exclamations in a breath, all tending to shew that she knew perfectly well what was coming, and was delighted with it. 'But you must excuse the poor Adèle,' she said, 'if this takes her so greatly by surprise as to prevent her receiving you with all the politeness *d'une jeune fille bien élevée*. I know she will be amazingly surprised, *pauvre enfant!* Yet who is there but me to dispose of her? It is a duty which has devolved upon me, and I perform it well, Monsieur Coventry, in bestowing her upon you. *C'est malheureux* that the establishment of my *aimable beau-frère* is broken up! *Mais que voulez-vouz?* — You, of course, heard of his noble *dévouement* and all that it has cost him? *C'est sublime! mais parfaitement sublime, sans doute. Cependant* — just at this moment it is unfortunate. However, *mon cher neveu*, if you will but give me time, I doubt not that I shall be able to manage our *trousseau* perfectly to the satisfaction of the Cordillac and Tremouille families; but time is every thing.'

'But unfortunately, my dear lady,' replied Coventry, stoutly, 'time is what I cannot grant you; and my Adèle must be contented to let her *trousseau* follow her, or await her return to Paris.'

The black, arched, and expansive eye-brows of Madame de Hautrivage mounted to the very top of her forehead, and a spirited remonstrance, beginning with the ominous words, '*Les Anglais!*' was about to burst upon him, when he cut the matter short by inquiring if Madame had been made acquainted with the very disagreeable business which had brought Mademoiselle de Cordillac to Paris?

'Oh, yes,' she replied, 'I know all that perfectly well. Adèle is come to receive her rents; and though it is possible she might have preferred receiving her income through the hands of her noble-minded *beau-frère*, I can hardly call the receiving the money herself a disagreeable business, especially as M de Servac is so old a friend, and so perfectly ready to arrange every thing for her.'

'Ah, madame!' returned Coventry, '*vous n'y estes pas.*' He then asked her, if she was aware of the situation in which Roger Humphries, Mr Hargrave's old English servant, was at present placed.

'*Mais certainement!*' replied Madame de Hautrivage, colouring violently, and with an accent of the deepest indignation; 'and a dreadful misfortune it is, that a man so every way estimable as my *beau-frère* should have so dreadful a villain in his service. – *Les Anglais,*' she began again; but once more he stopped her, and now informed her, as briefly and as clearly as he could, that Mademoiselle de Cordillac, knowing the old man to be perfectly innocent, inasmuch as she had herself sent him elsewhere precisely at the time when Madame Bertrand was robbed, was now in Paris, less for the purpose of receiving her rents, than for that of proving the innocence of her old servant. After allowing a short interval for Madame's violent surprise to evaporate in exclamation, he steadily pursued his object by saying, –

'That Mademoiselle de Cordillac is right in this, it is impossible that any person of honour can doubt. Nevertheless, madame, the appearance of the young lady in open court will be highly objectionable and equally disagreeable, I have no doubt, both to you and to me, without even attempting to say how dreadfully repugnant it must be to all her own feelings of delicacy. For this, my dear lady, there is but one remedy. Mademoiselle de Cordillac must never be summoned into a public court. But if it be found necessary that Madame Coventry should appear, there can be no kind of objection to it, especially as her husband will be summoned also. But even this will not, as I flatter myself, be necessary when she is my wife, as I believe her husband's statement will be considered as perfectly satisfactory. Thus, madame, you perceive that an immediate marriage is rendered necessary. And it shall be my care so to hasten the business portion of the necessary preliminaries as to prevent any inconvenience from this involuntary haste.'

There was such a mixture of decision, authority, and reason, in the manner in which this was spoken, that Madame de Hautrivage appeared totally at a loss what to reply to it in the way of opposition, and yet it was evident that there was something in this mode of managing matters which was greatly less than agreeable to her. Coventry, who was exceedingly anxious that this hasty and agitating proceeding should be rendered as little painful to Adèle as possible, watched her narrowly, in order to discover what part of the omitted ceremonies she seemed to consider as the most essential, in the hope of finding some means of supplying it; well aware that nothing would be more likely to harass the feelings of his already trembling bride than any avowed displeasure on the part of the only relative whom circumstances permitted her to have near her. Nor did he watch in vain; for, together with many dainty phrases concerning the solemnity which ought to be observed in all ceremonies connected with families of distinction, several slight allusions were made to the incorrectness, not to say indecency, of marrying, especially where the bride was a lady of fortune, without a *corbeille*; and the words *cadeau* and *cachemire* caught his ear distinctly, though the sentences of which they made part were too rapidly muttered for him to feel very sure of their purport. But Coventry, as we have said, was a quick-witted young man; and waiting not for further explanations, or wasting a moment in making compliments, apologies, or wordy work of any kind, he suddenly started up, seized his hat, and uttering, with a somewhat theatrical air, '*Adieu, ma tante!*' quitted the room and the house.

The head or the heart, or the *musée of speech* of Madame de Hautrivage was too full for her to endure being long left alone, and the agitated but delicious solitude of Adèle was soon invaded by a request from her aunt that she would *please* to come to her directly. To please or to be pleased in doing this was quite out of the question; but as far as obedience was in her power, she yielded; and, with shaking joints and a beating heart, Mademoiselle de Cordillac repaired to the presence of her aunt.

It would be a useless task to attempt rehearsing all the wisdom uttered by Madame de Hautrivage on this occasion. The catalogue of dresses — the enumeration of trinkets — the necessity of new equipages — all were dwelt upon with the most pathetic eloquence. That every thing *must* be had was asserted as a broad fact that could not admit of discussion; and that nothing *could* be had was declared almost at the same moment, in a tone no less positive. Adèle bore it all like an angel; in which, to say truth, there was no great merit, for she was far too happy to care greatly for any lamentations that could possibly be uttered upon the miseries, great and small, of human life. She did at last get a little weary, however, and having repeated, for about the hundred and fiftieth time, that unhappily there was no law to regulate necessity, she was making up her mind to receive the rest in silence, when a ring was heard at the outward door, and a minute or two afterwards the man-servant entered with an extremely large brown paper parcel in his arms, the maid-servant following with another, of hardly less dimensions, in hers. Both were addressed to Madame de Hautrivage.

'*Mais qu'est-ce que c'est, donc?*' exclaimed the good lady, with that sudden species of animation which is always produced on persons of her temperament by the sight and touch of such packages. 'There must be some mistake, I fear,' she continued, looking first at one servant, then at the other, and then at Adèle. 'I am quite positive that I have purchased nothing whatever, except those few things for you, my dear, which were brought home two hours ago. I suppose I had better open them, but I am quite sure that there must be some mistake.'

The two servants sang forth a duetto of reduplicated assurances that there was no mistake at all; for that the man who brought the packages had asked over and over again, very particularly, if Madame de Hautrivage lived there.

'*Eh bien donc!*' she replied, in terms of unmitigated delight. 'In that case you may cut the cords, one of you, and we shall soon see what it means.'

The meaning did not long remain a mystery. The cords were cut; one, two, three envelopes of paper (the first being very coarse, and the last very fine) removed, such a treasure of rich mercery was displayed as shook her philosophy to the very centre.

But exquisite as were the satins and the silks, the laces and the embroidery, which constituted the contents of the first and largest parcel, that which permitted its softness to be compressed into the compass of the lesser one caused a perfect scream of ecstasy to burst from the lungs of Madame de Hautrivage. Two cashmere shawls, of the very finest texture, the very largest size, the most perfect colours, and the richest patterns, either being worthy of becoming the state turban of the Sultan, lay before her; and between them both was placed a billet well deserving to be called '*doux*,' in which Mr Coventry respectfully requested her acceptance of whichever of the two shawls might chance to please her fancy best, and begged, as an additional favour, that she would have the kindness to present the other in his name to his fair *fiancée*. As to the other articles, he said that he had taken the liberty of sending them jointly to the aunt and niece, to spare them all unnecessary trouble at a time when every hour was precious, as he was sure she would have the kindness to feel, when he told her that the object which made her niece's immediate marriage necessary could not be achieved if the ceremony were delayed beyond the third day from the present. He should take care, he added, that every thing should be ready for this which could possibly come within his province to arrange, and he ventured to flatter himself that Madame de Hautrivage would employ the interval in getting the materials he had taken the liberty to send converted into such dresses for herself and her niece as her exquisite taste and judgment might approve.

It is a prodigious advantage to have to deal with people whose natures are sufficiently candid to permit their ruling passions to be discerned. From that moment there was nothing imaginable which Alfred Coventry could have asked for or proposed, which Madame de Hautrivage would have objected to or refused. Her very soul was touched and melted, as it were, before the all-powerful influence which his sagacity had set to work upon her.

'Dieu! quel homme!' she exclaimed, 'quelle perfection de noblesse, et de bon goût! Et puis, le choix à moi! Hélas! Comment croire que je n'avais pas, en quelque sorte, raison, quand . . . Mais il ne faut pas y penser! Pauvre Alfred! à ce moment même il me laisse le choix! Eh bien! Il a raison. Elle est riche, et moi, je ne le suis pas.'

It cannot be necessary to inform the intelligent reader that the greatest part of this was uttered not quite half aloud; so that nobody knew more of what was passing in her grateful and susceptible heart than was convenient.

From this moment Adèle was troubled no more with regrets and lamentations concerning the hurried pace at which the preparations for her marriage were to proceed; and when their tête-à-tête dinner was over, she was left to the enjoyment of solitary musing on the extraordinary change which had taken place in her circumstances within the last twenty-four hours, while Madame assembled in her bed-room as many artistes as it was possible to get together on so short a notice.

In their different ways, both the ladies were exceedingly happy. It might, indeed, be in some degree difficult to decide which was the most so.

CHAPTER XXXIII

The departure of Adèle, though her absence was not expected to be long, was a calamity which Sabina feared she should not bear well; and for the first hour or two after her departure she shut herself into the room they had shared together, less for the comfort of weeping unmolested than for the purpose of schooling herself into such a degree of fortitude and composure as might enable her to appear before her father in such a state as not to give him pain. She had already learned, poor girl! that the most strictly required, as well as the most difficult, duty she had to perform in their seclusion was such command of feature as might prevent him from supposing that she was thinking with regret of the past; and far from repining at the symptoms of temper which brought this sort of selfish tyranny to view, her heart ached as she thought how much her beloved father must have suffered to make him thus keenly sensitive. And it was in such thoughts as these that her greatest fund of strength lay. Without them it is possible that, left without the presence and support of the dear friend and counsellor to whom she had ever looked, in every joy and every sorrow, as the pilot who would keep her from going wrong, she might have sunk under the many sorrows that had fallen on her young head, and given herself up to hopeless melancholy. But what she could not have borne well for herself, she could bear well for him; and having bathed her swollen eyelids, combed her silken hair, and breathed a prayer to Heaven to strengthen her, she left her room, and stole out to take her best-loved solitary path to the well-known rock, determined not to re-enter the more than ever desolate walls of the residence till she felt able to meet her father with a smile.

Mr Hargrave, on his side, was as busily employed in preparation as herself; but his object held no great affinity with hers. Since the departure of those brilliant days in which he had felt within himself a consciousness of innate brightness, that made him feel his rising to be to his household what the rising of the sun was to the rest of the world, – since the departure of those blissful days, Mr Hargrave had fallen into the habit of lying in bed whenever he felt himself disposed to be 'gentlemanlike and melancholy;' and having no more inclination to bid Adèle farewell than she had to be bidden farewell by him, he resorted to this indulgence on the morning of her departure as a means of avoiding her. But the attainment of this object, if the first, was not the only motive for this retreat; and long after he was aware of her having left the house, he continued to enjoy the shelter of this favourite seclusion, for the purpose of digesting at his ease the immediate execution of a project towards which his thoughts had been for some time turned, but which, till now, he had not considered as of any pressing necessity.

Though not quite so very clever a fellow as he thought himself, Mr Hargrave had discernment enough to perceive that Adèle, notwithstanding the essential services she had rendered him, retained neither for his person nor character the slightest trace of the affection she had formerly borne him. The masterly manner in which she had managed his escape, and opened, by her admirable political insinuation, a vista for future manoeuvring (which was, by the by, more hit than wit on her part, poor girl!), all this induced him to form an extremely exalted idea of her ability; but this was unaccompanied by any thing like a just idea of the beautiful *morale* of her character.

He knew that she disliked him, and felt persuaded that, having become heartily (and naturally) sick of the desolate seclusion of their Mummel palace, she had seized upon the arrest of Roger Humphries as an excuse for being off. Her independent fortune, and the many noble connexions who would be glad to receive her, rendered this plan as rational in his eyes as he felt it to be probable; and the more he thought of it, the more fully he became convinced that Mademoiselle de Cordillac was gone to Paris, without any intention of returning, and that, whether for the emancipation of old Roger, or the gratification of universal curiosity, or because she would find it, one way or another, impossible to avoid it, HIS part in the Bertrand adventure, as well as in some others, would speedily become known, his hiding-place betrayed, and himself dragged out of it to condign punishment.

These ideas having once taken possession of his mind strengthened with every hour spent in the examination of them. He had learned to hate his step-daughter quite as heartily as he believed that she hated him, and, so far from seeing any thing improbable or monstrous in the course which he believed her about to pursue, he would, in truth, have been inclined to bestow these epithets on any other.

'Let her go, let her talk, let her recover her position, as she can. It is no more than I had every reason to expect. But as to making me the sacrifice, she will find herself mistaken if she expects it.' It was thus his recumbent meditations ended; and having perfectly decided what to do, he sprung with renewed activity from his bed, summoned his *valet de chambre*, Gertrude, and his running footman, Hans, – employed the first in aid of the sundry necessities of his reduced toilet, and the last in conveying a very earnest message to Father Mark, requesting to see him immediately, and then sat himself down with a cup of strong coffee to prepare for the business he had to perform.

There was one corner of Mr Hargrave's heart – for every animal has a heart of some kind or other – which was not entirely and altogether, solely and wholly, filled with himself. This was the corner in which the image of Sabina dwelt; but even from this, though he did not occupy it wholly and alone, he was not banished. Oh no! That any thought or feeling could exist in the heart or soul of Hargrave, unmixed with self, was as impossible as that a balloon should float without air, or a steam-boat be propelled without hot water. So, even in Sabina's corner, his own gratification, his own pride, and his own ambition, had found place, and nestled, side by side, with his paternal love.

All that can truly be said, therefore, of the share his daughter had in the schemes which now engrossed him, was that she was not forgotten.

On the entrance of Father Mark Mr Hargrave rose to receive him with much more than usual solemnity. He approached him with his arms crossed on his breast, – not in the 'sad knot of Jaques,' but soldier-wise, and with the aspect (admirably well *singé*) of a monk professed, and in the full-blown odour of especial sanctity.

'I have sent for you, Father Mark,' he said, 'that I might communicate to you the meditations of the past night, inspired, as I cannot fail to believe, by the most holy Dominic, the patron saint to whom I am dedicated. I have sent to you, father, to tell you what these meditations have been, and, also, the resolution at which I have arrived at in consequence of them.'

Father Mark was by this time so accustomed to the sanctified pomposity of his new penitent that he listened to this exordium without deeming it necessary to return any other answer than a meek bowing of the head. But when Mr Hargrave, after signing to the priest to take a chair, while he placed himself in another, began to explain himself further, his confessor found it necessary to listen with rather more attention than usual, in order to prevent his making some blunder which might speedily, as it seemed, be conveyed direct to the foot of the Papal throne.

'I can no longer, father,' resumed Mr Hargrave, 'resist, without sin, the inward impulse which leads me to repose the state secrets that burden my soul on those who are more qualified to convert them to good than either you or I, good father. My purpose is to set off immediately for Rome. My stay there will depend on many circumstances, into which it is at this moment needless to enter. But should any arise that might make it desirable for me, who have so deeply involved myself in the struggle of two rival dynasties, to retire at once from the busy scenes of life, and to bury myself, and the important secrets intrusted to me, in a cloister, I should wish to be prepared with such testimonials from you, holy father, as may render the usual ceremony of novitiate unnecessary. I must desire you immediately to commit to paper all the facts you know concerning me, and also your opinion of the strict sanctity of my life, and the ardour of my zeal to endow whatever holy society I may enter with the treasure (by no means contemptible), which I have still left from the ample fortune, of which I have hitherto dedicated so large a portion to the use of the elder branch of the Bourbon family. You will commit all this to paper, Father Mark, in case I may find it expedient to hasten the time of my profession.'

Having said this, Mr Hargrave rose, and sought for pens, ink, and paper, which he laid before the priest.

Father Mark continued to sit with his eyes fixed upon the ground, and without any intention, as it seemed, of employing the implements which had been set before him.

'May I ask, holy father, what it is which delays your compliance with my request?' said Mr Hargrave.

'Pardon me, my son,' said the good man, while the ruddy colour of his cheek mounted to his temples. 'But I was thinking how much it was I really did know of you. If I understand you right, the document you have desired me to prepare is to convey information to some of the highest depositaries of the holy authorities under which I am bound to live, and it needs, therefore, that I write nothing lightly.'

'Nay, father,' returned Mr Hargrave, colouring in his turn, 'I can proceed without your aid if you are thus scrupulous in affording it. It seems proper and natural that every man, knowing the value of confession, and resorting to it with unvarying punctuality, as I do, should wish, on such a sacred mission (for so I must call it), to carry with him from the priest to whom he has most recently opened his heart, some testimony of the spiritual opinion formed of him. However, I will not press this task upon you. I must state to those I go to seek with the humble piety of a devoted heart, that I have not had the good fortune to fall in with a confessor whose views corresponded with my own; and this will account for, and excuse, my appearing without such testimony. Fortunately there is no danger of my being long at Rome without receiving, both from the heads of the Gallican Church and from the royal exile himself, such letters as will furnish me with all the aid and all the authority I require. My only reason for addressing myself to you, Father Mark, was to make my entrance into a religious community as instantaneous as possible, for which there are reasons connected with the cause I serve which may, doubtless, easily be divined by you.'

'May the Pope and the holy college condemn me as a heretic,' murmured the unfortunate priest to himself, 'if I can divine, guess, or imagine, any thing about it.' But the poor man was frightened. He knew himself to be profoundly ignorant of all the dynasties, and all the politics, and all the cabals, of the earth, and had only been made obscurely to comprehend, by his conferences with Mr Hargrave, that the Pope and the holy Catholic religion were, somehow or other, mixed up with Charles Dix and that eloquent gentleman himself. But this was, of course, fully enough to make him amenable to the species of argument now brought forward to prove that he ought to do what was desired of him. He accordingly set himself to do it, but not without a sigh at the untoward fortune which doomed him for ever to be the advocate and eulogist of what he did not understand.

The document thus obediently framed was very nearly all that Mr Hargrave desired it to be, and trusting to the influence of his venerated uncle, the cardinal, for the rest, he told Father Mark, as he folded it up and placed it in his pocket-book, that he should not forget to speak favourably of him at Rome, and that he should set out for that venerable and venerated city on the morrow.

'To-morrow!' repeated Father Mark, in considerable surprise, but certainly not without a strong sensation of pleasure. 'Is it possible, my son, that all your worldly concerns can be thus speedily set in order? Your excellent daughter, and the unfortunate heretical young lady her half-sister? What may be your purpose respecting them?'

'I will tell you, my good and holy friend,' replied Mr Hargrave, 'and I rest much on your aid, and on that of your pious and excellent mother, for carrying into effect my plans concerning them. As to Mademoiselle de Cordillac, – whom you most correctly term unfortunate, for who plunged in the errors of heresy can be otherwise? – she has already disposed of herself, having left this house for Paris at day-break this morning. But my dear Sabina,' and here a pang of real feeling stopped him for a moment, 'as for her, Father Mark, I trust that you will extend your pious cares to her for a day or two, – in short, till I have been received into the convent I have named to you. After which, a letter, which I shall leave with her, will be forwarded to her aunt at Paris, who will, I doubt not, take care to send a proper escort to convey her to that city. In the meantime it would be an act of very holy charity if your inestimable mother would invite her to remain with her in the interval. But remember, holy father, that Sabina is not to suppose that I go without the intention of returning. After all it is extremely probable that I may return, – in fact, every thing will depend upon the wish and will of his holiness, to whom I shall submit myself in all things. But, in any case, I need have no lasting leave-takings, it would render me unfit for – for my duty.'

Father Mark promised, in his own name, and in that of his good mother likewise, that no service which it was in their power to perform for the young lady should be omitted. And so he took his leave, little disposed to speculate upon the actions of the man who had rendered his religious functions a most heavy penance, simply by boring him almost beyond his pious power of endurance by the weight of his pompous egotism.

As soon as he was gone, Mr Hargrave wrote a letter, which it was his purpose to leave with Father Mark, and which was to fix the fate of poor Sabina; and had it not been that the renewed terror of being followed, arrested, tried, and convicted, again seized upon him, it is probable that even his selfishly callous heart would have found the task nearly enough to master him. As it was, however, the lesser evil was swallowed up by the greater, and with little time lost in sorrow or uncertainty, he wrote the following epistle: –

'*To Madame de Hautrivage.*

'At the moment of quitting the busy haunts of a world which your charming society has so often contributed to render delightful to me, can you wonder, my charming sister, that some of my latest thoughts are devoted to you? Your niece, Adèle, informed you before our last hurried parting, how deeply I had involved myself by my enthusiasm for the cause of a CERTAIN INDIVIDUAL, whose name must not be trusted to the common post, which, I am sorry to say, is the only means I have of conveying these lines to you.

'Your intelligent mind and honourable feelings, my dear sister, will enable you to appreciate justly the motives which must now, and for ever, prevent my entering into any details respecting the confederation that has been formed for the purpose of restoring THAT PERSON to his rights. Over this an impenetrable darkness shall fall, as impassable and as sacred as that which is speedily about to envelope myself. All upon this unhappy subject that you will ever hear from me is, that the plan, noble, disinterested, and generous as it was, has totally failed, and the only successful effort belonging to it being that which has prevented any suspicion falling on those concerned in it, with the exception of my unhappy self. But think not that I repine at being thus selected, as it were, by fate as the only victim. I am contented, my dear Clementina, that so it should be. My spirit – my affections were, as, by the blessing of the most Holy Virgin, I have now learned to believe, too much wedded to the pomps and vanities of this lower world. All that is over! Weary of a state of things which I have not been able to amend, a short time only will pass before I shall be sheltered under the cowl of a monk, alike from the pleasures and the disappointments of life. I have, I think, fixed upon a beautiful but retired monastery in Andalusia as that in which I shall take the vows, and, as I hope, deposit my bones. Having said thus much of myself, I must add an explanation of my last wishes respecting my daughter. Tell her, dear sister, from me, that nothing could have endowed me with sufficient courage to leave her, not even the holy voice which has called me to the cloister, had I not been aware that the sentence which would have fallen upon me from the present tyrannical government of France would have been more dreadful for her to witness than even our separation. Tell her, also, that I know her to be too good a Catholic not to find consolation in reflecting that the part I have chosen must ensure me a place among the saints in heaven. Nay, if exemplary holiness of life, and the exertion of the talents which I have been led to believe that Heaven has bestowed upon me, if this can ensure the being elected as a saint on earth, I may not, perhaps, altogether despair of one day adding to the honourable names from which she derives her descent – that of a canonised father!

'Beyond such consolation as this assurance of my eternal well-doing will afford her, I have nothing to bequeath; and her affectionate heart will, I am well aware, require no more. From you, admirable Madame de

Hautrivage, I look for the personal care and protection which I am no longer able to give. But you are not rich, and I look not to you for any pecuniary means for her support. On this point I wish you to address yourself to your niece, Mademoiselle de Cordillac. Tell her from me, if you please, as well as from yourself, that if she permits the daughter of her mother to want any thing that her ample fortune can bestow, she will prove her newly adopted faith to be even of a worse quality than I think it. But I cannot say that I have any fears on this point. I feel perfectly satisfied that before Adèle de Cordillac marries she will settle the half of her fortune on Sabina Hargrave. It is to her, therefore, my dear sister, that you must apply for the funds necessary for despatching to Gernsbach (a small town only a few miles distant from Baden-Baden) such an escort as you and her sister shall deem proper for conveying her to you at Paris. If you inquire at the sacristy of the church at Gernsbach for *Father Mark*, as the good priest to whose care I have left her is familiarly called, you will learn where to find her.

'And now, farewell! and be assured of the constant prayers of one who trusts that he shall not be accounted the last in the society of God's saints.

'Your affectionate brother,

'CHARLES HARGRAVE.'

This task performed, he carefully examined the treasure still left in his hands, and had sufficient knowledge of precious stones to feel convinced that, let him bend his course which way he would, – to Rome, to Spain, to the light freedom of the United States, or the loose tyranny of imperial Russia, he should have sufficient wealth to be still a personage of some consequence in either. It is quite possible that had this treasure been in current coin, he might have indulged the only feeling of his heart not ending as well as beginning in self, by leaving with Sabina a share of it; but he was relieved from any combat of doubts and wishes on his head by the obvious necessity of carrying away whatever might tend to raise a suspicion against him. Of the small residue of his golden hoard he did design a part for her; and, having made the division of it in such proportions as he thought right and proper (in doing which he took into consideration the speedy replenishment of the little purse he was preparing by the sums which she would receive from her sister), he disposed of his own share, as well as of the jewels, into small and commodious divisions, to be secured in different parts of his dress. This done, he set about all the minor preparations for his departure, and had completed every thing just as he saw from his window the figure of Sabina slowly returning from her long ramble, or rather from her long repose upon the summit of the rock which jutted from the cliff above.

The heart of the father felt as keen a pang as it was possible such a heart could feel; and for a moment or two he felt that rather than take leave of her, he would set off without her knowledge, leaving to Father Mark the task of announcing his departure. For a short time this idea was a great relief to him; but when the thought crossed him that he had then seen her for the last time, he changed his mind. A longing wish to kiss her once again took possession of him, and, determining to spare himself the sight of her agony at bidding him a lasting, or even a long farewell, he mentally rehearsed a scene, which even then he pleased himself by thinking he should perform admirably; in which he should lead her to expect his speedy return, or, at the very worst, such a delay only as might oblige her to return to Paris for a short time, where she would rejoin her sister, and might remain in perfect assurance of his safety. But all this was planned solely to spare himself the pain of witnessing her grief, for he had no intention of leaving her many days in this delusion, being quite certain that as long as she nourished any hope of his return, she would, in all probability, refuse to take up her abode in Paris, where it was notorious that he could not come, and might, moreover, set inquiries on foot respecting him which might prove any thing but convenient.

Once more interview with Father Mark was necessary; and the good priest obeyed the summons with the less reluctance, because he had such comfortable reason to believe it would be the last. The hour Mr Hargrave fixed for this was at seven o'clock on that same evening. His *tête-à-tête* dinner with poor Sabina was sad enough, doubtless, for he was decidedly not gay, and she was as much the reverse as it was natural she should be, with the thoughts of Adèle's lonely wandering at her heart.

Immediately after the cup of coffee which always followed their dinner, Mr Hargrave rose and said, 'I have matters of importance, my dear Sabina, to discuss with Father Mark this evening, so I must leave you to your drawing and your books. Ah, my love! I shall never feel satisfied till things are so settled as to restore you to Paris, a brilliant fortune would be sure to open upon you there, but here you are lost!'

Sabina assured him, with the utmost sincerity, that if she could see him well and happy she should be perfectly contented, though certain of never beholding Paris again. But he shook his head incredulously, and, saying that he still hoped he should be able to manage matters for her better than that, he passed his hand, as he had done a thousand times before, over her silken hair, kissed her fair brow, and left her.

Hargrave rose on the following morning somewhat earlier than usual; for he chose himself to prepare the packages which were to convey the whole wardrobe of which he was now the master. Moreover, he had to dress himself with peculiar care; not indeed, as formerly, for the purpose of making five-and-forty years look like five-and-thirty; but he had his *treasure* to dispose of about his person, so as to be secure from observation, loss, or injury, and, above all else, to be so placed as not in any way to annoy his person. But all this was done, and Hans had received orders to be ready to attend him to Baden, before the light step of Sabina was heard at his door, bringing her to inquire where and when he would like to take his breakfast.

'Immediately, my love, if you are ready, and with you,' was the reply; and, taking her arm under his, he led her to their usual sitting-room.

Sabina had not rested well; the idea of Adèle pursued her, and she had not once dropped to sleep without waking with a start from some painful dream, which again and again came to torment her, by placing before her eyes the pale and terrified countenance of her sister suffering under some travelling misadventure.

Her want of bloom, and of the bright look which used to make her so lovely, was remarked by her father; but every effort of his mind was at that moment directed to the one sole object of sparing his own feelings as much as possible. He, therefore, took no further notice of this than saying, 'Yes, my love, as I told you last night, I must positively manage so as to get you back again to Paris as soon as possible.'

Sabina sighed, shook her head, but said nothing in reply.

'You really, my dear girl,' resumed her father, actively employing himself in preparations for eating his breakfast, – 'you really *must* get back to Paris. You have no idea of the pain it gives me to see you buried here. To say the truth, my dear love, this idea of your being speedily restored to Paris is all I have to console me under the first sorrow which I have to communicate to you.' Sabina started, and looked at him in great alarm. 'Yes, dearest,' he resumed, 'there is yet more sorrow in store for us. I have received notice, through the agency of our excellent friend Father Mark, that my presence is absolutely necessary at Rome or in Spain, and I must set off, Sabina, within an hour!'

An exclamation of great agony burst from the poor girl at hearing this, and, though as unselfish as her hardened father was the reverse, she did for one short moment feel the terrible desolation of her own situation beyond all else; but, in the next, the idea of his being about to encounter fatigue and inconvenience chased every other, and she inquired, with anxious tenderness, as to his mode of travelling and the probable length of his absence.

'I shall travel by public conveyances, my love,' he replied, 'which is the mode best suited to my fallen fortunes. But as to the length of my stay, it is impossible to answer satisfactorily. You are aware, Sabina, how much I have already done for the cause in which I am embarked, and having done so much, your good sense must teach you to expect that I shall hold myself ready to do more. In one word, Sabina, there is nothing which could be required of me to which I am not prepared to submit. From what I can learn from Father Mark – but be very careful, my dear girl, not to let him know that I have told you this – but by what I hear from Father Mark, the great terror of my royal friend arises at present from the probablity that I may be pursued and taken. He has, therefore, dictated that I should immediately repair to Rome, and afterwards to a certain convent in Andalusia, and there wait for further instructions.'

'Oh, my father!' exclaimed Sabina, 'can you leave me thus?'

Hargrave shrunk from the gentle eyes that awaited his answer, and then, for one solitary moment, spoke in the accents of truth and nature. 'Did you know, my child, how dearly my remaining here might cost me, you would suffer much before you would ask me to do it!'

'Oh! go then, go!' cried Sabina, with an instinctive perception of the truth of this. 'Think not of me, I shall do well, – perfectly well; Adèle will come back to me.'

'She will, Sabina, or else you will go to her. Meantime, good Father Mark and his excellent mother will watch over you; and if your return to Paris, or mine from Spain, be delayed, it may be that your best course will be to remove to the quiet shelter of their humble home. We must take no leave, Sabina, neither of us could bear it. Here is gold, my child, more than will be sufficient for your wants till you reach the protection of your aunt and sister. Adieu! adieu! fear not but we shall speedily meet again. Spare me, Sabina, spare me!' And with these words Mr Hargrave laid her gently on a sofa, and departed. Had he ventured to look around, he would have seen that he might have safely gazed at her for a few moments longer without any danger that her words should wound him, for she was senseless.

CHAPTER XXXIV

The last injunction given by Mr Hargrave to Father Mark was that his letter to Madame de Hautrivage, which he left in his hands, should not be consigned to the post till the tenth day after his departure. This order the careful priest registered on a slate, which hung conveniently in his mother's parlour, for the reception of numberless memoranda, concerning appointments for confessions, church-services, chanting practisings, and so forth; most of which would probably have been forgotten without them. There was, however, one duty, of which he never made any memorandum, but which, nevertheless, he never forgot, namely, the being near to all who wanted his good offices. Though his short acquaintance with his new penitents made it quite impossible for him to know or guess how terrible to Sabina was this separation from her father, his kind and gentle nature led him to pity her profoundly. Dearly as he himself loved to be alone, he could not well endure the thought of the sad solitude of one so young; and daily did the good man convey to her an humble-worded but most urgent invitation from his old mother, entreating her to take up her quarters with them, till such time as the friends her papa had written to in Paris should get the letter and come to Gernsbach to fetch her. But Sabina, who pertinaciously clung to the last words she had heard her father speak, which were, '*Fear not but we shall meet again speedily,*' as constantly declined the offered kindness, uniformly replying by quoting these parting words, and adding strength to them by observing that it was impossible any one could tell how soon he might come back again. 'I would not for the world, and all the glory of it, be absent from these walls,' she said, 'at the moment he shall re-enter them! No, good father! – no, I cannot go with you. I feel that it is my duty to remain here, to await the fulfilment of his promise; and while I feel it I must act accordingly.'

'There is no more to be said, my daughter,' replied the kind-hearted priest, after this, or something to the same effect, had been repeated to him half-a-dozen times. 'I will not persecute you with invitations; but should you at any moment fancy that you could find comfort from being with my good mother, come to us, my child, without waiting for further invitation.'

'God reward you, Father Mark, for all your kindness, both to my poor father and to me. It is a very great comfort to know that I have such friends near me.'

And so it unquestionably was; and though Sabina preferred gliding through the spacious solitary chambers like a ghost, with no human voice, save that of Gertrude, to break the profound stillness that surrounded her, she nevertheless did remember, from time to time, with a sensation like pleasure, that in case she felt her courage fail her, and the solemn, unbroken silence of her long days too terrible to bear, she might at any moment take the strong arm of Gertrude, and walk into Gernsbach with the assurance of finding safe protection and certain kindness.

The first event which broke the monotony of her life during this dreary interval was a letter brought to her by the Frau Weiber from Adèle. It was written with strict observance of the cautions agreed upon at her departure from the château, and therefore, of necessity, contained little more than an assurance of her safety, – that the lady she had gone to visit had received her kindly, – and that she had already seen the kind old lawyer, with whom they had all been acquainted in former times, who had willingly undertaken to help her in the business which she had to do.

This was not much; but it sufficed to comfort and cheer poor Sabina;

and it was read, and re-read, on the rock and in the castle, till every word was known by heart, and all the deficiencies which caution had left supplied by imagination, till it seemed to tell her *almost* all the Paris news she wanted to know.

But day after day wore away, and she received no tidings of her father. She remembered that he had not said any thing about writing to her, but she had never doubted that it was his intention to do so, and as no morning passed without her despatching Hans to inquire for letters at the post, at Frau Weiber's and at Father Mark's, so no evening came that did not bring disappointment.

At length the ten days appointed by Mr Hargrave for the retention of his letter to Madame de Hautrivage were expired, and the punctual Father Mark dropped the despatch with his own hand into the letter-box. On the day following he received from his departed penitent a note containing these words:

'Father Mark, – Nothing can save the secret on which so much depends but my immediately becoming a member of that strictest of religious communities where speech is forbidden, and I submit. Yet it may be that my name shall yet resound through the Vatican!

'Tell my beloved daughter that I had no courage to inform her how this journey was likely to end; but that now I send her my blessing with more assurance of its efficacy than I could ever dare to do before. Watch over her, till her sister or her aunt come to reclaim her. Brother, farewell! May the saints have you in their holy keeping prays one who, while in the world, was known as C.H., but who henceforward will be distinguished only as

'ANSELMO.'

Father Mark was in no degree surprised by this epistle, nor would he have cared three farthings about it, had he not remembered that he must perform the painful task of communicating its unfeeling contents to the lonely inmate of *the Residence*. Father Mark's reverence for the Church made him habitually abstain from all critical examinations of persons proclaiming themselves peculiarly pious; but in the case of Mr Hargrave, he felt, in spite of himself, that he was a hypocrite, selfish, and unfeeling, as well as being by far the most fatiguing penitent he had ever shrived; so that it was with no very kindly feelings towards the hard-hearted, intriguing father that he set off to perform this terrible commission to his child. Before he reached the castle however, he made up his mind to attempt nothing like circumlocution, or consolation either, but to put the letter itself into the hands of Sabina.

During the wretched hours which succeeded Adèle's first

announcement of Mr Hargrave's danger, and all the time marked by every species of privation and sadness, which had followed, no shadow of a thought had ever crossed the mind of Sabina, tending to cast a doubt either on the wisdom, goodness, or affection of her father. For one or two short moments, perhaps, this perfect reliance, love, and confidence, had received a *little shake*, when the political agent (as he declared himself to be) definitively declared to her his intention of sacrificing EVERY THING to the cause in which he had embarked. For a moment she thought that this could hardly be right, and that there was no cause for which she would sacrifice him. But the tenderness of parting sorrow had drowned all such speculations; and for days and days after he had left her, no feeling, no reflection of any kind arose to interfere with her pefect love for him. But then followed an interval of sharper anguish than even the first agony of parting had brought with it; for as she sat upon the seat she had formed for herself upon the summit of the cliff, she fell into a fit of meditation that lasted till she was startled out of it by perceiving that twilight was fast settling into darkness.

Sabina knew it not, but the five hours she had thus passed formed a most important epoch in her life. It was not, indeed, the first time, by many, that she had sat alone on that same spot, yielding up her young heart and imagination to both sweet and bitter fancies. But hitherto very little of serious reflection had mixed with her reveries; and, to own the truth, the hero of the rock, in his double character of prince and peasant, had been the subject of by far the greater portion of the thoughts which had occupied her.

But, on the evening in question, the state of her mind was wholly different. She indulged no longer in the rainbow meditations which had often followed the tears she permitted to fall in memory of departed pleasure, and during which the pertinacious elasticity of her young spirit often indulged her with vague but bright glimpses of a possible future; no such silly fancies amused her now. She felt her situation such as it really was, full of doubt and dread for the future, and of gloom and suffering for the present; and then came, involuntarily and irresistibly, a throng of burning thoughts, all testifying, as with tongues of flame, against the conduct of her father. She remembered her lost mother, and the watchful care which, as long as recollection could go back, she knew had been bestowed upon her in little things as well as great, so as to shield her from every danger and from every pain that human power could avert. She remembered, too, the species of idolatry with which her father had been used to treat her, the accumulated luxury with which it had been his will and pleasure to surround her, rendering her as unfit for the changes and chances of this mortal life as it was possible to make her; and then she thought of the manner in which she had been abandoned for the sake of a political intrigue.

Could Adèle have been made a party to these thoughts, could she have seen the deep expression of misery which they produced on the altered features of her sister, she would have felt how vain was the vanity of believing that she could spare the child of such a man as Hargrave the agony of discovering him to be unworthy. Gentle indeed, most gentle, and most full of pitying love, was the sentence which the heart of Sabina passed against her father. But she did pass sentence against him, and the moment of doing so was, perhaps, the most painful of her life.

It was on returning from this more than melancholy musing, that she found Father Mark waiting for her, to communicate the important letter he had received from her father. He had already been at the château for above three hours, and would have given up the performance of his painful errand for that night, had he not begun to feel seriously anxious for the safety of the solitary wanderer. Glad was he, and Hans and Gertrude also, as they decried her from the look-out which they all occupied together on the terrace; but the gladness faded rapidly, when on entering a room where there were lights, the extreme paleness of her face became visible. Father Mark felt frightened, and could think of nothing but telling her to go to bed, – to go to bed instantly. But, unfortunately, he unconsciously held in his hand, as he said this, an object upon which the eyes of Sabina had eagerly fixed themselves, and which caused her to give no other reply to his kind injunction than an exclamation which gave no sort of hope that she would comply with it. 'That is a letter from my father! Oh! give it to me – give it to me!'

Perfectly unable to invent any excuse to avoid doing so, he complied, put the letter into her hands, and turned his head away from her as she read it.

The meditations of the rock had been but a bad preparation for the fearful stroke which now fell upon her. Had she been thinking only of her own misery, the effect might have been more favourable, as it might have taught her to feel that it was hardly possible her situation could be made worse by any steps her father could take; but to a mind just awakened to the power of perceiving that it was possible he could act unworthily, the lines she read brought both sorrow and indignation to her heart through no palliating medium of self-delusion. She had lost her father for ever, – lost him doubly. It was tremendous to know that she should never behold him more; but it was a deeper pang still to feel that had she lost him but a few short weeks before, the loss would have been heavier still.

The first visible effect of this appalling news was an air of stupor, that fixed her features into an aspect so unlike her own, that Gertrude and the priest, who stood one on each side of her, felt terrified from thinking that her reason had left her. But she heard them express this fear in words, and immediately rousing herself, she said, 'No, no; there is no danger of it. I have been frightened, – perhaps a little stunned, by this news. But God will have pity upon me, and will not let me lose my reason. It is now that I shall have the greatest need of it. What is this about my sister and my aunt, Father Mark? I do not well understand it. How did my father know that they were coming here?'

'How did he know it? that is a question, my child, that I cannot answer; but the letter he confided to me, which, as I think, informed them that they would be wanted here, was posted by me yesterday; your father having so ordered it.'

'That is all well,' replied Sabina, composedly. 'I shall be more fit to meet them.'

Though relieved by this from his fears for her reason, the good priest was hardly satisfied to leave her; and once more urged her removal to his mother's house, as a dwelling less forlorn than the wide mansion she was in, and strengthened his arguments by saying that her father had recommended this removal. How amply sufficient would this argument have been a short time before, to make her comply with it! But now its effect was different. After a moment's silence, during which one or two strong heavings of the breast shewed that some powerful emotion was at work within, she said, –

'In my altered condition, Father Mark, it will not be wise for me to regulate my conduct by the judgment of any one who is not in a position to know what that condition is. I no longer expect to find the world a path of flowers, and I shall have to prepare myself for many things worse than inhabiting a house that is too large for me.'

'Well, my dear child, I would have you do whatever your own heart tells you will be least painful,' replied Father Mark. 'And now good night! you will let me see you to-morrow?'

This quiet yielding to her wayward longing to be alone did her better service than the most orthodox opposition to it; and poor Sabina shed some gentle, healing tears, as she thanked him for it. Nevertheless, though it soothed, it only confirmed her in her averseness to quit the spot where Adèle had left her; and when the morning came, and brought the good priest to her again, she repeated to him with so much earnestness that it was her wish to remain where she was till Adèle came for her, that once more he yielded, promising to see her from time to time, and making her promise in return that she would give him notice if she changed her mind. One favour only she asked of him before they parted, which was that he would let her have her father's letter.

To this request he could not make, nor did he see, any objection; and having complied with it, he left her with a fervent blessing, and a promise that she should be remembered in his prayers.

It may seem strange to say that the perusal of this letter many times repeated was beneficial to Sabina, and tended to reconcile her to the loss she had sustained; but it certainly was the case. The phrase referring to the possibility that his name might 'resound through the Vatican,' opened to her a whole volume of meditation; and that ambition would still continue to be ambition under every change of circumstances, was a truth which became stamped upon her mind in characters indelible.

'Adèle saw all this,' thought she, 'before it was plain enough to catch my undiscerning eyes.'

And then came home to her heart the dearest solace that her fate had left her, – the reunion with that dear Adèle, who now seemed a thousand times more precious and more beloved than before. Two days after the departure of her father, she received a second letter from her through the hands of the Frau Weiber; but written as it was with all the cautious ambiguity which had been so strictly enjoined, she learned nothing from it, save that all things seemed to promise well for the happy termination of 'more affairs than one.' What this might mean, it was, of course, impossible to discover; but as Adèle referred all explanation to their meeting, Sabina most contentedly did so too, and thanked Heaven for the favourable oracle, despite its obscurity.

But yet this meeting came not; and a whole fortnight had elapsed since the departure of her father's letter. What could this mean? How was it possible that such a letter could remain unanswered? Yet still her confidence in Adèle wavered not. She felt sure, oh! very sure, that she would come for her; and though her heart sickened by the hope delayed, her sisterly love was of a quality that sufficed to cast out fear. She remembered their last embrace, and was satisfied.

CHAPTER XXXV

A more able general than Alfred Coventry never stepped forward at a moment of need. From the moment that Adèle fairly consented to put herself and her friend Roger under his guidance, all things had gone well with her; and yet, like a spoiled child as she was, she grumbled, – grumbled because she had to confess to Sabina the startling precipitancy of her marriage, – grumbled because she could frame no excuse for doing exactly what she most wished to do, – grumbled, in short, because she actually was obliged to marry the man she loved in less than a week after he had asked her to do so.

Coventry, however, was not absolutely hard-hearted towards her; and having learned from M de Servac that his presence could not by any possibility be wanted in Paris till the day of trial, he determined to spare both himself and his bride as much of the publicity which the delighted Madame de Hautrivage was likely to bring upon them, as possible, by driving from the hôtel of the English Ambassador, where the marriage ceremony was performed, to Montmorenci; and the better to enjoy the interval of *honeyed* peace, he contrived to be uncertain as to which way they intended to drive, till after they had parted from their full-dressed aunt, who, though the weather was exceedingly warm, failed not to envelope herself in the adhesive folds of her beautiful cashmere.

Before leaving Paris, before having lost her right to the name of De Cordillac, Adèle wrote once again to Sabina; but, at the earnest request of her *almost* husband, she did not even allude to the momentous adventure which was about to befall her. 'Let us,' he said, 'appear so suddenly before her at her Mummelsee, with our liberated man, Roger, behind us, that she may believe, indeed, that the "good people" have been busy in your affairs, and brought all these wonderful adventures to pass.'

This was agreed to, on the part of Adèle, the more readily, because she felt that it would be very difficult, in the mysterious style of correspondence to which she was condemned, to render that clear which was really in itself extremely in need of elaborate explanation to make intelligible.

In fact, notwithstanding her grateful sense of exceeding happiness, Adèle still felt the necessity of such hurried espousals as an adventure, embarrassing to recount; and she remembered, too, having once fallen into a paroxysm of indignation, because a young acquaintance had 'transgressed the laws of civilised society' in the same manner; for the which Sabina had taken the liberty of laughing at her; so that, on the whole, she greatly preferred appearing as a bride before her sister, when the joy of meeting would overpower every other feeling, to sitting down and informing her by letter, that she had fortunately met Mr A——d C——y the day before yesterday, and was going to marry him the day after to-morrow.

MR AND MRS COVENTRY, therefore, were sentimentalising very agreeably amidst the shades so pleasantly redolent of the Swiss philospher, when Mr Hargrave's letter to Madame de Hautrivage arrived in Paris. That excellent lady, on perusing it, really felt very much as if the foundations of the solid world on which she stood were crumbling and giving way beneath her feet. Oh! it was a great blessing for Adèle that she was beyond hearing the myriads of interjectional bursts, equally expressive of admiration and astonishment, by which Madame de Hautrivage relieved her spirits! But if she escaped it, very few of her acquaintance did. What was Madame Bertrand's diamond adventure compared to what she had to tell? Mademoiselle de Cordillac, her eldest niece, married to one of the finest private fortunes in England! That '*âme noble*,' her '*élégant et aimable beau-frère*,' turned monk! And her youngest niece, Mademoiselle Hargrave, accounted only a few weeks ago to be one of the largest fortunes, as well as one of the greatest beauties, in Paris, left, forsaken, '*absolument abandonnée*,' within the precincts of a miserable little German town called Gernsbach; which, she believed, was buried in the depths of the Black Forest, or else in the farthest part of Bohemia, she could not exactly recollect which, but that made no difference. Here was '*un roman, – mais un roman inouï et sans pareil*.'

To her very particular friends she read the whole letter; for, as the *âme noble* was now in safe harbour, she had the immense gratification of knowing every thing and telling every thing without let or hindrance of any kind; and truly she made the *salons* of Paris ring with the tidings of Mr Hargrave's magnanimous adherence to 'the cause,' and the excellent chance there seemed to be of his descendants having hereafter the gratification of seeing his name enrolled in the sacred calendar among those of the saints made perfect here on earth.

Among the multitude of persons who eagerly listened to this wonderful history, Prince Frederic of —— was not the least interested. Having heard something of the matter at second hand, he honoured Madame de Hautrivage with a call at her residence in the Rue de Rivoli; and by means of shewing about one-twentieth part of the interest he felt in the business, induced her to enter at the fullest possible length into the whole history of the *âme noble's* devotion to *la cause* – the incredible sacrifices he had made – the ruin which had been its result – his magnanimous resolution to bury himself and his secret under the cowl of a monk, – and, lastly, the unheard-of state of matchless and romantic desolation in which he had been forced to leave *sa charmante fille* in the very centre of the Black Forest.

'Where, madame?' said the Prince, with a sternness which she thought looked more like the hauteur of royalty than any thing she had ever seen in him.

'*Mais à Gernsbach, mon Prince, au milieu de la Forêt Noir, à ce que je crois*.'

'*A Gernsbach?*' returned his Royal Highness, in a voice that trembled in spite of all his princely resolution; '*à Gernsbach, – près de Baden?*'

'*Mais oui, Altesse, mais certainement oui, – près de Baden*.'

The Prince rose to take his leave; but, ere he reached the door, turned again towards the loquacious lady, and said, 'May I take the liberty, madame, of asking if it be not your intention to go to Gernsbach immediately?'

'*Moi! oh, mon Dieu, non! Pour moi, mon Prince, ce serait impossible!*' And then she went on to inform him that she had no doubt but that her eldest niece, Madame Alfred Coventry, would repair thither with all the haste possible, as soon as her *mari* should be able to leave Paris.

'*Bon jour, Madame!*' said the Prince.

'*Bon jour, votre altesse!*' said Madame de Hautrivage.

* * *

To say that the tone of Sabina's spirits did not become more and more sad, as the days crept on without bringing any further tidings of her sister, would not be strictly true; yet she bore it well. Her mind had received a blow which seemed less to stun than to steady it. Never had she thought so deeply, – never had she weighed so justly, the value of real against ideal advantages, and never did she feel so capable of submitting meekly to the touch of sorrow as since she had been deprived of every support, of every friend, of every counsellor, save 'herself alone.'

Father Mark, probably from his own love of being left in peace, had contented himself with her promise of sending to him when she wished for his counsel or assistance in any way, and had ceased to importune her either with visits or invitations, so that her wide sitting-room in the château was as lonely as the forest, and the forest not a whit more melancholy than her sitting-room; and the hours of her long day were pretty equally divided between both.

On the afternoon of the fifth day after Mr Hargrave's letter had been despatched to Paris, Sabina, with slow and languid steps, once more climbed the steep and narrow path which led to the often-mentioned rock above the castle. Her heart was heavy, for Hans had just returned from Gernsbach with the oft-told tale of 'no letters,' and her eyes were full of tears despite her newly cherished philosophy. But the evening was enchanting; not a sight, not a sound, not a smell, that could make Nature, – unmixed, unadulterated Nature, – enchanting, was wanting, and Sabina suffered herself to be cheered; and when she reached the little platform where she so dearly loved to sit, she felt a throb of pleasure at looking down upon the lovely landscape that for a moment made her forget her desolation.

But not even the beauty of such a scene as that which spreads below the commanding point on which she was seated, could long avail to make her forget what, and where, she was, and what she had been. Yet still the tone of her sorrow followed that of her gentle nature, softened as it was by that species of womanly philosophy which shews itself in the endurance rather than in the battling with grief.

She had thrown the large flat straw hat, worn by the peasants of the district, on the ground beside her; and a soft warm breeze, that fluttered through the boughs which sheltered her, blew aside the curls from her forehead, refreshing without chilling her. Never, perhaps, in all the soft grace of the most becoming ball-room toilet had she looked so beautiful as she did then; her uncovered head bent slightly forward, and her deep blue eyes steadfastly fixed on the dark waters of the little lake below, might have been watching for the fabled sovereigns of its waves, or looking upon many other things which were not, save in the memory of the fair statue who thus sat, seemingly fixed in contemplation.

While thus employed, if it may be so called, in idle thoughtfulness, Sabina fancied that she heard a rustling amidst the leaves behind her. She turned suddenly round, but saw nothing; all was again still; and believing that it was only a capricious freshening of the evening breeze, she turned again to look upon the lake, and think, and think anew.

But this profound tranquillity of spirit did not last long: another sound was heard; but ere she had time to think whence it might come or what it might be, she saw standing before her the identical hunter youth whom she had seen nearly a year before exactly on the same spot. His dress was the same, his stature was the same; the same bright curls which had attracted Adèle's notice waved over his forehead. Yes, it was the same, and yet how different! The laughing light of the bright blue eye was gone. The gay and thoughtless smile which had curled his handsome lip had given place to an anxious, agitated expression, that shewed his very soul was moved by the thoughts with which he was occupied.

Sabina looked at him long and earnestly, but seemed incapable of uttering a word; and he too looked, and looked in silence, but by degrees the troubled aspect of his countenance softened. It seemed as if, during the short space in which each seemed perusing the eyes of the other, a world of doubt and uncertainty had passed from him to her. Instead of anxiety and agitation, his features now expressed nothing but gentleness and love; while hers, on the contrary, grew troubled as his grew calm, and at length the words burst from her, 'Are you Prince Frederic?'

'Sabina! tell me, ere I answer you, why is it that I find you here? Here on this very, very spot – this narrow spot – not easy to find, not easy to remember. Tell me, Sabina, why do I find you here?'

Poor girl! the feelings which she had never fully and honestly avowed to her own heart were now traced, discovered, and proclaimed, by precisely that being in the whole wide world from whom she would most have wished to conceal them.

'Oh, terrible!' she exclaimed, hiding her face in her hands, while her heaving bosom testified her suffering.

Her companion knelt before her, and gently drawing her hands away, said, 'Before you condemn me, Sabina, remember my position. It is that, loveliest and best Sabina, that is terrible! Nay, look at me again! Oh! you know not what I have suffered from trying *not* to see those lovely eyes.

Yes, Sabina, I am Prince Frederic. He who fluttered round you in the drawing-rooms of Paris; sometimes with an aching heart, but always with a steadfast spirit, — steadfast in the resolution of not running the tremendous risk of being loved because I was PRINCE Frederic. But now, Sabina, quarrel not with the dear precious gleam of light which, like a star in the midst of darkness, has led me to your feet. Your aunt told me you had taken shelter at Gernsbach. Why at Gernsbach? Why at Gernsbach, Sabina? Why do I find you on this very spot? If I am wrong,' he added, rising from the ground, — 'if I have falsely imagined the thoughts of my own soul were reflected in yours, speak but one word, Sabina! — say only "Leave me, Prince Frederic," and you shall see me start from your presence with a step, if possible, more rapid than that which brought me here.'

Either Sabina had lost her hearing or her power of speech, or else she did not wish Prince Frederic to leave her, for, most assuredly, instead of repeating the sentence he had suggested, she sat looking more like a beautiful statue than ever, and without uttering a single word.

'My wife, and my Princess!' exclaimed the young man, once more falling at her feet, and explaining, with very tolerable clearness, all he had felt and suffered, from the hour in which he had first seen her on the spot where they now met again. Nor did Sabina, though she listened to him apparently with very great attention, again exclaim, 'Oh, terrible!'

Of course Sabina was exceedingly shocked at being escorted to the door of her wild-looking home by a young man, especially as his dress differed very little from that of a peasant, and as, by some accident or other, they quite forgot the hour of the evening, and did not reach the gates till the light had very perceptibly began to fade. Gertrude, however, who saw them approach, behaved very civilly, for she said not a word about it to Sabina, though she did remark to Hans that she certainly never did see a young fellow make so fine a bow as this stranger did when he took leave of their poor young lady at the door.

* * *

Shortly, *very* shortly after daybreak on the following morning, Sabina astonished Father Mark and Father Mark's mother, exceedingly, by entering their little parlour, and telling them that as they had been so very kind as to invite her, she was come to stay with them for a few days.

Notwithstanding their surprise, however, both the good priest and his old mother received her with great kindness, the best proof of which was, that they neither of them said a word about her having changed her mind. It is probable, however, that Father Mark guessed what might be the reasons, and that he did not think the worse of her for it when the young hunter made his appearance a few hours afterwards, and gave the priest to understand that he was affianced to the young lady who was his inmate. On the strength of this assurance, which was gently assented to by the blushing Sabina, the lovers were permitted to have a tolerably long *tête-à-tête* conference, and many important matters were discussed and arranged in the course of it.

There is a lesson which Fate is often found to bestow on mortals, which if read aright might cure them of much presumption. How many among us may remember to have heard the young, and strong in purpose, declare that there were things which they were positively determined never to do, and other things which they were as positively determined that they would do, and how few among us have seen these purposes accomplished!

> '*L'Homme propose, et Dieu dispose,*'

is a pretty proverb.

It might have been difficult to find any two ladies in any country less inclined to join in the chorus, –

> 'Happy is the wooing
> That is not long a doing,'

than were Adèle Cordillac and Sabina Hargrave; and yet it would, perhaps, be rarer still to find any who had acted with, apparently, such decided approbation of it. Whether my sister-heroines ought to have been sturdy in their refusal to listen to any arguments which might lead to such a termination, their fellow-heroines must decide; but most assuredly both Alfred Coventry and Prince Frederic had very cogent reasons to urge in favour of the unseemly haste they proposed. Those of Alfred have been already explained; and Prince Frederic was not a whit behind him in proving an absolute necessity for the same measure. Sabina had in fact no alternative to propose that could be considered as eligible. Having startled her almost into the belief that he was jesting, by informing her of the marriage of her sister, he proceeded to state that her speedy arrival at Gernsbach was hardly to be hoped for; for that the bride and bridegroom being absent from Paris at the time Mr Hargrave's letter arrived, and having declared themselves at their departure uncertain in what direction they should go, Madame de Hautrivage was left with as little power as inclination to disturb the serenity of their happiness by communicating it contents.

What then was to become of Sabina? Prince Frederic confessed that he had travelled to Baden with too much speed to be cautious, and that he had little hope his incognito could be preserved, if indeed his attempt to effect it had not already proved abortive. Should he then leave her after a visit which, if he were known, was certain of being widely and loudly commented upon, what would be the inference?

Delicately, most delicately, he made her see and feel, that the only permanent and insuperable obstacle to his hope of giving her the place in society which his wife ought to hold, would be created by such gossip as this imprudence would inevitably produce. At the present moment Father Mark knew nothing but that he was her lover; and if she declared it to be her purpose to become his wife, the good man, who well knew her situation, must feel that he could not better perform the duty of a temporal as well as spiritual father than by joining their hands immediately.

That her sister, whom she had ever loved to make her model in all things, had felt that circumstances could justify a hurried marriage, was very clear; and this, together with the dread of throwing herself upon her and her husband, under appearances so painful as those suggested, sufficed to convince her that all he said, and all that he proposed, was

'Wisest, discreetest, best.'

★　★　★

Nothing could exceed the thankfulness of Father Mark when this immediate marriage was proposed to him; for his concern for Sabina was only to be equalled by his conscious inability to assist her. His mother had hinted, before the arrival of Prince Frederic, that as it was evident her Paris friends were in no great hurry to reclaim her, the best and safest course for her to pursue would be to follow her father's example, and embrace a religious life; — a piece of advice to which all his deference for ecclesiastic, as well as maternal authority, could not reconcile the kind-hearted priest. Joyfully, therefore, and without the slightest suspicion or scruple, he joined their hands as firmly as their hearts had been joined before.

The incognito which, as Prince Frederic truly stated, had been neglected before, was now assumed with such effectual care, that whatever might have been at one moment reported at Baden respecting the movements of Prince Frederic died away for want of confirmation; while he quietly prepared to convey his lovely bride to England, where a meeting with her sister could be more pleasantly and conveniently arranged than any where else.

Sabina was quite as anxious as her noble husband could be that her marriage should not be immediately published, especially at Paris. The adventures of their family must already, she thought, have made too much noise there to render it at all desirable that it should be increased. She was too, perhaps, a little *piqué* by Adèle's silence towards her; and, in short, she agreed to address such a letter to her, under cover to Madame de Hautrivage, as might prevent her being *too* much alarmed, and yet leave enough of obscurity to ensure the concealment which they at present wished to preserve.

It was thus she wrote:—

'My Dearest Adèle, — You must have ere this learned the decisive step which my poor father has thought it necessary to take, in order to shelter the secret which he holds to be more sacred than any other earthly tie. This is a subject upon which I can enter into no discussion; nor is it necessary. You will be able to guess but too well what it has cost me.

'Reasons, which I will explain when we meet, have rendered it impossible for me to remain with propriety at the Castle of the Lake; and other circumstances, the explanation of which I must also refer to our meeting, have led me to take refuge in England rather than in Paris; where the strange termination of my poor father's career would render me the object of more curiosity than I should like to encounter.

'This sounds strangely, Adèle, does it not? Coolly to tell you thus, that I am about to leave Germany for England; and as coolly to tell you that I expect you will meet me there. But so you will, dear sister; nor do I think that you will particularly dislike my choice of England as a place of meeting. Inquire at Mivart's Hotel for a letter addressed to A.C. as soon as you conveniently can, after reaching London, and you shall know thereby where to find me.

'Our good aunt does not appear to make herself very particularly anxious about me, but I will beg you to tell her that I am perfectly well, and will do myself the pleasure of writing to her as soon as I feel sufficiently settled to be able to send any satisfactory intelligence. And now farewell, my dearest sister: doubt not that I love you dearly, and let me not wait for you in England longer than is absolutely necessary.

'Ever affectionately yours,

'SABINA.

'P.S. Be not anxious about my mode of travelling — I shall go under respectable protection.'

It is impossible to imagine astonishment much greater than was felt by Mrs Coventry on receiving this letter. It reached her hands only a few hours later than that of Mr Hargrave to Madame de Hautrivage, and while she was suffering the most pungent anxiety on account of her forsaken sister whom she figured to herself as sinking beneath an agony of grief at the loss of her beloved, but unprincipled and most selfish father, and trembling with all the timid sensitiveness of her character at her own desolate position.

Was it possible that Sabina could thus decide upon setting off upon a long journey, to a country where she was utterly unknown, where there existed no friend, no protector, to welcome her? Again and again she told herself that it was impossible; and then re-read the letter and was compelled to believe that so it was.

Coventry could give her no help in explaining this most mysterious and tormenting document; for though he saw, or fancied he saw, that in the mention of Adèle's approving England there was reason to suppose that by some means or other she had become acquainted with their marriage, the seeming impossibility of this robbed the suggestion of all its value, and left them both exactly as much puzzled as they were before.

There were moments when Adèle thought it possible that, despite all the efforts she had used to prevent it, Sabina had perceived the total change of her feeling towards Mr Hargrave, and felt her sisterly affection chilled by it; but the remembrance of the fond embrace on the last evening they had passed together, which seemed to have been given and received as a pledge that they were still dear to each other as ever, drove this painful idea away. But it only left her to torment herself anew in efforts to explain what was inexplicable.

The only relief to be found for this state of feverish uncertainty was furnished by making themselves ready to leave Paris within the shortest time possible after the trial of Roger Humphries should be over, determined that if Sabina could be found by means of an application at Mivart's, she should not be long lost to them.

Nothing could be better than M de Servac's management of the worthy Roger's affair. His *alibi* and his innocence were proved to the satisfaction of all the world; and if a most triumphant acquittal could atone for his imprisonment, it was atoned for. But a good deal of police blundering followed; for no sooner did it become clearly evident that Roger Humphries was innocent, than the logical inference that somebody else must be guilty threw the minds of all men, and of all policemen in particular, into a state of the most violent activity. Nor was the Bertrand robbery the only mystery of which M Collet had hoped for an explanation during this trial, and in which hope he had been disappointed. He fully expected that Roger Humphries would be convicted, and was prepared to follow this up with what he considered as a very pretty chain of evidence to prove that if not the actual thief, he must have been connected with those who were in the affair which had taken place near Riccordo's. Not only, however, was his innocence of the first charge satisfactorily proved, but the large sum of gold found in his possession was shewn, by Mr Coventry's statements concerning his length of service, the amount of his wages, and his quiet mode of life, to be no more than he would be likely to have amassed; while the testimony of Madame de Hautrivage, who had known him since the period of her sister's marriage, placed his character quite beyond the reach of any further suspicion.

In spite of all Madame Bertrand's assurances, therefore, that it was absolutely impossible Mr Hargrave could have had any share in robbing her, it is more than probable that M Collet's suspicions would again have settled upon that gentleman, had not the evasion of Signor Ruperto, together with the infamous character he had left behind him, pointed him out as more likely still. The circumstance, too, of only a few pieces among many of the gold found being marked, so lightened the suspicion against him on that score, that, together with the extreme improbability that a gentleman filling such a place in society should have committed the act, it turned all evil thoughts away from him, and directed all the energy of the baffled law towards tracing the course of the supposed culprit. Signor Ruperto, however, was at that time making arrangements for opening a large confectioner's shop at St Petersburg in the most respectable style, and was in no more danger of being troubled by M Collet than M Collet was in danger of being troubled by him.

Roger Humphries' affair, then, being thus happily settled, and the old man consenting to attend the grateful Adèle to England, in the delightful persuasion that her marriage would never have taken place if he had not taken such particular care of her letter, they set off in a style which contented even the *exigéante* Madame de Hautrivage, and as strong a desire to annihilate both time and space as ever propelled a fashionable pair.

Hardly had the foot of Mrs Coventry touched the pavement before Mivart's Hotel before she forestalled the voice of her husband in asking for a letter addressed to A.C.; but it was some time before a document, which had reached the house by the undignified channel of the post, and with so very unpromising an address, could be found; even though inquired for by the elegant traveller who had stepped from a finished equipage with all fitting appurtenances of attendants and so forth to prove her claim to attention.

While the search for the A.C. despatch was going on, the impatient Adèle declared that she could not mount the stairs, as the doing so would evidently place her farther from the intelligence she felt sick with impatience to obtain. Coventry, who pitied the unfeigned agony of suspense which had seemed to increase in its intensity as it approached its end, said not a word against this waiting scheme, and only placed himself before her in a corner which she occupied, so as to shelter her from the bustle of the goers and comers who filled the hall.

As he stood thus his eye was attacted to a very elegant equipage which displaced his own travelling carriage by driving up to the door. The floating feathers of the *chasseur* who sat behind it shewed that it belonged to a foreigner of distinction; and, making a step forward to get a sight of the armorial bearings, he recognised the escutcheon of Prince Frederic of ———. The discovery was immediately announced to Adèle, and her first feeling at hearing it was a wish to escape seeing the Prince, while his name so vividly recalled the remembrance of the poor wandering Sabina in her brightest and gayest days, that tears started to her eyes at the idea of having to tell her erstwhile admirer in answer to any inquiries with which he might honour her, that she knew not either how or where she was.

'Perhaps we had better go to a room upstairs to wait,' said Adèle to her husband; 'they are so very long in finding this letter.'

'Shew us into a sitting-room,' said Mr Coventry to one of the servants of the house, who at that moment passed by.

'In a moment, sir,' was the man's reply, as he stepped towards one in authority, who would settle the delicate question between the claims of handsome carriage, stylish servants, and so forth, against the no claims of people arriving without having bespoken rooms.

During this interval a movement was perceptible among the attendants who filled the hall. They stood back leaving space for a personage of handsome person and of lofty bearing, who was descending the stairs, while 'the Prince,' 'the Prince,' was whispered among them.

Adèle stood so near the door that it was impossible she could escape being seen; and Coventry, unconscious of her wish to do so, changed his position and placed himself beside her.

It was, indeed, Prince Frederic of ——— who was thus passing to his carriage; but as he walked forward with his eyes directed towards the door, as those do walk who have no inclination to return all the staring they receive, Mrs Coventry began to hope that they should escape his observation. But she was mistaken. Wishing to give some order to the servant who followed him, the Prince stopped and turned his head within three feet of the spot where she stood.

His recognition of her was instantaneous, and the bright smile that followed shewed that, to him at least, this recognition was full of pleasure.

The terms they had been on in Paris made it perfectly natural that he should come towards her with an extended hand; and as he immediately addressed her as 'Madame Coventry,' the cordial manner in which he greeted her companion was in like manner intelligible; but both the husband and wife certainly felt rather surprised when, instead of passing on, he continued still firmly to clasp both their hands, and exclaimed, –

'This meeting is, indeed, delightful! Let me lead you to the Princess!'

Adèle had too much the *usage du monde* not to know that such an invitation approached very nearly to a command; but her anxiety about Sabina, which nothing could for a moment set aside, superseded every thing else; and in defiance of *etiquette* she said, 'Your Royal Highness does us great honour, but at this moment I fear it will be impossible for us to profit by it, as we are in search of a dear friend of whose abode we are as yet ignorant.'

'Nay, but I cannot be refused!' said the young man, gaily seizing the arm of his unconscious sister-in-law; 'the Princess will not detain you a moment longer than it may be convenient for you to stay; but I cannot deny myself the pleasure of introducing you!'

Rank has its privileges. Had simple Frederic *un tel* ventured thus, *nolens volens*, to march off with his bride, it is probable that Mr Coventry might not have followed so quietly; but, as it was, he took his hat from his head and stepped on in the wake of his lady and the Prince without betraying any symptoms of dissatisfaction.

Ere he reached the first landing-place, however, his own man made a long stride or two after him, for the purpose of inquiring what was to be done with the carriage, and whether the luggage was to be taken off. The moment which it took to say in reply that it must wait sufficed to take the Prince and Adèle out of sight; they had passed through a door near the top of the flight, but it was left open, and Mr Coventry without ceremony passed through it also.

Great was his astonishment as he entered the apartment to perceive his wife fast locked in the arms of a lady at the upper end of the room. For a moment he stood still and stared at them, but in the next the mystery was explained, the two lovely faces ceased to conceal each other, and he beheld Sabina! Whether this explanation lessened or increased his astonishment may be doubted. Prince Frederic, however, left him not much leisure to meditate upon this unexpected discovery; but, approaching him with a look of 'measureless content,' he said, as he once more extended his hand, 'Let us mutually congratulate each other, dear Coventry: we have both managed our love affairs with exemplary discretion; but as our respective romances have ended in sober matrimony, we may now venture to speak openly concerning all our marvellous adventures. Look at our two dear wives! How very like the double cherry of which your poet tells! Think you not that it would be charity to leave them *tête-à-tête* till dinner-time? In the meantime you shall come with me into the next room while we inquire about your accommodation near us. And this point settled, you shall be indulged with half an hour for your toilet, and then I will put myself under your guidance, either to walk or drive, as you like best, for the rest of the morning.'

Coventry, who had recovered his astonishment sufficiently to pay his compliments with a very good grace to his new sister, gallantly kissing her hand, when he had done so (a salutation which might, perhaps, have been exchanged for a brotherly kiss had the lady been less than royal), accepted the Prince's offered arm, and they walked off together.

There is no need to listen to all that Adèle told Sabina, or that Sabina told Adèle, during the happy hours which followed; for we pretty well know it already. And it would have been well for us if we had enjoyed it all as much as they did.

*   *   *

But little else of importance remains to be told. The morality of poetical justice was not infringed in the destiny of Mr Hargrave. At any rate he thought himself considerably more than enough punished for all his sins, by learning the news of his daughter's marriage immediately after he had put it out of his power to profit by it; for, getting alarmed by a paragraph in the Paris papers about the renewed search making by the 'unrivalled police' for the perpetrator of the Bertrand robbery, he gave a considerable portion of the jewels which remained from it for permission to dispense with the ceremony of novitiate and to take the vows as a brother of one of the strictest religious societies in Spain; in which country he thought he should be less likely to be traced than at Rome, where his respected uncle, the Cardinal, might have been apt to prate of his whereabouts under a more questionable name than that of 'Anselmo.'

The whole thing, however, turned out to be more disagreeable and vexatious than he had power to bear; for, instead of keeping his promise to Madame de Hautrivage and getting himself canonised, he was more than once threatened with the censures of the Church for various breaches of monastic discipline, so abominably ill-managed that they became subjects of scandal, which was of course more than his superior could overlook, especially after the last diamond had been lodged in his reverend hands as the price of absolution. So Mr Hargrave fell ill and died; a circumstance made known to the Princess Frederic of —— with much ceremony, and over which she shed more tears than the object of them deserved.

The exalted position of many of her Royal Highness's maternal connexions greatly assisted the work of reconciliation between the Prince and his brother; and, this once effected, the beauty, grace, and goodness of his lovely wife soon gave her the position in his family which he wished her to hold.

The intercourse between the sisters was frequent and delightful in every way; Mr Coventry's speedy succession to the English peerage, as well as the noble lineage of his charming wife, rendering the connexion welcome in every way.

The affair of the robbery near Riccordo's remains a mystery to this day; though Count Romanhoff has hardly yet ceased his efforts to discover the culprit. But though he continues to maintain a frequent intercourse with his friend Coventry, and perpetually discusses this interesting subject in the presence of his wife, she has never favoured him with any hints upon the subject; her superior information, or, at any rate, her superior right of *guessing* upon it, being the only subject on which she has a secret either from her husband or her sister. But there is every reason to believe that all she knows, more than other people, concerning Mr Hargrave, will die with her.

Madame de Hautrivage is not forgotten by either of her nieces, and is quite as happy as such sort of old ladies can be; but, at present, it but rarely happens that any one makes positive love to her, and nothing could enable her to bear this, but the number of new dresses received from her sister's dutiful children.

Roger would have been sadly perplexed as to how to decide the choice offered him between the houses of the two sisters, had not that of Adèle been in England, but this settled the point; and as the Prince and Princess make occasional visits to that country, the honoured and happy old man has already held the offspring of both sisters upon his knee.

Hans and Gertrude hold excellent situations in the household of Prince Frederic; and Susanne is again the *femme de chambre* of Adèle.

Madame Bertrand has been presented by her husband with a new set of jewels. And Father Mark is growing easier in his mind, and has never again been tortured by so illustrious a penitent as Mr Hargrave.

THE WIDOW
BARNABY

FANNY TROLLOPE

'The Barnaby is such a heroine as never before has figured in a romance. Her vulgarity is sublime. . . . Such a jovial, handsome, hideous, ogling, bustling monster of a woman as maid, wife and widow, was never, as we can recollect, before brought upon the scene.' *The Times*

'Mrs Barnaby was really very sorry for the death of her husband, and wept, with little or no effort, several times . . . but she was not a woman to indulge long in so very unprofitable a weakness; and accordingly, as soon as the funeral was over . . . she very rationally began to meditate upon her position and upon the best mode of enjoying the many good things which had fallen to her.' So it is that Mrs Barnaby, whose boldness is only matched by her social ambitions and who finds herself unexpectedly a woman of means, sets out from the small Devonshire town of Silverton to achieve that which her heart most desires: a rich and fashionable husband. Having determined upon her path of action, Mrs Barnaby, with her beautiful niece, Agnes, makes for Clifton to begin her assault on the world of society. . . .

DOMESTIC MANNERS OF THE AMERICANS

FANNY TROLLOPE

Pursued by debts, Fanny Trollope, mother of the famous novelist, emigrated to Ohio. Here she was assisted by her husband — a poor provider — in a fancy goods bazaar, a venture which failed as surely as others before. But when, on her return to England, she published *Domestic Manners of the Americans* in 1832, she achieved profit and fame overnight, and was able to support her family ever after by her pen.

Her candid and sometimes critical observations were bitterly resented in the United States. Throughout Europe, however, the book was quickly admired as an authentic account of a novel society where momentous change and expansion had already begun. The New World, with its contrasts powerfully described, already seemed foreign to the Old . . .

FANNY TROLLOPE

TERESA RANSOM

FOREWORD BY VICTORIA GLENDINNING

Born in Bristol, the daughter of a country parson, Fanny married a barrister in 1809, and produced seven children in eight years. In 1827, with her husband in financial trouble, she decided to take three of her children to America where living was cheaper. She also hoped to set up her son Henry in business there. The bazaar she built was a disaster and, penniless, she started to write a book about her adventures in America. With borrowed money she returned to England. *Domestic Manners of the Americans* was published in 1832, and became an instant bestseller. At the age of 53 Fanny Trollope became a celebrity.

She wrote until she was 77, producing forty-one books in twenty-five years. Critics labelled her writing unfeminine and vulgar, but the public loved her. A freethinking and observant woman, she provided a contemporary picture of Regency and early Victorian life. Her importance in contemporary literature, and as a formative influence on her son Anthony's writing, is only now beginning to be recognized.